CW01500639

OPERA'

ST◎RM'S
EYE

The Silent Codename Series Book One

First Published by Mushroom Millie May Publishing

Copyright © 2022 by E.S.Benton

Cover Design and Typesetting by SpiffingCovers

First Edition Published 2022
Paperback ISBN: 978-1-7392516-0-4
Hardback ISBN: 978-1-7392516-2-8
eBook ISBN 13: 978-1-7392516-1-1

Second Edition Published 2023
Paperback ISBN: 978-1-7392516-3-5
eBook ISBN: 978-1-7392516-4-2

This novel is a work of fiction. Though based on historical fact the incidents described and dialogue are drawn from the author's imagination and are not to be construed as real. The author holds all rights to this work. It is illegal to reproduce this novel without written expressed consent from the author, except in the case of brief quotations embodied in critical articles or reviews. All rights reserved.

OPERATION

STORM'S
EYE

The Silent Codename Series Book One

E.S.BENTON

Acknowledgements

This is the point in a book which most of you will likely overlook (unless you're hoping for me to mention you). But in truth, there are more people who have got me to this point than I can count. For that reason, and through fear of missing someone out, I am not going to list you, but am simply going to say *Thank You*.

Whether you've had to live with me, support me financially, given me the confidence to move forward, and had to be the first to read my story, suggesting excellent alterations (even if we disagreed half the time).

Whether you've worked to make this book the best it can be, made it look like a book, given it a perfect front and back cover, and helped it to sell.

Or whether you have dedicated your own time to reading this, no matter if you are the only person or are among hundreds.

I cannot convey enough of my gratitude. I hope I've provided you with an excellent book to start showing my thanks. So please, flick the lights up high, settle down, turn the page, and allow this story to take you on a journey...

Contents

Prologue – The Beginning
December 29th
16:02 GMT

"To keep your promise, is to keep your honour. And to keep your honour, is to keep your humanity," said Echo Two.

"That is so unfair. I never agreed to clean the truck," argued Echo Four, in a timid voice.

"Joining Echo team means you must clean the truck for a month. You knew that when you agreed to join last month," added Echo Two, in a much deeper voice.

"Stop messing with him. And stop putting that deep voice on, we all know you sound like a mouse," said Echo One. He had a very calm and soothing voice, matching his laid-back personality. He was the complete opposite of the 6'8"-brute of Echo Two. Nothing on Echo Two's face seemed to match, especially when compared to his naturally squeaky voice. It would also be a lie to say good looks were on his side with the grotesque look about him. Echo One had instantly silenced his team without breaking his gaze through his scope. Over in the distance was a building, standing alone in the centre of a barren-looking wasteland. The clearing was over four miles in diameter and had no cover. If they simply walked up, they'd be spotted straight away. All four of them observed the building, trying to see anything of interest, whilst they waited for their assistance.

There was no sign of any guards around the building, nor could any be seen through the windows.

"Adrian, are we sure this is the location?" asked Echo One, as he continued to see nothing more than an abandoned building.

"Whoever is responsible for attacking the civilian sites after those natural disasters was definitely tracked back to that location. It should be a simple capture. Just stand fast for the moment, our drone is almost overhead and Blindspot should be in position soon," said Adrian, who was back on their plane, coordinating their assault.

"I am in position," said Blindspot, hidden even to Echo team. As soon as everyone was ready, and they had their drone overhead, Echo team began to move in. The sun had set only a couple of hours prior, so the darkness would give them their best possibility of staying hidden. The grass was longer than it looked, as it brushed up to their knees.

The two-mile trip was going to take them a while, so Adrian and Blindspot had to stay as focussed as if they were in the middle of a fight. Blindspot's flat voice wouldn't help to keep anyone focussed, but as he stayed quiet, watching from afar, it was the adrenaline that kept them all on point.

"There's a lightning storm overhead. Because of the clearing, you'll need to stay as low to the ground as possible. I'd recommend going prone for the final few hundred metres," said Adrian, as he continued to watch over them. He had a friendly personality with a warm and welcoming voice. He was the kind of person you felt you knew well, even after the first time meeting him.

Echo team hit the floor and crawled the final few hundred metres on their bellies. About fifty metres away from the building, they stopped.

"Echo Four, I know you only joined our team last month and this is your first operation with us, but remember this, you've been training since you were born, so don't fight your natural instincts and trust those around you," said Echo One.

Echo Four didn't speak, he simply swallowed hard and nodded his head a few times. He was the youngest amongst them with his pale complexion and giant blue eyes. Echo Four seemed to always give the impression he was scared but was rarely anything but fearless.

"Let's move out," concluded Echo One, as they split directions, but stayed prone.

Echo Three was the first to split, as she headed to the right side of the building with the intention of securing the back. She rarely smiled, laughed, or spoke, but always insisted she had fun on the inside. No matter how she lived her life, Echo Three was among the best operatives within their organisation. She was able to adapt to any situation, and could take on all of Echo team in hand-to-hand combat, which is why she was often the one to go alone.

Cracks of thunder and strikes of lightning bombarded the grounds surrounding the building, so once in position, Echo team didn't hang around. Echo Three had crawled around the building and was waiting by the rear door. Echo One started to count them down.

"Breaching in… three… two… one… Execute."

Echo Three bashed down the door and entered the building. She swept her rifle right, and then left, seeing no one. Holding her rifle up, she continued to flow through the building. Just as she started to get complacent, two armed guards emerged from her right. She wasted no more than a second in identifying them as a threat, before placing two suppressed bullets into each of their foreheads without giving them the chance to even fire a single shot. Another guard jumped out from her left. But, before the guard could thrust his polished knife towards Echo Three, she bent down and allowed the guard to roll straight over her, landing on the floor with a thud. She put another two bullets into him, as she kept count of the number still in her magazine.

The building was only two stories high, and whilst Echo Three cleared the ground floor, the first floor had been cleared by Echo Two and Four. They regrouped at the base of the staircase, with the building cleared before they'd even got going.

"There's no sign of anything here. Just a few guards," said Echo Four.

"If there are guards, then you have to ask yourself, 'What are they guarding?'" replied Echo One, trying to teach his new operative to not jump to any conclusions.

"Two things. One, there are multiple vehicles approaching from the east. And two, there are multiple heat signatures above you, perhaps on the roof," said Adrian, still calm and relaxed. Echo One didn't need to ask for assistance, as they really did know what each other was thinking.

"I've got the vehicles covered, but there are no enemies on the roof," said Blindspot, as he homed in on the fast-approaching vehicles.

"Then they must be below us," agreed Echo One, as they all fanned out to search for an entrance to a basement.

Echo Four stayed in the kitchen, as he started moving every item around, twisting the knives, pressing the chopping boards, and turning on the taps, all in the hope of finding a hidden door. But as he removed a mirror from the wall, he caught sight of a door under the stairs in its reflection. It was designed to disappear into its surroundings and look like a wall. Echo Four approached it, slowly, and started pressing its seams and joins. Eventually, with the pull of a coat hook, the door swung open.

"Good job, kid," said Echo One, as they all regrouped. Echo Three kept watch on the ground floor, whilst the other three all descended to the floor below.

They moved down the stairs and held their position by the closed door at the foot of them. Echo One removed a grenade, pulled the pin out and flung it into the room, whilst Echo Two held the door ajar. The grenade let out a bang, indicating the room was ready to be cleared. Echo Two opened the door, allowing Echo One to immediately take cover behind the closest table, flipping it on to its side. Echo Four took cover beside him, whilst Echo Two stayed in the doorway and opened fire immediately. Once the initial cluster of guards was down, they began to take cover. Echo team's tactics were more of an art, as they allowed for Echo Two and Four to suppress any guards by shooting near or at the cover they cowered behind, whilst Echo One held back and saved his bullets. As soon as one guard poked their head out, as they thought it was safe, Echo One returned one bullet at a time, taking them all out. It didn't take long for the dwindling number of guards to completely diminish, apart from just one, left all alone. The guard could see he wasn't going to make it out so yielded and threw his rifle to the floor. He slowly stood up with his hands in the air.

"Echo Four, go and detain him," said Echo One, as he kept his rifle pointing at the guard. Echo Four approached quickly, as he put his rifle behind him and moved to seize the guard. He got within a metre, when he reached up and grabbed the guard's right arm but, as he clutched it, the guard suddenly rammed into him. Before Echo Four could react, he went tumbling to the ground, a knife heading for his face. But just as quickly as it started, it ended, with the guard lying dead on the floor with two bullet wounds to the head.

"Don't let complacency cost you, kid. You should've seen the knife in his left-hand sleeve," said Echo One, as he helped him back to his feet.

With the room cleared, they moved over to the only laptop in the hope it would provide some information. Echo Two inserted a large device, in the style of a memory stick, and started a data transfer which would be received by Adrian. It only took a minute to complete, and they were back upstairs just after.

"Outside is clear of enemy vehicles," said Blindspot.

They stepped outside to see the storm still pounding the barren surroundings. Echo Four stopped and looked to the east, where he saw a trail of over fifty guards lying on the ground. They were all close together, so had clearly been dropped in short succession of each other.

"How did Blindspot have that many rounds for his sniper rifle?" asked Echo Four, as they all started to lie prone to make the trip back to the surrounding woodland.

"Ask him yourself when we get back..." answered Echo One, knowing that Blindspot would fail to comment. As they continued through the field, he added, "The operation might've been simpler than we thought, but you still did good today, kid."

"Who knows, maybe you'll even earn yourself a seat in the meeting room," added Echo Two with a deep voice, followed by a slight giggle.

It took longer to get back, but they were eventually out of the grasp of the building storm. They started to pick up speed, as they headed back to the plane, while Adrian made it clear their operation wasn't quite over.

"We've got more vehicles approaching from the east," he said.

"I've got them covered. Head back to Adrian and take off. I've got to meet Alpha team, so I'll see you back at the Molehill," said Blindspot, marking the longest utterance Echo Four had ever heard him say. Echo team knew he'd be more than alright and headed back to Adrian.

They travelled on foot, to reduce the chances of being tracked, and eventually arrived back at the exfil site over an hour later. Their comms had also been shut down, ensuring nobody could trace the signal as they returned. As they got to the runway, their private jet came into focus. It was all black and capable of flying off the radar, making up for its lack of firepower. The door was already down, and Echo

One led the way onboard. As they got in, Adrian stood up to greet them.

"Blindspot has dispatched the convoy, and there are no signs of anyone tailing you. As for the data, well, I've passed it on to Bosse to be analysed, but there didn't seem to be much there. I'm no hacker, but the only thing I could find was the person who supposedly organised the attacks. A... Mr Wilson. But aside from that, we've got nothing to go on," he said.

Adrian was short and thin with a round head. He had ginger hair and eyebrows, and always had a happy expression, even when he was concerned. The door was sealed, and they were in the air within minutes, heading back to their base.

During the flight, Adrian shut himself away where he could coordinate the assault for a different team. The other members of Echo team decided to rest, with Echo Two and Three sleeping and Echo Four unable to stop talking about their operation. Suddenly, the plane began shaking irreparably.

Adrian rejoined the others, asking, "What's going on?"

Echo One didn't have an answer, so they both started to head for the pilot. Through the window, Echo Four could see they'd hit heavy turbulence through the storm they were suddenly amongst, but then, without warning, a bolt of lightning struck one of their wings, tearing out a chunk. The lightning was persistent and continued to strike the plane. Before long, the jet couldn't keep its altitude and, with just one wing and a damaged engine, the plane started hurtling towards the ground.

"This is Adrian to the Molehill, do you read me?" he shouted, before his laptop was torn from his hands, as they picked up speed heading towards the ground.

Adrian was thrown against the back wall, whilst the others braced themselves in their chairs. He was desperately trying to reach a button, just out of his grasp. Echo One let go of the chair he was holding and crashed to the back of the plane. Within a second of arriving, he pressed the button, launching a drone. The drone sent out an instant distress signal, as it started to record the plane plummeting to the rocky terrain below. It was unstoppable, colliding with the ground and bursting into flames. Seconds after crashing, the storm simply cleared up and vanished, its work done.

Chapter 1 – The Compound
February 2nd
03:28 GMT

It was a crisp and clear night with not a cloud in sight, just the stars glistening in the sky. Moving through the barren wasteland without a sound, the huge and modern complex came into view, lit up like a sports field. Their night vision was on, it helped them to see in dark conditions, making everything green. They also had a light filter fitted, which was able to reduce the strength of the night vision, preventing them from having to remove the goggles every time they came into a bright area. Should the need arise, their goggles could be flipped up, above their heads, to give a clear view in front, whilst keeping their face masks on. The most noise they ever made was the occasional breath of the cool air. The masks they wore covered most of their faces, leaving only their mouths exposed.

They reached a wall that stretched the entire perimeter of the compound. All five operatives fired their grappling hooks into the very top of the fifteen-foot, rough stone wall and with the specially designed hook, it just stuck to the surface by acting as a sucker, supporting up to 400 pounds. They glided up as one, climbed over the top, and jumped down the other side, as if they were landing on a soft pillow.

The complex itself was Mediterranean in style with white, coarse walls. They moved through the shadows and passed the few guards patrolling the grounds. When Alpha team goes on a mission, they plan everything. No questions, no doubt, no hesitation. But this time, something was different, something didn't feel right. Alpha One was usually right about his instinct. It stemmed from the lack of guards. Their intel wasn't just a couple of guards over, there were about five times less than when the intel was obtained, yesterday.

The target hadn't left through any known exit, but that didn't mean he hadn't left through an unknown one. Despite this, they had to continue, through the shadows. They knew to only take the guards out if they had to, a dead or unconscious body could draw unwanted attention and that wouldn't help to keep a low profile.

At this point, they split up. Alpha One and Two moved to the back door, whilst the other three headed to the roof. The two that headed to the back door got there without seeing a single guard, and they waited behind the hedge next to the door, watching for a green light. They ensured the door was unlocked and let the others know they were ready. Their masks sealed in their ears, so they could only hear each other through their earpieces, as well as any external sounds picked up by the microphones on the sides of their helmets, creating a 3D audio within the mask to help them identify the direction of any sounds.

***

Alpha Three received a short ring in his earpiece to let him know the other two were in position. They climbed the external ladder without making a sound, their boots absorbing all the noise. Upon reaching the summit – five floors up – the wind had become stronger, sharper even. There were no guards on the roof either and, because it was still dark, the distant city could be seen as if it were right next door.

They approached the giant skylight and set four black, round charges on each of the corners of the glass. Next, they set up metal fixings which stuck to the roof just as the grappling hooks did. Attaching a cable to each of the three metal hooks, they sent a signal back to the other two which automatically started a three-second timer. Then, they took several steps back.

THREE, their shoes twisted in the dirt and gravel. TWO, Alpha One's fingers pulsed over the door handle. ONE, Alpha Three placed his hand over the detonator, and Alpha Two clonked a lever down to shut off the power inside. There was no ZERO, no GO, and no START, they all knew when to go and, within a split second of each other, they began to move in.

***

Alpha One turned the handle, and with a clunk, it came free and began to creep open. Without a squeak, it opened to reveal two guards facing away from the door. Without hesitation, both Alpha One and Two released their rifles to swing them out of the way on their straps, swung their left hand around the guards, and placed their index finger behind the guards' gun's trigger. Whilst their right hand slapped around their mouths, their thumb pushed down on the tip of their noses. The guards' arms flailed around and their lungs gasped for air, but before long, they went limp, some would even say lifeless. They laid them on the floor in an adjoining empty room, still alive, just unconscious.

***

34 SECONDS EARLIER
Alpha Three detonated the charges, and they ran towards the skylight. The gravel kicked up behind them, as their shoes pounded the roof. The charges vibrated the skylight to such a degree that it shattered into thousands of little pieces, raining down to the floor below. When they got to

within a step of the skylight, they jumped up and spun around 180 degrees, the momentum carrying them above the newly formed hole, and they were engulfed into the lightless room below. The cable whistled through the metal hook and, near the bottom, it tightened, swinging them away from the broken glass. With a slight click, they unclipped their cables and flung themselves towards the edges of the room, landing again as if the floor was a giant pillow.

They knew the floor plan and knew the order to clear the rooms, so they wouldn't miss anything. Every room had the same routine, they checked straight ahead, they checked left, and they checked right, along with under and around all the furniture. This was enough to take in the whole room; even if they didn't directly look at something, it would have been taken in. Inside, the complex was very different, going from a modern Mediterranean outside to a decor inside that changed from room to room.

***

The first room which Alpha One and Two came to was a study which looked like it was from a murder mystery set in the old English countryside. Despite everything looking like it was made of wood, the entire room was fitted with high-grade steel, capable of withstanding most explosions. This seemed easy to clear, with a bookshelf on each side and a desk at the far end by the window.

They checked behind and under the desk and whispered, "Room one clear."

Alpha One found it easier to give the rooms numbers rather than names, this way they only had to remember room one was the study instead of the study being the first room. This might not seem like it would make a bit of difference, but to them, it made it easier, and it was these small details that made them so efficient.

***

Alpha Three, Four, and Five cleared a giant, open-plan room. The room consisted of a lounge, kitchen, dining area, and even a second seating area, looking through a vast expanse of glass, overlooking the whole of the left side of the complex's grounds, and the brightly illuminated city in the distance. The glass wasn't what you could call a window, perhaps it would be better described as a glass wall, and was so clear that, during the day, it couldn't even be seen. They checked everywhere. All around the furniture, under the table and chairs, under the cushions of the sofas, in the cupboards, and they even checked for loose floorboards. This wasn't just because they were checking for security or looking for the target, but they also needed to find a hard drive that could have been hidden anywhere. Whilst the contents of the hard drive were a mystery, they knew it must have important information, which would prove useful, no matter what those contents were.

***

Alpha One and Two entered the next room – a gym – and again, swept through it. They looked around all the equipment, snapping their rifles around every corner. There was one of each piece of equipment, suggesting only one person would use the gym; their target. Most of the rooms seemed to be designed without practicality in mind and didn't even look lived-in; it was more of a show house than a home.

Throughout the hallways and corridors, the walls were littered with paintings of all shapes, sizes, and artists, most of which had been reported stolen or had simply vanished. The rest of the paintings had probably also been stolen and just not reported because the so-called owners didn't want to admit they 'owned' them.

Once the ground floor was cleared, they moved up the glass, spiral staircase. Alpha One had his rifle pointed directly ahead and angled slightly up, whilst Alpha Two looked straight up. Upon reaching the summit of the tightly curled staircase, their rifles clicked to point in opposite directions. Alpha One looked to the left, towards the bend in the wide corridor, and Alpha Two stared down the long expanse of the corridor on the right, not moving his eyes. Although Alpha Two was looking at a fixed point at the very end of the hall, his eyes were taking in the entire surroundings, and anything that moved could be spotted immediately.

They headed to the left, went around the corner and towards a pair of frosted double doors. They were heavy to push, yet they were still made to look effortless to move. The doors opened together and the two figures, dressed all in black, emerged into the room. Their heads darted all around the room, their rifles remaining still. The room was large and mainly taken up by a crystal blue swimming pool. The lights were still off, all except the ceiling light, creating a moonlit atmosphere, which illuminated the entire room. Alpha Two began to wonder whether the power might have been turned back on, but then saw a generator and realised it likely had the pool on a separate circuit, along with the waterfall on the right. The pool itself reflected the light, which made the room even brighter, so they both removed their night-vision goggles. Although it was more than capable of reducing the strength of the night vision, it seemed far quicker to remove their goggles altogether. Whilst the pool was crystal clear, it was somehow difficult to see to the bottom, just like an illusion. Alpha Two flicked up a little screen on his right arm, known as a computerised arm terminal or CAT for short. The screen showed a thermal image of the pool and its contents. Although it was heated, it would still show a person in there. It was, however, empty.

They moved along the pool, their boots softly squeaking on the wet floor. This told them that it had been used recently, because the target wasn't someone to let others use his pool, but where he was, remained the question. At that moment, Alpha One heard footsteps down the corridor. Their eyes darted around the room, looking for a place to hide. If the guards were alerted to their presence, the whole operation could be over. It was far safer to strike with immediate effect, without the guards even knowing they were in danger, before it was too late. There's no point in taking a risk, not if you don't need to. And if you do need to, it isn't a risk, it's a chance, a chance that must be taken. Splitting up would give them a better chance of success, so Alpha Two headed towards a metal cage, scrambled up like his hands and feet were covered in glue, and jumped up with his arms stretched, wrapping his fingers around the metal pole which ran the full length of the room. He pushed a ceiling panel up and disappeared into the darkness, replacing the panel behind him.

The footsteps came closer and closer still. Only one set could be heard, but they didn't break rhythm. Alpha One spotted the wide flow of water going from the ceiling to the pool. It looked smooth enough to be a water wall, yet behind the smooth, cascading waterfall was a small space, just big enough to stand behind. Alpha One only knew this space was there because of the extensive reconnaissance that had been done prior to their operation, where there really wasn't a single stone that was left unturned.

Alpha Two could hear the pounding footsteps had got even closer and continued to get closer, and louder. Alpha One used his CAT to look at the door, as the water was too loud to hear through and almost impossible to look through. Although it was deafening from behind the waterfall, its noise couldn't be heard from the outside. Fortunately, the water flowing downwards was at room temperature and was a very thin layer, so his thermal camera would work, it just didn't provide nearly the same crisp picture it would in the open. Alpha Two had moved directly above the door and used his CAT for the same reason. There was just enough room to crouch in amongst the cables and pipes within the ceiling.

The thumping had become stronger but then, it suddenly stopped. The doors were insulated to keep the pool at the perfect temperature for the cheapest price, but this meant whoever was on the other side remained a secret for longer than the two would have liked. After a moment, the doors opened, scraping along the floor, and not one, nor two, but six guards came through, with their knees slightly bent and their rifles up, before the doors came to another thud as they sealed again. It was clear that the guards were looking for an intruder, so taking these six guards out seemed the best thing to do, and indeed was what they planned to do next.

Chapter 1.2

The guards split in half to head around the pool in opposite directions. Whilst Alpha One waited for them to move closer to him, he was faced with a dilemma; whether to use lethal force or not. Despite their suppressed weapons, taking anyone out non-lethally was always the desired option, as a dead guard couldn't provide any information, but Alpha One knew that it couldn't be allowed to jeopardise the mission.

Alpha Two moved back along the ceiling, until he was about halfway between the door and the wall, and raised one of the ceiling panels, before waiting patiently in the darkness. It didn't take long for the shadows to move below the removed panel, shortly followed by the guards themselves. Two guards had passed and, as the third stopped right below, Alpha Two dropped down. He landed just behind the guard, ensuring his rifle knocked him on his head, dazing him for only a split second, but that was all he needed. Alpha Two raised his rifle and whacked the guard on the back of his head with the stock again, causing him to drop to the floor. Alpha Two charged forward, as the other two guards turned around, kicking one of them to the floor and grabbing the rifle in the other guard's hands, twisting and ripping the rifle over his own shoulder. The guard still had hold, but his arm was outstretched, and Alpha Two jabbed the guard in the ribs with his elbow, causing him to release his grip on the rifle as he took a step back and slightly curled up in pain. Alpha Two spun around, curled his fist up into a tight ball and used his own momentum to hit the guard square on the nose. As this was happening, the other three guards, who were now over by the waterfall, began turning around to take aim at Alpha Two.

Alpha One's arms emerged from the water, hard to see because of the reflection from the lights. These long arms wrapped themselves around one of the guards and caught him off balance, pulling him into the water. From the outside, nothing could be heard, but moments later only Alpha One reappeared from the water and kicked one of the guards in the back of the knee, causing him to kneel. He grabbed hold of the other guard, pushing his rifle to the sky so he didn't hit anyone with a stray bullet. As the guard went to get off the floor, Alpha One kicked him in the face, knocking him back to the ground. Both of his hands were occupied by holding the rifle up, so he had to raise his knee to knock the guard off balance and catch him in the torso, causing the guard to loosen his grip just enough for Alpha One to rip it out of his hands. He flung the gun around and propelled it towards the other guard, who was again getting back up. The gun caught him on his left cheek and threw him on his side. Just as Alpha One lowered his body to tackle the guard that was still standing, he caught sight of another guard over on the other side of the pool, grabbing his rifle and raising it towards Alpha Two. As soon as he'd shunted the guard into the waterfall, he grabbed the knife from under his bulletproof vest and threw it, sending it hurtling towards the guard. It hit his hand, embedding itself within, causing the guard to release his grip on his rifle and shriek in pain.

The cry echoed around the room and alerted Alpha Two to his presence. He kicked his leg out, as if breaching a door, sending the guard flying back and into the pool. The guard, who had previously been shunted out of the way, jumped out from the waterfall and threw himself forward, pointing his knife toward Alpha One. As the knife lunged towards him, he managed to push up on his wrist, sending the knife flying above his head. At the same time, he twisted to turn his back on the guard and braced his legs; the force of the guard crashing into Alpha One's back caused the knife to slip out of his hands. Alpha One caught it as it headed towards the pool, his fingers wrapping around the handle, implanting it in the guard's leg. Alpha One then crouched to flip the guard over his shoulder and slammed him down on the poolside. The other guard was still staggering to get to his feet, before Alpha One clenched his fist and swung it around to hit the guard square on the side of his face, knocking him back to the floor, but this time, he didn't get back up. Alpha One looked up to see two guards lying on the floor and Alpha Two dragging a third unconscious body out of the pool. They'd managed to take all the guards down without killing them, but the scream one of them had let out could've alerted the entire compound to their presence. They tied the guards up and put them behind the waterfall, where nobody could find them, so a clean-up crew would have the chance of retrieving them for interrogation.

At that moment, they heard numerous footsteps travelling down the corridor. Without thought, Alpha One ran over to the locked door leading out to a terrace and used the stock of his gun to break the handle and lock. Then, he moved back over to Alpha Two, who was climbing back up to the ceiling, and followed him up, replacing the ceiling panels once they were through.

The guards flooded through the double doors and filled the room in seconds. Fourteen of them swarmed around, searching everywhere.

Just as one of them was shining their torch up at the ceiling, another found the broken lock and alerted everyone that, "They've gone out the back!"

They moved out onto the balcony and through the door of the adjoining room. Alpha One and Two saw their opportunity. Removing a ceiling panel, they jumped down to the floor. They placed their night-vision goggles back over their eyes and headed out of the room, whilst keeping an eye on what, and who, was behind them.

***

Meanwhile, the other three had cleared the giant room on the top floor and had breached a smaller room next to it. It was tucked out of the way and could easily be missed through a lack of planning. Alpha Three and Five went in, whilst Alpha Four stayed in the doorway, looking out and down the glass staircase. The room was full of computers and giant screens on the walls, and in the corner was a server with hundreds of blinking lights. Alpha Five sat down in the black, office, swivel chair and started pounding away at keys. He was looking for the data they had come for on a hard drive. He was scanning and flicking screens up and down so quickly that nobody could keep up with what he was doing. He did, however, find traces of where the data had been, but it appeared their intel was unfortunately correct; the data was solely on a hard drive. In fact, all their data had been transferred to the hard drive and then wiped off everything else just two days ago. The system did contain the entire security system, which was shut down by Alpha team prior to entry, as well as the security code that could be used to activate or deactivate it.

Alpha Five uploaded the code to activate the security system to a remote detonator that they took with them. The detonator itself had no connection to their own system. This made it safer than uploading it to their private servers in case there was some sort of virus within the code. Whilst waiting for it to upload, Alpha Five noticed an order to double the number of security guards from just two days ago, the same time everything was put onto a hard drive. The guards seemed to be from a private security force, but it was unclear who had hired them, the target or the organisation he worked for.

But they did know that time was short, so they got moving. They travelled down the stairs and continued to clear all the rooms, from sitting rooms, to bedrooms each with their own bathroom, not an en suite but an entire bathroom, and then they even came to a room with a huge round table that looked to be used entirely for meetings. The so-called 'meeting room' had sixteen chairs around the table and many more around the edge of the room. The room was empty, but each of the chairs had a small computer in front of them, built into the table.

Alpha Five checked to see if they had anything of use, but they had also been wiped. He did, however, manage to find something called 'Operation Storm'.

It was from a message simply saying, "*It has been built, now we must test it. It is time to initiate Operation Storm.*" It seemed that this had been forgotten about when cleaning all the data, a careless mistake, or something they hoped would be found. Either way, it couldn't be ignored. Once the message was recorded, they moved on and continued to clear out all of the other rooms.

On the third floor, all five Alpha team members regrouped. Alpha One and Two were a little bit later than they had planned, but the others were waiting in the final room, crouched, with their rifles poised. When Alpha One and Two entered the room, everyone was able to identify whether someone or something was a threat. The stripe on the top of their helmets helped to speed up the identification. It was a white stripe which was unique to each team member, with varying thicknesses. With all the rooms cleared, very few guards found, and no sign of the target or the data, they considered their next move. Whilst they were thinking, they all sat in the dark room, with their night-vision goggles still on, each pointing their rifle at a slightly different angle, but all pointing towards the only door. The entire compound had been under surveillance since the recon had been completed, and nobody had been in or out, so the target was likely still inside, at least that's what they had to assume.

Alpha One and Three got the floor plan of the complex out and rolled it over the floor. The floor was good enough to spread the map out on and it was a lot quieter than swiping a desk clear and flinging all the contents onto the floor, potentially drawing unwanted attention. The floor plan was printed in such a way that it could be read with night-vision goggles on or off. But after checking it, they couldn't find anything out of the ordinary and nothing that they could have missed. Alpha One paused, in thought, before reliving the events of their search, trying to think about whether there was anything he could have missed. Alpha One was the best at remembering everything, with his photographic memory he could remember every single thing that he needed to for all their ops. Despite this, his recollection turned no results. The only thing that he could think of trying was to go back to the room that was completely different from the rest – the office that looked like it had just come from a murder mystery – and this did seem the most appropriate place to put a secret room or hidden basement.

They all travelled down the two flights of stairs, single file, taking nothing for granted. Even if they thought there were no guards, it could be a mistake that would cost them everything, so they treated the place as if they hadn't cleared it at all. Upon entering the office, they swept the room clear, in the same manner as before. The room was still clear, so whilst Alpha Four and Five stood just outside the door, watching both ways, the other three proceeded to look for something that could be a trapdoor or a door to a secret room.

They lifted the rug off the floor and found no door, nor any loose floorboards. They opened the draws in the desk and felt for some sort of button or lever, but still had no luck. The final place to look was the bookshelf. There were hundreds of books spanning the entire length of the office on both sides. All the books were the same size and colour and were sorted in alphabetical order. They pushed, pulled, and lifted every book as quickly and quietly as they could, but before they could finish, Alpha Three noticed four light switches on the wall. With Alpha One's permission, he started flicking the switches from one end to the other. One was for the main light, one for the desk's side light, the third turned on a strip of lights on each shelf which illuminated all the books, and finally the fourth switch was clicked. There was a clonk, before one of the bookcases began moving forward. It had runners underneath the bookcase that slid along, and they moved within the cracks of the floorboards to not scratch the floor and give its secrecy away.

Behind the bookcase was a staircase, spiralling down. The stairs were within the walls of the office, so there wasn't any empty space on the floor plan to cause suspicion. Everything behind the bookcase was still lit, so it looked to have a different source of power, seemingly along with the office itself. They removed their night vision, expecting they would no longer by required, and allowed their eyes to adjust to a new light, before moving down the stairs. Alpha Four and Five stayed watching the entrance to the office with their night-vision goggles remaining on.

The stairs were completely enclosed down the sides, so they could only see directly ahead and had very little time to react to anything around the corner. Once Alpha One reached the bottom of the stairs, about two floors down, he stopped and stared down the wide, empty corridor ahead of him, made entirely of concrete, whilst he waited for the other two to catch up. Alpha Three was next, who stood to Alpha One's left. Then Alpha Two came down and stood to Alpha One's right. Both Alpha Two and Three touched Alpha One on his shoulder to say they were down. Alpha Three was left-handed, so it worked much better for him to stand to the left. They moved down the corridor, as spread out as possible, to a great big, reinforced door. The door looked like it was protecting a vault, but Alpha Three seemed confident he could open it.

First, he asked Alpha Two to grab the bag that Alpha Four had, he was the backpack guy; anything they needed, he had. Then, he placed seven of the charges, used on the skylight, at equal distances around the perimeter of the seal. The charges were made with a strong magnet so when Alpha Three activated them, the bolts all slammed against the door. The bolts perpendicular to the door were now unlocked, but the parallel ones were trickier, as they weren't magnetic. In fact, it was the perpendicular ones that secured the parallel ones, just to try and confuse people.

Alpha Two returned with the bag. Alpha Three rummaged through it and pulled out several items. He then began constructing them into a powerful drill with a fifty-centimetre-long and five-centimetre-thick drill bit. He began drilling next to one of the charges, at full speed. The drill had ice-cold cooling jets to stop the drill bit from getting hot so it wouldn't break or blunt, and he could drill without stopping. Once he had drilled in as far as he could, Alpha Three removed the drill and emptied a packet of silver powder down the hole. Thanks to the slight angle put on the hole, the powder made it to the back. Alpha Three did this for all seven of the bolts.

Once all the holes were drilled and filled, he put a tube of ice, that was in a thermos bottle, into each of them, before covering each with a cream-coloured patch, pushing on them to begin heating them up. The patches acted the same as a hand warmer, just bigger and better, and instantly began giving out heat. Once this was done, they ran back up the stairs and sealed the bookcase door behind them. Every cream-coloured patch caused the ice to melt and began seeping into make contact with the powder which in turn reacted with the water and exploded with a crippling force. The bolts bent out and the vault door gave a loud '*pop*' which echoed through the concrete corridor and up the stairs. Alpha Three then detonated the charges which rattled the door free. It fell to the floor with a crack.

All five of them moved back down the stairs and along the corridor. They glided down the corridor, again, spreading themselves out as wide as they could. Alpha One led the spearhead-shaped charge, as they clambered over the door and went inside. As soon as they entered the room, it became clear where most of the guards had gone.

They were spread out across the entire room which appeared to be some sort of modern-styled nuclear bunker. As they stepped in, a second door slid shut behind them, sealing the room and making it airtight, as the seals fastened themselves over the edges of the door. It was fitted with computers, TVs, and cupboards that stretched all around the room, and in the back corner there was a giant freezer door that probably kept most of the food. The guards were positioned in a semicircle around the room, using all the tables and furniture as cover. Alpha team stood still with their rifles aimed at some of the guards. Whilst everyone was poised, waiting to make the first move, a figure emerged, parting the guards as he went.

Chapter 1.3

The man looked about sixty, with the little amount of hair he had left being short and grey. He walked through the guards with a slight limp to his right leg, looked of an average weight and seemed fit and healthy for his age, with blue eyes and an oval head. Although the picture Alpha team had been given showed the target with a grey beard, the man in front was clean-shaven. Despite the lack of facial hair, Alpha One didn't need to review the picture; he had it firmly in his mind and knew the 5'11"-man ahead of him was the target. The target began talking, making them an 'offer'.

"You have a choice, lay down your weapons, and we will…"

By this point, Alpha One had phased the droning Los Angeles accent out of his mind and had begun looking for a way out, as his eyes darted around the room. For the room to be used as a nuclear fallout shelter there were certain necessities, such as fresh or filtered air. At the back of the room, there were canisters that looked like giant milk barrels. There was a valve that connected several tanks to pipes that went into the wall, and likely came from some sort of a filtering device. Alpha One slowly moved his rifle to the right, so that it was pointing at the canisters.

"Am I boring you, Mr…?" questioned the target.

Alpha One's reply was blunt, "I honestly couldn't tell you; I wasn't listening. But thanks for the distraction, Mr Wilson."

Before the word 'Fire' could even leave Mr Wilson's mouth, Alpha One fired a single bullet towards the canisters, making a slight clank as it ruptured the valve. All the guards turned around as the valve was completely ripped off the top of the canister through the quickly releasing pressure, and whilst the guards were distracted, Alpha team took the opportunity to put their gas filters on, which attached to the front of their full-face masks, preventing the need to remove anything, and costing them unnecessary time. The compressed air, once held within the giant canisters, filled the room, increasing the pressure so much that all the guards dropped their guns to cover their ears because of the pain, the same sort of effect you get when flying, just much, much worse. It didn't affect Alpha team, as their masks were pressurised now the gas filters were attached. Alpha Four then took out two smaller, white canisters, pulled their pins, and flung them into the middle of the room. A white smoke filled the room until Alpha Three created a hole in the second door using a blowtorch. The blowtorch was able to burn at such a temperature, thanks to the extra compressed air, that it cut through the door like a hot knife through butter.

The gas slowly cleared from the room, and the pressure returned to normal. As the smoke cleared, it uncovered all the guards, and the target, lying unconscious on the floor. Alpha Two picked up the target and threw him over his shoulder, whilst Alpha Five moved over to the computer on the table. Next to the computer was a hard drive which Alpha Five plugged into a small device he carried around with him. The device scanned the hard drive and gave a green light to say that it contained the data they were expecting. Just as Alpha Five packed the hard drive into a bulletproof pouch, the power came back on and, with it, a deafening alarm sounded throughout the complex. Their time was up, and they had to act quickly.

"Should I switch the security alarm off?" asked Alpha Five.

Alpha One gave it a short amount of thought, before saying, "No. It might give us the distraction we need."

Alpha Two flung a Kevlar sheet over the target to try and prevent him taking a bullet, before they all charged up the stairs with Alpha One leading the way.

Alpha One radioed through, "Exfil will be hot, we need covering fire."

They moved out of the office, with Alpha Three covering the right-hand side, and away from the front door. Alpha One kicked the outside door open, which swung around and slammed against the wall, almost coming off its hinges. Alpha One, Four, and Five came out of the door, their rifles pointing forwards, before Alpha Two came out with Alpha Three watching his back. To leave, they used the gate on the east side, opening the huge steel bolts and scraping the gate open onto the granite path leading to the beach.

Once they had got out of the compound, they could hear an ever-closing whistle. Alpha One looked to the right to see four dune buggies and two trucks tearing up the sand. Their recon team had already laid a small set of charges in the sand just up the beach, but first, they had to get there. All of them scuttled along the beach, passing the ridge of charges with next to no time to spare. When the buggies were nearing the charges, Alpha One turned and held his rifle scope to his eye. He zoomed it in towards a cross marked in the sand with a special paint that could only be seen through their scopes. The cross marked where the pile of C-4 charges had been buried. It was between two higher mounds of sand which would make it a likely place for any vehicle to go.

As the buggies got to the cross, Alpha One detonated the charges, sending two of them high into the sky before crashing down, crushing the roll cages, and ripping the bonnet of one clean off. A third was sent hurtling towards the sea, crashing into the once sedate, dark waters. The final buggy flew through the freezing air, the coarse sand peppering the scorched bodywork. It landed down on the sand, its suspension pushed to the fullest, which caused it to bounce back up. As soon as it had returned to the ground again, its wheels began spinning, chewing up the sand and throwing it out as it tore back along the beach. The mounted machine gun began firing at Alpha team, who immediately fell to the floor. The bullets came roaring past their heads. Each pound of metal came whistling past and embedded itself into the sand behind. Alpha One flicked a switch on the side of his rifle, turning it into a fully automatic gun capable of ripping through a metal frame, and that's exactly what he did.

As soon as the buggy rose above his horizon, he emptied all 31 bullets into its bodywork. Slicing their way through, smoke began billowing out from the engine, before one bullet cut through the top of one of the suspension springs, causing the left side to suddenly drop to the sand and bury itself, as the buggy to come to a shuddering halt. The passenger at the front flew onto the bonnet, as sand was thrown into the buggy from all angles. The gunner on top was propelled forward, the gun digging into his ribs, as his face was pivoted down and hit the gun itself, whilst the driver's head hit the steering wheel, rendering them all unconscious. All five members of Alpha team jumped back up and continued along the beach, with the two armoured trucks bounding across the dunes behind them, digging the sand up in front of them, and kicking it out behind.

Alpha team didn't have much further to go, but the trucks had already caught up with them. Both dipped down and came to an almost instant stop, pushing a small amount of sand out in front of them. The doors swung open and slammed against the side of the trucks. Alpha team continued to move along the beach but were still aware of the security force flooding out of the back of the trucks. All of Alpha team were fitted with specially designed camouflaged suits which were perfect for combat at all times of the day. They absorbed most of the light, rendering them almost invisible, especially at night, which made them incredibly hard to hit.

The trucks likely had some sort of thermal imaging camera to lock on to them, but the security didn't. The private security force didn't stop though, as they opened fire towards Alpha team. Their suits offered some protection against stray bullets, but they quickly had to dive into cover because the suits didn't stop the pain. They found rocks, mounds, and holes to give them cover, and Alpha Two lay on top of the target to protect him as much as possible. Bullets pounded the ground around them, eating away at the rocks they used for cover. The cracking of the rifles hid the noise of the hundreds of empty shells tinkling on the sand as they clashed against each other. Suddenly, the guns stopped, they reloaded and took aim back at Alpha team. Instead of continuing their bombardment of bullets, one man stood forward.

Whilst most of them were all in black, one had green stripes, one had red, and the one who stepped forward was half in black and half gold.

The one with gold stripes barked, "Surrender or die!" as if giving an order. He said nothing else.

Alpha One replied, "If you lay down your weapons, you may leave with your lives."

The security force chuckled, obscuring their hearing from the ever-loudening rumbling that came from behind them. Alpha One caught sight of a symbol on the side of their trucks which he couldn't quite make out but knew he would remember it. Once the scoffing and chuckling had subsided, the gold-striped leader held his left hand in the air and flicked it forward. The bullets again filled the sky but, by this point, the rumbling had got even closer.

Alpha team threw smoke grenades out to land in front of the security force, creating a thick screen of white smoke.

Over the radio, they heard, "This is Alpha Six," followed by, "Er… what are you doing down there?"

A scout attack helicopter burst through the smoke wall, leaving a plume of smoke in its wake. It flew so low that some of the security forces were lifted off the ground, before plummeting back down. The pilot tilted the cyclic pitch control to the left and pulled back hard, spinning the helicopter around to face the smoke. Alpha team were already up and heading towards a flat open space up the hill.

The scout helicopter spooled its twin-mounted Miniguns and fired, spitting out hundreds of bullets in seconds. The bullets flew along at waist height, keeping all the security pinned to the floor. As Alpha team reached the summit of the sandy hill, the helicopter tilted forwards and launched all twelve rockets into the sand in front of the guards. Throwing sharp sand into the air, it created another wall and kept the security guards down for even longer. The helicopter was quickly out of ammunition, so it flew to the top of the hill and hovered, side-on to the security force. Alpha Six emerged from the side with only a metre-long barrel sticking out. Alpha Six wasn't the pilot; he was the sniper.

He locked the bolt of his custom-made sniper rifle in place, looked down the sight and pulled back on the trigger. The rifle made the noise of thunder, just louder, as the bullet was propelled towards one of the trucks, ripping its way through the steel grill and into the engine, disabling the truck. Alpha Six did the same to the other truck, before switching weapons to a smaller semi-automatic marksman rifle. It wasn't as powerful, but it could release bullets in a shorter succession to each other. Alpha Six aimed down his sights and began firing at anyone getting back up. The bullets went at such a speed that the helicopter blades had little effect. Each shot was placed in the exact same place, an inch above the knee. Whilst the compound may have been private, the beach was technically public property, and even though Delta team had prevented any civilians getting close, killing was certainly a last resort to aid in the interests of keeping a low profile.

Alpha Six was using the last traces of the smoke, blowing in the wind, to work out the direction and strength of the wind, and the distance was short enough that each bullet had very little fall on it. This rifle wasn't on a bipod but instead just rested on his knee, pinned against the side of the helicopter, yet it still had hardly any recoil, allowing him to place each shot exactly where he wanted, as quickly as he could. Alpha team scrambled to the exfil and crouched down; a huge black hawk helicopter filled the sky seconds later from over the water. As it approached the ground, it flared to reduce its speed and land as quickly as possible.

The doors swung open and they all clambered in, throwing the target on the bed at the back and strapping him in to stop him from falling off. As the black hawk began to take off, the blades' thudding got louder and quicker. The blades got to such a speed that it looked as if they couldn't go any faster and the helicopter wasn't going to take off but, eventually, the wheels lifted from the sand. The scout helicopter flew off first, followed by the much bigger black hawk. They launched flares, which flew out from each side of the black hawk, to try and prevent anyone looking on with any sort of missile or rocket. The flares were also so bright that anybody looking at them would quickly turn away. They flew off as low to the sea as they could. From where the security detail were standing, who were now climbing back to their feet, only the black hawk could be seen, completely obscuring the smaller scout helicopter. As the sun began to rise above the horizon, they flew off, out of danger, to return to base.

Chapter 2 – The Accountant
February 2nd
09:58 GMT

"…921 you are cleared for landing."

Alpha One swung the door open, whilst they were still in the air, and dangled his legs over the side. Alpha Three joined him shortly after. He had a very big build and was muscular, only just fitting into his tactical gear. All the time he was out of his gear, he wore black T-shirts which were clearly two sizes too small. He was 6' tall and could always be seen coming, although his most distinguishing feature were his amber eyes. It looked almost as if he wore coloured contact lenses, but the unusual colour was perfectly natural. He removed his helmet and threw it back into the helicopter, revealing his blond, curly hair. He was in his late twenties and watched as they flew over the bright green hills and into a once abandoned airfield. The only thing around was a giant C-17-style plane at the very end of the long runway. Whilst it may have looked similar, their version had eight turbofan engines, rather than four. The added length of the wingspan also aided in getting the transport off the ground, due to its larger cargo bay and increased length and height. It had been designed back at their base and was called a C-8, nicknamed The Donkey. As they landed, it was clear just how big this plane was, towering above everything and creating a shadow that stretched all around it. It could hold both helicopters with plenty of room to spare.

As they jumped out of the black hawk, they were greeted by a dozen armed guards who collected their, still unconscious, guest. Entering the plane, they saw an older man walking towards them. At about sixty years old, he had short, grey hair which was going thin in places. In some ways, he looked a little like Mr Wilson. He was a bit shorter than average height, had a round head, and looked a little overweight in places, but nothing that was noticed too much in the dark blue, pinstriped suit he always wore. As Alpha One continued to get closer, his short, grey stubble and faded, blue eyes came into view. The impression he gave wasn't that of a businessman but, instead, of just someone who took the upmost pride in their appearance.

"Success?" he asked in his husky, French accent.

They had been on radio silence, to keep their location a secret, so he had no idea whether the mission was a success or not.

Alpha One replied, "I need a word, in private…" whilst swiftly moving him into the middle of the C-8. "They knew we were coming," whispered Alpha One.

"What do you mean?" replied the older man, who was seemingly in charge.

"They knew we were coming, Bosse; they had already wiped their database and were hiding in the bunker. They'd also sent for some sort of special military security force," said Alpha One.

Bosse questioned, "What are you suggesting?" whilst lowering the tone of his own voice.

Alpha One replied, "Well, they knew exactly when we were going in and made sure the security force held back so that they weren't picked up by Delta team on their recon. Whoever it was knows how we operate, so we might have a data leak. Well, either it's a leak in our system or we have a mole."

Bosse lowered his eyes in deep thought and replied, "I'll look into it."

"But yes, we did get both the target and the data," concluded Alpha One.

He turned to see the two helicopters being put into the back of the C-8 and Alpha team unloading their gear into individual crates. The target was secure, the hard drive was being decrypted, and it was a long flight back to base. Most of them went to sleep, with Alpha Three being the first to go. Although he would never admit it, his mouth was wide open, and his snoring could be heard throughout the plane, just like a cartoon dragon in a cave. Alpha Six, Anthony, was the tallest of them all at 6'3" and was about thirty with a long face and piercing blue eyes which stood out from everything else. His body was wrapped around crates and netting, like a snake, with the main part of his body lying on a row of hard, metal chairs. They were able to sleep under the noise of exploding shells, but Alpha Six's snoring was the hardest to sleep through without any sort of rhythm and a whistle that sounded like he was calling a dog. He tended to be at his noisiest whilst sleeping, as he was the quietest member of the team. During the rare occasions he did speak in his flat voice, his North London accent was unmistakable, but to those who heard him speak more often, they could detect the hint of his Cornish accent from when he was a child. Anthony always had short brown hair, so short it wasn't far off being completely shaved, but no matter when they saw him, it was always the same length.

Alpha One was cleaning his rifle about twenty seats away from the rest of his team. Normally, he would choose to sleep first, but he had a lot to think about. The possibility of having someone leak information, or worse, was troubling. He started running through all the possibilities in his head, but the more scenarios he ran through, the faster he began cleaning his rifle. He'd chosen all the operatives who worked there from a list created by Bosse. If someone had infiltrated their force everyone would be in danger, and Alpha One would blame himself. Yet, at the same time, he knew how ridiculous it truly was. Alpha One was aware there was no way someone could betray them, but despite that, he was unable to stop considering it, no matter how hard he tried.

Alpha Two could see him frantically cleaning and knew why, as he'd known Alpha One for longer than any of the others.

He moved over and touched him on his shoulder to stop his train of thought, before saying, "Scott? You don't know how they knew we were coming. We don't have any moles; everyone chosen by you is dedicated to the force. You've nothing to worry about."

About a month ago, Scott wouldn't have been thinking so negatively, but since losing Echo team and Adrian, he couldn't get out of the deep hole he'd put himself in. Alpha team had picked up the case where Echo team had left it, but deep down, Scott knew something wasn't right. He knew something ran deeper than their deaths just being a coincidence, and that was what he intended to find out. Scott laid his rifle down and moved over to his hammock. It took someone else to tell him what he already knew, but that still didn't put his mind to sleep. He threw his legs in and lay back, staring at the metal ceiling whilst he slowly drifted off, thinking about the past, the present, and the future.

***

Scott wasn't sure how long he'd been asleep but was awoken by a tannoy message, "Five minutes to landing."

They'd hit some turbulence, as the plane began rocking whilst making the noise of it falling apart.

Scott turned to Alpha Two, who was just getting up, and said, "Daniel, secure the target, we're almost there. Take Samuel with you," whilst nodding towards Alpha Three.

Daniel nodded his round head, before raising his big, thick eyebrows towards Alpha Three. Daniel walked with a slight limp to his left leg, but never seemed to limp when in the field. His round head was covered in black hair, which was always kept short and tidy, and his dark brown eyes often had contact lenses in them, giving the option to change the colour of his eyes, should it be necessary for a mission. He might've lived in London for almost ten years, but just like Scott, he was able to put on a whole range of different accents, helping him blend into multiple environments. Daniel was around 5'11" and was the oldest member of Alpha team, aged in his late thirties. Scott might've been the wisest and smartest leader they knew, but even he occasionally needed help, and it was Daniel who had to know what Scott was thinking. He was the one who'd known Scott the longest and had been by his side for many years, but rarely needed to step in. Daniel's main task was to keep Scott on the rails, rather than pick him up and put him back on. But lately, Daniel's job had become more challenging, as Scott blamed himself for something which was completely out of his control.

Scott moved towards the front of the plane and up the stairs, passing a square, steel box, about two metres tall with one window, where Mr. Wilson was sitting on a chair, the only piece of furniture in the box. Scott continued up and into the cockpit. One of the pilots had his hands on the controls, hardly moving at all, whilst the other was radioing through a long number, their clearance code. Looking out of the narrow cockpit window, Scott could see the runway getting bigger and bigger. The wings were flexing up and down, like a bird. Eventually, the plane touched down, with squeaking wheels, before tearing down the bumpy runway.

Once slowed down, the C-8 maintained a steady speed. Due to its extended size, the wings needed to, and were able to, fold in. This couldn't be done whilst airborne but could halve its wingspan once on the ground. The wings sounded creaky, as they jolted back into a fixed position. Just as they were narrow enough, the pilot swung the plane into an open hangar. It was the biggest at the airfield, yet it was only just big enough to fit the plane's still vast wingspan through the doors. The doors scraped shut behind them and locked. The whole hangar was completely bombproof, made of a combination of layers of steel, reinforced concrete, and tungsten, with small, spherical, black objects plastered all over the wall. These strange objects switched on, scanning the entire hangar for heat signatures and any other objects. This was done by releasing a sound not heard by the human ear and worked the same way as bats 'see'. If the sound bounced back, there was something in the way. A thermal imaging camera also helped to give them a clear look inside. With these two pieces of information, the entire hangar could be scanned for anything out of place, to ensure nobody had got in, or put something inside that shouldn't be there.

After this was done, the hangar floor jolted, as if a mechanism kicked in. Instantly, the floor began lowering. It didn't go very quickly and couldn't be felt from within the plane, so from the cockpit, it looked as if it was the walls that were going up. They went down about thirty metres, almost the height of a ten-storey building, before the walls vanished and they were in their hidden base, the Molehill. The giant lift shaft opened into the true hangar, which was the size of a large airport, where you needed a car just to get either side. Everything in there was parked at the edges and ran the full stretch. There were troop carriers, including another C-8, fighter jets, stealth planes, helicopters, tanks, and everything else you could think of with a few experimental vehicles which the world hadn't seen.

The platform thudded to the floor, before a car hooked onto the front wheel and began pulling the plane forward. From the ground, the car looked like a big 4x4, but it looked almost insignificant from the cockpit, more like a toy car. Whilst the plane was being dragged into its space, Scott headed back down towards his team, who were already standing at the back, ready to leave. Scott picked up his bag and joined the others.

"Well done today, that was a close call, but you came through. All of you..." said Scott, as he looked at each of them, before continuing. "Sorry that we don't get a break, but there's still more to do. Daniel, take Mr Wilson to the interrogation room and prep him, I'll be along in a few minutes..." Whilst turning to Alpha Five, he went on to say, "Mike, I need you to take the hard drive down to Tech and try to get into it. Samuel and Anthony, you've got to head over to reception with Bosse to meet with the new sponsors. Bosse was saying they wanted us for some security op. It shouldn't take too long..."

Anthony's shoulders sank, whilst Samuel interrupted with an exasperated voice, "Seriously? We've got to be bodyguards for yet another rich person, adamant they're in danger just because they have money! The only reason they're going to give us any money is just so they're part of a super secret organisation. I mean, they don't even realise how big our organisation is. They've only been chosen to give us money because they're so easy to keep tabs on and will do anything for power."

His face started going red and his fists were clenched. Mike and Daniel began smirking, knowing that if they said anything it would make everything worse.

But this didn't stop Scott, who replied, "Correct me if I'm wrong, but I get the impression something's made you a little tense. Is there something you need to get off your chest?"

"No, I can't wait," said Samuel sarcastically.

Scott replied, "Good, I needed someone to go to some 'meet-and-greet' event for those 'rich people' a little later, so you'll be okay with that, won't you?"

Scott began moving out of the plane with a sly smile, not expecting an answer. Although Samuel was born in the UK, he'd spent most of childhood growing up in America which resulted in his strong New York accent. For the past few years, he'd lived in South London which had already caused a slight change in his accent, as every few words were spoken in a very South London tone.

Mike swung his arm around Samuel and squeezed, as they headed out, with Anthony following closely behind. Mike was short and skinny with spiky black hair and brown eyes. His height was the only thing which didn't make the others jealous, despite him only being 5'9" and not much smaller than the others. He had perfect features, with nothing broken or out of shape, and had a smug smile, showing he knew it. Although he wasn't posh, he was very well spoken and always walked around with a very straight back and upright posture. Whilst changing his accent wasn't one of his talents, he was able to speak eleven languages fluently, and many more in a lesser capacity. He was twenty-seven, so this gave some of the older members even more to be jealous of.

Alpha Four moved off towards Scott, turning his amble into a slight jog.

"What about me?" Alpha Four questioned.

Scott said, "I need a favour." Alpha Four looked quizzical but intrigued. "Back at the compound, there was a symbol on the side of the security trucks of some sort of a bird with a message in, I assume, Egyptian hieroglyphs. Here, I drew a picture of what I thought I saw... but it was dark, and they were trying to kill us," he continued.

"I'll see what I can find... And I assume this is to be kept quiet?" Alpha Four replied.

"Yes. And Kenny, tell Suzy that those suits are almost perfect," said Scott.

Kenny smiled, as he replied, "She'll be pleased, but I do know she's in the process of making them even better.

Suzy also hopes our rifles can be made the same way, but I haven't a clue how we're meant to see them."

Kenny was the same height and age as Samuel but looked very different to him. He had green eyes and big, thick, brown hair which was always swept back to fit in his helmet. He had a very large, muscular face but was of average build. Kenny was from Southampton, where his mother grew up, despite his father being Belgian, although you wouldn't know it to look at him. Although everyone called him Kenny, not Ken or Kenneth, it was actually his middle name, preferring not to be called by his first name, Trevor. Scott gave him a couple of little pats on his shoulder before they moved off in different directions.

Scott swung his duffel bag over his shoulder and raised his hand as if calling for a taxi. An open-backed pickup truck turned up, and Scott hopped onto the back. The truck trundled down the long hangar until it reached a set of double doors. He jumped off without the truck even stopping, went through the doors, and headed down the long, stark corridor.

There were rooms of all sorts spread across the whole compound but all full of plants. The compound may have been underground, but the plants, natural-coloured lights, and the ventilation made it just like working above ground with the added security that comes from being under metres of reinforced concrete.

The room he was heading for was the evidence room. It was rammed with paperwork, weapons, clothes and everything else you could think of, yet it was still perfectly organised. Scott knew what he was going in there for and moved over to the exact spot he wanted without glancing elsewhere. He picked up a small pocket watch with an inscription on the back saying, '*Making the difference*'. Scott slipped the watch into his pocket and started to head towards the interrogation room.

Mr Wilson was already sat in a chair with its back right up against the wall and a cold table pressed up to his chest. There was a mirror on the opposite wall, staring down on those in front. There was nothing but a solid wall behind the mirror, but Mr Wilson wasn't to know that. If he thought someone was watching him from behind it, then he would direct his true emotions away from it, and towards one of the many hidden cameras that lined the room.

Scott swayed in, not as Scott, but instead as Alpha One. He didn't want to intimidate him by standing up or raising his voice, but instead relied on a more subtle approach which included everything from the positioning of the room to Alpha One and Two changing into clothes slightly smarter than Mr Wilson's dirtying suit. He let Mr Wilson intimidate himself.

Alpha One dragged out the seat and sat down next to Alpha Two. Alpha One asked the questions, starting with the most obvious.

"Who do you work for?"

And of course Mr Wilson replied with the expected, "No comment." Alpha One went through tens of questions, asking everything from where he grew up to who his boss was, with the same, "No comment," as an answer for all of them.

Alpha One then broke the pattern of questioning and asked him a random question.

"What colour are your socks?"

To which Mr Wilson replied in his usual way of, "No comment," without even thinking.

Alpha One then proceeded to joke about it with Alpha Two, saying, "Well, would you believe it? Even his socks have to be kept a secret. Still, at least we have a lead. Alpha Two, take his socks off and get them down to evidence."

Alpha Two began standing up, replying, "With pleasure."

By this point, Mr Wilson knew he had made a mistake and couldn't have his socks taken, as it would make him feel vulnerable. So, he quickly shut Alpha Two down by snapping, "Yellow and black striped. Like a wasp."

Alpha One then tilted his head towards Alpha Two and chirped, "Or a big fluffy bumblebee. Still, at least we got something other than a no comment," whilst maintaining eye contact, as he had throughout the interview.

Scott continued with this momentum, like a dog that wouldn't release its bone, building on each question. Over time, the questions became more and more relevant. It was taking time, but they were getting the answers they needed. Although Mr Wilson had no idea how long he had been in there, everyone else did and, after precisely eight hours, Alpha Two got up and left. He didn't say anything, he just gave a glance to Mr Wilson to show him that he wasn't getting out. It was to make him crave freedom which was something that Mr Wilson no longer had. Alpha One continued, unfazed by the planned exit. Every question answered let Mr Wilson's guard down just a little more.

Eventually, they came full circle, and Alpha One returned to his original question. He leant forward, gave a slight frown, and asked, "Who do you work for?"

This time round, Mr Wilson gave quite a different answer. "I work for no one. We work together. We work in the shadows, all around you. We are M.N.G.W.A."

Alpha One paused for a moment, before questioning, "Mngwa? As in the mythical beast?"

Mr Wilson smiled, almost pleased to prove his knowledge, and replied, "Yes, a giant feline which never fitted in. It looked like a domestic cat but was bigger than most lions, and yet it moved like a leopard. It was almost a hybrid, combining everything great about all felines. But can you honestly say that it is a myth? That is our organisation, able to work in the shadows because the few people who do hear about us don't believe in our existence, and those who come face to face with us aren't able to speak of our existence."

"Working in the shadows. Well, I guess that explains why you're not on any database," added Alpha One, trying to make Mr Wilson think he had the upper hand.

Alpha One focused elsewhere, asking, "How many head this organisation?"

To which Mr Wilson swiftly replied, "Five."

Alpha One smiled. "Five people who all want to make the difference."

Mr Wilson's demeanour changed instantly, before Alpha One flung the pocket watch onto the table with the inscription facing up.

"Where did you get that?" trembled Mr Wilson, before removing an identical watch from his pocket.

Alpha One leant further forward with an even larger smile, saying, "This isn't the first time we've had one of you five sat in that chair. Didn't they tell you? Well, they weren't nearly as talkative as you, so will you inform the others of our conversation, or will it be our little secret?" Mr Wilson continued to look worried, as Alpha One didn't wait for a response before concluding the interview by saying, "You're going to stay in here with another interrogator and you're going to answer all their questions, and if I have more, I'll be back to ask them. And if I don't like any of your answers, you'll be released, and I don't expect your 'partners' will be so understanding."

"You're very sure of yourself, aren't you?" said Mr Wilson, trying to have the final word.

Alpha One then stood up and walked towards the door, opened it, and left without a single glance at Mr Wilson, slamming the door shut behind him, confident he had no need for the final word. Scott travelled back down the stark corridors, but this time towards his quarters. The room was entirely for practicality without much more than a bed. He lay down, still dressed, and fell asleep within minutes.

Chapter 2.2

After just four hours of sleep, Scott awoke and began moving to their office. Inside, there were six desks, all identical and laid out in three rows, apart from one that was completely clear. Beyond the desks was a separate room, with an all glass wall, which was Scott's office. He moved over to Kenny, who was sat at one of the desks, and tapped him on his shoulder.

With a soft voice, Scott said, "Have you found anything?"

And with the press of a few keys, Kenny replied, "The inscription seems to translate to 'making the difference'."

Scott looked deep in thought before saying, "Just like the pocket watch. They must be a part of this organisation."

"Not necessarily. The inscription might be the same, but the final symbol here isn't any sort of letter or word. It seems to be an emblem for a private security force. They've been around longer than us. In fact, the first reference to them was back in 1918, formed after World War I. They call themselves the 'Night Vipers'," said Kenny.

Scott stood back up and patted Kenny on the back, saying, "Good work. Best get some rest. We'll hopefully be moving back out soon."

Scott then moved into his office, closing the door behind him and sliding his hand upon a touchscreen panel. The entire glass wall began getting darker until the whole thing was smoked, and nobody could see inside. His desk was neat and tidy, with every piece of paper straight and stacked up to one side, and the one blue pen parallel to the paper. The monitor and laptop were lined up so their bases were straight against the back of the desk, and the keyboard was at a perfect forty-five-degree angle over to the monitor's side. He sat down with the smoked glass in front and a world map behind, filling the entire wall. Scott spun his chair around and stared at the map, full of pins and red string lines. He then placed one more pin in the exact spot they had just been, at the compound. There were pins in all the continents and most of the major countries. Each pin represented where this secret organisation had been spotted, but Scott still couldn't find any connection or pattern between them. He still didn't think M.N.G.W.A. was behind it, more like yet another pawn. He sat back, staring at the map, and let his mind wander, wondering what they even wanted. A knock at his door startled him, making him sit bolt upright. His reaction time was as near to instant as anyone could get, but he didn't reach straight for his gun, as he could distinguish a threat from no threat just as quickly.

At the press of a button, Scott released the door.

A disappointed Mike poked his head around the corner, exclaiming, "I've got a bit of bad news. I think you should come and have a look."

Scott nodded his head and followed Mike out of the door, towards his desk.

Mike picked up the hard drive, before saying, "This can't be accessed without a key, well, an electronic key to be precise. We've managed to reverse trace the only key we can find back to a building here," as he pointed to a location on one of his three computer screens.

"Well, can't we just move in and pick it up?" asked Scott.

To which Mike replied, "It's a little more complicated. The building is used as a nightclub. Well, that's what it's meant to look like. It appears to actually be a safe house for a group of people called the Night Vipers."

Scott lowered his head and released a huge sigh, before saying, "The Night Vipers were the group we went up against on the beach. But if we need that key, then we're getting that key. I'll put a plan together with Daniel. You need to get some rest before we move out."

Mike agreed and headed back to his quarters, whilst Scott moved over to a small, square panel on the wall and pressed an even smaller button next to Daniel's name. His name went green, so Scott knew he was on his way.

Once Daniel had arrived, Scott filled him in, and they began planning their assault. The building was within the public domain, so there was a no-kill order in place. It also turned out that the nightclub was even more of a front than Scott first thought, as the only people that were allowed in were those who worked for the security force. That meant everyone in the building was highly trained, and they could only enter with a certain type of watch. The watches every member entered with appeared to be different, according to the only surveillance camera outside which Alpha Five had hacked earlier. But there was something about them which had to be specific and identical to each other, as the guard on the door seemed to know exactly what he was looking for. Either way, they could let Delta team get the watches so they continued with the plan.

There was a multistorey car park opposite, so they agreed to station Anthony in the back of a van, giving him a prime position to observe the nightclub through his thermal sights. Daniel would oversee their exfil and would wait in another van a couple of blocks away; he could even pace the path in front of the nightclub to watch for any reinforcements. Samuel could get himself a bartender's outfit to keep an eye on most of the people, whilst Mike would stay on the floor and blend in with the majority of the security force. Samuel and Mike would be close enough to help, but it would be down to Scott to get the key.

As soon as word spread that the data had been stolen, the key could be moved to a separate location, so there was no time to waste. They had no time to wait for any sufficient reconnaissance to be done, so they would be going in blind. Going in blind wasn't something Scott liked doing, especially when they wouldn't have any weapons on them, but if it meant the difference between getting the data or not, he had to take that chance. That was why Scott would be the one to get the key and be in the most danger. Judging from their limited intel, it appeared that everyone who entered got frisked, so there wouldn't be a way of bringing anything in, well, not anything suspicious anyway.

"Get Delta team to head to the nightclub and obtain a few of those watches, then make sure we have transport to get there and back. I'll get the rest of the team, and we'll meet in the hangar," said Scott, whilst nodding his head to show they had finished.

"Did you ask Mr Wilson about the assaults after the weather disasters?" asked Daniel.

"No, I wanted to make him think there was something he knew that we didn't. Anyway, we know they're behind the attacks. Destroying ships and planes full of relief aid isn't something they'll get away with, but right now, we need to find who's pulling their strings," answered Scott.

"You don't think they're at the top?" questioned Daniel.

Scott shook his head, answering, "Whoever they work for knows exactly when there's going to be a natural disaster, a tsunami, tornado, tropical storm, anything. They have people on the ground instantly. I want to know how and who."

They both left the room, deep in thought. Scott collected the other four and told them to head to the hangar, before he moved on to meet Bosse.

When Scott entered his office, Bosse was on the phone, and Scott gave him a look that told Bosse to put the phone down, immediately.

He got the message and swiftly ended the call with a short but sharp, "I'll contact you when I have more."

Scott went straight in with, "We've found a way to open the data, but there's something we need first, a key. We know where it's being held and will be ready to move within the hour."

Bosse replied, "And you think you can get this key?" whilst lowering his eyebrows. Scott nodded which was enough to reassure Bosse of their impending success.

"Best of luck," he replied, before immediately shifting his gaze to his computer.

Both Scott and Bosse had the same level of clearance and, whilst Bosse was more of a face as the head of the organisation, it was Scott who ran it, despite Bosse being able to give the orders and have the final say. If there was something Bosse wanted to change, he would be allowed to change their operation thanks to the strange and confusing way their clearance codes and authority worked. Scott might have run the organisation, but it was Bosse who was in charge, although, he rarely changed anything. Bosse never gave his permission for a mission; it was always more of a blessing.

"Before you leave…" Bosse started, lifting his head back up to Scott, "there's been another natural disaster. This time it was a volcano erupting. We've no idea how many casualties and there is no sign of any relief forces being targeted this time. Despite the break of pattern, the odd thing is that the volcano was extinct. Not dormant, but extinct. There shouldn't be any way that it could have erupted."

Scott shared Bosse's confusion, not only could a secret organisation predict any natural disasters with perfect accuracy, but now, a volcano had erupted that shouldn't have been possible.

"Bit of a coincidence, isn't it?" Scott asked.

Bosse began nodding his head, giving a slight shoulder shrug at the end but said nothing, concluding the conversation. Scott knew there was nothing further to say and Bosse had clearly finished his side of the conversation.

He left the room and made his way to the hangar, so he could join the rest of his team. Back in the hangar, Kenny was loading one last bag on top of half a dozen others into the back of a private jet. They had the official landing permit and could slip under the radar as just an ordinary private jet taking someone to their private yacht. The rest of Alpha team were already inside and, as soon as Scott and Kenny were in, the door was closed. They could stay in a nearby safe house until Delta team had their equipment ready, meaning they could move in without delay. The jet then began moving towards the lift, wasting no time.

Chapter 3 – The Voice

February 4th
22:02 GMT

Alpha One waited patiently amongst the other seven people queueing for the nightclub, watching what everyone else did as they entered. By the time he got to the front of the queue, three further people had joined behind him. He stepped up and held a card in front of the guard's head with his left hand. The card was irrelevant, even though everyone who entered had that identical card. It was the black watch, strapped to his left wrist, which got them in. Whilst everyone's watches appeared different, on closer inspection, the hour hand was actually identical to each of the others. Made especially for them, the guard on the door took little time identifying the hour hand before being satisfied. The guard briefly frisked him, finding nothing more than an elastic band. He replaced the elastic band and stepped back, shifting his focus to the next person in the line, allowing Alpha One through and into the nightclub. But stood at the side of the road, under a flickering streetlamp, was an unfamiliar figure. Wrapped up, with a great big hood covering much of their face, unseen, the figure watched… everything. Alpha One pushed the left saloon door open and let it swing closed behind him. Without looking back, he entered the huge room ahead that was already full of people. Alpha One's eyes scanned the room, left to right. He took everything in, whilst he continued to walk, so as not to draw any attention to himself.

Moving over to the bar, a familiar face greeted him. Alpha Three handed him a dark drink in a tall glass, making it look like his regular. There was a key card inside the serviette, under the glass, which was subtly slipped into Alpha One's pocket whilst he took a gulp of his sweet drink. At the bottom of his glass was a tiny, white bottle. Alpha One finished his drink and allowed the bottle to roll into his mouth. Making his movements slow and discreet, he held the serviette up to his mouth and pretended to wipe his lips. Alpha One flicked the bottle into the serviette, with his tongue, and placed the bottle, wrapped in the serviette, into his pocket. He nodded at Alpha Three, before turning his back and leaning against the bar, looking for any doors which had 'Private' above them. Only one door had a sign above it, saying 'Private', and any door inside one of the most private places that existed that said 'Private' must be worth a look.

Alpha One wandered over to the door, negotiating the huge crowds of people, whilst still not drawing any attention to himself. To the right of the door, there was a large swipe panel. Alpha One removed the key card from his pocket and swiped it through the panel, resulting in a beep that could have easily been missed in the deep thumping of the music. With a firm pull on the door handle, it swung open, and Alpha One moved through. He didn't look behind, because Alpha Five would have had his eyes on Alpha One the whole time and would have known if anyone else had spotted him.

The door clunked shut behind Alpha One, who was staring down a short and narrow corridor. On this side of the door, there was no noise that could be heard, so no footsteps would be masked. Alpha One knew he had to find a staircase and head down, as the largest energy draw came from two floors below ground which was likely the server room, and Alpha One hoped the security room would be with it. He headed through the first door on his left. It seemed to be some sort of empty staffroom, but in the adjoining room, Alpha One could hear talking.

He stood there for a moment, listening, until he was convinced there were only two people inside. Needing to create a distraction, he picked up an apple from the fruit bowl on the table and went into the next room, a locker room. There were four rows of lockers in the middle and benches surrounding them, pressed up against the chipped, cream paintwork. The two were on the other side of the second row of lockers, so Alpha One threw the apple to the left and moved around the row of lockers on the right. One of the two went to see what the noise was, and Alpha One took advantage of their separation. He crept up behind the stationary one, swung his arm around his neck and squeezed as hard as he could. The flailing arms of the panicking cleaner smashed against the lockers before going limp. The second man flew around the corner, but it was too late. Before he could even work out what was going on, Alpha One's clenched fist thumped into his temple, knocking him straight to the floor.

Whilst both were unconscious, Alpha One took the time to rifle through their pockets, taking everything of interest. He took a set of six keys from the cleaner, as well as another key card, a screwdriver, and a hammer from the other worker. He dragged the cleaner's body into a giant laundry bin and, after changing into the other man's clothes, who was an electrician, he flung his body on top, covering both with the unfolded towels which seemed to fill the laundry bin. The electrician's clothes were a close enough fit, and should offer him entrance to most of the areas, which was just as well because the cleaner was tiny. Alpha One just had to hope there wasn't someone who knew everyone's face. He looked down to see a clipboard and a piece of paper on the bench with a jobsheet ordering the repair of a printer in the security office. Alpha One smiled at his turn of good luck, letting out a slight chuckle over the coincidence. He left the room and went back into the corridor.

As he approached the next door, he could also hear talking inside, but after trying the handle, without success, there was no going back, so he knocked on the door. A set of footsteps came closer, then the lock snapped open, and the door squeaked inwards. A woman with long, blond hair emerged from behind the door with a stark expression. Her left eye was blue, and her right was brown, catching Alpha One's attention and causing him to hesitate with a slight stutter.

"I'm... er... I'm looking for the security office," he said, whilst handing her the clipboard.

She was quite tall, at around 5′12″, and had a long face, but a tiny nose. It was clear from her complexion that she wore a large amount of make-up, and her eyebrows appeared to be drawn on with an eyebrow pencil. She looked down at the document before pointing to the left, followed by a quick flick of her wrist, directing Alpha One to turn left at the end of the short corridor with her long, thin fingers. She'd gone back into the room, closed and locked the door without saying a single word. But just before the door closed, Alpha One caught sight of a large, muscular man sat down, dressed in security gear with a red stripe down his shoulder. It was the same person as at the compound. He had a square head and jaw, surrounded by a thin, wiry beard, thick eyebrows, and mid-length, brown hair sitting around his ears. The officer was slowly wiping a knife he held in his hand, taking a lot of care over it. As much as Alpha One knew he could force his way in and take them both down, that wasn't the time for confrontation. The risk of taking them out far outweighed the reward.

Alpha One followed the directions, taking the door on the left, whilst subduing any thoughts that the data key could have already been moved. The door on the left led to the staircase Alpha One was looking for. He took the stairs down two flights which then opened into a room almost as big as the nightclub floor. The room seemed to be the server room, security room, and armoury all in one place. There were ten guards in the giant room, one of whom strutted up to Alpha One with a face that was clearly asking 'What are you doing here?'.

Alpha One handed the guard the piece of paper, who then examined it and handed it back, saying, "You're not meant to be here until tomorrow, so come back then."

Before the guard could turn his back, Alpha One stepped in, saying, "There's been a change've plan. I was told to come today, guv'nor," with a cockney accent.

He wasn't entirely sure why the adopted accent was cockney, but it was already too late to change it. The guard went to shut Alpha One down again but was interrupted before he even spoke.

Alpha One continued, "'pparently you're goin' on full lockdown tomorrow, so now's the last chance for me to fix the printah," after raising his eyebrow to make his statement a question.

The guard paused, thinking, then beckoned Alpha One over to the side of the room where the printer was. Alpha One gave a slight hint of a smile in appreciation, then crouched down and took the tools out of his pocket, laying the only two next to him. The guard stood right behind Alpha One, watching his every move, and tried to intimidate him which, of course, didn't work. Alpha One saw the door on his left as his only option to thin the herd but had to think about how to get in there. The door didn't look reinforced so probably didn't have anything of any value or importance. Alpha One didn't like guessing, but he had no choice so hoped it led to some sort of storage room or, even better, an altogether empty room.

He picked up the screwdriver and took all the front panels off, and then began ripping out a thin metallic sheet from within the printer. Although hitting a printer may get it to start working again, they are fragile pieces of machinery. Alpha One, however, had no intention of fixing it, all he wanted was to make as much noise as possible, and he succeeded. He began hammering away at this piece of metal as if he was changing the shape of it.

The other guards quickly became irritated by the noise and, after just a few seconds, the guard tapped Alpha One on the shoulder, exclaiming, "If you're going to make that sort of noise, follow me." He pushed the printer over to the door, opened it and went inside, closely followed by Alpha One.

Inside the much smaller room were a few empty shelves and an empty, wooden desk. The guard slammed the door shut, plunging the room into complete darkness, before switching the lights on. He then stood behind Alpha One, again, watching his every move.

Alpha One turned around and pointed to the table, asking, "What is that?"

The guard didn't want to be fooled but the curiosity was too much, as he turned to the table. There was nothing there, so the guard spun around to confront Alpha One, but he was greeted by the metal sheet knocking him square on his face, sending him falling to floor, almost as if it was in slow motion.

Changing into the guard's outfit wouldn't work as the other nine would likely all know what he looked like, so Alpha One took the taser out of the guard's pocket and slipped his baton up his sleeve. He then thought about how he could take the others out quietly. If there was one thing Alpha One knew he had to adopt, it would be patience. He hid the guard's body under the table, then flipped the table down on its side to cover the body. He then proceeded to open the door by just an inch and started hammering again.

It took a few minutes, but another guard eventually came sauntering round the corner.

"You need to keep the noise down," said the guard.

What Alpha One really needed to do was to close the door before the takedown.

"Pass me the screwdrivah would ya mate," exclaimed Alpha One, making the guard move over to the table. Alpha One silently closed the door, before the guard looked behind the table. Seeing his unconscious colleague, he froze for only a moment, but by the time he went to spin around, Alpha One's arms wrapped themselves around his neck and squeezed tightly. The guard's instincts were to grab Alpha One's arm, but he wasn't strong enough to do anything other than gasp, before eventually losing consciousness.

Alpha One dragged the guard over to the table, as if it was his prey, and slumped him over with the other body. Alpha One then opened the door again and wheeled the half-dismantled printer back into its original place, plugged it in and, with two exposed wires, he tripped the circuit, taking down every computer in the room. He quickly unplugged the printer and carried on as if nothing had happened. All the computer screens went black, causing the other guards to look around in confusion.

They looked towards Alpha One, asking, "What have you done?"

Alpha One answered a short, "Diddly-squat," whilst moving over to the desks.

The guards were visibly confused by his answer, as they looked at one another, hoping someone could help. Even Alpha One started to find the lengthening silence awkward, unsure how to proceed.

He looked at the black screens, as if he didn't already know what he'd done, and then calmly said, "I'll fix your primitive little computahs. Where's ya fuse board?"

The guard in front of tens of security screens stood up, looked at Alpha One, and said, "Darren, Pierre, go and show him where it is."

The two nodded at the French guard and directed Alpha One back towards the stairs. Whilst it had broken the silence, the guards were still unsure what Alpha One's previous comment had meant.

Behind the stairs was yet another door. This one led to another small room full of fuse boards, metal pipes, and even a mop propped up in the corner.

Just as the door was closing, Alpha One could hear the head security officer say, "Go and check on…" before the door slammed shut.

One of the guards pointed to the fuse board labelled 'Security Room' and crossed his arms.

"Cheers, mate. I doubt I would've ever worked that out," said Alpha One with a sigh and a long look up to the ceiling. He simply flicked the switch up and the power came back on. Alpha One then began turning around, whilst saying, "I'm surprised you couldn't do that." He then looked directly at one of the guards and added, "Hmm, I dunno though," under his breath, but loud enough so they could hear him.

Ensuring Alpha One was in the middle, the guards began moving him back to the main room. Just as the guard in front reached for the door handle, Alpha One grabbed the taser from his pocket and fired at the guard behind. Immediately after, he grabbed the guard in front, again wrapping his arms around the guard's neck and squeezing until they were both lying on the floor. Turning to the one behind, he lifted the guard by his collar and knocked him back to the floor, ensuring he was rendered unconscious as well. Alpha One then searched through their pockets, again looking for anything of use.

He moved back into the security room to see only three guards left. He walked over to the head of security, stood in front of him, and turned his back to him. This angered the guard, and Alpha One could almost feel the guard's muscles tense. He was hopeful the increased anger would make the guard reckless, and Alpha One was usually right. The three guards were all staring at him, trying to intimidate Alpha One, as if they knew his true plan. In truth, however, they were exactly where he wanted them. A click of the guard's keyboard echoed around the room, before all three stood up and a fourth came bursting out of the first room, drawing his handgun.

Chapter 3.2

Keeping a cool head, Alpha One let the baton slip down the inside of his sleeve and caught it in his hand, before throwing it towards the guard holding the gun. The baton hurtled towards the guard and caught him on the forehead, sending him falling back. The head of security threw his arm around Alpha One's neck, but that was also what Alpha One wanted, it meant one less person with a gun. The other two had begun to draw their handguns, but Alpha One beat them to it, whipping two tasers from his pockets and firing at the guards. Both fell to the floor, shaking. Finally, Alpha One quickly dispatched the head of security by taking a small pin out of his watch and stabbing it into the guard's leg. The sedative-laced pin affected the guard within seconds, as he was suddenly overcome with an incredible sense of fatigue. He staggered around, before falling to the floor.

Alpha One checked the two tasered guards wouldn't be getting back up any time soon with a not so gentle tap to their faces. He looked around at the unconscious bodies and didn't waste any time in moving them all into the empty room. He searched through all their pockets and took out any key cards, keys, and anything of interest. After finding a guard that was a similar size to him, Alpha One changed into their uniform and went back into the security room to access the cameras and other security details. He was sat there for less than a minute, and had just about switched the computers back on, when he heard footsteps coming down the stairs. He had enough time to hide under one of the desks, where he'd be out of sight. Four armed guards moved down and fanned out across the room. Alpha One risked a little look above the desk and saw two of them were originally from the security office, so he knew there was a chance his cover had been blown.

Their weapons were suppressed, which meant Alpha One didn't have to worry about them firing their sub-machine guns, he just had to make sure he didn't get hit. Alpha One took the taser out of the pocket of the guard lying at his feet. A pair of feet moved past, heading straight for the back of the room. It was the next pair that moved past slowly, checking everywhere, before turning and bending down to look under the table. Alpha One leapt up and grabbed the guard's gun to hold it down with his right hand, whilst his left, clenched fist caught the guard on his jaw, sending him staggering back. Alpha One swung around and fired the taser at the approaching guard, who also fell, shaking, before returning and hitting the first one on the nose to finish him off.

"Freeze! Drop the weapon and place your hands on your head," came a bellowing voice from behind.

Alpha One knew he couldn't outrun a bullet, but they seemed to want him alive, rather than dead, which did give him the advantage he needed.

He could hear the shuffling footsteps creep closer and closer in fear, their fingers twitching over their triggers. It wasn't the first time Alpha One had witnessed tough guards becoming scared, but it did make him start to wonder whether his presence was expected. Eventually, Alpha One felt a hand clasp his wrist and, as soon as he heard the gun being holstered, he spun around. The guard, who was now holding Alpha One's wrist even tighter, ended up facing in the other direction with an arm wrapped around his neck.

Alpha One then stared at the second guard and shouted, "Drop it!" as if he was talking to an animal.

The guard clearly had a plan, but he lost concentration for just a moment. Alpha One took the baton from the guard, clutched in his arms, and flung towards the other one at such a speed the impact was enough to instantly knock the guard out. With just a few moments of constricting the guard's breathing, the final one fell to the floor.

Alpha One then began dragging the remaining guards into the tiny cupboard, one by one. Once all the bodies were hidden, he got back to the computer and continued pounding the keys. He brought up the login screen and went to look at the head of security's badge. There was a long number which was successfully used as the ID number. The screen then flashed up, requiring a passcode. Alpha One observed the room, looking for anything that could help. Above the computers he was currently using was a board full of documents and sticky notes. Alpha One scanned the board, finding only one sticky note that didn't look old. It displayed another number that Alpha One plugged into the system. The passcode was accepted, and he was into their system. It seemed obvious that the passcode was changed frequently, meaning nobody could remember it, the only thing that allowed Alpha One into their system was their overcautious security. First, he turned off all the security cameras and deleted the past twenty-four hours of footage. Alpha One then searched through all the data on the 'key' he was looking for. There were no files that seemed to give anything away, but he did find a directive ordering most of the guards to the 'secure room' in just one hour. Shaking his head at their hubris, Alpha One got up the floor plan and planned his route to stay out of corridors as much as possible.

The last thing he did was place a grenade, from one the guards, next to the servers. The grenade had its pin pulled out and had Alpha One's elastic band wrapped around it. He then took the tiny white bottle from his pocket, which Alpha Three had given him earlier, and dripped all the contents onto the band. With the band now laced in an acid, it would corrode the rubber and give him about thirty minutes.

Alpha One got to the foot of the stairs, adjusted his outfit so it would look right, and began moving upwards. He ascended as if he knew exactly where he was going, whilst listening for the slightest noise of foreign footsteps in case his cover had been blown. There were no alarms or charging guards, which gave Alpha One some confidence that his cover remained in place, but he knew there was no room for complacency. Once the stairs were cleared, he headed through the first door on his left, striding in with confidence. It was a bathroom, which had a doorway at either end, with someone at the sink washing their hands. Alpha One strolled past as if he was meant to be there. The opposite bathroom door led to a communal lounge, which led to a locker room, and then to a dining area, all of which were filled with guards and other workers that didn't even see Alpha One as being out of place.

The following room was another communal lounge, but with three doors this time. There were five guards in there, but one of them didn't recognise Alpha One as part of the normal security team. The guard looked square at Alpha One, refusing to hide her suspicion. Thinking quickly, Alpha One headed straight for one of the doors, slipping through and closing it behind himself. The room was a set of sleeping quarters with twelve beds, all recessed into the wall. Alpha One stood behind the door so, when it opened, it would hide him altogether. The suspicious guard strutted in, edging her head around the room. Slowly, Alpha One crept the door closed, before stabbing her in the back with the tiny, sedative-laced needle from his watch, also rendering her unconscious. Alpha One placed her body in one of the beds and covered her with a blanket, before picking up a key that fell out of her pocket.

He then headed back out, just as confident as before, to find the other four guards in the same place with no suspicions. He unlocked the final doorway with the key and moved up the stairs it was hiding. The spiral staircase was tightly packed into a space no larger than a closet, so it didn't take any more room than was necessary and didn't register on the floor plan.

"They like their secret rooms, don't they?" he muttered to himself, as he started his ascent.

As much as he tried, Alpha One found it hard to move up the creaky, metal staircase silently with the big, clumpy boots he had acquired from the guard's outfit. With every creak and crack of the stairs, Alpha One had to become even more vigilant, relying on all his senses to work together, and not just his eyes.

At the top was a wooden door, completely out of place with the rest of the building. It must've been thin, because he could clearly hear a conversation from the other room, but with no recording device, Alpha One relied on his keen memory.

The first to speak had a strong, but high-pitched, Dutch accent, who said, "The key is in my possession and ready to move."

After a slight delay, another voice leapt in, clearly angered, yet still soft, saying, "Well, what are you waiting for?"

The delay made Alpha One assume the other person wasn't there but instead on a call, maybe video, maybe just a voice call.

The Dutchman chirped back, "As soon as the security office gives the all-clear, we'll be on our way," pleased with himself for taking so many precautions.

"When was the last time you had any contact with them?" asked the soft-voiced man in his Irish accent.

The Dutchman began to lose confidence, quickly, as he continued, "Well. We… Er. We lost contact with them a while ago after some sort of disruption, another team was sent down there, who... who haven't quite got back in contact just yet. But we do expect... Sir? Sir? He just hung up."

Just as Alpha One was reaching for the door handle, a huge arm came tearing through the door, grabbed hold of Alpha One, and ripped him into the room, before he'd had any time to brace himself. Alpha One's borrowed rifle slid across the floor, as he looked up, and then looked up some more, to ultimately see a tiny head, surrounded by masses of fat and muscle, on top of a huge, towering giant. He was wearing only a sleeveless vest and trousers, with no bulletproof or stab-proof vest, and no protection, other than the natural armour his body provided. He looked the sort of person that could lift a car and make it look like it weighed as much as a book. The giant just stood there, almost 7' tall, waiting for Alpha One to move, as if it was an animal teasing its prey. Behind the giant, another man was standing back. He was much smaller, at about 5'10", and had a small face and build. Judging from their appearances, it was the smaller man whose voice had been heard only moments prior. The Dutchman had thick, brown hair, which was in no obvious style, and was all over the place. But before Alpha One could take in any further details, the giant drew all attention back to himself, as he let out a huge snort, just like a fierce bull. Alpha One tried to draw his stolen sidearm, which the giant stopped, effortlessly, before the man mountain intentionally aimed it at his own torso. Alpha One pulled the trigger, firing the bullet into the giant's body, before the gun was crushed and the giant revealed the bullet had entered about two centimetres into his body, halted by the many layers of muscle. The pain seemed non-existent, protected by layer upon layer of fat and muscle, despite blood oozing from the wound. Still clutching Alpha One's hand with his left, the giant swung through with his right fist, catching Alpha One below his stomach. Alpha One flew across the room, crashing through a table full of computer screens. He crumpled up in pain, desperately trying to find something to help. Big heavy footsteps began getting closer.

Alpha One saw a chain not too far away with what looked like a pickaxe on the end, that was hanging up in a cabinet full of ancient weapons made with a modern twist. Alpha One crawled over to it without looking behind him. He climbed to his feet, smashed the glass door and began swinging the weapon around his head. The giant man stood back, as the weapon swung around, before it was released and sent hurtling towards him. He casually stepped out of the way and watched it wrap itself around a metal pole, fastening itself with the pickaxe. The pickaxe was only inches away from catching the Dutchman's hip, who swiftly moved through the door and out of the room, holding a small, black box in his hand; likely the data key itself.

With a smile, the giant said, "Missed!" in a voice that echoed throughout the room. He then grabbed Alpha One and tightened his grip around his throat, draining the life from his head.

It felt like Alpha One had been gasping for air for minutes but, just when he needed it, the building gave a slight rumble, before alarms were sounded which were so loud you'd probably want to cover your ears if you were in the building opposite. The noise startled them both, with the giant losing his grip on Alpha One and stumbling back. Alpha One quickly took advantage of this and, without a second thought, he wrapped the chain around the giant's leg, punched him under the chin, and pulled as hard as he could on the chain. The momentum of his weight caused the giant to crash to floor. At that moment, the alarms quietened down, and sprinklers hidden in the ceiling turned on, covering the floor in water instantly.

The giant man mustered all his strength to get back to his feet and squinted through the large amount of water flowing down his face, to see Alpha One holding a silver dish. The giant man began running towards Alpha One as if he were a bull charging towards a red cape. *Bang! Bang! BANG!* Heard Alpha One as the giant man's footsteps got closer. When he was within a couple of feet, Alpha One flung the tray into the giant man's face and curled up into a tiny ball on the floor. The tray was just enough to distract the man, as he stumbled over Alpha One and tore through the wall. A couple of seconds later, the chain went tight.

After he'd caught his breath, Alpha One leant out of the newly formed window to see the man, once thought to be an unstoppable giant, hanging next to the building with the chain tight around his ankle, unconscious from knocking his head on the wall. Relief flooded Alpha One's body, but it was to be short-lived.

He looked up to Alpha Six opposite, who'd been following most of his journey with the thermal imaging camera, and who was now flashing a light on and off. It was a message in Morse code, which was short, and kept repeating itself. It read, ".-. ..- -." which simply translated to 'run'.

Alpha One looked up, as he heard a helicopter approach. Thinking quickly, he grabbed a rope from the floor, tied one end in a knot, and slid down the chain. When he got to the bottom of the chain, he looped the knotted end of the rope over the unconscious man's other leg and continued to slide down, until he reached the end of the rope. Alpha Six shot the chain, causing it to break, sending Alpha One down the final part of the drop, followed by the huge guard, who somehow survived the fall.

Alpha One ripped the preplaced earpiece out from under one of the bins, to hear, "Everyone's out," from Alpha Two's much welcomed voice.

Alpha One ran for the alleyway, as some sort of specially designed, armoured helicopter flew into sight. He could see the blond-haired woman and security officer in red and black flee from the building as well, but Alpha One had no time to chase them, as the helicopter fired countless rockets at the building. He continued his straight path as fast as he could, as the building he had been in, only moments before, was torn to shreds by this helicopter. The building crumpled into just a pile of debris in a matter of seconds. It was followed by a massive explosion, with the shockwave propelling Alpha One even further along the alleyway. He was thrown to the floor, and he stayed there protecting his head as, what felt like, a huge fireball erupted over him.

By the time Alpha One felt it was safe enough to get back up, he raised his head to see the hooded figure, who had been watching earlier, rush past in front of him. This was the first time Alpha One was aware of this mysterious figure, so he stumbled to his feet and gave chase. Just before rounding the corner, he gave one final look at the raging inferno that was the pile of rubble. Alpha One began picking up speed, as he was led through the rabbit warren of back alleys until, finally, he caught up to the figure. Standing facing Alpha One, his face still obscured by the hood, the figure, who looked over 6' tall, lifted his right arm and fired a grappling hook out of his hand which quickly became apparent was a prosthetic arm. The figure shot up and climbed atop one of the buildings, revealing both his legs were also prosthetic. Before Alpha One thought about continuing his pursuit, something caught his eye; something in the shadows.

As he moved closer to a swinging, shaded object, it became clear what it was; the Dutchman, strung up by his neck, hanging. At first, Alpha One thought the hooded figure was sent by the other person on the video link to recover the data key, but then he saw something taped to the Dutchman's hand; it was the data key. Alpha One removed it from the man's hand, taking an unlikely risk that it could be a trap. He reviewed it by plugging it into a tiny memory drive stored in his watch, confirming this was what they were after all along, before slipping it into his side jacket pocket. He looked up to the roof, where the figure had last been sighted, to see nothing but black smoke billowing into the sky. As he turned back to the Dutchman, he saw his brown eyes, clean-shaven face, and noticed his black shirt had been taped up above his abdomen. The raised shirt revealed a tattoo which he swiftly recognised as being of a mythical beast, the mngwa.

Alpha One then re-established radio contact with his team and said, "I have the package. I'll meet you at the rendezvous."

He took a picture of the Dutchman's face to run it through their database, as well as a sample of his DNA, fingerprints, a picture of his tattoo, and a retinal scan.

Alpha One then left the scene and continued through the twisting and turning labyrinth of alleyways, now almost completely in darkness as the black smoke covered the lights. When he eventually got out to the other side, he acted as if he was an ordinary person out for a walk. All kinds of vehicles shot past, their sirens crying out. Crossing two roads and entering the car park, he kept his head down but still looked around as if he was curious so that he didn't look out of place should anyone spot him. Alpha One walked up to a plain silver van, gave four knocks, then climbed into the back to find all five members of Alpha team waiting patiently for his arrival.

Alpha One's quizzical look gave away something was wrong, but before anyone could get a word in, Alpha One shut them down by saying, "We've a lot of questions, and hardly any answers. But before we start speculating, let's get this data key back, and then we'll try and find out what happened."

They said nothing, but clearly accepted his proposal. They were also a little taken aback by the volume of Alpha One; he'd clearly been affected by the explosion. Although nobody said anything, they thought it was for the best if Alpha One didn't go shouting their next plan from the back of a van. Alpha Six climbed out of the side door and moved into the front. They set off for their ride home, whilst Alpha One lay back to rest his body. His mind, however, stayed very much awake.

Chapter 4 – The Lie
February 5th
17:27 GMT

After countless security checks, they were finally back in their hangar. Daniel was the first out, and he walked straight over to a set of double doors and went through, holding them behind him for the others to follow. Daniel didn't ever look back, he just knew that everyone was going to the same place, to get the same answers. They swiftly walked down the long, stark corridors in complete silence, the only thing making a noise were Scott's worn and borrowed boots scraping along the floor. Daniel led the way into Bosse's office after just two short knocks, not even waiting for his permission to enter.

Bosse didn't look puzzled by their unannounced entrance. In fact, he got straight to the point.

"Sooo… not everything went to plan then." Without waiting for a comment, he continued, "We were able to listen to that conversation between the Dutchman and whoever the other person was, whose voice, by the way, doesn't match anything in our database. We couldn't trace the call, but another call was intercepted just moments after, to someone who goes by the name of Hailey. He told her to 'get out', along with 'Red Viper' due to an 'imminent strike'. So, it would appear it was this person who had the nightclub blown up to try and prevent the data key from being stolen."

Daniel then stepped in saying, "If he would rather destroy the key, than lose it, and to go to those lengths to destroy it,

79

then it must hold something important, perhaps more so than we originally thought."

Bosse began nodding towards Daniel's frowned expression before he continued. "Yes, and that's exactly why I need that key taken straight down to Tech." His gaze shifted towards Mike, who gave a single, but slow, nod before heading back towards the door with the data key in hand.

Bosse went to conclude the conversation with, "So, if that's all…?"

But it was Scott who then stepped in, saying, "Actually, there was something else, or rather, someone else…"

Mike stopped leaving the room and moved back towards the others, who all looked to Scott to continue.

"After the building exploded, I was a little dazed, but I could make out a figure in front of me whose was face was completely covered. I gave chase and caught up to them, right where I think they wanted me to catch up. They were just standing there, waiting for me, and as soon as I got there, they used some sort of grappling hook and zipped up to the roof. The grappling hook seemed to come from a prosthetic arm, and they also looked to have prosthetic legs. But, to my left, the Dutchman was there, hanging by his neck; dead, obviously. The data key was still in his hand, so whoever strung him up was either just there to kill him, and did nothing else, or decided to help us as well. But whoever they were, they seemed good, skilled, and not someone that would get sloppy." Scott then directed his concern at Bosse, before continuing, "So, try and find something if you want, but I doubt anything will turn up. Also, they seemed to know who we were, or at least, that we weren't a threat."

Daniel could sense Scott's concern, mainly because Scott had felt helpless against someone who had got the upper hand.

"I'll see what I can do," concluded Bosse.

Before Scott also finished the discussion with, "It's been a long, few days. We should all get some rest…" As he led the way out of Bosse's office, he turned to face the others and added, "…outside the compound. It'll take a little while before we turn up anything useful with the data key. I'll be in touch when we have something to work with."

Daniel watched as Scott, followed by Mike and the others all finished filing out of the room.

Daniel then turned to Bosse, who was already burying his head in his computer, either trying to find answers, or avoid any further questions. Either way, Daniel didn't wait to ask, as he followed the others out of the room, and then proceeded to go his own way. Through the maze of corridors, and what felt like a hundred doorways, Daniel finally came to the entrance of a tunnel. There weren't many people to be seen along the way, but here, the place looked more like a military checkpoint. There were about twenty armed guards scattered all over the place, two of them up high where nobody could see them. Even though all the guards knew who Daniel was, he still handed over his pass, let them scan his eye, and take a fingerprint scan before he was able to leave. The fingerprint check scanned as deep as possible, mapping every layer of skin, right down to the blood vessels in his fingers which were uniquely his. There was no way of lifting a print from a door handle and getting through undetected, the only way was with the fingers themselves which had to still be attached.

Once everything was clear, they let him on his way, down the well-lit, straight tube. About half a mile down the tube, a bright light, at what seemed like the end of the tunnel, could be seen. It got closer, brighter while he moved onwards. As it got into view, it could clearly be seen as a tube station, just with no connection to the outside world. Daniel sat on a bench and waited, looking as if he was a normal commuter, not that he had any need to as the public had no way of getting in. Not long after, a train arrived.

Daniel got in and scanned his pass on a little panel on the door. The automated train then left the station, without waiting for anyone else, as a translucent door sealed the train within the tunnel it had entered, separating it from the platform. Shortly after leaving the station, the train was up to its maximum speed of 120 miles per hour, so there was no point in trying to stand to see if you could keep your balance. It used a combination of magnets and pressurised air to throw the train through the tunnel without friction to slow it down. Once within the sealed tunnel, the air in front of the train was sucked out, reducing any air resistance, and was pumped out behind, helping the pressurised air to propel the train forward.

Ten minutes later, the train came to a stop, spending only a couple of seconds slowing down, as the air was removed from behind the train and pumped out in front, creating a huge amount of air resistance. Daniel left the tube and headed up a spiral staircase that stood right in front of a door. As he got close to the top, his thoughts began to be drowned out by the booming noise of a bustling London above. The doorway at the top of the stairs led into a tiny, cold room which had another door, opposite, which opened into a freezer room. From there, the huge stainless steel doors led into the kitchen of a restaurant. Everyone who worked in the restaurant was combat trained and acted as a first line of defence. The restaurant itself was owned by their organisation, although not officially, and could be easily monitored for threats or potential security leaks.

Working in the kitchen was Daniel's cover for the outside world. It explained the irregular working hours and ensured that nobody would be able to see where he worked to notice his absence. He changed into more ordinary clothes and replaced them, where they had sat in the room behind the freezer, with his specialist outfit. He then entered the kitchen and picked up a set of chef's whites hanging up, which would fit Daniel perfectly, swinging them over his shoulder as he left. Hanging the whites up in the kitchen meant that they would smell as if he'd worn them in the kitchen all day, with aromas of spices, fish, and fats clinging to the clothes. Daniel left the kitchen and passed the guests, as if he was the one who had just cooked them their meals, and even stopped to help a woman get her pushchair through the doorway. He had instantly become a completely different person, from someone who could hold others' lives in his hands, to a kind-hearted and overworked chef.

It was hard to tell which was Daniel's natural personality, as he had played both for so long now. Even he didn't know which character, if either, was truly him. He bounded through the crowds, with a smile on his face, whilst putting just one earphone in his ear. Putting one in helped him to blend in without compromising his hearing. He never travelled the same way home twice. Sure, many of the ways were similar but even if it was just walking on the other side of the Thames, or approaching the apartment from the other side, it was never the same way. Again, this wouldn't stand out to an ordinary person, but to anyone trained, they would find it hard to set up any sort of ambush and couldn't track him nearly as easily. Although he tried to hide it, his limp was present. It was only very slight, but it was noticeable, so a reasonable explanation had to be created. The best kind of lie is a simple one, close to the truth, preventing you from tripping yourself up or forgetting part of the story. Whilst nobody had ever asked, Daniel was prepared to tell them that the limp came from a car accident when he was a child.

Daniel's body showed every sign of being just another ordinary person, despite his mind working overtime, scanning everyone who passed him, trying to take in as much information as he possibly could. He continued through the crowds, all of whom seemed to be heading against him. He dived into one of the many apartment blocks and climbed all twenty floors to reach his apartment at the very top. Inside, the apartment was dark, but Daniel still knew exactly where to go. He moved over to a hidden panel in the wall and went through the same process as leaving and entering their compound. As soon as the verification was approved, all the lights sprung on, revealing a large and modern studio apartment.

Although it was just one room, it was divided into compartments by thick, white screens that didn't reach the ceiling. This was to allow him to hear everything within the apartment, but still offer some protection and cover, should the apartment get compromised in any way. The penthouse was surrounded by quadruple-glazed, bulletproof glass, overlooking the vibrant city. The glass was able to withstand any known bullet or small projectile and, with a safe room that could be accessed through a chute under the kitchen sink, the apartment was safe from almost anything. To a casual observer, it might have looked a little strange, seeing a chef enter the penthouse of a London set of apartments that overlooked the Thames. Anyone who tried to look, however, would see that his father owned the apartment and restaurant he worked in, and it was only the people that tried to look who became dangerous.

After hanging his chef's whites up, next to a clean set of the same size, he flung a giant ice cube into a whisky tumbler and cooled the glass down. Before the ice had a chance to melt, it was tipped back out and swiftly replaced with whisky, filling almost half the glass. It was an unusual way to serve it, but holding a cold glass, and letting it touch his lips, gave his body a closer sensation to drinking a more refreshing drink, despite its burning nature, whilst not diluting the flavour. Daniel then moved towards the window, flicking the lights off as he went, and stared out, looking at the huge expanse of land and people. A vast array of lights coloured the thick blanket of clouds, hovering just above the tallest buildings London had to offer.

He took one huge gulp of his drink, making enough noise to echo around the room, which tensed his jawline and burned all the way down, as his eyes tried to take in the sheer number of people heading in all directions, for all different reasons. He realised that although there seemed to be an endless number of people, it was only a fraction of the world and all the people they swore to protect. It was this kind of realisation that gave Daniel conflicting feelings, with both a warm feeling of pride and sadness from everything he had left behind.

With a second reverberating gulp, he'd finished the drink and slammed the glass down on the nearby table. Suppressing his emotions, Daniel left the apartment again and headed out to try and fill his head with noise. He had to go through the same security process to leave the building, just to confirm it was him leaving, and eventually made it back outside, where it had started to rain. The rain started off delicately tickling his face, as each drop landed softly. But he'd only taken a few steps before the rain became harsher. The drops got bigger and more frequent, as they bounced off his nose and trickled down his forehead into his big, thick eyebrows. He flicked his fur-lined jacket collar up, tucked his head into the jacket, and submerged his hands deep into its pockets, before purposefully moving towards the closest bar. When outside the Molehill, Daniel didn't just play the part of a chef, he had to be him. Everything from the way he walked and held his posture, to the way he spoke and acted. Even the way his brain worked had to be changed, which was by far the hardest thing he had to do, but it made the difference between acting the part and living it.

The bar he approached didn't have too many people inside. *At least it's dry*, thought Daniel. He stepped in, only to see the entire left-hand wall full of all different kinds of alcohol and mixers; everything you could think and more. The bar looked more American in style, with 'Route 66' plaques all over the red walls and rams' skulls hanging above them. And just in case you still didn't get the whole American vibe, it was called the Kentucky Gambler. Daniel moved over to the bar, flicking his damp collar back down, and took a seat.

He stuck his hand up to signal the bartender, who was cleaning a few empty glasses at the time. Daniel made a mental note of her description, as he did with every person he met, sometimes without even realising it. The first thing he noticed was her hair scraped back and resting behind her shoulders. It was greying, but had ginger highlights which were done a while ago, as the ginger hair had clearly grown out. Her face was quite long, but with its chubby appearance, it looked a little rounder. She had a freckly face and looked a little on the overweight side. Although her appearance made it hard to work out her age, she did look in her forties, despite her greying hair.

She was in no hurry to tend to him, but did eventually saunter over and asked, "What can I get for you?"

She sounded like she came from Kentucky but also seemed to have an East London accent almost fighting to get out.

Daniel hoped she was the owner, as he stared at the endless bottles in front of him, and asked, "What do you suggest?"

The bartender began to crack a smile, as she pointed to a board advertising a 'Mint Julep' for £7.99, and then went on to say, "It's the best tasting one outside the Kentucky Derby."

After staring longfully at the board, Daniel said, "Isn't it a little... safe?"

The woman took a step back, stood upright and continued, "Well feel free to play it a little unsafe. I mean, I've got bottles of things even I don't what they are, and I've had them for years now. I'd love to get shot of 'em. Plus, you do look like a man of adventure, and yet, you want more, don't you? You've got the world on your shoulders, and the first thing to help is to have a drink, so what's it to be?"

Daniel began to question how someone he'd met only one minute and twenty-three seconds ago was able to see through him so easily. At least he knew his cover as the chef fitted her comments; he'd taken the restaurant from his father, but always knew he wasn't running something of his own. He had to carry on, brushing any comments aside, hoping she'd only said that to try and make him have a drink, not that he'd gone into the bar for anything else. But that was when Daniel noticed a young woman sat to his right. She seemed to be looking towards him, but without letting on, so he decided to try and make an impression.

He said, "Let's try something new. How about a double measure of dark rum and a single of Scotch whisky, stirred, then poured on top of a single measure of grenadine and topped with lemon juice to taste."

The bartender stared back at Daniel with a face of uncertainty, which didn't shift, as she said, "That sure as hell ain't safe," before turning around to get the ingredients.

"You've got unusual taste, haven't you?" came from a soft, tender voice to Daniel's right.

He turned to see a tall, brown-haired woman in her late twenties. The harsh, red lights reflected off her soft skin, highlighting her deep green eyes. She gave a smile, enough to draw Daniel's full attention.

But, before he could engage her in conversation, the bartender interrupted.

"I've got something called Kahlúa that I've just opened for some strange bloke who asked for something nobody has ever heard of; you'd probably get on quite well. I mean, who would want coffee-flavoured alcohol? One makes you sleep, and one keeps you awake. They just shouldn't be mixed. But anyway, if you'd stop interrupting me, how much of it do you want in the drink?" she asked, as she stared at Daniel, not at all fazed by her intrusion.

Daniel was completely caught off guard by the comment, as his gaze remained fixed on the other woman, and blurted out, "A teaspoon will be fine."

The bartender took little notice of his comment and replied, "Yeah, whatever. I'll put a double measure in... Just to be sure. And anyway, how much lemon juice do you want?"

"I prefer a sweeter drink..." started Daniel.

"Should I sit down whilst I wait for an answer or are you goin' to get to the point today?" interrupted the bartender.

Daniel saw one last chance to make an impressive alteration to his drink, as he said, "A dash, but I would like the Kahlúa poured on top of the other three ingredients, followed by the lemon juice. It then needs to be stirred four times, before a small ice cube should be placed in the centre."

"Alright, but I'll charge you extra," concluded the bartender, as she moved off to make the drink.

Daniel hoped the interruptions with his drink were over, so continued to speak to the younger woman.

"I think we've all got unusual taste in something, because if we haven't, then we're just boring."

The woman looked down at her Mint Julep and asked, "So, am I boring?"

"No! No, just because you've chosen the only drink on the menu which people here are made to drink, it... well... it doesn't mean you don't have unique taste in something else," replied Daniel, unsure whether he was digging himself a deeper hole.

A drink was slammed down on the bar. It was served in a tumbler and looked a similar colour to blood but, no matter how disconcerting it was, he knew there was no going back.

The bartender said, "I'd say 'enjoy', but… well, I guess you could try. Oh, and the restroom is out back when you need it," as she moved back to the other end of the bar and continued polishing the glasses.

Daniel let out a timid, "Thank you," as he picked up his drink and moved his full attention back to the woman. "Are you waiting for someone, or just drinking alone?"

"Both," replied the woman, pleased with her secrecy.

Daniel paused for a moment, pretending to work out what she had just said, before replying,

"Am I the person you were waiting for?"

The woman then gave a tiny nod, as she said, "Maybe. I guess only time will tell."

Daniel then went on to try and start a proper conversation with her, simply asking, "Do you come by here often?"

"No, I'm actually only here for the week, over on business," she replied, offering Daniel little scope to continue the conversation.

"What kind of business are you here for?" asked Daniel.

The woman gave nothing away by saying, "If I told you, I'd have to kill you. But that's enough of me. You look like someone with a secret or two."

Daniel then ensured his mind was still clearly focussed on being the chef, before saying, "Well, I'm only a chef. My dad inherited the business from his family, and now I run it for him, working as many hours as I can. I'd always hoped to do more for people, maybe even find something I can do that's actually mine, not just… living in someone else's shadow."

He then took a sip of his drink, expecting to have to pretend to like it, but as the sweet and sharp flavours all fought for dominance, he was left with a pleasant taste heightened by the coffee liqueur.

"I've always had this dream of starting up my own great restaurant from scratch. Not that anyone dreams of opening a bad restaurant," he continued, before sharing a short laugh with her at his comment. "But that's enough of me," said

Daniel, as he threw her own words back, before continuing, "Is there anyone special in your life?"

The woman again smiled and replied, "No. But I am always on the lookout for people... People I feel are a 'match' for my lifestyle."

He took another sip of his drink, whilst trying to work out why she was using such specific words, as if she never lied, but instead clouded the truth.

Daniel was intrigued by her presence, but before he could ask her anything else, she got up from the bar and began heading for the door.

As she stood in the doorway, she turned and said, "If you are the person I was looking for, then I'm pretty sure we'll meet again. But until then, I hope you find what you're looking for."

She turned and disappeared into the crowds on the streets.

Sitting back, he contemplated what had just happened, before letting out a small laugh. He didn't know whether he'd just found someone that he wanted to be with, someone he had to help, or whether it was her mystery that intrigued him more than anything else. Daniel looked at her untouched mint julep and pondered what any of it even meant, as he asked, *What's just happened?* in his head.

Under her glass laid a white serviette, he picked it up to see writing scribbled on the other side in black pen. It said '*LoLa, 6673 253049*'.

"So, you've got the girl's number," came from the bartender, before she continued with, "Well, don't say I didn't warn you."

"But you didn't warn me," said Daniel with a quizzical look.

"Well, I meant to, okay!" she barked, before muttering, "Can't be expected to remember everything."

Daniel then moved back to the writing on the serviette. He first noticed the unusual way of spelling 'LoLa', with two capital letters, but brushed it aside as it seemed very fitting for her curious nature.

He also seemed confused by the number. *Could it be her mobile number?* he thought. *Maybe. But it isn't a format I recognise*, he continued. By this point, his mind was wandering away from being the chef and towards the mind of Alpha Two.

"You 'avin' another one?" demanded the bartender.

Daniel looked down at his empty glass, unaware that he'd finished his drink, and said, "Sure, why not?"

The bartender turned away to make the next drink, muttering, "I can think of several reasons."

Back to being the chef and leaving Alpha Two behind, he tucked the serviette inside one of his pockets and watched the bartender make his second drink. Daniel's mood had changed dramatically, and now he didn't really care what people thought. He felt, quite literally, on top of the world. The bartender proceeded to make the exact same drink in a clean glass, not altering her method one bit.

The drink was placed in front of Daniel, before the bartender said, "One Blood Thirst."

"Shouldn't I be the one to name the drink?" asked Daniel, as he raised his glass.

The bartender made no comment. Instead, she stood staring at Daniel, making her answer clear.

"I think 'Blood Thirst' is an excellent name," he concluded.

Daniel drank the second at twice the speed of the first, thinking of nothing but LoLa. Standing up, he then threw a £20 note on the bar and left, grinning the whole time.

As he left, the bartender mumbled, "You're too generous, a 20p tip and she didn't pay for hers. But don't you worry, you thievin'…" The door slammed shut and he was once again on the street.

By the time he got back to his apartment, after a long stroll in the brisk winds, it was long past midnight and the streets had become far quieter. But as he lay on his bed, his mind was solely focussed on what had happened that night, and who he'd met. Usually, he could get to sleep in minutes, but this time, it took him hours. In fact, it took so long to get to sleep, that he didn't wake again until later in the afternoon. When he did finally wake, he still had just one thing on his mind. It was a welcomed change from their operations. But he couldn't turn his Alpha Two brain off, the more he thought about the previous night, the more confused he got; she'd never asked for his name or anything. Daniel then began thinking it was because he stopped her from asking questions, and perhaps, because of that, he would never see her again. Weirder thoughts then started creeping in.

"Maybe I had too much to drink, and she wasn't actually real," he said aloud. "Maybe I was just hallucinating because of stress or something."

He then began to calm back down, knowing that she was real, and realising how ridiculous he sounded.

It's strange really. I can look at that door and know nobody is standing in front of it. But when I turn away, I can no longer be 100% sure. Even though nothing has changed, and I know nobody is standing there, I just can't say I definitely know, he thought, trying to justify his confusion. He'd tried to calm himself down as well, but only ended up confusing himself even more.

After minutes of letting his mind jump from thought to thought, he'd completely taken his mind away from LoLa. He climbed to his feet, wondering how he could fill his day with 'ordinary' things. After throwing on some clothes, he headed down to the shops, bought some flowers, and went to the local cemetery. The place was full of thousands of headstones, all representing a memory of someone and how they had affected those around them. Weaving between the stones, Daniel finally found the one he was looking for: *'Daisy Longman, born 14 January 1912, died 9*

June 2003, Loving wife, mother, and grandmother'. She was from the family they had chosen for Daniel to be a part of. He placed the yellow flowers down at the foot of the stone and stared. Whilst placing the flowers would keep up his identity as the chef, the true purpose for his visit was to see the headstone two rows in front.

From where he was standing, Daniel could see the headstone saying, 'Mark Simons, *born 8 March 1964, died 13 September 2013, Rose Simons, born 8 March 1964, died 13 September 2013, and Daniel Simons, born 27 August 1985, died 13 September 2013, always together, never forgotten'*. The stone was for his real parents and himself. His parents always told him that they were meant for each other, as why else were they born on the same day in the same hospital? They'd likely feel the same about dying together as well. Daniel, however, felt he'd cheated death and should also be with them. But, obviously, it was never meant to be. He stayed a while, thinking, remembering.

Eventually, he left the frosty graveyard and started walking back to his apartment in the frozen February afternoon. Just as he got to the foot of the apartment stairs, his phone buzzed in his pocket. He took it out to see a message from Teddy which read, '*Angel's gone sick, wondered if you could cover her shift? Thanks'*. Daniel knew he was wanted back at base, so charged upstairs, grabbed his chef's clothes, and went straight to the restaurant.

He got to the restaurant just as it was starting to get busy, so headed straight to the kitchen, hung his chef's whites up and changed into his tactical gear. Then, without a word to the other members of staff, Daniel went through the freezer and down into the tube that was already waiting for him. Inside was Mike, who was also travelling back to base. They said nothing to each other but instead reflected on their 'other' lives. Once they reached the checkpoint, they both went through the same security checks as when they left, leaving nothing to chance.

Chapter 5 – The Future
February 6th
18:45 GMT

Scott was already waiting in the gigantic meeting room. There was a table so big that you could hardly see one end from the other. There were also twenty-three swivel chairs, all padded with fabric cushions, big enough to curl up in, and five TV screens that took up most of one wall. Every piece of furniture in the room was so big that it even made the glass, double doors look small. One by one, Alpha team walked in and took a seat, took their own seat. Bosse was the last to enter, and once the door was closed, he smoked the glass so nobody could see inside the soundproof meeting room. As Samuel sat on his chair, he stretched down to adjust the height. Instead of gently pushing the lever down, he punched his hand down with all his strength, dropping the chair to its base. Now with only his upper body above the table, he began pumping the chair back up, until it was at its original height, doing none of it quietly.

Bosse didn't seem to find any funny side to the incident and was clearly angered, as he growled, "Can I have your attention!" directing all his fury towards Samuel.

Bosse had no time to mess around, what he had to say was time sensitive and his slight outburst told them that.

Bosse then went on to say, "We managed to get into the hard drive. Whilst it didn't have as much as we'd hoped, it does give us a lot to work with. We have a list of safe house locations, as well as some of the higher members of a third, unnamed organisation. Unfortunately, it doesn't tell us exactly who is at the top of the food chain, but with some cross-referencing, we've been able to identify most of the members. It seems the Night Vipers are also run by them. I would like to add, at this point, that M.N.G.W.A. seems somewhat unrelated to this organisation and the hard drive has no direct reference to them, so how Mr Wilson fits into both, we still don't know. At the top, we have two members, unknown to us, but it did strike me as odd that such an organisation could be shared equally. Either way, just down from them, there are three members, again unknown, who all seem to act as the boss in their own area. We expect one of them to be the voice you heard on the video call, as it's this person who indirectly commands the security agency, but is the direct superior to the Dutchman, Mr Wilson, another person, who goes by the name, The Vesper, and someone I'll get onto in a moment. It appears the unknown person is also the one to oversee this 'Operation Storm'. It seems the head of the security force answers to the Dutchman… well, answered, and directly to Hailey. Judging from the intercepted call, this is the woman with the different coloured eyes you mentioned in your report. But that does seem to make the Dutchman slightly redundant, as we've found no other purpose for his presence."

"So, M.N.G.W.A. isn't the same organisation whose information was on the hard drive?" questioned Samuel, unsure whether he could've missed something. Whilst Bosse wasn't pleased with the interruption, even he could see the potential confusion.

"That is correct. They appear to be separate. As far as we can tell, both M.N.G.W.A. and the Night Vipers have been hired, to some extent, by the one I think we are truly trying to catch. But as I said, how Mr Wilson can be a part of both organisations is what seems the most confusing. And whilst we're on the subject, we've also had an unusual request."

By this point, they had all sat upright, listening carefully to what was coming next. After a deep breath, Bosse continued.

"We've had an assassination order, a hit, on The Vesper. Now before you all jump to an answer, the hit has come from someone called Heartfell. We can't find anything on them; they quite literally are a ghost. However, in my opinion, Heartfell could be a great ally. They've already given us information on this organisation, which filled in the hard drive's blanks, and helped us to identify most of the members. Once the job is complete, they're going to give up the names of those in charge. They've also given us a lead on someone called Kale, who worked for this organisation and might be able to help us. But again, I'll get to that later. They have also shone a little more light on Mr Wilson's involvement, although still not enough to clear up the confusion…"

"We can't do it," dismissed Daniel.

"What is it they've done? The Vesper, I mean," inquired Mike.

Bosse then replied, clearly trying to sway their opinion, "The Vesper has killed countless people with his own hands. He doesn't care who they are or what they've done, if they're in his way, he kills them; and not in a nice way."

Samuel began frowning, before putting his hand up and asking, "Can you kill someone in a nice way?"

Bosse ignored Samuel's remark and continued, saying, "He's also untouchable. No criminal charges seem to stick. Only one person has got close to catching The Vesper and they were killed… after being tortured."

He then brought up an image on one of the five screens. It was hard to make out the image at first, but after a little time looking, they all realised it was of a butchered person. They had few distinguishing features left and barely resembled anything human.

"Look, either we kill him, someone else kills him, or he murders more innocent people," added Mike.

Kenny then joined the conversation, saying, "We've all killed people before, it's not like we've kept our hands clean. It's always been in a 'my life or theirs' kind of way, but if this is going to save anyone's life, even just one person, then I think we've got to consider it."

"We all swore to protect people," said Daniel.

"We are not soldiers! We were not soldiers! We have no book to go by! We save as many people as possible, by any means necessary. Imagine how many more he'll kill if we don't intervene…" erupted Mike. He then calmed his voice slightly and continued. "None of us have served in any military. Anthony was a gun for hire, often hired by militaries and governments but still not working for them. Scott and Daniel were spies. Kenny just worked in the armoury. And Samuel was nobody. We've all taken different paths to get here, but now we are here… we can save lives."

"We weren't exactly spies," said Daniel in a soft voice.

"First of all, saying I was 'nobody' is a little on the rude side, I was a chemist. And second, why don't you remind us again how a computer expert became a trained killer," said Samuel, ignoring Daniel's remarks.

"I'm a fast learner, and I only killed people who killed first. That's what we're doing here," concluded Mike, showing a sly smile.

"We weren't spies," insisted Daniel, still being ignored.

Bosse had sat back, knowing he'd done more than enough to convince the team, and they would be enough to convince Scott. Scott hadn't said a word. He was just listening, trying to balance the skewed opinions of his team.

"Are we sure this information is worth it?" asked Scott.

"No, but it should help us to uncover the identities of those running this organisation."

Bosse's answer gave no confidence, but it was at least truthful.

Scott summed up the most likely possibilities, before saying, "If we'd known the names of those in charge a week ago, maybe we could have stopped them blowing up the nightclub. And we can't take that chance again. I think we must do it. But there is one thing I want to know first. Why now? Why not a week ago?"

Bosse gave little thought, before saying, "They want to take them down, just like us. But after what happened two nights ago, they've realised they're not strong enough to stop them, only we are. It was also Heartfell who provided us with the intel on Mr Wilson's compound. Apparently, Heartfell used to work for the organisation as well, but left and is now being hunted by them. I think I should also add that, recently, The Vesper has been inviting certain rich people to invest in his vineyard. They often travel there to visit, and all seem to miraculously disappear two days later. In those two days, nobody sees them, it's merely a data trail likely intended to divert suspicion away from The Vesper. Unfortunately for him, it hasn't worked with us."

Scott then sat forwards, almost ashamed of what he'd decided, and said, "So, when do we do this?" with the others all looking at Bosse for an answer.

"Not yet…" Bosse started. "First, we have a rescue mission: Kale. We've uncovered information to suggest he's been taken and is being held in a deserted part of the Sahara Desert."

"What? You mean some parts of the Sahara aren't deserted?" questioned Samuel.

"It used to be used as a nuclear testing site. No nuclear bombs were ever dropped there, but the place has become abandoned, and we expect has fallen into some sort of disrepair. As I said, the target used to work for this organisation, before betraying them and trying to leave, much like Heartfell. In fact, the hard drive seems to suggest he had the same level of authority as the Dutchman, Mr

Wilson, and The Vesper. It's likely they are going to make an example out of their captive, and because of the time-sensitive nature, we have no time to do any recon. In fact, all we have is a satellite image, and it doesn't show much," continued Bosse.

Scott then added, "And just to get this clear, we're not rescuing them out of the kindness of our hearts, we're rescuing them because they might have information we need. Isn't that right?" But before Bosse could say anything, Scott added, "And one more thing. If this was so time sensitive, why did we lead with the assassination contract?" Bosse went to ignore Scott's questions, but before he had a chance, Scott concluded, "Don't bother answering; we've got a mission to plan."

"I'll leave you to it," said Bosse, as he left the room, leaving all the paperwork he'd brought in on the table.

Scott flicked through the pieces of paper, familiarising himself with their objective.

"Okay, first things first. How do we get in? There's barren land all around, so we'll be spotted ten miles off if we go on foot or by car. That's why I think we've got to go by air," said Scott.

They all gave it some thought, before Daniel asked, "What if they've got radar?"

"That's why it's going to be a HALO dive, the high altitude will stop us being picked up on any radar, and the low opening should allow us to arrive unseen," Scott replied.

"Supposing they do see us?" questioned Kenny.

Scott thought hard about how to solve the problem but began to think it was a risk they may have to take, before Daniel suggested, "What about the active camouflage suits? They're still experimental, but they worked at Mr Wilson's compound, and if we get our parachutes made from the same material, we should be almost invisible."

By this point, Kenny had started making a list of everything they would need.

"So, we've landed, then what?" Mike asked.

Anthony then stepped forward and pointed to a building on the satellite image, saying, "This building here, it overlooks the entire place. If we can take it, then I can provide overwatch. It'll face away from the sun, so there shouldn't be any glint from my scope."

"What if there isn't a window facing the right way?" asked Mike.

Anthony gave a wry smile, then said, "Then I make one."

Scott knew Anthony had more than convinced them, in his own way, so continued, "Okay, once Anthony's in position, we head to this central building here..." He then pointed at the biggest building there and, based on the original blueprints, it was meant to portray a casino. "It's the obvious place to keep a hostage. The building is the easiest to keep secure, with plenty of spots to cover it from, and there's a vault. So, assuming the hostage is in the vault, Kenny and Mike will head into the building next door as, looking at the number of generators around it, this is likely to be where their security operates from. If there are any surveillance cameras, shut them down. You will then meet back with the rest of us outside the side door. Apparently, this is meant to be designed the same as this casino here, and if the blueprints are the same, it should just be a quick dash across the floor, down the stairs, and into the vault. Obviously, our suits will still help to keep us hidden but, if for any reason we do get spotted, they'll likely lock the vault, so we may be blowing it open."

Mike then raised his hand. He didn't wait for permission to talk, but as soon as he had everyone's attention, he said, "What happens if we do get spotted? Earlier, I mean."

"Don't worry, I've got just the things," said Kenny, jotting even more down on his tiny scrap of paper.

Kenny's secrecy didn't worry any of them, they trusted him, and if he said not to worry, then he had a plan that would work.

"Alright, now let's just say, by some miracle, we get to the hostage, then what?" asked Samuel.

"We get out the way we came in," said Scott, before looking directly to Kenny and saying, "So, make sure we pack an extra suit, or just something camouflaged to cover the hostage."

Kenny nodded and continued to scribble on his piece of paper, now on the other side of the paper to make more room.

Scott continued, "Once the hostage is secure, we'll head back up the stairs and go out of the side door, making our way towards Anthony's position. As soon as we've regrouped, we'll head to this point here."

He was pointing to an area without any buildings, just on the outskirts of the abandoned town. There were two very faint lines running through a point he'd circled in bright red pen.

"Are they train tracks?" asked Samuel.

Scott was a little disappointed that he couldn't surprise everyone with the way out but was equally pleased with Samuel's keen eye.

"That's right. We're going to catch the train that passes through," said Scott, as he leant over the table and picked up one particular piece of paper, adding, "The train only comes through once a day, so our timing will have to be perfect. The train isn't too bad timing wise, it's apparently never more than ten minutes early or five minutes late, so we'll have to be there at its earliest time of arrival, at 11:11 local time. I know fifteen minutes is a long time to wait if we're under fire, but we don't want to miss it."

Daniel stood up and pointed to the red circle, asking, "Is this where the train stops then?"

Scott lowered his head, wondering how the team would take the next bit of news.

"No. The train doesn't stop anywhere nearby. So yes, we'll be getting on a moving train," he said.

Daniel then took the piece of paper and scanned through it, "Thirty miles per hour?" he said.

Scott's voice softened as he said, "Yes, but it's either that or we walk."

Everyone's demeanour changed, with Kenny, who was now writing with very small letters, saying, "I'll get us the stuff we need."

"Good. If there are no questions?" Scott said, as he scanned the room.

When nobody said anything, Scott finished the conversation by saying, "Then let's get to work. We've obviously missed the train for today, but we'll be setting off first thing in the morning. Wheels up in eight hours, we can circle around to kill time if we need to," before taking his leave.

They all went to their respective stations, getting everything they needed together and delivering it in a huge pile on the hangar floor, before getting whatever minimal rest they could grab.

Scott went to see Bosse, to inform him of their plan, but was unable to find him in any of the places he looked. It was unusual for Bosse to leave the Molehill, but on the rare occasions he did leave, he would always inform Scott of his location in case something happened. With no clue to his whereabouts, Scott got a couple of hours' sleep, before meeting the others back at the hangar when they were close to taking off.

Kenny was the last to arrive, followed by a container on the back of a truck. As the truck pulled up, they began offloading the container and squeezing it into the back of their plane. The plane was still a prototype but had been tested many times before. It was designed and built by their engineering division, overseen by the head of engineering, Suzy. The plane, named the S-4 *Pin-Drop*, was dark in the Molehill, but once in the air, the bottom of the plane could project the image above it, and the top would project the image below it, thanks to the hundreds of tiny cameras fitted all over its shell which rendered it almost invisible. An early design of the plane, the S-1, used blue paint underneath and left the top black, but with their advances in technology, a more sophisticated method could be adopted. Inside, the stealth plane was spacious, with plenty of room to move around and sit close to, or away from, everyone else. Every single part of the S-4 was open, maximising its interior space. The cockpit could also be sealed off from the hold, allowing for it to be both pressurised and unpressurised, depending on the need. Whilst it was a stealth plane, which shouldn't get into any combat, it was able to carry several small payloads, either AAMs or AGMs, just in case they were needed. Once in, the doors swung closed, and they started their ascent.

Kenny got to work, attaching parachutes to the only container. It was two metres tall, with a metre squared base, and had been wrapped up in a black plastic bag. Once the bag was removed, and the parachutes were attached, it became clear why Kenny wrapped it in a black plastic bag. It was almost completely invisible, so he stuck one line of high-visibility tape on the outside, preventing them from misplacing it.

Whilst Kenny kept busy with his invisible container, Scott explained, "When we get there, we'll have twenty-three minutes until the earliest time the train will come through. There's no time to waste, so make sure your suits are on and you're ready to go when we're over the drop site."

Kenny then stood up and took over, saying, "These suits absorb over 99% of light, along with your parachutes and this container here. It's the same concept as our old suits; they're just a lot better. Now, just in case you're wondering, although I doubt you are, when I say the suits absorb most light, they're not black, they just become almost invisible.

I'm obviously not expecting you to understand how, so that's all you need to know. Everything is currently in black plastic bags, so we don't lose anything…" He began chuckling, but when nobody else joined him, he gave a slight cough to clear his throat and pressed on with what he was saying, adding, "This container here has the rest of our gear. Each person has a rucksack full of what they need; the rucksacks are obviously camouflaged as well. Also, these suits are bullet resistant, up to a point, and can absorb a lot of impact, but getting onto that train will still hurt. And finally, in case it's not obvious, we don't leave any of this gear behind, Suzy wants to make them better, well, perfect. Whilst our weapons aren't made from this material, I have taken the liberty of wrapping them in a thin sheet of it, so they should blend in as well as our suits. Just treat them with care because the material is only stuck on with a bit of sticky tape. Oh… and before I forget, I shouldn't have to tell you this, but please remember to discard the black plastic bags before we leave the plane. They're not quite as effective inside them."

"One final thing, we've been given the order to kill, so if someone's in our way, well, you know what to do. I know it's not how we usually go about missions, and I'd hoped to change Bosse's mind on the order, but he was nowhere to be found and Bosse's orders are… well, the boss' orders. The flight there won't be too long, so if any of you want a rest, now's the time to do it," concluded Scott, before retaking his seat.

The S-4 could travel quicker than the speed of the Earth's rotation. In fact, flying east to west, the plane could give the illusion of the sun moving backwards. Of course, the direction they were heading in made the sun rise, and set, slightly quicker. A flight that would take a commercial airline four hours could be done in under two.

"How good are the suits?" Mike asked, directing his question to Kenny.

Kenny smiled, before answering, "You tell me. Can you see the guy sat next to you?" before moving to take his seat at the other end of the plane.

Mike turned slowly to see what looked like an empty chair next to him. He had a face of fear, not knowing whether Kenny told the truth.

"Morning," he muttered, before turning to face the other way as if to get some sleep.

The sleep never came as he sat in his chair, motionless, with his eyes wide open, still not sure whether someone was sat next to him, watching him.

***

Eventually, the five-minute light flashed up in the hold. Scott, Samuel, and Anthony had already got their suits on, but with five minutes left, the others began to copy them. For a while, the pressurised hold had provided them with pure oxygen, the same as they would be breathing from the tiny oxygen tanks within their suits. And by the time Mike had clipped the final buckles together, and everyone who would be making the jump had their suits on and their oxygen masks fitted, so the hold depressurised. They couldn't hear whether it made a noise or not, but before long, the hold doors opened. The bright sun illuminated everything, too bright to look at, especially at the high altitude they were flying. They all flipped their tinted visors down, making their entire bodies covered by the light-absorbing material. Their visors also adapted to the light, so with the sun penetrating the plane, their visors tinted, but by the time they returned to the surface, the visors would be a little clearer. At the point the indicator light on the inside of the plane went green, they all piled out of the plane within a second of each other.

Kenny flew down on top of the container, although he had his own parachute. He was mainly on top to get their gear in the same low opening the rest of the team would land in. They'd managed to prevent any spinning as they left the plane, but all the way down, they were entirely focussed on the ground, getting closer and closer. Despite the fact they were just falling from the sky, it felt like there were hundreds of things to concentrate on. Everything from watching their altitude, trying to stop the wind pushing them off course, and even breathing became a voluntary action, as they needed to control the levels of oxygen they were consuming, rather than letting their bodies take in its usual amount. Their oxygen tanks, built into the suits, were completely separated from their visors, so they didn't steam up, but the view they had was so limited, they could only distinguish the land from the sky, everything else was too small to see.

They continued to fly like bullets through the sky, tempted to pull their chutes, but it was something they knew could only be done at the last possible moment. They knew that when they saw the buildings, they had to carry on. It was only when their altitude hit the optimum level that they had about a second to pull their chutes. They all had slightly different altitudes to aim for, due to their weights, but it was only Kenny on the container who you would notice had pulled his chute slightly earlier. Finally, they'd all pulled their chutes. The force of the air resistance slowed them down, feeling as if they'd stopped suddenly, but in reality, they were still travelling at a speed that would break bones without landing properly.

Kenny was pulling at two 'wings' on either side of the container, raising the right 'wing' to go left and vice versa. Although the 'wings' looked tiny compared the container, they could move it by miles and needed expert precision. Kenny was the first due to land. Still on top of the container, he pulled another cord, inflating a giant pillow underneath. He bent his knees and prepared for the harsh thud as they hit the burning sands. The pillow underneath had both helped to soften the landing, but also reduced the noise for any nearby guards. The others all came floating down, gracefully, but quickly. Their visors had been designed to pick out the material the suits were made from and display them with a solid black outline and a hazy centre, but still prevented others from seeing them.

Once everyone was down, they proceeded with the plan, heading towards the lonely building on the outskirts of the town. Alpha One and Six secured the building, with nobody in sight, whilst the others brought the container up to the top. The building was half destroyed with no door and a few of the steps missing on the staircase. Getting the container to the top wasn't too much of an issue, with Alpha One only needing to knock a few of the concrete blocks out from around the doorframe with his rifle's stock. Within a minute, they were all at the top and Alpha Six lay prone next to a hole in the wall.

"Twenty-four minutes until the earliest time the train arrives," said Alpha One, handing the four labelled rucksacks to each member of the team, taking his own, and leaving the container lying in front of the wide, broken window with Alpha Six. They all headed back out of the building and onto the sand, leaving Alpha Six to provide overwatch. He observed his surroundings and placed his rifle on its bipod, so the barrel was pointing through the hole made by a missing concrete block, before peering through the scope. With the sun behind him, his scope wouldn't glint, and anyone would find it hard to look towards the building due to the blinding light of the sun, almost absorbing the building itself.

As he lay there, a small '*ting*' rang out beneath him. It was an empty bullet casing, dented and burned, with a bird symbol scratched into the side. It slowly rolled over the few grains of sand on the concrete floor towards the edge, eventually being stopped by a brick. Then it lay there, with the bird symbol facing Alpha Six, as if it was looking back at him, almost judging him.

Chapter 6 – The Past

10 Years Ago
June 18th
11:32 GMT

Hidden in the tall grasses was Anthony, who gave himself the call sign Chameleon for this one mission. His ghillie suit helped to obscure him from the patrolling guards.

"Chameleon, I have eyes on you. One guard is peeling off from the others, two o'clock, he's yours," said a voice over the radio with a strong North London accent.

Chameleon crept forward, silently, as he emerged from hiding. Only the leaves rustled in the wind, as his head slowly moved out from under them. He was already within a foot of the guard, so leant up and placed a cloth over the guard's mouth. The guard slumped down instantly and was dragged back into the tall grass like a predator taking its prey back to its den.

"Not bad, for an apprentice. Two more beyond the gate. Time to see what the master can do," continued the voice.

"When you're ready, Pigeon," said Chameleon.

"Remind me again why I'm Pigeon," he asked.

Chameleon laughed, before answering, "I'm Chameleon because I blend in with my surroundings. You're Pigeon because you're sat in the roof of an abandoned block of flats, using the floor as your only toilet, and eating literally everything you find. Anyway, cheer up. It's only for this one mission."

As he crept through the gate, the two guards in front of him dropped to the floor, only a split second between them.

Pigeon wasn't just a good sniper; he was the best of his time. As he watched through the heavily magnified scope of his two-metre-long, custom-made sniper rifle, he saw Chameleon drag the guards back into the tall grass. He continued scanning the nearby area for any more threats, before giving the all-clear.

Chameleon moved back through the gates and into a small yard. As he looked around, he saw a watchtower with a guard stood outside. Before Chameleon could even identify the guard as a threat, he fell off the watchtower to the floor.

"You're welcome," said Pigeon.

Whilst Chameleon lay in wait for the proceeding doorway to be guard-free, he asked, "If I'm the apprentice, why am I down here? Wouldn't it make more sense for me to learn next to you, whilst someone else went in?"

Pigeon chuckled at the comment and said, "Before you master the bow, you must first master the arrow. You'll never know what a true threat is from hundreds of metres away unless you can place yourself in the shoes of the person only one metre away. And try not to talk so much, you'll give the game away."

Chameleon rolled his eyes, as if to say, 'Thanks, a great help!' Just then, the doorway became free.

Whenever heading inside, the nerves always got worse, for them both. Chameleon knew he had to watch every direction, with no chance of a slip-up, and Pigeon had nothing to do but wait, for what felt like forever.

Chameleon headed through the doorway, and into a large, factory-type room full of guards. The problem with ghillie suits is that they're hard to take off quickly, and they don't really help you to blend in inside a factory. But Chameleon figured that if he was high enough, nobody would look up. He pressed himself against a huge pipe, going from the floor to the ceiling, before moving to sit behind it, whilst he looked for a distraction.

Over on the far side of the room, there was a giant furnace, and next to it, a load of canisters. Chameleon didn't know what they were for but, given that they were connected to the fuel gauge on the furnace, he took an educated guess and assumed they contained pressurised gas. Raising his suppressed rifle, he fired just one bullet at the valve. With a clang, the valve blew off and the canisters exploded. The explosion was a little bigger than expected, and it was only thanks to the fans above that the massive fireball went up and blew the roof off, rather than towards Chameleon.

He immediately began climbing.

"Did that explosion have anything to do with you?" asked Pigeon.

"Well, I might have been lightly involved," said Chameleon, still climbing the pipe.

At the top, or what was left of it, was a thin metal pole, acting as the roof's support. Chameleon shimmied along it, right up until he got to the hole. There was a little more attention than he had hoped on the roof, but after leaping up and onto the roof itself, he was clear.

"Your ghillie suit is on fire," said a very relaxed Pigeon, before shooting the same metal pole Chameleon had just walked along. Water sprayed up at a great pressure, almost knocking him off the roof, but it did turn his red ghillie suit back to green, or as close as the charred suit could be.

"You do realise that was the sprinkler system you just walked along, right?" asked Pigeon, already knowing the answer.

"Yes, obviously I did. Who would walk across a sprinkler system thinking it was secure enough to hold the whole roof up? I'm not stupid!" said Chameleon.

"Sure. Just remember, I can't see all of the field you're about to cross, so don't get spotted. And don't forget that your ghillie suit isn't as green as it was earlier," said Pigeon, still staring down his sights.

Chameleon, lying on the roof, observed the trucks coming across the field. The grass wasn't that long, so passing all of them on foot was unlikely, but there was a chance he could crawl. Chameleon slid down the drainpipe on the side of the building and began descending into the field below. But as he moved down, each of the clips started tearing out of the wall, before the drainpipe ended up leaning away from the building at about 60 degrees, held up by only a couple of remaining fittings. He fell to the floor instantly. He crashed down on his back and instinctively rolled over, lying prone for a moment. He listened for anyone coming close. When he was sure he hadn't been seen, he started his journey.

"I don't even drink tea, but I could really do with a sweet cup of it after this," said Chameleon.

Pigeon made a sound of approval, before replying, "A cup of tea sounds lovely. I can't wait until I hear the sound of the boiling water as it trickles into the cup. The aroma of the tea leaves tickling my nose. That warm feeling from the steam. The delicate taste of the tea refreshing my mouth…"

"Okay, that's starting to sound a little creepy now," interrupted Chameleon, as he brought the conversation to a stop.

Crawling on his belly, he slowly made his way around the outside of the incoming vehicles, several of which pulled up early to search the field. Not once did Chameleon dare a peek, he relied entirely on his ears, as he snaked through the longest parts of grass.

Suddenly, Chameleon could hear a pair of guards getting close. He stopped, and became a part of the field. The guards came closer and closer, until they were finally right in front of him. They'd also stopped, one being only a couple of inches from Chameleon's head, who was more than prepared to strike if they got any closer. The closest guard unzipped his trousers and began weeing, on Chameleon. No matter how tempted he was to jump up and attack, if nothing else to see the look of panic in the guard's face, he had to remain still. The wee went on, and on, and just when Chameleon thought it had finished, there was another splash on the back of his head. He focussed on his breathing, trying to ignore his dampening clothes and the stench of urine.

Eventually, the guard was finished, and to Chameleon's surprise, and slight disappointment, they headed back away from where he was lying. He carried on, weaving through the field, avoiding any sort of confrontation. When they originally scoped the field out, they were unsure if it was full of mines, but at least the huge presence of guards gave him some sort of reassurance as he moved through. A truck then started to get close, too close for comfort, but because of its speed, Chameleon had no chance but to wait and react quickly if he needed to. The truck was still getting louder, but a little peek over the grass wasn't an option, no matter how quick it was. As he lay motionless in the grass, the truck suddenly came into view. Chameleon rolled to the right, and the truck drove straight over him, straddling him and spitting mud as it went.

He took a moment to relax again, clearing his head and refocussing his attention. One thing was clear though, he'd have to stay between the truck's tyre tracks which would get him to the compound without having to keep his bearings. Chameleon travelled the length of the rest of the field without any disturbances, crawling the entire way.

"I have you in my sight," informed Pigeon, as Chameleon stood up at the very edge of the field. He retrieved a small pair of bolt cutters from inside his suit and snipped only a quarter of a large circle in the wire fence. Chameleon slipped through the small opening and bent the fence back in place to not draw any unwanted attention to his presence.

Inside the perimeter, there were hundreds of guards, some patrolling with dogs, others high up in watchtowers scattered all over.

"One guard, seven o'clock," said Pigeon.

Chameleon lay flat again and removed a knife from one of his many pockets, waiting for the guard to get closer. He was lying down a narrow alleyway, so when the guard got close enough, he swung his hand up, plunging his knife in the guard's knee. Just as the guard was about to call out, his screams were silenced by a cloth laced with chloroform. The limp guard was dragged into cover and the knife was cleaned as he placed it back in its holder.

He leaped forward and scaled the wall in front of him, as if he had sticky hands and feet. Two floors up, he grabbed a ledge and pulled himself on top. As he inched his way along the ledge, with his body pressed up against the wall, a guard fell past from above and crashed onto the concrete floor below.

"That's twice this 6'2" pigeon has saved your life now," said Pigeon, with still no change to his calm and relaxed persona.

Chameleon continued up the building, trying to ignore Pigeon's remarks, and stopped at a window five floors up. Pigeon had a very small view of the room, but his silence gave the all-clear from his perspective. Chameleon gave a brief glance through the window and saw nothing, so he entered, cautiously.

Still with great vigilance, he crept over to the other side, his rifle up, and got to a computer terminal. Plugging away at all the keys, he brought up information on an impending nuclear strike.

"Bingo," he said.

"Nobody your age should say 'bingo', and that's coming from a forty-year-old," added Pigeon.

Still hitting the keys, he began reading the details of the launch, saying, "It's been brought forward. The launch is today, just seventeen minutes away."

"Download the information then get out," said Pigeon.

"We both know I'm not going to do that; I have to stop the launch. As soon as the data has downloaded, I'm going for the nuke. The launch pad is in the building opposite, twenty-two floors down," said Chameleon, plugging in a small device and starting the download.

The download was being transferred directly to the cloud, as well as the device itself, just in case they didn't make it back out. But transferring such a file would bring up red flags. About halfway through alarms were sounded, and the base went on to their highest level of alert. Chameleon scanned the room, identifying two doors, a foam fire extinguisher, due to the only potential fire being electrical, and not much else.

First, he stuck a pack of Semtex, from under his suit, on the hard drive. He then went to reduce their breach points; he stuck the only chair under one of the door handles and taped the fire extinguisher upside down above that the same door.

"Tell me when you can see the hard drive," said Chameleon, as he began slowly moving it to the right.

"Got it," replied Pigeon.

He then moved down the corridor, placing a line of wire widthways at about fifty-centimetre intervals, before charging back into the room and lying prone, facing the open doorway.

As soon as one of the guards' heads popped around the corner, Chameleon took a shot, one was all he needed. The guards came through quicker and quicker, trying to avoid the incoming bullets, some crawled around the corner, others ran, but they were all caught by Chameleon's catlike reactions. Thirty bullets down, and thirty-one guards down, he had to reload. He rolled to the left, out of sight, and reloaded in only a split second. He then rolled back, a few guards had already rounded the corner, but they had never seen where Chameleon was lying, which gave him just long enough to take them all down. The guards were treading lightly, in between the wires, to not set off any explosives. Of course, there were none there, but they didn't know that.

As he continued to tear through the oncoming guards, the other door handle began to twitch. He could then hear the guards on the other side trying to charge towards the door before it all went quiet. Chameleon had to focus on the guards in front of him, but he never neglected the responsibility of the other door.

"We're at 82%," said Pigeon. Chameleon continued to shoot everyone that came round the corner, but as there were more and more of them, they began edging closer. The dummy tripwires helped to slow them down, but they were constantly closing the gap. Then, a huge bash came from the other door, followed by another, and on the third, the door broke from its hinges and fell, crushing the chair under its weight. The fire extinguisher was torn free of the tape and, after a complete turn, landed on the slightly angled door. The valve ruptured, sending the fire extinguisher flying up and into the closest guard, catching him on his cheek. The fire extinguisher spewed foam over everything, and everyone, giving Chameleon just enough time to rise up and throw a stun grenade down the left corridor.

It gave no time to return it before exploding, stopping anyone who was too close, catching them in a daze. He had a quick look at the progress of the download, reading '98% complete', before heading back towards the window and diving out. The grenade down one side, and the dummy tripwires on the other, gave him ample time to escape. Chameleon grabbed hold of the floodlight just one floor down after falling on it, dropping his rifle in the process. He then slid down to the base and submerged himself back into the tall grass, retrieving his rifle and waiting for the best moment to move.

As Pigeon saw the green light flash on top of the hard drive, he told Chameleon to, "Blow it."

And with the press of a button, the room was emptied, sending a plume of fire out of the nearby windows. The alarm was still sounding and, as the second battalion of guards charged into the building, Chameleon used his only opportunity and took off. Stealth wasn't his friend at this point, speed was. He bounded across the courtyard like a gazelle, with Pigeon preventing anyone from raising another alarm, using just one bullet per threat. It didn't escape Chameleon's notice, despite his eyes being fixed on his destination, how the guards were being taken down in the order they became a threat.

As he reached the other side, he stopped and looked back towards Pigeon. Out of the corner of his eye, Chameleon could see the guards converging at the other side of the courtyard and heading towards his own position. Before Chameleon could even dive into the building, a bullet clanged off a metal post in the ground and whizzed past his head, missing it by only a couple of millimetres. He turned to see the bullet had flown through a guard, stood right behind him, holding a pistol to Chameleon's head. The guard keeled over, revealing a bullet embedded in the stone behind. Chameleon became slightly dazed, he'd been close to dying before, but something about this time really scared him.

"Do you want to get a move on? I know I'm good, but they are getting closer," said Pigeon.

This brought Chameleon back round to full focus, and without a second thought, he took off towards the stairs, taking the burning hot, crumpled bullet with him.

From the top floor of the abandoned block of flats, Pigeon was under the cover of a mesh net. It was grey on top, fitting in with the urban setting of the building, and green inside, so it could be used in more rural areas. Whilst it was easy for Pigeon to look out of, from the outside it perfectly blended with its surroundings. Pigeon continued to thin the vast number of guards following Chameleon into the building, but his bolt-action rifle couldn't keep up with their numbers. Every shot fired hit a different guard in an identical place. As Pigeon pulled the bolt back into place, another empty shell casing was released. They all lay beside him, all with an identical marking on the side. It wasn't anything artistic, but instead, a badly drawn pigeon. As all the shell casings would be taken back, he knew Chameleon would find out about the mark and would be pleased that he'd taken the first call sign Chameleon had given him, despite Pigeon's reservations.

A few seconds later, Chameleon got to the stairs and started leaping down several steps at a time. After two flights, he leapt down the third, landing on a guard at the bottom, knocking his head against the wall, rendering him unconscious. Chameleon could hear more guards approaching from behind, so he continued down, placing his rifle on his back. Seventeen floors down, there was still no time to rest, and when he spun around the corner to descend further, he ploughed straight into another group of guards. They weren't travelling at anywhere near the speed of Chameleon, but neither him nor the guards had time to brace. Like a bowling ball, he was able to take out all eight guards, who got tangled up with each other. Chameleon managed to regain his balance, just as he smacked into the wall, stomping on a few guards as he went.

"They're about to start their launch sequence," said Pigeon, over the now crackly radio.

Chameleon didn't bother answering back, or making sure the guards stayed down, he just continued bounding down several steps at once as if nothing had just happened. He finally got to the bottom and ran out into the open.

"Freeze!" shouted one of the many guards forming a perimeter around him. Chameleon stopped dead in his tracks, like an animal caught in headlights. They were clearly trying to take him alive, which struck Chameleon as a bit odd, but it did give him his only chance of escape.

Moving slowly, he raised his arms, clearly showing a grenade with the pin pulled out. He held it up and moved towards a junction box on the wall. Chameleon hadn't a clue what the box connected to, but by the guards' sudden panic, it was clear it must've been something important. Despite his ultraslow movement, nobody dared to open fire, giving him a slight advantage and a little time to think.

Chapter 6.2

More guards entered from the stairs, their fingers twitching over their triggers, wanting to fire, but not wanting to at the same time. The only possible way out was the door right next to the junction box. He kicked it in and moved inside, still holding the grenade as close as possible to the box, closing the door when he was safely inside. The room was nothing more than a medical cupboard, and it wasn't even well stocked. He took only a moment to catch his breath and focus, whilst he looked down at the crumpled bullet. Before he became too mesmerised with it, there was bashing on the door, as the guards tried to force it open, immediately refocussing his mind.

He scoured the room, looking everywhere for everything. He took a half empty bottle of whisky, hidden under a spare uniform. Then he rolled up a small rag and stuffed it inside the bottle, tipping it upside down to soak the rag. He then got a plastic bucket and all the instant ice packs and split them, tipping the contents into the bucket, and grabbing a bottle of water. Carefully, he placed the grenade into the bucket and tipped the water in just after. The contents of the bucket froze, holding the grenade in place and preventing it from going off, until it melted. Chameleon then moved the bucket over to the door and turned his attention elsewhere.

He continued to rummage around the room until he finally found a half empty box of matches. He didn't have much, but it would have to be enough. Taking out his knife, he unscrewed the panel to the ventilation shaft and climbed through. It was a tight fit, but he fitted, and that was all that mattered. He squeezed up and along the tiny tunnels until reaching the following hatch, the sides of the tunnel pressed tightly against him. The hatch was already loose and, after just a small amount of pressure, he fell through and landed on the hard floor below. With a crash, Chameleon rolled over and climbed to his feet, ensuring the bottle of whisky hadn't cracked in any way.

Somehow, the bottle looked untouched. He didn't bother to wonder how, he just continued through the doorway, checking every direction as he tiptoed down the adjacent corridor. There were no guards around, as they were still watching the cupboard door, waiting for it to creak open. There was a little flutter of worry, as he moved down the corridor, *Maybe they heard me. Maybe they know I've gone around the other way.* But no matter what he was thinking, he had only one objective, and that was where he was heading.

There was a terminal over to the right side and Chameleon headed over to it.

Once there, he started pounding the keys, asking Pigeon, "How do I stop it?"

There was a slight delay, before Pigeon's voice came back over the very crackly radio, saying, "Use... radio..."

Chameleon thought about what he could have meant, before remembering that their radios could be used as an EMP. *If I set off the EMP just as it's ready to launch, it should shut down its targeting computer.* He logged into the launch cycle and brought up the countdown, informing him there was just one minute until launch. He got his radio out and placed it on the table.

He tore it apart, removing a small, black box. With just thirty seconds left, he pressed the small, round button on the black box which triggered the EMP. Chameleon had no clue whether it had worked or not but was taking no chances. He charged over to the other side of the corridor and watched as the nuclear missile sat there. The entire launch pad had been sealed, including the place Chameleon was standing. He tore the panel off the door sensor and stuck the bullet, which saved his life, into it. With a little spark, the door thought it was open, and thanks to his insulated gloves, he didn't get any sort of an electric shock. If the missile hadn't been stopped by the EMP, he'd hoped that short-circuiting the door might prevent a launch, for safety reasons, in a kind of ironic way. Chameleon really was clutching at straws, but he was prepared to risk everything, just for the smallest chance of stopping the launch. He waited well over the thirty seconds, probably closer to a couple of minutes, but when the missile still hadn't launched, he decided one of his methods must have been a success.

There was no need to do anything but delay the launch, as there was another team heading in in just a few hours. The second team would go in with a heavy assault, so the hard drive was his priority, and so long as they couldn't launch the nuke before the others arrived, Chameleon's mission was a success. Now, he just had to find a way out, with no radio and no workable plan.

The guards clearly still thought he was hiding in the cupboard and hadn't even realised the launch had been stopped, because there were still no guards to be found. This did mean that the only set of stairs was also blocked, so whilst the distraction had helped, it had now become more of a hindrance. He spent a couple of minutes looking in all the rooms, cracking the locks of any that wouldn't open. Most of the rooms seemed to be used as living quarters but were empty, which was just as well as he went stumbling into most of them. There was an office, a restroom, a kitchen, and a giant room with a round table in it. One room seemed to contain all the ventilation for the compound, and Chameleon decided this was his best chance of escape; not just to climb up, but to create another distraction.

He opened one of the vents, lit his match, and set the Molotov cocktail alight. Chameleon held it in the vent and dropped it, which allowed it to fall about ten metres to the bottom. He then grabbed a huge stack of paper from one of the offices he'd found earlier and dropped it down on top of the burning alcohol, resealing the vent behind it. The ventilation pushed white smoke around the entire floor, and before long, smoke was coming from all the vents. Because of the dangers of being next to a nuclear missile, as soon as any sort of heat or smoke was detected that area would be locked down. And with the smoke billowing from all the vents, one by one, each sector was locked down, with huge steel doors slamming down and making things airtight, preventing anything from getting in, or out.

The compound had one straight pipe going up to the surface, stopping at everyone floor. His boots had rubber soles which would stick to sides of the vertical pipe. He then proceeded to pour water on his, now gloveless, hands, making them just as adhesive. Chameleon climbed in and placed his body as if he was desperately trying to keep the two sides of the pipe apart and began edging up. Every step, he kicked his feet against the sides and tested the grip by slowly adding his weight. He did the same with his hands and, when the water dried, he braced his legs and poured a little more water on them. It took a long time and a lot of effort, but eventually, he got to the top.

There was a steel grate blocking his exit, so he braced his legs again and took out his suppressed handgun. He fired a bullet at every bolt, creating a small flash of sparks with each one. By the time he'd finished, some of the smoke had reached him so, after reloading, he raised the grate and raised his head just above the surface. The stench of stale urine had also filled the thin pipe, so the fresh air was a welcomed change. As he looked out, he saw guards running in all directions, covering the courtyard like ants. In the distance, Chameleon could see the tall, abandoned building

Pigeon was camped in. There was a flash of light from the very top, from Pigeon's scope, which told Chameleon he was still being watched over, despite their lack of radio.

He watched as the light focussed on him, before it started flashing. Without thought, Chameleon knew it was Morse code and began translating the flashes, first into dots and dashes, "-- -.--   --. ---   --- -." and then he translated the repeating message into letters, *"my go on"*, constantly repeating. It would usually be easier to just know what sounds corresponded to which letters and ignore the dots and dashes, but this way, he could understand the flashes for Morse code as well. Chameleon rearranged the order and created something that made sense, *"on my go"*. Holding his hand up, the message stopped being repeated, Pigeon understood it had got through.

Chameleon waited, patiently, for any sort of signal, ready to go in an instant. As he waited, there was a slight rumble from below, shortly followed by all the sirens and alarms switching off. *I guess the water melted*, he thought to himself, as he realised why the guards were so concerned about the grenade going off near the junction box. Suddenly, something erupted behind him, bursting into flames. That was the signal.

Chameleon leapt out of the tube and bolted towards the hole in the fence. Pretty quickly, the guards saw Chameleon and began firing in his direction. Before they could get a hit, Pigeon cut through them, causing the others to go into hiding and dive for whatever cover was available. One guard dived behind a load of fuel barrels; it was a mistake he wouldn't make again. Chameleon just ran, not stopping for anything, putting all his trust in Pigeon's ability, as explosions filled the courtyard. His feet were pounding the ground as stray bullets flew past, some only inches from Chameleon. He had no time to duck and dive, it wouldn't help with the element of luck that had to be adopted. But eventually, a stray bullet did tag Chameleon, catching his left shoulder. He felt the bullet hit, but the adrenaline flowing through his body masked the pain, making him more animal than human.

Chameleon scurried through the cut fence and continued towards the field, running for his life. As the abandoned building hid behind the factory, Chameleon was once again alone. To say he wasn't scared would be a lie, but it was being scared that made him better and far more deadly. Fortunately, most guards had returned to the main compound at some point, which meant the field ahead was empty. It also meant that all the guards were now chasing him. Trucks, motorbikes, and dune buggies with mounted machine guns all tore up the turf behind. Because of the uneven surface, it was hard for anyone to get a shot on target, as the vehicles seemed to find every dip and mound, and the bikes had to slow down to just a crawl. The buggies were by far the quickest and, before Chameleon could even reach the halfway point, they were right behind him.

His rifle was still strapped to his back, to help him move quicker, with his handgun clasped tightly in his fist. As he pelted across the field, he took only a second to spin around and shoot the tyre of the closest buggy, sending it rolling and flipping down the field, buckling its roll cage. The next buggy revved up its engine and bounced towards Chameleon, trying to knock him down. As it got close, Chameleon jumped up, slamming into the glass windscreen, cracking it with his shoulder.

The impact dazed him, but not enough to dull his instincts. He raised the handgun, still clenched in his fist, and fired at the passenger. As Chameleon took aim at the unarmed driver, the driver threw his foot on the brake, sending Chameleon sliding off the bonnet and back onto the field. He landed on his feet and was sent at such a speed, he stumbled to regain his balance, just picking himself up without crashing to the floor. One of the trucks ploughed straight into the back of the stationary buggy, demolishing the rear half of it, and sending the truck high into the sky. Some of the passengers tried leaning out of the window to take a shot at Chameleon, but thanks to the constant supply of bumps and holes, most of the bullets either buried themselves in the mud or flew straight up and away from the field.

The buggies were keeping a steady distance from Chameleon, not knowing when it would be safe to attack. The next one saw its chance and pulled up alongside Chameleon. The passenger pulled out his gun and went to take aim. Chameleon holstered his handgun and removed his knife. He leapt at the passenger, digging the knife into his shoulder. Using him as support, Chameleon climbed onto the front of the buggy and yanked the squealing passenger onto the field.

Chameleon swung into the buggy, pointing his unholstered handgun at the driver and ordered, "Get out!"

Without time for a second thought, the driver heaved himself up and rolled out of the vehicle, falling to the field below. As Chameleon planted his foot to the floor, he heard two helicopters fly overhead. One of them with billows of smoke pouring from its engine.

It was clear that Pigeon was trying to take them down, by targeting their weakest spot. Chameleon's buggy continued to bound over the ground, as it headed towards the half blown-up factory. He lined up the open doorway and pushed his foot as far as it would go, trying to push it through the floor. The buggy squeezed through the gap and roared through the factory. The open space in the middle could just about fit the buggies through, but then one of the trucks tried to follow. The truck punched a hole in the wall and was instantly stopped by the turned over steel barrel, much like a giant beer vat, that once stretched to the roof, sending shards of metal flying everywhere.

The first time Chameleon braked was to angle the buggy out of the factory and into the final courtyard, replacing his foot on the throttle as soon as he was lined up with the gate. Three other buggies made it through the factory, with everything else being stopped by what was left of the truck. By the time they got back into the open, the smoky-engined helicopter had begun spinning around, getting quicker and quicker as it fell towards the ground. Chameleon watched as the muzzle flashes of Pigeon's rifle got closer in succession, desperately trying to take down the final helicopter. The spinning helicopter finally hit the ground, its blades ripped off by the mud and thrown in all directions. One of the loose blades embedded itself in a guard's buggy, flipping it over.

The second helicopter hovered motionlessly, looking at Pigeon, before releasing a bombardment of rockets at the base of the building. Pigeon continued to fire at the helicopter, even when the lower framework of the building began to collapse. Before long, the whole building folded in on itself, absorbed into a huge cloud of smoke.

"Westbrook!" shouted Chameleon, before being covered in the same cloud.

As he emerged, his face was emotionless. His foot eased off the throttle as he looked meaninglessly in the distance. As the remaining two buggies caught up, Chameleon caught sight of the helicopter. He was instantly filled with anger and rage; he was fixed on nothing else but revenge. His foot returned to the floor, pushing the throttle further than it would go. Chameleon's determination was unrivalled.

They travelled across gravel paths, more fields, and small rocks for over a mile. Eventually, the rocks got bigger and bigger. One of the buggies began to back off, not as brave, or fearless, as Chameleon. The other buggy went over a large rock, tearing out the entire underneath, including the steering column. It was still going at full speed as it smashed into the edge of the cliff face, which was getting taller and taller. Before long, Chameleon was on the sand, where his buggy belonged. The helicopter had hovered alongside him the whole time, still refusing to open fire, but as they got to the sand, it had no speed in comparison, to what was now a plume of sand, due to its damaged engine.

He splashed through some crystal clear, shallow water and continued flying along the beach until he reached a path leading off the sand. Chameleon spun around the corner, heading up, and turned up the huge circular path. He'd turned a complete circle and set off straight through the light foliage ahead, and with perfect timing, clattered into the helicopter, crippling into its tail rotor.

The helicopter spun out of control, heading left, right, and all over the place. Eventually, just before the pilot could regain control, the already damaged engine packed in, not able to cope with the stress of its out-of-control body. As it fell to the sand below, there was still a little left in the blades. The helicopter was dragged along the sand towards the frantically reversing enemy buggy. Before they could pick up any speed, the blades chewed through the buggy's roll cage, sending debris flying in all directions. There wasn't any explosion, just two unrecognisable heaps of metal lying in the sand.

Chameleon heaved himself out of what was left of his own buggy and staggered towards the carnage. There was little left of the buggy, and the helicopter pilot sat motionless in the cockpit, slumped over the metal pole that impaled him. By some stroke of luck, the helicopter gunner was still alive, although he likely wouldn't see it that way. His scrabbling body was already hanging out of the helicopter when Chameleon grabbed his jacket and dragged him onto the sand.

"Why did you not kill me!" he shouted, spitting in the gunner's face as he bellowed. "Why?" he continued.

Chameleon saw a small piece of glass embedded under the gunner's arm, he began pushing it, causing him to groan in pain. There was nothing that could be done to prolong his life, so Chameleon needed all the answers he could get, quickly.

"There was no nuclear missile. It was staged to catch you… Crabble…" the gunner started, spluttering as he tried to get his words out. "Crabble… wants you," he said.

"Why? Why does he want me!" Chameleon demanded.

"You have been… chosen," he mumbled.

The gunner's mouth began filling with blood, before all the life rolled out of his eyes. Chameleon dropped the gunner back to the sand and stood up. He knew this wasn't over, not until he avenged Westbrook, putting Crabble six feet under. Chameleon took the bullet from his pocket and observed the bent and scorched lump of metal.

Chameleon gave a false smile as he spoke out loud, as if speaking to the bullet itself. "I will make this right, no matter how long it takes… I promise," he mumbled, frantically trying to clean it as best he could.

To his left, he caught sight of the waves crashing into one another, all racing to reach the sand first. In the distance, more vehicles were coming closer, likely locked on to the helicopter's last broadcasted signal. Chameleon immediately headed up the path and towards the exfil site, leaving a wake of destruction behind him.

Chapter 7 – The Present
February 7th
07:49 GMT

A loud, piercing alarm refocussed Alpha Six. The noise began digging its way to his eardrums. Alpha Six turned a dial on his CAT, rendering the noise silent again.

"I don't know what that noise was, but now we've sealed our earpieces, we can't hear it. That also means we can't hear anything other than each other, so don't forget to open them again," said Alpha One.

"We must've tripped an alarm, probably a proximity alarm, or motion sensor, or something like that. So yes, they know we're here," added Kenny.

They never planned for if a mission went sideways, they didn't need to. Our minds don't need the memory during high adrenaline moments, they need instinct, and it was instinct that would get them through it, not some plan they didn't have time to try and remember, but instinct.

Alpha Six's sight wasn't magnified at all; he could see the entire place which was now a battleground. Because of the open land surrounding the town, the wind was harsh, but Alpha Six knew what to look for. He could see the sand being blown from the tops of the roofs, the cloth blowing from where it had been caught in the shattered window, and even in some cases, how the enemy's hair blew in the wind. Alpha Six wasn't just good, he was among the best, like all of them in their own elements. Alpha Six had his crosshairs lined up about an inch to the right and a centimetre above his target's head. There was a click of his trigger, followed by the sound of thunder from his rifle, as the long bullet was propelled from the barrel. An instant later, most of the person flew back and dropped to the floor.

Despite his bipod and heavily modified sniper rifle, the gun still jumped up. This kind of thing didn't faze Alpha Six, in fact, he didn't even notice it. When the gun had lowered, his next target was already lined up. There was another clap of thunder, as the bullet flew through the hot air completely unstoppable. Every time someone else stepped into Alpha Six's line of sight, they had less than a second to hide, but once a hunter has their eyes on their prey, they never lose sight. One of the security guards moved back behind a small stone wall and into cover, moments later a bullet blew a hole in the wall and took a chunk out of his lower abdomen.

***

The other five trusted Alpha Six with their lives. They headed straight for their objective without moving for cover or stopping to fire their guns. The security guards were still finding it hard to see anyone because of their suits. The footprints left behind, the flicking of the sand, and the hazy figures, where not all the light was absorbed, helped the security to see, but Alpha Six didn't give them long enough to lock on to any targets. Alpha Four and Five continued with their original plan and headed for the outbuilding.

Kicking the door down, they entered as one. Alpha Four checked the right and Alpha Five checked the left. They cleared the room in seconds, killing seven people in total, one shot to the head, in the exact same place. As Alpha Five moved over to the computer, another security guard leaped out, thrusting a knife at his head. Alpha Four caught it only millimetres away from Alpha Five's head, but the knife was stopped instantly, with Alpha Four cracking the guard's elbow, sending the knife back. It buried itself deep in the guard's arm. He tried to shriek in agony, but Alpha Four's hand was clasped tightly around his mouth. Alpha Five never flinched; he just carried on towards the computer as if nobody had just threatened his life.

He plugged away at the keys, whilst Alpha Four dragged the squealing guard over and smacked his face against the retinal scanner which they'd seen on entry.

"Okay, I'm in. Security cameras disabled. The front door is unlocking, but I don't know how long it'll take," said Alpha Five.

Alpha Four slumped the unconscious guard over the chair and added, "Look in your rucksacks. You should all have something that will help."

***

They each took the rucksack from their backs and looked inside. Alpha Three took a barrel of a gun, about half a metre long, along with the magazine and the main part of the gun itself. He quickly clipped in the magazine and attached the barrel, creating a machine gun capable of chewing through tank armour. The stock was an unusual shape, which wrapped around his arm, to reduce the strain of the recoil.

He pulled back on the trigger, allowing the machine gun to spit out hundreds of bullets in seconds. It slashed through the walls, sending bits of broken stone one way, and spraying a red mist the other. The giant magazine could hold one thousand bullets but, because of its weight, only one magazine could be carried. Both Alpha One and Two covered their faces from the empty shell casings and decided to wait until Alpha Three was finished, pressed up against the unlocking steel door. There was little point in all of them wasting their bullets when a machine gun of that calibre could take buildings apart.

***

Whilst Alpha Three demolished the surrounding area, Alpha Four and Five headed to the side door, ready to breach. Alpha Four took his special weapon from his rucksack, a drone. The drone wasn't small, it was roughly the size of a paving slab, and he attached sets of small rockets underneath and loaded ten rounds into a top hatch for the rifle that stuck out of its belly. Alpha Five then looked in his bag for something to help and took out a water pistol.

"What is this?" he asked, clearly infuriated.

"It's a water pistol," Alpha Four replied with little emotion to his voice. There were a few sniggers over the radio, from those who had time to listen.

"If we get stuck in this desert, under the burning sun, and you all run out of water, I'm not sharing mine," said Alpha Five, trying to swing the embarrassment in his favour.

"You do know we all packed enough water to last until tomorrow, so I think we'll be fine," said Alpha Four as if he'd already planned what to say.

"Why did you do this?" demanded Alpha Five, directing his question to Alpha Four alone, hoping the others wouldn't join in.

"Well, I thought it would be funny," replied Alpha Four, as he pretended to become compassionate and feeling.

Alpha Five knew there was little he could do to save his broken ego, so threw the water pistol back into his bag and watched, as the drone cut its way through the wall with what looked like a tiny laser.

It flew into the casino and scanned all the targets in sight. One brave, or stupid, guard fired at the drone, emptying all thirty of his bullets. The drone hovered for a moment longer, completely unaffected by the impact, before releasing all its rockets. One by one, the rockets were propelled towards their targets, turning the whole place into a ball of fire. Each rocket packed only a small number of explosives, but together, they were able to turn the three-storey casino into a one-storey wreck. As the rockets pounded the steel supports, the entire floor above came crashing down. Although the rockets seemed persistent, they did eventually run out, but that wasn't the end of the drone. With its ten rounds of ammunition, it identified anyone still alive, and made sure that changed. The bullets were nothing special, but the already injured guards couldn't survive such an accurate shot. By the time all ten rounds were emptied, what was left of the casino was now flooding with more guards.

Alpha Four wasted no time in getting the drone out and returned it to his backpack.

"The door's unlocked," said Alpha Five.

Alpha Four then added, "There're a lot of enemies in there now, so it's probably a good time to use the item right at the bottom of your backpacks."

***

Alpha Three's gun finally ran out of bullets, and with little left around, Alpha Six was able to cover their backs whilst they made entry. Each of them rummaged around in their rucksacks for the next item, and they all took out a grenade launcher, all except Alpha Two, who had an extendable shield. The grenade launchers were filled with canisters of gas which would render anyone within their grasp unconscious. Their full-face masks would stop any of the gas getting in and their visors could pick out heat signatures, so they could see everything through the smoke.

Once Alpha Two had extended the shield to cover all three of them, Alpha Five opened the doors. The steel doors scraped open and, before there was even a clear sightline, the guards opened fire. The bullets clanged against the shield, which stood strong against the firepower, as they slowly advanced. Once in, Alpha Five closed the doors behind them, whilst Alpha One and Three began launching their gas-filled projectiles into the air. With a hiss, the white smoke began to fill the room and both Alpha Four and Five came flying through the door on the right, sending even more canisters into the air. The once constant firing had now slowed to almost a complete stop, with just the odd bullet rattling past and the gasp for air within the white clouds. The thermal imaging showed the guards falling to the floor, one by one. One guard made a final effort to charge through the smoke, their rifle still raised. Alpha One lowered his grenade launcher slightly and fired his final canister. It hurtled across the room and caught the guard square on their head, sending them crashing to floor quicker than the canister itself.

With the room cleared, Alpha Two and Three stayed behind the shield, watching for any more potential threats, whilst the others made their descent down the stairs. Before turning the corner, Alpha Four fired two canisters of the gas blindly through the doorway. After only a couple of seconds, they rounded the corner with their rifles raised, and advanced. They stepped over the limp bodies, which littered the floor, and made their way to the, now locked, vault door. Alpha One watched the bodies on the ground to be sure none of them would get up.

"The vault door is fake," Alpha Four stated.

He knew they didn't understand, not through his keen sense of intuition but through the silence on the radio. Alpha Two and Three turned to each other, shrugging their shoulders as if to say, 'Were we meant to understand that?'

Alpha Four then continued, explaining. "The vault is made from the same materials as normal but, in a nuclear explosion, there's no point in locking it. That'd be like throwing a spider out of your house, and then locking the door just to make sure it can't get back in. All…"

"Hold on, hold on. What's wrong with that?" asked Alpha Three.

Alpha Four began to laugh, as he said, "Do you seriously lock the door to ensure they can't get back in?"

"I see nothing wrong with that. I don't like spiders," replied Alpha Three.

With a shaking head and a smile still stretched across his face, Alpha Four concluded, "Anyway, all they would've done would be to put the same materials into the vault and then add some cheap locking mechanism to hold it closed. So, if we can get some water into the CPU, which would be in the middle of that box, then it should short circuit the whole thing. Oh, and the box can't be tilted in any way, it'll trigger a fail-safe. Don't ask me why, but for some reason that's how they were designed." He then pointed to a square box on the floor and looked at Alpha Five.

He tutted before taking the water pistol from his backpack and spraying it into the box, sending the water further in than just pouring it. After a few sparks and a little bit of unnerving fizzing, the lock on the door failed.

"See. And people say I'm just a comedian," joked Alpha Four, as he pulled open the lumbering vault door.

"Nobody says that," said Alpha Six, watching as the security presence got ever bigger outside.

Alpha Five stepped in, scanned the almost empty vault, shouting, "Clear!" as he looked down to the blindfolded hostage, sat all alone on the vault floor.

"We've got him," said Alpha Four, as he began taking a light-absorbent sheet from his bag and proceeded to wrap it around the man sat in the vault, taking his blindfold off in the process.

The hostage's dilated pupils started wandering, unable to focus on anything. His teeth were yellow, and his hair was completely shaved. Along with the scars, which covered his face, it seemed clear he'd been their captive for a long time, and certainly longer than they'd been led to believe. So much so, his face had few features left. Alpha Four then cut the ropes, which bound his hands together, noticing the skin surrounding his wrists had been completely torn away, leaving only dark red, infected wounds.

"What's your name?" asked Alpha Five. The man looked dazed and failed to answer, so Alpha Five repeated his question with more force. "What is your name?"

"Mieko. Mieko Kale," the man said in a timid and shaken voice.

"That's the right name and, as we've no picture to go by, we'll have to assume we've got the right guy," said Alpha One, still watching the unconscious guards on the floor.

***

Meanwhile, in the only other building still standing, Alpha Six had ensured the huge container was in front of a window and he pulled a lever on the inside. From underneath the padded cover came a turret with a mounted Minigun on top.

***

"Okay, remember, the whole thing is automated. It should fire at any heat signature, unless they are wearing this material. It is a little experimental, so I hope it works," said Alpha Four.

Although they couldn't see each other's faces, they all looked equally concerned.

Alpha One added, "Let's hope it does work, because I imagine it might sting a little if it turns fire on us."

The comment maybe wasn't reassuring, but it was enough to relax the others. After rejoining the other two, they laid the hostage down on a little ledge on the shield, and Alpha Three and Four picked it up from either end, with Alpha Five stood right next to the hostage. They then reopened their earpieces to hear the alarms had all stopped.

Alpha Two looked back in his rucksack and pulled out a shotgun. There was a little lever, which moved the choke, on the side of the gun, adjusting the spread of bullets. It could kill someone at point-blank range, or up to about twenty-five metres, so long as the shot was well placed. Alpha One then leant into his backpack and took out two handguns. They were revolvers in style and mechanics, just with the power of a shotgun. There was enough room for twelve rounds in each, compared to the traditional six, so he began clipping each of the giant rounds into an even bigger cylinder.

"Those bullets look more like suppositories," joked Alpha Two, as he looked down at the guns.

Alpha One finished loading the handguns, which were almost the size of their rifles, and said, "I'll know where to aim then," before cocking the guns and moving into position.

"There will be no offer this time, you will all die, but I'll ensure it's by my hand," came a voice booming out of what was left of the speakers dotted around the place.

"Well, at least it's a different cliché. I wonder whether we should switch the external sounds off again," said Alpha Three.

"My position is about to be overrun. Should I activate the turret?" asked Alpha Six.

Alpha One waited, not saying a word, as they took deep breaths, filling their lungs. It was unlikely they would have time to stop and catch their breath, so they ensured their lungs were full before leaving.

Alpha One kept his eyes locked on the door and said, "Now."

This was both a signal to Alpha Six for the turret and to Alpha Five to reopen the doors. With the flick of a switch, the turret began throwing bullets everywhere. With little left of the buildings already, most of the guards were exposed, and the turret had little difficulty in dispersing them. As the doors opened, the first person Alpha One could see was the security officer with the green stripes, cowering behind a wall. The officer's sniper rifle was pointed towards the opening doors, but in his moment of hesitation, Alpha Two fired his shotgun, catching him in his left shoulder. He went down, but they knew he wasn't finished.

Alpha One was the only one to flick his thermal imaging off, preferring to look with the naked eye. They left the building, shooting anything that moved. Alpha One pointed his revolver at one guard and fired, the recoil sending his gun up at 90 degrees, the impact sending the guard back through the wall behind him. He fired the revolvers alternately, firing the right, whilst the left recovered from the recoil. Each shot could take chunks out of the enemy. Alpha Two's shotgun was equally powerful. With the lever pushed to its maximum, it was able to blow people off what was left of the first floors. They stood together, back to back, shooting anything that moved, under the constant spray of bullets from the turret above. One by one, the guards came out of hiding, and one by one, they were all sent back.

The green-striped security officer climbed back to his feet, using his knees to steady his rifle. He wore a full-face mask and his security outfit, meaning nothing was exposed except the bleeding hole in his shoulder. He aimed his sniper rifle straight at Alpha One and pulled the bolt into place. Alpha One just caught the glint of the rifle's scope in the corner of his eye. Without thought, he dropped to the floor, letting gravity do all the work, and twisted his revolver round. He didn't have enough time to line up a proper shot, but it was on target. The giant bullet went straight through the officer's mask and into the left side of his face, shattering the bone and biting a chunk out of his cheek. The officer was sent back down and out of sight. As quick as the violence had started, it stopped. There was no gunfire, no footsteps, only the smell of gun smoke.

The others left the room, with the hostage still behind the shield, whilst Alpha Six moved back over to dismantle the turret. Just as he bent down to pull the lever back, the turret spun round and fired about fifty rounds in only a couple of seconds. Alpha Six turned, to see two of the security guards fall through the doorway with more holes than body left.

They continued through the desert and out onto the open sand, with Alpha Two at the front, and Alpha One protecting the rear.

"Two minutes," said Alpha One after looking at his watch. Alpha Five moved to the bottom of the final standing structure and helped Alpha Six carry the container. The sand quickly became difficult to walk through, as the further they got from the town, the softer it became. Wading their way through, Alpha Two eventually got to the train tracks, at the earliest time the train would arrive, and immediately began strapping the hostage to his suit. Each of them offloaded their rucksacks back into the container, sealing it up tight afterwards. Alpha Two finished tightening the final cords not a moment too soon, as the tracks began rattling just four minutes after their arrival. It was only very minor, but it was there. The train came into view shortly after, as they stood ready and poised, waiting for the only perfect moment.

The train came closer and closer, but they all knew the exact point to aim for, the whole thing was planned, and the plan was perfect. As the train got to about ten feet away, Alpha Three fired his grappling hook. At five feet, Alpha One fired the grappling hook belonging to the container. When the train got level with them, Alpha Four and Five fired their grappling hooks, latching on to anything they could. Alpha Two was next, and fired his just a split second later, with the hostage braced against him. The hostage had no idea how much it was going to hurt, and that was probably for the best, the more relaxed he was, the lower the chance of injury. The train rattled past, almost falling apart. The cords on their grappling hooks slowly became tight, trying to reduce the sudden increase in speed. Even with the slow increase in speed, it still felt they were being launched into space. As Alpha Three was lifted from the ground, his body was instantly thrown against the side of train, and then again, and again, until he could eventually grab a hold of the door and stabilise himself. The container was much the same, but instead of it being in pain itself, it inflicted the pain on the train. It bashed into the side of the train, buckling the door of the second carriage. The grappling hooks were placed in exactly the perfect places; Alpha Three was able to hook onto the container, whilst Alpha Four and Five got the bent doors open. The doors only went to about halfway before they got stuck on the buckled metal, but that was enough for them to angle the container in, secure it, and then detach the grappling hook.

It fell to the floor and slammed against the back of the cargo carriage. Alpha Three immediately went to Alpha Two, who was still thumping against the side, trying to shield the hostage as best he could. Alpha Three grabbed the cord and began pulling it inside the carriage, attaching it to the weighted container and letting all three of the team begin to reel it in. Alpha Two was pulled along, heading towards the front of the train, before he was grabbed and yanked into the rattling and shaking carriage. Alpha One and Six waited until the train had almost gone past. Twenty-four carriages later, they fired their grappling hooks, clutching the poles of the final carriage. The length of their cords was much shorter, offering less time to gradually increase their speed. Both leapt at the train, allowing their safety lines to catch them. They swiftly grabbed the sides, and heaved themselves onto the back of the train, still outside, where they could look back at the town and watch for anyone following them.

But what they couldn't see was the green-striped officer, crawling to the edge of the rubble. He tore the shattered mask from his head and threw it to the floor. His left arm was unusable, and his left eye full of blood, just above his bloody cheek and shattered jaw.

"This is Green Viper. I have eyes on the target," said the officer, hardly able to form his words through the blood and pain.

He focussed down his sights, tracking the second carriage. After a few seconds of judging its speed, the distance, and the wind direction and strength, Green Viper squeezed his trigger. The gun cracked, as the bullet emerged from a plume of smoke. The bullet tore through the air, clanging as it went through the closing door of the second carriage. The clang was shortly followed by a thud.

"No, no, no, no, no! Alpha One, we're in need of immediate medical attention," said a panicked Alpha Four.

Alpha One spun round and began charging towards the front of the train, jumping between all the carriages.

"Who is it? Dan? Sam? Mike? Is anyone there? Talk to me."

Chapter 8 – The Plan
February 7th
08:18 GMT

The last thing Daniel remembered was the carriage door being torn open and Scott flying in. Their voices sounded muffled to him, as if he wasn't there, losing his grip on life. Scott leant over him, applying a large amount of pressure to his lower abdomen. The pain was never really there, but he could see his eyelids roll closed. They felt heavy, like huge iron shutters. No matter how hard he tried, they closed, only for a couple of seconds for him, but an eternity for the others. Daniel could hear his heart slowing down, feeling as tired as he did.

He woke up moments later to bright lights. They started to hurt his eyes, almost as if they were burning. But eventually the pain subsided, and his eyes were fully open. He was staring at a plain, white wall without knowing why.

"So, you decided not to leave then?" came a voice next to him.

It was a familiar voice, and he turned to see Scott. Still unsure of his surroundings, Daniel went to sit up but was flooded with an almighty pain in his intestines.

"I wouldn't do that if I were you," said Scott, lying back in his chair.

"Don't lie, if you were me, you'd definitely be trying to get up," said Daniel, causing Scott to let out a little laugh. Even in Daniel's pained state, he knew something wasn't right.

"Was the mission a success?" he asked.

"No," Scott replied, not wanting to expand.

Daniel didn't say anything, he just gave a look; a look that told Scott to go on, so he did.

"We lost Kale, the hostage. According to the surgeon, he saved your life, even if it was unwilling and somewhat unbeknownst to him. The bullet penetrated his inferior vena cava, he died pretty shortly after that," said Scott, lowering his head.

Daniel also sank in his bed, asking, "The whole thing was for nothing then?"

Scott then looked up, giving Daniel a little hope, and said, "Before he died, he did tell us something. He said, 'They can control the weather', and then gave the classic, 'You can trust nobody'. And before you ask, no, we've no idea what either mean."

At that moment, Scott's phone buzzed.

"They've got something," he said with the smile reappearing on his face.

"That was quick, wasn't it?" asked Daniel.

As Scott was getting up to leave the room, he stopped. He didn't know whether to break it to Daniel gently or just be blunt, and no matter how much thought he'd given it, he still didn't know.

"You've been asleep for four and a half days, Danny," said Scott, tentatively, but seemingly with the direct approach.

Daniel went quiet; he just stared at the plain, white wall in front of him. Scott didn't really know what the best help would be but decided to listen to the doctor, as he was the most qualified.

"Doc said you need to rest. I'm not sure they know you've been asleep for over four days, but they still say rest. I'll fill you in later," said Scott, realising a joke didn't help as much as he'd hoped.

Scott left the room, turning back to see Daniel still looking at the same plain, white wall.

Scott re-entered the meeting room and seemed to bring silence with him, as the conversations were muted and everyone inside turned to Scott.

"He's fine. It'll take some time to come to terms with what happened, him not being around to help, but he'll back with us in no time," assured Scott.

There were many more faces in the meeting room, despite Daniel not being there. Bosse was sat in front of the wall of computer screens with piles of paperwork in front of him.

He started by introducing a new face to the room, saying, "This is the person who'll be in your ear, helping you every step of the way."

Bosse then sat down and let the man in his mid twenties, beside him, introduce himself.

"I'm VOICE, the Very Overly Intelligent Computer Expert. I will be the voice in your ear," he said, letting out a strange laugh that sounded more like a cross between a short alarm and the noise you'd make if someone just stepped on your toe.

As soon as he started speaking, a strong smell of mint filled the room. It didn't take Scott long to realise the smell came from chewing gum, as he noticed the large amount of plaque building up on VOICE's teeth. He had no visible spots on his face and was very skinny, which was even more noticeable in the oversized T-shirt and shorts he wore. VOICE had brown hair, which looked longer than most in the room, with it falling about shoulder length, and looked unkempt.

There was an uneasy feeling around the room, as they began laughing awkwardly and with no energy.

"I can hardly contain myself," said Samuel quietly, but still loud enough for those near him to hear.

"Was that meant to be funny?" asked Anthony with no sense of a joke in his voice.

Bravo One was sat directly opposite Scott with his mouth wide open and a face of confusion. It was clear Bravo One had no clue how to take VOICE. Not only was VOICE someone to laugh at his own jokes, but he was also someone to find those jokes funny in the first place. Bravo One was big, muscular, and scary, and was somebody you wouldn't want to meet on a dark night. He was about 6'2" and had an oval head with a big, square jaw. His brown hair was the same length as his short, brown beard, making it look like it was all connected and flowing from one to the other. Even his bright blue eyes looked scary, as they drew attention to the imposing stance he always adopted. Bravo One went by the name Liath, preferring to forget his given name, Martin.

VOICE hadn't exactly filled the teams with any confidence, but Scott knew what he was taking on when he agreed to hire him.

VOICE then continued, "To tell you a little about myself, I'm 6' tall…"

"Maybe we can skip that for now," interrupted Scott, knowing full well that he was only 5'10".

VOICE then moved on slightly and continued, "Now, I know I've taken over from a dead guy, but I'll…"

Scott then leapt to his feet, saying, "Alright, now we've all met you, shall we get on?"

Scott's attempts to move the conversation along were not subtle, despite VOICE not picking up on this subtlety, but Scott knew how VOICE had managed to touch a somewhat tender nerve, without even realising it, and if he continued, it was likely he'd end up with a broken nose. The person before him, Adrian, had only been killed recently, along with Echo team, and VOICE clearly didn't know the circumstances.

Around the table sat all six members of Delta team, next to Alpha team, followed by three empty chairs, four of the twelve members of Bravo team, VOICE, then Bosse, then two members of Charlie team, who basically acted as the organisation's cavalry. Finally, there was Alpha team with Daniel's chair left empty.

Bosse started the conversation.

"We've been looking some more into the hard drive and what Kale said before he died…"

"Just before you continue, how long was Kale held captive?" interrupted Scott, making no apology for his intrusion.

Bosse looked a little confused, but still answered, "According to our intel, he was captured at the beginning of the week. Why?"

Scott shrugged his shoulders and replied, "Just wondering."

Bosse wasn't sure what Scott could be inferring but carried on with his original statement, slightly angered he'd been interrupted without being given a clear reason.

"As I was saying, with Delta team's help, we think we might have something…" he said, before holding his hand towards Delta One, and concluding, "…Diana will fill you in."

He took his seat and fixed eye contact with Scott, despite getting no response.

Diana was relatively short, at around 5'2", with short, brown hair, tied back behind her ears, and no distinguishing features. She was in her early thirties and was very slim with eyes that were hard to tell if they were brown or green. Delta team primarily acted as the organisation's recon team, and as such tended to not be as skilled in combat as the others but were rarely seen when on a mission. They were the closest team to being ninjas and were all extremely agile. Diana and her team usually wore full-face masks, whilst in combat, to aid their ability of keeping a low profile in the shadows. Although she used her natural disguise in the Molehill, Diana would always wear a different wig, contact lenses, and volume of make-up every time she went on a mission which wasn't combat involved and required a slightly more natural appearance.

Samuel stared at her, looking deep into her dark greeny-brown eyes in her ordinary-shaped head. He wasn't discreet, yet still thought his feelings were a secret. She stood up, looked around the room, and directed her findings to the computer screens in front of her.

She began by saying, "Kale said 'they can control the weather', so we've been looking into their organisation from the hard drive, and we have found these two assets. They seem to own a satellite, which orbits the Earth, obviously, collecting data on weather, or more specifically, how weather changes. We've also found a submarine with a similar purpose; it scans for any anomalies under the water. Although the satellite is listed as that very thing, we have managed to obtain a few images from the ground. In size, it seems far bigger than an ordinary satellite, and capable of having a large presence of crew."

Bosse retook the lead, breaking his long stare at Scott, and powered up the wall of screens behind him.

"Alpha team, you will oversee these two operations in capturing their assets, along with the assassination, and one more operation. We've been able to track the helicopter that, shall we say, made a statement at the nightclub? It's located at an airfield, along with a lot more of their equipment, including tanks, missile launchers, and so forth. I shouldn't have to tell you, but taking down the airfield will deal a great blow to the Night Vipers. Everyone's been brought in on this because we know you'll be stretched, but it's your lead, and your plan. I'm sure it's on all your minds that if they can control the weather, we may be able to finally shine light on what happened last month, which might prove we were right all along. Only time will tell whether Echo team were targeted or whether it was just a freak accident. Just don't get your hopes up, okay?" said Bosse, now passing the lead to Scott.

Samuel went to ask whether Bosse intended to make a pun as he said 'shine light', knowing full well Bosse had no intention of doing so. But even he was able to refrain from making jokes at that time. Talking about Echo team and Adrian was something only Bosse seemed to do, although still without mentioning their names. They all took responsibility for something they couldn't control and made a silent agreement to not mention them until the truth had been uncovered.

"Okay, first of all, I was thinking we would all need to play a part in the assassination…" started Scott.

"Well, I was actually hoping to do this solo…" interrupted Mike.

Everyone in the room turned towards the hacker, with surprise plastered across their faces. Mike could see he would need some justification but had nothing he wanted to offer.

"Please, I need you to trust me," continued Mike.

Scott knew what he was doing but was still surprised by Mike's omission. There was a sense of confidence in Mike's eyes, not like anything Scott had witnessed before.

With reservations, Scott said, "Okay, but Blindspot will go with you and act as backup, should you need it."

Anthony hadn't been called Blindspot in a while, but Scott felt it was time to bring him back. In fact, Anthony had dropped the title after the plane crash, feeling he should've been with them when it happened, even though his presence would have had no impact on the outcome. Blindspot was more anti-hero than man, able to kill anyone, usually in their blind spot. Both Anthony and Mike gave their approval, despite Mike being a little unimpressed by not having the mission solo.

Scott then continued, "Kenny, you'll take Charles, Carol, and the rest of Charlie team, and destroy the secret airfield. How you do it is entirely up to the three of you but, remember, you will be taking on a high-tech army, so take nothing for granted. It will be capture, not kill where possible though, so plan accordingly."

"Accordionly? Like an accordion?" whispered Charlie One, as he leant over to Charlie Two.

"No, accordingly," whispered Charlie Two with a slight grunt.

Scott waited patiently for them to finish their short, whispered conversation, before calmly carrying on, as if nobody had just interrupted him.

"Samuel, you'll be on the submarine with Bravo team. Again, the plan is yours, but try to take as few casualties as possible. And finally, that leaves me with the satellite, the only one trained to go to space. Di, you said something about having a way up there?" he asked.

Diana gave a short nod but said nothing.

"We'll discuss it on our way out. Everyone else, you know what to do," concluded Scott as he moved to get out of his chair.

They all took their own respective pieces of paper and moved out of the room. Scott watched VOICE leave next to Alpha Four, confirming that VOICE was only 5'10". Bosse slid another file towards Scott, titled 'M.N.G.W.A.', which was clearly to aid him in his further interrogation with Mr Wilson.

Bosse was the last to stand up, ensuring he would also be the last to leave. As Scott went to leave with Diana, and the other members of Delta team just behind them, Bosse began to follow loosely. He trailed the tail end of Delta team around several corners before he rounded the final turn and came face to face with five of them. He casually strolled past, as if he had no idea they were there, but Scott and Diana were nowhere to be seen.

They had split from the pack at the very beginning, allowing the rest of Delta team to act as a distraction for a suspiciously curious Bosse. They had travelled to Scott's office, to talk in private.

"I need a favour," he said.

She looked around the soundproof room and said, "Off the record, I assume?"

Scott nodded, saying, "Bosse is investigating a potential internal threat; he has to suspect everyone, including you and I. But recently, he has started taking information from an anonymous source, in return, he's authorised the assassination contract. We know nothing about this person, who goes by the name Heartfell, and it's unlike Bosse to take such a risk. I'm not sure if he knows who this is and won't let on, or he is just taking a risk with more immediate things on his plate. Kale had been held captive for what looked like months, and again, I don't know if Bosse is lying or being lied to."

"So, what do you need from me?" asked Diana.

"Find out everything you can about this Heartfell and see if there's any connection to Bosse. I don't think Bosse is the bad guy, I'm just not sure if he's made, or is making, a mistake. And let's be honest, Bosse is known to keep secrets, he always has been," said Scott.

"Sure thing. And this is what you need to get to space. Oh, and one last thing, tell Samuel to stop staring at me; he's hardly discreet," she concluded, handing Scott a file on something called, '*Operation Star Rocket*'.

Scott gave a slight smile with more troubling things on his mind.

He watched as she left the room, uncertain whether he'd done the right thing. He then shifted his focus elsewhere, concentrating on the file in front of him. '*Operation Star Rocket*' was a plan and design for a plane that could take off from the ground and fly to the moon, with enough fuel to then fly back and touch down on its landing gear. It was something that had been kept a secret since the late 20th century and had only recently been handed over to a Swiss company. Where the original designs had come from was still a mystery, although the Swiss company was quick to take credit. The file detailed a prototype that had been built and held at their Swiss testing runway. Scott looked further down the file, to see that the company were not only reluctant to sell the prototype but were prepared to destroy it if it got into the wrong hands. The satellite, or whatever it truly was, would likely have an external hatch for docking, given its expected size. But, as he looked at the prototype's specifications, it seemed to lack any ability to dock, with its more plane-like structure, adding yet another complication.

He turned and stared at Switzerland on his map, trying to think of a way of getting the plane. After hours of thought and hundreds of tiny ripped up scraps of paper, Scott had finally come up with a plan. He walked down to see Daniel with the intention of including him in the plan as someone to run it past. But by the time he'd got down there, the doctor stepped in his way.

"Daniel is resting, he can't have any visitors at the moment," said the doctor with his heavy German accent.

He was short and round, filling his doctor's white coat. He had short, black, curly hair and a matching beard, both of which always seemed to be the same length. The doctor had worked in the Molehill for years, yet his name and age were still a mystery to everyone. To them, he was simply called 'Doctor' or 'Doc' and they'd never been able to even estimate his age. No matter how long he had worked with them, he just never seemed to age. It was almost like he'd been frozen in time, with his hair no longer growing and his age remaining the same.

Scott looked down to the small German doctor and asked, "Has something happened?"

The doctor glanced back at the room Daniel was staying in and answered, "There was a complication. It seems the bullet was specially designed, as it released tiny pieces of itself, shrapnel, shortly after impact. Unfortunately, the bullet was in Daniel at the time."

"What happened?" Scott demanded, becoming more frantic with each moment.

The doctor then carried on, saying, "Of course, there is nothing to worry about now, it is all okay. But we had to leave one piece of the shrapnel in Daniel, as it was plugging a hole in his liver. In the state he was in, we had no time to operate, so patched him the best we could and scheduled to remove the shrapnel when he had further recovered. We expected that to be sometime next week, because he'd certainly find it easier to recover if he wasn't so injured in the first…"

"Doctor! You're getting sidetracked. What happened?" persisted Scott.

The doctor continued, saying, "Of course. Earlier, the shrapnel was pushed out by his body, and he was left with internal bleeding. So, we rushed him down to surgery and removed the shrapnel, we also repaired any damage caused, which was quite extensive, which we could have repaired earlier, but he was in no state to do so. So, we scheduled an operation for later this week but…"

"GET ON WITH IT!" shouted Scott before they both fell into silence. Scott then continued, trying to backtrack, saying, "I am so sorry, I meant to say that in my head, NOT that that is any better, but… er… sorry. What I meant to say was, 'Could you hurry things along a little please'."

"Of course, the stress, I suppose," replied the doctor.

Scott nodded, happy he'd found some sort of an excuse for his outburst and said, "Yes. Yes, that's probably it."

The doctor began moving closer to Scott, examining his eyes, and said, "Of course, what I'd recommend is a few days rest, out of this place. Maybe even somewhere warm, with…"

"Doctor, we were talking about Daniel," interrupted Scott, this time without raising his voice.

"Of course. We operated and, like I said, it is all okay now, he just needs rest," said the doctor, happy with the outcome.

"Thank you, Doctor. Wish him well when he's next awake, would you?" asked Scott.

The doctor gave one long nod, saying, "Of course."

Scott turned and went to leave again, muttering, "Talk about getting to the point quickly," as he left the ward and moved off towards the interrogation room.

Scott familiarised himself with the details of the file on his way. By the time he'd got to the interrogation room, Mr Wilson had already been sat in there a few hours. Alpha One strutted in, quietly clicking the door closed behind him.

"The true fool is not the person who acts it, but the person who believes the act, right?" began Alpha One. "I trust you like to play the fool, knowing that there will always be a 'greater fool', someone more foolish to buy the act. Well, that person isn't me," he continued. Mr Wilson looked both puzzled and intrigued, hooked with what Alpha One was saying. "I like to play the fool, there's a certain… power that comes with it. After all, in medieval times, the court jester, or fool, was made to try the king's food, to make sure it wasn't poisoned. But nobody checked the food after the fool had touched it. So, with some exceptional timing, the fool was always the only person who could poison the king. In many ways, he had more power than anyone else. And why? Because he was underestimated. He was always thought of as being stupid. So, they entrusted him with the most power. The same worked for you, didn't it?" he said, raising his eyebrow in question.

Mr Wilson said nothing, he just sat there, so Alpha One tried to make him his talkative old self, saying, "A good lie has a grain of truth to it. You are one of five members of M.N.G.W.A., true. You don't work for anyone, false. M.N.G.W.A. is just another pawn in this game, a game where you don't even know who's playing."

Mr Wilson sat forward, saying, "M.N.G.W.A. was hired

a year ago for a job. There was a tsunami which hit a couple of small islands. The richest countries in the world sent relief aid to help. We were sent in to cripple all that came. As the jobs went on, the predictions of these natural disasters became better and better. We began getting a little, concerned, as the weather devastations could be so accurately predicted and were becoming more frequent. Before long, we'd grabbed your attention, so we started to gather a little information on the organisation who had hired us and stored it on the hard drive. I kept the hard drive safe, whilst Gert…"

Despite Alpha One's strong poker face, Mr Wilson could see he didn't know who Gert was.

He smiled and started to laugh, as he leant forward and clarified, "Gert was the Dutch guy, at the nightclub. You remember? The one you killed. Anyway, I held the hard drive and Gert held the data key."

Although Alpha One already knew Mr Wilson was behind the attacks, it gave him the perfect opportunity to make Mr Wilson think he still had control over the information he was providing. But what he didn't like was being unaware of who the Dutchman was. Their scans on his DNA, fingerprints and so forth had all given no results. Although the information on the hard drive showed the Dutchman to be of the same level as Mr Wilson in the unnamed organisation, he now knew the Dutchman was also a member of M.N.G.W.A., much like the man sat in front of him. But it did seem as if every answer created new questions, as he now knew two members of M.N.G.W.A. were within the unnamed organisation for no obvious reason.

"How did you know he'd been killed?" asked Alpha One, trying to swing the conversation towards what he knew.

"I have my connections, even in here," replied Mr Wilson, still trying to get into Alpha One's head.

"Well, clearly they're not very good. I didn't kill Gert, somebody got to him first," added Alpha One.

Mr Wilson also found it hard to hide his surprise, as he went quiet. Within a couple of seconds of deep thought, Mr Wilson returned his persona to normal, giving the impression he knew who the mystery figure was. But that wasn't the time to ask, as Mr Wilson had no intention of giving up the name.

"How come you weren't caught?" asked Alpha One.

Mr Wilson started grinning, saying, "It's like you said, the fool has the most power. Gert and I told our 'superior' what we were doing, and he had no problem with it, because he underestimated us."

"Speaking of Mr... Gert, I noticed a tattoo on his stomach. You wouldn't happen to have the same one, would you?" asked Alpha One, already knowing the answer.

Mr Wilson lifted his shirt and displayed the same tattoo of a mngwa on his stomach. But unlike Gert, Mr Wilson's tattoo was alongside numerous scars, all at different angles and different depths. Before Alpha One could get a closer look, Mr Wilson lowered his shirt and tried to prevent Alpha One from making him feel vulnerable.

"And who is this 'superior' which you speak so highly of?" asked Alpha One, as if nothing had just happened.

"We've met a few times. He goes by the name... Crabble. And that is all I know," answered Mr Wilson.

"I see..." Alpha One replied, before saying, "...and what of 'Operation Storm'?"

Mr Wilson's eyes lowered as he said, "I'm afraid I don't know. All I do know is that it is now in operation, whatever 'it' is. But given its name, and the time it came into operation, I'd say it's likely connected with the natural disasters and sudden change in weather."

Alpha One stood back up and went to leave the room, now he had everything he needed.

As he reached the door, Mr Wilson raised his voice, saying, "M.N.G.W.A. wants to take over the world. But there isn't much point if there's no world to take over. There are a few others who are trying to leave, most get killed. Oh, one more thing, myself and Gert are the only members of M.N.G.W.A. who assisted with this other organisation. The other three would've gone into hiding, waiting for someone to deal with this threat before re-emerging. Someone... like you."

Alpha One left the room satisfied with the answers he'd been given. M.N.G.W.A. wasn't a threat... Yet.

Chapter 9 – The Storm
February 13th
14:33 GMT

In the depths of the deep, dark blue waters, a submarine lay motionless and floating. Not a sound could be heard from within. Everything that made a noise was shut down; they were as stealthy as they could be. About two hundred metres away was their enemy, and their target. Alpha Four was down in the torpedo bay, along with all twelve members of Bravo team. It became a little cramped as they all jostled for space, trying to squeeze into their wetsuits. They then clipped their rebreathers onto their suits and wrapped their fins around their feet, before climbing into one of the two torpedo tubes, one by one.

Alpha Four and Bravo One were the first to enter their respective tubes. They climbed in and placed their rebreather masks over their faces. The tube was tiny, restricting any sort of movement. As soon as the doors were sealed shut behind them, the tubes began filling with water, equalling the pressure outside. Once this was done, the outer doors were opened, allowing them to climb out and wait, clinging onto the front of their submarine. The outer doors sealed, and the tubes began emptying to allow the next operatives in. The process was slow, but under the radar.

After about five minutes had passed, they were all out into the dark and icy water. Because of their radio silence, there was no way of using any system other than radar. Alpha Four used his CAT to ping any short-range radar. The signal was faint, but the direction of the target submarine could just about be seen. They pushed off from their sub and swam into the distance, shortly becoming invisible from where they had been floating only moments prior. They had to stay close together and swam in a long, straight line, only about half a metre from the person in front. As they swam, not far above the seabed, a slightly shallower part of water separated the two submarines, hosting a cold-water coral reef. They stayed in a line as they travelled through the vast array of colours. Fish shot from side to side, moving from cover to cover. An octopus began coming closer, eyeing up a potential threat, before gliding off in fear, as it used its ink for cover. It slipped between two rocks, its red body mimicking the colour, shape, and texture of them perfectly, as it became a third rock. As they continued on, they all had the uneasy feeling of being watched. Hundreds of eyes all pointed in their direction, hiding from their unwelcome guests.

As quickly as the coral reef began, it ended. They were once again alone, in the dark water. Alpha Four had been leading them through the water for a couple minutes, when doubt started creeping into their minds, wondering whether they'd swum past the submarine. But just then, a hazy object began to come into view. The submarine looked very much like the one they had just come from but, assuming they hadn't made a complete turn, it must've been the enemy submarine.

Alpha Four got to the very front of the submarine and placed a jet-black, square device on its nose. Bravo team headed to the top and placed several charges on the escape hatch, all in one place. They then moved behind the tower and hid, waiting. Bravo One detonated the charges, ripping a hole in the submarine, as it created a huge bubble of air containing the explosion. Water rushed in, forcing the submarine to surface. According to their intel, the enemy submarine was far more advanced than their own, and that seemed to be the case as the compartment which the water was rushing into appeared to instantly seal. After only a couple of seconds, the water stopped flooding the submarine, but repairs still needed to be made.

"Comms are online," informed Alpha Four, now they had made their presence known.

The submarine flew to the surface, lifting all of Bravo team out of the water. Alpha Four flicked the only switch on the device as soon as he was also above sea level. It was fitted with a laser which sliced its way through the thick metal carcass of the submarine with ease.

Bravo team then set a charge on the sub's second hatch, which was at the top of the tower, and detonated it as soon as they were clear, blowing it off completely. It crashed onto the surface of the water and was slowly dragged down to the depths of the ocean. Bravo team slid down the ladder into the submarine, one by one, leaving Bravo Two, Eight, and Eleven patrolling the top. They flooded in, covering all directions with their rifles. Two robots came stomping forward, their rifles aimed towards Bravo One. The five operatives that were looking at the robots all opened fire, sending sparks everywhere. The robots fell back, falling to the floor.

"Okay, I have just done a full sweep of the submarine. Other than you, there are no life signs," said VOICE, now able to speak with them.

"Well, we've just taken down two robots, maybe they act as security," said Bravo One, in his deep, throaty voice.

"That is interesting. A submarine operated by robots. I expect they will be better security than people because they can take so many hits," said VOICE.

"And that helps us how?" questioned Bravo One, becoming angry.

"I do not think I can help you; the place is full of electrical surges. I would guess that the entire submarine is full of robots. Oh, could you hang on a minute..." said VOICE.

They all shared uneasy glances at each other, knowing what they were all thinking.

"And what was the point of him?" asked Bravo One, voicing their opinions.

Bravo team were there to create a distraction, and that's exactly what they did. They moved through the narrow walkways of the submarine, destroying every bit of machinery they came across. There were more and more robots closing in. As Bravo team got to a central area, it was clear where a lot of the robots were stored. There were about thirty robots, all pinned against the wall. They seemed to be charging but, after a short ring of an alarm, they all began to move. Their heads jolted forwards, followed by an arm. They dropped from their respective charging stations and surrounded Bravo team.

"Lay down your weapons," said one of the robots.

Bravo team did exactly as they were told. Whilst it would've been possible to destroy all the robots, the best distraction would be to draw them all into one space.

***

Back at the front of the submarine, Alpha Four had removed the device, revealing a perfectly cut circle. It was no more than one metre in diameter, but that was more than enough for Alpha Four to slip through with all his gear. He landed in an empty room, full of huge steel pipes, creating a maze to the door on the other side. Alpha Four shimmied past and heaved himself over the pipes, eventually reaching the doorway. He observed the passageway ahead before creeping through, making his footsteps as quiet as possible. He continued to move through each doorway, checking for anyone, or more, 'anything', as he went on, maintaining his secrecy.

"There are three large power draws from the submarine, one is where Bravo team is, one is a likely place for the engines, so the third should be your destination," said VOICE, again joining the conversation.

"Why would there be a large power draw in the engine room? Surely the engines would have a limited power draw?" said Alpha Four, confused, but still focussed on keeping a low profile.

"The entire submarine seems very 'high-tech', so I suspect the submarine has an entirely computer-based engine block, as there is nobody around to do any maintenance. And do not call me Shirley!" replied VOICE, again laughing.

Alpha Four gave no comment, he just shook his head and released a long sigh.

Alpha Four continued to take his only available path, his boots rattling the metal grates he walked on. There were no guards in sight, the distraction was obviously working, but this gave no time for complacency.

"Behind you!" shouted VOICE, startling Alpha Four, as he spun around and fired his gun. He saw nothing; there was just an empty corridor.

Alpha Four wasn't sure what had just happened, but before he could ask, VOICE said, "Sorry, that wasn't meant for you," before switching to a different frequency and leaving the conversation.

Alpha Four still couldn't contemplate what had just happened, but after lowering his heart rate and calming back down, he flung his arms in the air and shook his head, continuing along his path. The layout of the submarine was different from their own. The entire place was laid out for practicality, with no sleeping quarters taking up excess room. The space saved from the lack of recreational facilities was mainly taken up by the storage of weapons, mostly torpedoes. The central control room was also in a different location which could be found at the core of the submarine. It could be secured quickly, with only one way in and out of the room.

It wasn't the easiest of places to find, despite Alpha Four being on a one-track path. His only way was to carry on and execute the mission, hoping that VOICE's instructions took him to the right room.

"You would've thought the last place to have a robotic, or electric, crew would be on a submarine, under the water," said Alpha Four, trying to make conversation but still expecting a full 'well-structured' answer.

"Well, it is entirely possible that these robots are waterproof. Even if they are not, though, each compartment can be locked down with no requirement for air. There will obviously be air in there now, but that is only to delay any surface leaks by a crucial second or so," replied VOICE quickly, before clearly leaving his conversation with Alpha Four yet again.

He finally got to a locked door; it led the way directly into the control room. Alpha Four laid a square beige pack on the door and moved back a few paces.

"There is somebody at the door," said one of the identically voiced robots.

"Moving to intercept," said another, or perhaps the same one.

The metallic footsteps got close to the door and, as soon as they stopped, Alpha Four pressed the trigger clutched in his hand. The door blew in, clearing everything in its path.

"We have a breach in control room one," said another robot.

Alpha Four entered the room with his shotgun raised. He moved through the door slowly, hitting each robot as they came into view, removing their heads.

There was one robot left, but Alpha Four knew he'd run out of shotgun shells. He spun his shotgun up, revealing the axe attached to the front. Releasing a roar of fury, he swung down at the robot, slicing into its chest. There were more sparks covering Alpha Four, but he didn't settle for the two-inch deep scar down the robot's chest. With his face tightly screwed up, he swung the blade back up, and then down, cutting its head clean off. The robot stood, motionlessly, for a second, before its knees buckled and it dropped to the floor. Alpha Four leapt to one of the control panels and plunged his hand down on the big red button. All the doors slammed shut and sealed tightly, making the entire room safe. There was still a large hole where Alpha Four had previously made entry, so he moved back down the narrow passage and placed his only claymore down on the floor.

Back in the room, Alpha Four began trying to find what he was looking for, as he noticed what seemed to be thousands of buttons and switches, with no obvious explanation to any of their functions.

"Three things…" started Alpha Four, ensuring VOICE was listening. "One, is Bravo team okay? Two, how am I meant to work any of this out? There are millions of buttons, none of which are labelled. And finally, there are actually three doors in here, not just one," continued Alpha Four.

"Well, I didn't say there would only be one door…" started VOICE, before being interrupted.

"Yes, you did," argued Alpha Four, knowing he'd done more than enough to get under VOICE's skin.

"And I told you how to close the doors…" demanded VOICE.

"No, you didn't," continued Alpha Four, not expecting an answer.

"Just in case you're still interested, we are fine. The bots are just stood in a circle around us, staring. It's kind of creepy," added Bravo One.

Alpha Four stared at countless buttons, switches, and dials, not knowing what to do.

"The system is laid out for robots, so plug the encryption key in and I will do it all," said VOICE.

Alpha Four rummaged around in his watertight backpack and pulled out a tiny device, similar in style to a memory stick. He plugged it in and stood back. There was no sign of anyone in their system, but Alpha Four knew by the silence that VOICE was doing what he needed to.

Down the hall, Alpha Four could hear footsteps, big footsteps, which sounded more like a hydraulic press. They became so loud that he even had to lean out of the doorway just to ensure they hadn't bypassed the claymore. At that moment, they all came to a sudden stop, all at precisely the same time.

"Front toward enemy... Processing... Processing... Item identified... Claymore detected... Attempting detonation has predicted outcome of causing external damage... RBT19 you will sacrifice your parts to create a controlled explosion," came from one of the robots around the corner.

One robot stepped forward. There was a click, followed by an explosion echoing around the submarine, and then metal parts rattling along the floor.

"Detonation successful, proceed," said the same robotic voice.

"If you're going to do something, you need to do it now!" shouted Alpha Four, trying to get VOICE to speed up. He was frantically loading shells into his shotgun, whilst taking position behind one of the desks.

"You need to get closer," said VOICE.

"What?" demanded Alpha Four, too preoccupied to listen.

"Your shotgun will not be enough to penetrate their armour at that range. The ones coming around the corner have more armour," replied VOICE, still trying to gain access to their system.

Alpha Four didn't ignore the advice and moved right next to the doorway.

As soon as the first robot rounded the corner, Alpha Four pulled the trigger, sending the cluster of pellets straight into its head, tearing it clean off. As each one came towards him, Alpha Four did the same, but they were coming through quicker than he could recentre and fire his gun. When the fourth robot came round, Alpha Four swung the axe, again decapitating it. He then continued swinging the axe in close quarters, close enough to prevent the robots ever getting a clean hit, now he knew their weakest spot. The next lost its arm, before being kicked to the floor. The robots continued to fall, one by one, but Alpha Four's strength was also depleting. He swung his axe at the next robot which caught the gun in mid-air. He used all his strength to lower the gun as much as possible, lining it up with the metallic face in front, and he pulled the trigger, clearing everything in its path.

After finally clearing the last robot, with no shells to spare, Alpha Four headed back into the control room. The robot he had previously kicked to the floor was no longer where it had landed, it was inside. The robot was pressing most of the buttons within reach, before turning to Alpha Four.

"Come one step closer and I will detonate the submarine," said the robot.

"Okay, so that system they have is a little simpler than the traditional one. The two keys must be turned, not simultaneously, but as soon as one is released, the other will revert to its original place," said VOICE, unable to help any further. The robot turned one key and held it.

"All I have to do is turn the other key and you will all die," said the robot.

Alpha Four began nodding and moving closer.

"And how are you going to do that?" he asked, almost showing a smile.

"Like this," replied the robot, whilst going to grab the other key, but with no luck.

The robot's arm was still missing, and after a glance at his sparking shoulder socket, the robot began to realise its failure. Behind Alpha Four, the missing arm was moving around on the floor, its fist tightening and releasing its grip, trying to grab a switch that was metres away. Alpha Four gave no time for anything else as he sliced the robot's other arm off, ensuring he could do no more damage, causing the first key to return to its original position.

"Almost," said Alpha Four, looking at the robot, knowing how close he was to failure.

At that moment, the entire submarine began to shake, it was only light, but Alpha Four could feel it.

"What was that?" he asked.

"It was the waves out here. It's just become really choppy, out of nowhere," replied Bravo Two.

"Alpha Three and Charlie team have just reported a storm that came out of nowhere as well. I have just finished downloading everything, so it is probably best if you get out of there. I have also shut that robot down. Give me a moment and I can disable the rest, but they are all on different circuits, so it will take time. It's quite clever, really, they have no connection between one another, not even a back door, so a virus can only affect one of them. I guess the only drawback is they must speak to each other, but it still seems to be more of a help than a hindrance," added VOICE, again switching his channel to move onto a different conversation.

"You heard him, Bravo One, forget about waiting for him to disable them, you're clear to detonate. Bravo Two, get our exfil sorted," said Alpha Four, removing the tiny device.

***

Back in one of the midway storage rooms, Bravo team was still held in a tight circle in the centre. Bravo One slowly slipped his hand backwards and placed it inside one of his pockets. He removed a small, spherical object, still moving slow enough to not be noticed. He had managed to bring the device in front of himself and clasped it with both hands, as they swayed from side to side in the building storm. The robots' feet had magnetised to the floor, preventing them from moving in the rocking submarine.

"Device identified as an EMP," said one of the robots, as close as his voice could get to panicking. Bravo One twisted the top, releasing a pulse that wiped out all electronics within a close range. All the robots fell to the floor as if they were statues falling from their plinths. The EMP had wiped out the submarine's entire system, as well as their radios, but their plan was still being followed. They all jumped up, grabbed their equipment and headed back towards the open hatch.

***

On top of the submarine, the other three members of Bravo team were struggling to keep their balance. The waves had become higher and stronger within seconds, to the point they were in a tropical storm. Bravo Two crouched down, trying to keep a lower and more stable centre of gravity. Along with Bravo Eight, they began inflating two rubber dinghies, fastening them to the submarine, ensuring they couldn't get swept away. Bravo Eleven unclipped two small devices from his back and attached them to the dinghies. The two devices drew air from the front which then turned the blades inside. This allowed the water, which was drawn in from the bottom, to then be passed through the device and fired out of the back, as a pressurised jet, allowing it to move across the sea. It wasn't the quickest of machines, but the two devices were small which allowed Bravo Eleven to carry both without being at any risk of sinking. As the final device was clipped in place, a huge wave smacked against the side of the submarine. Bravo Two and Eleven were thrown into the dinghies, Bravo Eight was just about able to cling onto the lower hatch, as she fell back onto the submarine's shell.

***

Back in the control room, Alpha Four had just about removed the robot's head, as the wave crashed into the submarine. The head was ripped from his grasp, as he got thrown over the control table. The submarine then filled the void made by the wave, as it tipped the other way, rolling Alpha Four off the table. He quickly gathered himself and the items and headed out of the door, aware that the submarine was likely filling with water. He continued to stumble and fall as he made his way back down the corridor. Suddenly, the shaking stopped, and the rocking quickly got softer. Alpha Four hurdled the pipes and leapt through the small hole he'd used to enter.

Bravo team were already in the dinghies, one of which stayed back to wait for Alpha Four. As he stood on the, now swaying, submarine, there was a deafening crack. Everyone looked up to see several meteorites hurtling towards them. Alpha Four jumped into the dinghy, and they immediately headed for their submarine. Their lightweight, portable motors weren't what they needed at that point, as they all dipped their hands into the water to start paddling, desperately trying to speed their boats up.

Their submarine had surfaced, as the first dinghy was offloaded. As the others got close, one of the meteorites slapped into the ocean behind them. They were all thrown out onto the submarine, as the dinghy landed upside down. They were being dragged inside before they could even get to their feet. As Alpha Four ran back to pick up the head rolling towards the sea, he caught sight of one of the meteorites before it crashed into the sea. It was perfectly round, almost the shape of a plate. It ploughed into the enemy submarine, as Alpha Four was pulled through the doorway. Alarms rang out as the door was sealed. The submarine dived as quickly as it could, trying to get out of danger. Despite their extensive radar, it would be luck that would keep them from being hit. Fortunately, luck was on their side.

Chapter 10 – The Enemy
February 13th
13:57 GMT

Concealed by the undergrowth, vigilant eyes lay motionless. They all observed the giant compound ahead, scanning everything.

"Okay, just remember, you wait for my signal. And if these bullets don't work, don't blame me," muttered Alpha Three.

"Just remind me again, how do these bullets work?" asked Charlie One, in his gruff voice.

"They work like normal bullets, they travel the same, they look the same, but instead of killing, they act as tranquilisers. Exactly as we were told two minutes ago," said Charlie Two, raising her softer and more tender voice in frustration.

"We weren't told two minutes ago; I would have heard. The problem is people don't include me in the conversations... And they mumble," replied Charlie One.

Charlie Two was becoming even more frustrated, as she said, "What do mean, people don't include you? You were the one who started the conversation. I'll tell you what the problem is, the problem is that you don't listen!"

Charlie One shifted his focus back to the compound; still adamant he hadn't been told. Alpha Three had blocked the bickering out; he was busy waiting for the only perfect moment to move.

"The air is thin today. It's cold," whispered Alpha Three, almost as if he was talking to himself.

"You're not old, you're younger than me," replied Charlie One, before laughing and continuing, "That one was a joke."

There was a convoy of cars and trucks bouncing down the dirt track. Alpha Three moved to the side of the road, not acknowledging Charlie team around him. He climbed through the ditches and lay parallel with the road. The trucks moved past, pushing the cold, slushy mud onto him. Alpha Three rolled to his left, slotting in behind one of truck's front wheels. He got into position and grabbed hold of the following truck's underside. Wrapping his feet around anything he could find, he pulled himself as far up from the ground as possible.

The trucks continued towards their destination, unaware of the extra passenger they had just collected. As Alpha Three focussed on nothing but ensuring his arms stayed strong, the convoy began to slow. Their brakes squeaked in the damp weather, as the trucks stopped, ready to enter the compound. One by one, the trucks drove through a scanner which could scan for explosives, weapons, and heat signatures all at the same time.

"When you're ready, VOICE," said Alpha Three, keeping his voice low.

Alpha Three's truck got to the scanner and crept through. It wasn't easy to trust their lives to someone they had just met, especially for someone who found it so difficult to trust people, but Alpha Three was always willing to let someone earn their trust and VOICE did get him through the checkpoint with no issues. The cleared convoy headed towards one of the many outbuildings within the compound. They parked up, all side by side, and allowed the armed guards, who were waiting, to inspect the contents.

Alpha Three had to hold his nerve, as the entire truck was offloaded with the equipment and armed passengers all taken to their respective stations. Once most guards had moved away, Alpha Three slowly lowered himself, until his small rucksack was pressed against the damp, cold ground. He crawled out from the truck, surveying his surroundings. With bent knees and soft footsteps, he slipped, unseen, into the closest outbuilding. Inside, the building was bare, used entirely as a hangar for several tanks. He was on a narrow mezzanine, with a metal staircase leading down to the tanks. Over to Alpha Three's left was the only other doorway. He moved over to it, silently, and went through. The room was also empty, with a few shelves and one desk full of paperwork. Over in the corner of the dirty yellow walls was a narrow, metal locker. Alpha Three cracked the padlock off with the butt of his gun and looked inside. There was a jacket and a cap, both in the style the other guards wore. He flipped the cap over his head and put the massive jacket over his own clothes and rucksack, with his rifle now strapped to his back, obscured by the jacket. With a little bit of tucking and folding, he eventually made the jacket look closer to his size, although not perfect. On the table, there was a collection of handguns, all thrown on the desk. He grabbed one and tucked it into his jacket pocket. Although the handguns weren't loaded, Alpha Three had no intention of using it in such a way.

His rucksack had an easily accessible pocket underneath, nothing fell out, but every time Alpha Three positioned his hand at the pocket, the next item was already in place. Taking a small, black device from the rucksack, Alpha Three walked down the metal stairs, his boots making no noise, and headed over to the tanks. There were six tanks, all neatly packed into the room. Alpha Three couldn't identify their type and realised they were likely an experimental class. Although, from the outside, they were black and had only one visible hatch, it seemed they were high-tech, making it easier to disable them with the devices in his rucksack, EMPs. He slid one across the floor and under the front, central tank. The friction of the ground slowed the device down, until finally stopping almost in the middle of it. As soon as it stopped, it then flew up, magnetised to the surface above, by the strongest magnet they'd created.

Alpha Three casually strolled out of the building and turned to the left. He walked at the edge of the wide roads, designed to get planes through, so as not to draw attention to himself by hiding or get noticed as he got in the way. The compound was massive, too big to see one end from the other, but Alpha Three still had to walk almost its entire length, back and forth, planting charges on all the vehicles that could hinder Charlie team's assault.

With five outbuildings down and six charges used, Alpha Three finally caught sight of his star prize, the helicopter that attacked the nightclub. He approached slowly, trying to make out that he wanted to just walk past, knowing the guard presence would likely be high. Etched into the side of the helicopter was 'Heavily armoured helicopter attacker'.

HAHA, Alpha Three thought, before tutting and muttering, "Hilarious."

There were seven guards surrounding the HAHA, likely with more out of his sight. Alpha Three knew he'd struggle to get close, so he strolled past one of the guards, letting his stolen sidearm slip from his jacket pocket and fall to the floor.

The guard facing him saw and moved over, shouting, "You dropped something!"

Alpha Three turned, trying to act surprised, as he gave a little stagger back in shock. His acting wasn't up to much and the already suspicious guard began to reach for his gun. Alpha Three picked up the handgun and replaced it where he'd found it, before going to move on. "Wait! Your identity papers," added the guard, clearly not messing around.

"I haven't dropped those as well, have I?" said Alpha Three, turning back around and looking down at the floor.

The guard wasn't laughing, he just held his hand out, beckoning for the papers. Alpha Three removed the papers and handed them over. Delta team had already fixed him up with the necessary documents with his picture on, but this would be the first time they were tested. The guard scanned the documents, looked up to Alpha Three and then again read the documents, trying to find anything out of the ordinary. As the guard looked back down, Alpha Three flung the small device towards the HAHA. The EMP stuck to its rotor blade, but the guard caught sight of Alpha Three's movement. He continued to lift his arm and began scratching his back, as if it was his original movement.

The guard thrust the papers back towards Alpha Three, saying, "Get out of here!" looking a little disappointed that the papers checked out.

Alpha Three did as he was told and moved away, knowing the device had been safely planted.

"Now might be a good time to disable the radar, Charlie team are ready to bring in their big guns," said VOICE, as he watched through the many security cameras the compound had.

VOICE had looped the footage, so he was the only one who could see the live feed. He'd looped it from a day earlier, so there was plenty of footage and they alternated their guards at the same time each day, so nothing would look out of place. Alpha Three followed VOICE's suggestion and headed towards the largest building in the compound. He walked across the roads and runways with confidence, giving the impression he had purpose and didn't need stopping or questioning.

Alpha Three strode into the building and went straight up the stairs to his left. He saw no guards standing around, so took the opportunity to remove his own suppressed handgun which he kept under his jacket. He knew the room he was going for and pressed his left ear against the cold, steel door. He heard nothing to identify how many guards were the other side.

"Five guards," said VOICE.

Alpha Three stood up straight, ensuring his face was in full view of the peephole, and gave four firm clouts on the door. He left no chance for the guards to not hear the knocks, and one of them approached. Being in full view of the tiny peephole allowed Alpha Three to remain seemingly normal and didn't arouse suspicion.

"He is reaching for the door handle... Now!" shouted VOICE.

A split second later, the handle twisted, and the door creaked open.

"Time to test the bullets," mumbled Alpha Three, as he raised his sidearm.

The door opened, revealing the guard, looking straight down the barrel of his gun. Alpha Three fired before the guard could even make a noise. The bullet hit the guard on his forehead. It didn't penetrate the skin, it stopped the second it hit anything and spread out, creating a smudge of green gel. The poison worked its way through the guard instantly, causing him to fall to the floor in a deep sleep that would last well into the next day. The bullet had worked, but Alpha Three had no time to celebrate. As soon as the first guard was down, Alpha Three aimed at the next closest guard, who was starting to turn to see what the huge thud was. Alpha Three fired the bullet into the guard's temple and proceeded to move his gun around the room, from left to right, hitting each guard with a shot to the head.

"One behind the door," said VOICE swiftly, before leaving Alpha Three to focus. Alpha Three stepped back, allowing the rogue knife to scrape against the steel door, knocking it out of the guard's hand with the contact. Alpha Three then lunged forward, cracking his head into the guard's face, startling him and sending him stumbling into the table behind. Alpha Three lifted his gun and fired one last bullet at the guard sprawled over the table, pleading for his life.

With every guard unconscious, Alpha Three got to work on the control panel. There were buttons, levers, rocker switches, multi-position switches, dials, and sliders which were all fixed on one table, stretching the entire width of the eight-metre-long control room. First, he plugged in a small USB device, fitted with a thick aerial.

"VOICE, you should be getting the data through now," said Alpha Three, moving on to his next objective.

"I am getting it now, and do not forget those EMPs work on the amount of electrical output rather than just within a certain range," replied VOICE.

Alpha Three then placed three of the small devices at an equal distance under the desk. Over in the corner, there was a square hatch in the ceiling with a ladder leading to it. Alpha Three moved over to it and began climbing to the top. He used all his strength to turn the wheel, which was attached to the hatch, before pushing it up. With a couple more steps, he could lift himself onto the roof which, unsurprisingly, was where the radar tower was located. Alpha Three stared up at the towering metal structure, holding several metal dishes at the very top. Inside the metal maze of the tower, there was a ladder and a space just big enough to fit a person.

He climbed to the top, not missing a single step, as he clutched the ladder tightly. Alpha Three was still clinging on to the side of the ladder as he hesitantly placed his feet on the rattly, metal-grated floor. The wind was far stronger where he was, so he refused to remove both hands from the structural supports at the same time. Alpha Three slowly stood up; his eyes fixed on the electrical box in front of him. With his free arm, Alpha Three placed another small device on the box. Although this time, he also removed a small detonator and pressed the tiny button next to the

'11' marked on the side. The device made no sound, it just disabled all the electronics that it was in contact with.

"The EMP has disabled the radar, get down when you're ready," said VOICE.

"If you insist," replied Alpha Three, sliding his foot towards the ladder, still clasping the railings.

It took him just as long to descend, feeling for each rung as he went. Eventually, Alpha Three reached the bottom, flushed with relief. He knew Charlie team would be bringing in their gear, ready to assault, so Alpha Three continued to plant the EMP devices on the most dangerous equipment. It took him twenty-seven minutes, but he was eventually finished without anyone questioning his presence.

With no more EMPs left, he headed to the far corner of the compound, where he would make both a distraction and the signal for Charlie team.

"Alpha Four and Bravo team have entered the submarine, so you might be on your own for a while," said VOICE.

Alpha Three tutted, ensuring anyone listening on his radio could hear him, before saying, "Typical. Why did we have to execute these ops simultaneously? Well, almost simultaneously." Despite nobody answering, Alpha Three went on the assumption that someone must've heard, as he chuckled to himself, saying, "I'll laugh for you."

The place he was heading was where all the power generators stood. There were ten generators in total, each a different size and all providing power to a different location. The ten-foot fence that surrounded the plot was electrified, but Alpha Three had no intention of going inside. He removed his borrowed jacket and cap, so Charlie team could easily identify him, and removed his rucksack, throwing it on the floor afterwards. The rucksack lay on the grass, pressed up against the electrified fence, as Alpha Three walked away. He lifted the detonator up to shoulder level and pressed the button on the top. The backpack exploded, sending a huge fireball into the air, providing a fiery-orange backdrop to Alpha Three, imagining himself strolling away from the explosion just as they do in the movies.

***

Charlie team saw the signal and moved in. Four tanks trundled down the dirt road, filling the entire one-way track. Mud was being flung back as it got caught in their tracks. They were providing heavy armour for the trucks behind. As the four tanks got close to the gates, they spread out and ploughed into the fences. They took the ten-foot steel fences down, making them look like paper. As soon as they had been flattened, the trees came alive. The rest of Charlie team began emerging from the shaking trees and bushes. The camouflaged Charlie team held their rifles up and started firing at everyone they saw. Each shot was aimed and hit their prey on the head, releasing the sedative and causing them to drop to the floor instantly. The four tanks didn't fire their turrets, but instead moved into a defensive position, providing cover against those who were using real bullets with the intention to kill.

***

Alpha Three began heading back inside, getting to an elevated position. As he hurried along the open runway, he heard a brief cry of pain from behind. He spun around, lowering his body and drawing his handgun simultaneously, as he looked behind. There was a guard, on his knees, with a green chest. He keeled forward and smacked onto the floor.

"Behind you!" shouted VOICE, before realising his lateness.

"Thanks for the advanced warning... Still, at least we know these bullets do work through clothes as well," said Alpha Three, whilst lifting the guard up and observing the effectiveness of the bullet.

"Why did we have to do these operations together?" asked VOICE, starting to get a little flustered.

Alpha Three had already made his way back to the main building and held his position just inside the doorway.

"Because you should be able to cope with it," said Alpha Three, who was starting to raise his voice.

He held his hand up as he stood in the doorway, indicating his thanks to the sniper who was watching over him and had just saved his life.

Back inside, Alpha Three raised his handgun and moved back up the stairs. The building was still quiet, as all the armed guards had rushed to the front gates, showing their inexperience and lack of training. They weren't the Night Vipers, but instead just guarded their equipment. As Alpha Three moved off the top step, he saw two guards running towards him. They weren't expecting to see their enemy in the building, unaware they had got so far. Alpha Three fired two bullets, in less than a second. The two guards dropped to the floor, still cradling their guns. Alpha Three moved back into the control room, finding nobody else in there. The room was designed to see everything in the compound, to keep control, through the extensive windows which panned around the room. As he stood there, observing everything, he watched as the vehicles came into use.

The first was the HAHA. Two pilots leapt into the cockpit and began spinning the blades. Alpha Three waited, watching everything they did, and just as it started to lift from the ground, he detonated the EMP. It dropped back onto the ground; all its electrical components fried. The tanks then caught his gaze, ploughing out of the building. Alpha Three detonated their EMP, stopping all of them in their tracks. The component radius was big enough to take down all six tanks without compromising Charlie team's equipment. As each vehicle was powered up and started moving, Alpha Three shut them down, rendering every piece of enemy weaponry useless. With all the vehicles down, Alpha Three removed the data stick and blew the final three charges, after leaving the room. They crippled the compound's server, leaving every remaining guard alone and helpless.

"Blow up the backup generator," said Alpha Three, no longer needing its power.

Charlie One held his hand up and flung it towards the generator sat on top of the main building. The tank just behind him on his right aimed up and fired one shell at its target. The generator exploded, sending shrapnel into the sky and plunging the main building into darkness, due to its lack of windows. The remaining enemy forces were soon surrounded and hugely outnumbered by Charlie team's swift assault.

Alpha Three made his way back out of the main building, now full of members of Charlie team, and met back up with Charlie One and Two. They were waiting for Alpha Three over by one of their tanks, using it to protect them from any ambush from behind. Charlie One was stood bolt upright, with his rifle hanging down in front of his stomach and his arms resting on his rifle's stock. It never looked comfortable to Alpha Three, but it was a stance that had always been adopted by Charlie One. To his right, Charlie Two was in a far more relaxed stance, leaning against the tank with one leg bent back, pushing against its tracks. She was in her mid thirties, about 5'9", and had delicate, hazel eyes. Under her helmet was long, golden-brown hair, contrasting with her almost spherical head. All the time Charlie One wasn't annoying her, she displayed a warm, relaxing, and sympathetic smile.

"The compound is ours; the final guards are being rounded up as we speak," said Charlie One in his deep, gruff voice.

He was forty with big arms, big legs, and a muscular physique, and was around 6′ tall. He had green eyes, a prominent jawline, and although it couldn't be seen under his helmet, his head was always shaved, as well as any facial hair. Alpha Three started nodding his head and turned to Charlie Two. Before he could even ask the question, she knew immediately what he was going to ask.

"As we began our assault, there was a distress signal sent by the compound that we couldn't stop. So, it's likely they'll send over a drone, see we have the base under our control and probably won't send any reinforcements," said Charlie Two, in her much softer voice.

"Er… Well, I was going to ask you to get your boots off the tank. But thanks anyway," replied Alpha Three, taking no time to think of his sarcastic remark.

Charlie One began laughing, knowing the joke wasn't at his expense. Alpha Three was visibly pleased that he had finally witnessed someone laugh at one of his jokes.

At that moment, a huge gust of wind blew past, enough to lift one side of the tank's tracks off the ground for a second. It was swiftly followed by a crack of thunder, echoing around the compound.

"VOICE, are you picking this up? A storm has literally come from…" started Alpha Three, before a flash of lightning hit only metres away from them.

It hit one of the enemy tanks that sat motionlessly in the open. Alpha Three was the only one facing the tanks, as the flash caught his left eye, too quick for him to blink. His eye stung as he turned away from the strike. Every time he closed his left eyelid, all he could see was a white, jagged line running the full stretch of his eye. The image burned into his retina.

They wasted no time in running for shelter, as rain began pouring down.

"I can see the storm on the radar, but there were no traces of it a minute ago…" said VOICE, before continuing, "Hang on, Alpha Four is getting in contact."

They got inside and instantly started beckoning for the others to get in quickly. The final two members of Charlie team headed for the door, dropping everything to run quicker. As they got to the door, Alpha Three dragged them the final part, pulling them both inside and slamming the door shut. They all paused, catching their breath, before VOICE got back to them.

"Alpha Four and Bravo team are saying the same as you; a storm came out of nowhere. I have no idea how they started, but I did pick up a unique signal just before it happened. It seems to be the same signal we picked up when the volcano erupted, so I suspect it was also the same for the other natural disasters that occurred out of the blue. I'm trying to understand what this signal is, but it is nothing like I have ever seen before," said VOICE.

Alpha Three couldn't understand whether VOICE sounded worried or confused, but it was almost like he was excited with what was happening.

"I'm not really concerned with how it started. I just want to know how it ends," said Alpha Three, again getting no answer.

The wind and rain continued to batter the building they were huddled in, as if there was a hurricane outside. The lightning pounded the compound, almost drawn in as if it were a lightning conductor. Every time the lightning thrashed the building, it sounded like a bomb going off. The few windows that were in the building were quickly being shattered, with Charlie team staying in the windowless rooms to not catch sight of the lightning. With the wind still picking up speed, the steel door they had bolted shut was torn out, causing the few that were sheltered in the hall, to hide elsewhere. Even the building itself started shaking, unable to withstand the harsh winds the storm was throwing around.

Then, as quickly as it started, the storm died down. Going from a storm that none of them had ever experienced, to the clear skies and bobbing clouds that were present before.

"Stay inside. It might be the eye of the storm," said Alpha Three, keeping everyone in the central room.

"No, the storm has gone, it has just… vanished. I am not sure… Er, I am going to have to get back to you on that one," added VOICE, before leaving the conversation completely, raising more questions than answers.

Alpha Three cautiously stepped outside, looking up at the blue sky, ensuring the storm had gone. He started looking around at the devastation. The tanks were nowhere to be seen, the bodies gone; it looked more like a clean-up crew had worked for hours to make everything spotless. There were what seemed like hundreds of black spots all over the ground and the building's walls, caused by the powerful strikes of lightning. Two of the outbuildings also couldn't be seen, only their foundations remained. Out of the corner of his scarred eye, he saw one of their tanks, thrown up on top of the main building.

Charlie One rushed up the ladder and climbed onto the roof. The tank was resting on its side, crumpled up against the tall tower that was still standing. The top hatch flung open just as Charlie One leapt through the debris. It was the tank they had previously been standing by, and he watched as all four crew members crawled out and got to their feet, wounded, but alive. Charlie One was filled with relief, as he looked out over the compound, trying to find anything else.

Back on the ground, Alpha Three finally received contact from VOICE.

"Bosse has sanctioned an emergency mission for Alpha team, so there will be a helicopter to pick you up and take you to a rendezvous point in two minutes. He will explain everything when you are all together, until then, collect your gear and get ready to move out," said VOICE.

VOICE's change in personality surprised Alpha Three, as he had suddenly become very forceful, allowing no time for Alpha Three to object to the plan. He thought it was likely Bosse was in the room with him, but why it had changed VOICE's whole personality, Alpha Three couldn't work out.

"Charlie One, this is Alpha Three. I've got a helicopter pickup in five minutes, so how do want my help until then?" asked Alpha Three.

Despite the pickup being in only two minutes, he didn't want Charlie One to feel compelled to refuse his help.

"I'm not sure you can do anything. Your help was invaluable. We'll continue to look for the other five members of my team, so I guess you could help with that in the meantime. Four of them were the crew of one of the tanks; last known signal was in the woods. And the other is one of the snipers we positioned in the trees," answered Charlie One, after a slight pause for thought.

"Then I'll start there," said Alpha Three, knowing he wouldn't get on the helicopter until every member of Charlie team had been accounted for.

Chapter 11 – The Vesper
February 13th
08:18 GMT

Past the depths of the murky, green ocean lay a group of islands. As the central island came into view, the waters began to clear, maintaining a soft blue tint. The island played host to a mansion larger than most, covering much of its once green surface and buried deep within its rocky base. There were four neighbouring islands, each with a purpose. The closest was used defensively, armed with various weapons capable of destroying ships and planes. The largest of the neighbouring islands acted as a port, documenting any visitors to the residential island. The other two appeared to be uninhabited but were likely used as lookout islands, as well as used to grow line upon line of grapevines. Perfectly positioned, they had the longest and widest sightlines.

Alpha Six had been smuggled aboard the daily shipment of food and supplies. About half a mile from the port island, he jumped from the ship in his diving gear and made his way through the clear waters. Despite everyone on the surface being able to see the bottom of the shallow water, it would be hard to spot Alpha Six, moving like a shadow through the tranquil ocean. The islands seemed close together from the satellite image but swimming the stretch between them was quite different. It took him thirty-six minutes to swim the three-mile pool, but eventually, he was where he needed to be. Alpha Six was floating at the very bottom of a three-storey cliff face. It was completely vertical with few bulges and divots to cling onto. But due to its difficult nature, it was the only place that offered a way into the compound, because nobody would be crazy enough to try it, nobody except Blindspot. He removed his rebreather and fins, placing them into a net bag he had carried with him, but left his black wetsuit on. The bag fell straight to the seabed, with a little help from some borrowed rocks, meaning it could still be retrieved when he returned.

Blindspot moved up the rock face, grabbing everything he could, as he hauled himself up. Each foot was carefully placed, knowing that a fall would give his location away. Wherever there was a lack of a foothold, Blindspot angled his foot to be almost parallel with the rock and pushed his weight forward, holding his feet in place long enough to move up. As he climbed over the top of the rock face, Blindspot immediately dived for cover, as he was faced with several patrolling guards. He lay between the rocks, his black wetsuit helping to conceal him. Blindspot edged his way towards the structure to his left and waited, patiently. Blindspot was by far the most patient of them all, he never got flustered and didn't make any stupid moves; he just waited, until he was ready to move. Minutes passed, as Blindspot continued to lie prone in amongst the rocks. His suppressed sidearm was drawn, ready if he needed to strike. Eventually, Blindspot's moment came. The guards all started to move towards the jetty, down on Blindspot's right. He didn't wait for an invitation, and as soon as the guards had moved, Blindspot was inside the small building. There was nothing but a ladder inside, so he climbed up, making each step silent. Three floors up, he finally reached the top.

He carefully placed his foot up onto the top-floor's base, slowly applying pressure. Blindspot floated up, silently, as his other cushioned foot steadied his balance. There were two guards leaning over the side of what seemed to be a watchtower. They were completely unaware of what lay behind, as they scanned the grounds ahead. Blindspot holstered his handgun and crept closer to the two guards. He removed the rifle strapped to his back and swung the stock at the guard on the left, and instantly wrapped the gun around the other guard's neck, squeezing tightly. The guard desperately tried pushing the weapon away, but Blindspot had no intention of releasing his prey. As the guard went limp, Blindspot again knocked the guard on the left on his head, before applying pressure around the guard's neck, using his rifle, as he pinned them to the floor. Although all the guards wore balaclavas, Blindspot knew the guards' faces were full of fear as they lost consciousness. Once the guards had been tied up and their radios and masks removed, Blindspot placed his own balaclava on and aimed his rifle's sight out into the ocean. He waited for over two hours, his sights still fixed on the ocean, until he finally caught sight of movement in the distance.

***

"Blindspot in position, I have eyes on you," he said, zooming in on an incoming boat with seven passengers.

On the boat, Alpha Five sat and observed the three businesspeople all trying to prove they had the most money. Two guards also accompanied them, both armed with assault rifles and wearing balaclavas. The pilot concealed a small handgun under the belt securing his shorts. The handgun bulged at the back, making it obvious he wasn't highly trained and had likely never fired it at anyone. The pilot of the boat also didn't wear a balaclava and dressed more like he was on holiday in Miami, with his flowery shirt and white shorts. One of the businessmen strolled over to Alpha Five.

"It's Mr Gemini, right?" said the businessman.

Alpha Five didn't want to engage with him but saw no

alternative to keep up his businesslike appearance.

"It's just Gemini. And you are?" asked Alpha Five, trying to sound like he cared.

"My name's Marcus, that is Kyle, and she hasn't given her name away yet," he answered.

Gemini looked past Marcus towards the other two. Kyle was dressed much the same as himself, in a dark grey, plain suit with black shoes, whilst Marcus wore a dark blue suit, a tie to match, and deep brown shoes which probably cost more than the boat they were travelling in. Whereas the woman wore a short, black dress, almost too tight to move in. As he looked at her, something about her wasn't very businesslike. She was completely ignoring the drone of Kyle's posh British accent, which would be exactly what Gemini would do. But that was what was odd; she was too much like Gemini. She'd kept her back to him most of the journey and had partaken in little conversation, succeeding in distancing herself from the group.

"You can't trust Kyle; he'll try and turn you against everyone but himself. I know his type, eyes very close together, far too deceitful," said Marcus.

Gemini had lost his train of thought but turned to look back at Marcus. He was very tall with a thin face, spiky, brown hair and eyes that were pretty close together. He was clean-shaven and stood very upright, pushing his chest forward. Gemini didn't say anything to Marcus, choosing to see if he was telling the truth. As Gemini looked at Kyle, he noticed that his eyes weren't nearly as close together as Marcus'. He was also a completely different build, his muscles filling the jacket that was clearly two sizes too small. Most of his face was filled with a curly, black beard, making it hard to see whether his lips were moving or not, matching his black, curly hair.

"He's also got a very suspicious accent, almost as if it's put on," added Marcus.

Gemini was once again taken by surprise, as he tried to block Marcus' identically posh English voice from his head.

"What's that got to do with anything?" asked Gemini, hoping it would end their conversation. It, however, didn't work.

"I'm not sure yet," answered Marcus, thinking he'd almost won Gemini over to his side.

The boat got close to the island's jetty, and Gemini took the opportunity to move away from Marcus. Gemini headed to the front of the boat but was closely followed by Marcus, unaware of the obvious hint to stop talking.

"Are you excited?" asked Marcus.

Gemini wasn't sure whether to burst out laughing or break his perfect nose. But before he could decide, the boat's engine was switched off and they started to drift into place. Marcus and Kyle leapt onto the wooden structure, whilst Gemini stood back, held his hand out and gestured for the woman to go first.

She accepted his invitation and stepped off the boat, saying, "Thank you," in a very tender voice.

It was the first time any of them had even heard her speak. Gemini wasn't doing this out of kindness, but instead to find a way of making her talk. As she turned to smile at him, it was also the first time he could see her face. She had a very round head which she tried to offset with long, blond hair. She also wore bright red lipstick to match her very short nails. She was about 5'9" but wore high heels to make herself look taller. But what was more troubling was how familiar she looked. Gemini finally hopped onto the jetty, and they made their way up the steep wooden structure, passing a small square building on their right. It had 'guardhouse' written in big letters above the door, but clearly only housed two guards, as they could be seen through the only window.

"I think they're trying to give the impression they have more guards than they actually do," said Blindspot, who had been watching their every move.

As they reached the top of the wooden path, Marcus had started to get out of breath. Instead of hiding it, he decided to turn to Kyle.

"What's the… matter? Those steroids… not… doing you any… good," he said with a slight pause between every few words whilst he took in a huge breath of air.

As Gemini got to the top, he felt almost as if he was in someone's back garden. There was a giant pool, with tiles surrounding it, and even a square patch of grass leading to a tall structure in the corner. There was a man, stood with outstretched, welcoming arms. He couldn't have been more than 5′4″ with his hunched back and short, little arms. He looked very thin, with nothing more than bones under his oversized T-shirt and jeans. His feet were one of the few things visible because of the sandals he wore, which left his crooked toes exposed, showing all the scabs and dead skin on them. With his long, greasy, grey hair and creepy smile on his very pale face, he didn't give a very welcoming appearance.

"Welcome to my home. I am The Vesper, and you are here so that I can show my… undying gratitude for such a generous donation from each of you," said the man.

Next to him was another guard, armed with an assault rifle, but this was the first guard Gemini had seen without any sort of mask. Instead, he wore a baseball cap, allowing only a few strands of brown hair to stick out underneath. The cap was pulled down to his big ears which stuck out from his muscular face. He looked to only be in his early thirties and wore a tight, black T-shirt and matching tactical trousers, identical to the other security guards. The tight clothes made his muscles look bigger, much like Kyle's.

"I have a question…" stated Kyle.

"Well go ahead, don't let me… kill the mood," replied The Vesper.

"Have you always been called The Vesper?" asked Kyle.

The Vesper didn't know what to say, as he struggled to

find words.

He turned to the security guard behind and whispered, "Mark the idiot at the front for the first test." He then continued to the group, as if happily answering the question. "No. I changed my name as soon as I was allowed. I named myself after my favourite drink, but when one crucial ingredient stopped being produced, I stockpiled it and have now started to produce it myself, thanks to your generous donation, but we'll get to that later."

The guard behind him made no movement the entire time, not when he was asked to make a note, nor every time The Vesper made a joke about dying, his gaze was fixed on the four visitors.

"Shall we begin our tour then?" started The Vesper.

Who was then interrupted by Marcus who yelled "Yes!" at the top of his voice.

"It is sure to be a tour of thrills, excitement, and one you'll never relive," concluded The Vesper, as he turned and headed inside.

The four of them all followed him in, surrounded by guards, with the unmasked guard bringing up the rear. As Gemini walked into the villa, he felt the hairs on his neck stand on end, as the guard stared at him as if he was an uninvited guest.

"On this floor, the only room that will concern you is the guest lounge, where you can rest after our tour. But what we are interested in is what is downstairs," said The Vesper, waving his hands in all directions.

The Vesper had a very creepy nature to his personality; everything from the way his little voice breathed down their necks, to the way he took tiny steps with his hands clasped in front, when they didn't look like they were conducting an orchestra. They continued down the narrow corridors and headed towards the only door that was already open. The corridors were only wide enough for walking single file, but both Kyle and Marcus seemed to be side by side, each fighting for their spot at the front. Their shoulders pressed tightly together, scraping along the pristine paintwork. They were locked together, trying to edge closer to The Vesper before the walkway narrowed even further. The Vesper walked through the doorway and onto a set of stairs. Marcus went to push Kyle over but met an unmovable force as Marcus bounced back, ending up two steps right of the doorway. He slapped his foot down on the floor, desperately trying to slow himself down before reaching the looming wall. He stopped only an inch from the wall, his heart pounding. Everyone else just moved past and down the stairs, ignoring Marcus completely.

All the flooring was marble, including the staircase, but as they got one floor down, the flooring changed into dark, wooden boards. By this point, Gemini had moved up the order of people and was just stepping off the bottom stair, when The Vesper sprung open the tinted double doors in front. The open doors revealed a huge room, big enough to be a car park, which was almost the size of the whole villa. The room was open but had clearly been split into different sections, with one side containing giant vats covering the wall. There was also a deep shelf, behind crystal clear glass, filled with bark. And finally, there were two huge, cylindrical machines in the centre of the room. Over in the back left corner, there was a spiral staircase going up and an odd-looking box attached to a set of ropes. The walls were also bare, having nothing but shelves pushed against them and one mirror in the back right-hand side. The Vesper began smiling as he entered the room and admired its contents, a reaction he likely had every time he went in.

"This is the Wine Room," said The Vesper, refusing to lose his smile.

One of the staff members stepped forward and began saying his, clearly rehearsed lines.

"Welcome back, sir. Shall I show our guests the winery?"

asked the staff member.

He appeared to oversee the operation, as he was the only one dressed in a shirt and bow tie, setting him apart from the overalls in which the others seemed to be attired. The Vesper nodded, not saying a word to someone who was so menial to him.

"My name is Felix and I run the winery," stated the smartly dressed winemaker, as he began moving around the giant room. "As you can see, the entire process doesn't happen on this island. In fact, the growing of the grapevines, as well as the crushing, all happens on one of our neighbouring islands," continued Felix, stopping at the vats on the left-hand side.

His French accent was very strong, yet his English was fluent, and he could pronounce every word perfectly.

"These are called vats; they are used to age the liquid. All of them are made of oak and are temperature controlled. The aromatised wine must age for about one year, a very key part of the making process. In fact, this is very similar to making a Bordeaux wine, except of course, we are not in Bordeaux," added Felix, as again he moved the group on to another section.

"I guess it's the same as a Cornish pasty has to be made in Cornwall," said Blindspot, ensuring he was still a part of the mission.

Gemini stopped for a moment, frowning, as he tried to find the vague similarity between a sophisticated wine and a Cornish pasty.

"Over here, we have a storage chamber. Again, it's all temperature and light controlled, but we use it to store the bark from a cinchona tree. It is a key ingredient when making Kina Lillet. In fact, the tree is often referred to as a quina tree," said Felix.

Although by this point, he had clearly failed to keep their interest, as they all started looking around and fixing their eyes on the full bottles of wine stored in the next room.

"Now, if we turn our attention to…" began Felix.

"Actually, I wondered if I could use the bathroom?" interrupted Gemini, desperate to speed his recon up.

Felix looked straight back at The Vesper, unable to make such important decisions.

"That won't be a problem," said The Vesper, as he snapped his fingers and directed two guards out of the door.

One of them waggled his finger, beckoning Gemini closer, as they took him back up the stairs.

He was directed back along the corridor they were on earlier but travelled straight past the door they'd entered through. At the very end of the corridor, which felt a little wider with fewer people in, there was another closed door. It was opened, allowing Gemini into the guest lounge they had been informed about earlier. There were a further three doors in the room, and the one at the back provided access to a tiny, commercial-style bathroom, even with urinals and a cubical.

Gemini went inside, informing the guards that, "This might be a long one," as he slammed the door in their faces and went into the cubical.

"The window there should take you outside, from there you can move along to other rooms," said Blindspot, looking at the collection of photographs he'd been given prior to entry.

Gemini prised the metal bars off from around the window, ripping the weakened framing from the wall to take the whole piece out as one. He then opened the window as far as it would go and squeezed out of the tiny gap it offered. After pulling himself out, there was a thin ledge which he carefully placed his feet on. He shuffled them into the safest place and edged along, using the rough rock wall to balance. The next window was also barred, so Gemini continued edging along, trying to move past the window as quickly as possible, as the two guards were stood talking with their backs to the window. Gemini was past but didn't breathe a sigh of relief, as he latched his hands against the next window. This one wasn't barred and could be opened a lot further. So, thanks to it being unlocked, Gemini was able to pull himself in without making a noise.

The room he was now in was small, but full of weapons. It was clearly used as some sort of armoury and allowed Gemini to change his clothes without being seen. There were five sets of identical garments hanging in the room, and after choosing the closest fitting one, he became one of the guards, completing the look as he picked up one of the rifles. Because of the balaclavas they wore, he was able to blend in with nobody asking any questions. The only thing he couldn't prepare for, however, was what was on the other side of the door. Gemini carefully pulled the handle down and peeped his head around the corner, making no sound. The next room was much larger, yet it had hardly anything in. There was one long desk stretching its way across one wall, housing two guards, a few computer screens, and a stack of paperwork in a thin, plastic tray. Gemini went to close the door, ensuring nobody would be any the wiser to his presence. But as the door slowly crept closed, it let out a loud squeak. Gemini knew there wasn't a chance they could've missed the sound, but he couldn't help but freeze on the spot.

"Oh John, good, you're back. Was the patrol good?" asked one of the guards casually.

Gemini knew he had been handed a golden opportunity but had little clue how to use it. Without any idea as to how John spoke, Gemini tried to use little dialogue, hoping the questions wouldn't continue.

"Uh-huh," said Gemini, his eyes on stalks behind the balaclava.

"Same as usual then? Ha, ha, ha. You get it? Same as usual?" said the same guard.

He was clearly directing his comments to the other guard, who was taking no notice of anything. Gemini didn't dare make a sound as the fate of his cover still hung in the balance, trying to think what could've been funny about what the guard had just said.

"Just me then. I'm stuck with two people that don't talk. I am going crazy!" shouted the guard.

Gemini had no thoughts about starting a conversation or disagreeing with the guard, so carefully moved backwards. He edged away until reaching a staircase going down, he didn't know where it would take him, but going down was his best chance to find out.

Gemini moved down the stairs, whilst the guard continued to talk to himself. The room below looked much the same, with bare walls and empty floors. The only difference being the number of guards. Compared to above, there were seven guards occupying the space. Three of them were sat looking at the surveillance cameras, flicking through the images, hardly watching any of the feeds. The other four were all stood over at the far wall, looking through a tinted window. Gemini knew that if his bearings were correct, they were all looking through a two-way mirror in the wine room, and his bearings were never wrong. He noticed the mirror last time he was in the room but had thought nothing of it. The voices of the people in the wine room were being played through the speaker system, allowing the guards to keep a check on their guests, and their staff. Knowing that they had the room bugged, Gemini made sure he would check every room he went in. Checking for audio devices, hidden cameras and two-way mirrors wasn't something he'd previously thought needed to be done, which could've given away his cover. He strolled over to the mirror, leant against it and blended in, keeping his eyes on the people within the wine room, listening to everything being said.

Felix continued rambling on for almost another ten minutes. It was clear to anyone watching that the guests had no interest in what was being said. Gemini could also see the businesswoman slightly apart from the others, watching the stairs out of the corner of her eye. He still couldn't be sure what it was, but something about her didn't strike Gemini as entirely honest.

"Well, I think that's everything from me. I believe Frank, our master mixologist, will now take over and make this legendary drink," said Felix, creating a sense of relief throughout the room.

One man stepped forward and took the three remaining guests into another room. Gemini remembered seeing two sets of doors leading to the room, a perfect way to keep its content at a perfect temperature. The doors closed and they were all sealed in the room, out of sight, with no audio devices.

The Vesper had joined them in the room, but had left all his guards outside, likely to prevent the temperature changing too much. Gemini noted his first opportunity to catch The Vesper, alone. But if this were to be his chosen location, he'd need one of the winemakers' outfits and an excuse to get The Vesper back inside. Gemini knew there was a lot more of the building to cover and perhaps better opportunities of taking out The Vesper. He headed back up the stairs and left the security office with enough confidence and haste to prevent any more questions.

He re-entered the guest lounge, trying not to make eye contact with the same two guards who'd escorted him in there. They had both moved over to the sofas and were lounging on them, both reading magazines, oblivious to their surroundings. Gemini continued through the lounge and tried one of the two remaining doors. It led to a tiny room, with a spiral staircase leading down to the wine room, and some sort of platform with a pulley system. It appeared that the pulley was a dumb waiter and would be used to transport drinks up to the lounge, without the need for the staff to ever leave their working spaces.

With no new intel, Gemini moved back and tried the other door. There was a lot more activity behind the final door, so as he opened it, he walked straight in, confidently. It was a bustling kitchen, full of chefs jostling for space, some hiding amongst the steam. To Gemini's left was a staff changing room, perhaps a perfect place to acquire some uniforms. Unfortunately, there were no uniforms lying around and breaking into lockers wouldn't help to keep a low profile, so Gemini continued through the kitchen. As he left, he caught sight of one of the chefs entering a room at the back. It wasn't a room Gemini had been in, but as the chef passed through, Gemini could clearly see it was nothing more than a freezer room. Making the decision to not search the freezer room to save time, Gemini hastily headed up the stairs.

As he moved away from the staircase on the next floor up, Gemini was immediately faced with yet another narrow corridor. It had the same perfect yellow paintwork with a pristine cream carpet. Gemini started with the room furthest away from the stairs and planned to work backwards. There were no guards in sight, and it didn't sound like anyone was in the rooms, but Gemini still opened every door cautiously. The furthest room hosted a giant open-plan space, offering sections for a dining room, living room, and even a small corner space with a desk that seemed to be used as an office. There were two open archways dividing the room in half, isolating the dining room. There was a giant table, surrounded by twelve chairs, in the middle of one half. It was a dark, rustic, wooden table, full of candelabras and was sat underneath two glass chandeliers, in some ways making it look like Gemini had walked into a haunted house. He gave a quick glance at the chairs, looking for any indication that one seat was used more than the rest, trying to find another potential place where Gemini knew he could find The Vesper. But to his disappointment, all the chairs looked identical, and he saw little point in guessing. The other half of the room looked a little more homely, with one long, U-shaped sofa surrounding a huge open fireplace on the far wall.

With nothing new, Gemini moved back out of the room, and tried the next. His luck didn't improve as the following room was a bedroom. It had nothing more than a bed and a couple of bedside tables. The room was immaculate and didn't look at all lived-in, so again failed to provide a secluded place to get to The Vesper. As he left the bedroom, there was a set of small double doors facing him. Gemini grabbed the handles and pushed the doors in. There was a tiny cupboard, full of brown boxes. As both doors were swung in, they hit the far side wall. As Gemini closed them, he noticed something odd. There was a lot more wall space on the outside compared to the inside. There was no bulge in the dining area, and no immediate reason for this lost space could be thought of. Gemini paced out his steps, revealing a further two paces on the outside. He went back into the cupboard and inspected the wall. It was hollow, which wasn't uncommon for such a small room, but as Gemini continued to strike the hollow wall, he could also hear a faint metal clang. He swept the boxes out of the way, and began pressing the wall, but it didn't budge. He looked around the room, finding two light switches. He flicked them simultaneously. The cupboard lights flickered on and the wall he was stood by gave a quiet clonk. Gemini tried pushing the door again. This time, he moved it, but as the door gave another clonk, the closest light switch flicked back. Gemini repeated his last few steps, but instead chose to pull the door, rather than close it, which opened to an even smaller room behind. The tiny room was lined with a metal sheet, likely helping to maintain its secrecy. It was stacked high with open crates of weapons, ammunition, and grenades. The room might have been packed, but it was still easy to get to any weapon in there, something Gemini knew might be useful. He clicked the false wall back in place and quickly placed some of the boxes back in front, before leaving the cupboard, switching off the light as he left.

The final room on the floor was around the L-shaped corridor and past the staircase. Gemini opened the door and went in. It was a bathroom. There was one extra door, leading back to the living area, and a giant double sink. The room seemed to be set out for just one person, with one shower, one bath, and one toilet, yet everything in there was triple the size of any ordinary furniture. With no obvious use for the bathroom, Gemini swiftly left, knowing his time would be running short. He headed down the stairs and retraced his steps. Before long, he was back on the thin ledge, climbing into the restroom. He slipped back in again, wearing his suit, and carefully replaced the bars on the window, balancing them in place. He left the cubical and hid the guard's uniform in the cupboard under the sink, making it easier to obtain than before. Gemini ensured his suit was straight and smart and strolled out of the bathroom.

The two guards were still sat on the sofas, entirely focussed on the magazines they were reading. Neither had noticed Gemini leave the bathroom, it was only the slamming bathroom door that brought their attention to Gemini's imposing stance. The two guards placed their magazines down and climbed to their feet with no sense of haste. They led Gemini back to the wine room, where the others had almost concluded their tour.

"So, we are the only people who can make a Vesper cocktail to the original recipe after the discontinuation of Kina Lillet. And that concludes our tour," said Felix, who had retaken the lead at some point.

Everyone in the room looked relieved about the tour

being over, as they all headed for the door as quickly as possible. As they started to go upstairs, Kyle stopped and looked down the next set of stairs.

"What's down there?" he asked, directing his question to The Vesper.

"You will find out soon enough," said The Vesper, smiling again, as he looked deep into Kyle's eyes.

Kyle was clearly spooked by The Vesper, as he pushed his way to the front of the line, knocking everyone else out of the way as he went.

"Okay, the rest of the tour will continue a little later. So, in the meantime, relax in the guest lounge where you'll be given complimentary drinks and snacks. We will of course be having our meal later tonight, but I'll show you to your rooms before lunch which will be served at precisely one o'clock. So, take a break here and we'll see you later," said the head guard, speaking as if he was their guide, despite it being the first time he'd spoken.

His voice was soft and friendly, the complete opposite to what was anticipated. He left the room with The Vesper, as Gemini was once again with the other three guests. Marcus instantly took a seat and began reading one of the many magazines on the table. Kyle sat beside him, on the edge of his seat, waiting for something, whilst the unnamed businesswoman moved over to the window and stared into the distance. Gemini approached her, eager to find out anything.

"You still haven't told me your name," said Gemini, hoping it would start a fruitful conversation.

"I know," answered the woman, keeping her gaze fixed in the distance.

Gemini gave a little chuckle, trying to buy himself time to approach the conversation differently.

"What is your name?" asked Gemini directly.

She was clearly shocked by the directness of the question. "My name is Aqua…" said the woman. Gemini instantly stepped back, knowing the implications of what had just been said. "…That's right, I'm just like you, here for a job… here to kill," she added.

Gemini had so many questions and no time to ask them. He knew who she was, one of the most skilled assassins around, but he had no idea how she knew who he was. As far as he was concerned, she should never have seen or heard of him.

Chapter 11.2

"Do you know why they called me Aqua?" she asked, leaning towards Gemini, but still looking out of the window.

He nodded, answering, "Because you're patient and you cannot be stopped, despite your calm persona."

She smiled, admiring her reputation.

"Are you here for The Vesper?" asked Gemini, hoping for a 'no'.

"No…" she answered. Gemini began to relax, relieved they wouldn't be competing for the same target. "I'm here for you," she added, as if casually dropping it into the conversation.

Gemini took a moment to think. He'd been watching her every move, just as she had his, but now he had to watch her even more carefully. He knew how she worked, preferring to lay traps and wait for them to work. Most of her recent targets had been poisoned, but how she did it every time remained a question. Gemini thought back to the period he didn't have his eyes on her, whilst surveying the building.

"I have never failed. Can you say the same?" asked Aqua, already knowing the answer.

"You've never gone against me," said Gemini, as he left the window and took a seat next to Marcus, knowing her only weakness was her hubris.

At that moment, one of the doors swung open. A figure approached, dressed in a waiter's uniform, holding a giant tray of drinks. His arms were shaking under the weight. The heavy tray also caused him to have a false smile across his face, as if he was straining. The next door then swung open. An even bigger tray squeezed through the doorway, followed by an identically dressed waiter. This tray was full of food. As soon as Kyle caught sight of the two trays, he leapt up, first going for the drinks tray. On the tray were twelve Martini glasses, all filled with an identical drink. The food had a little more variety, but it was clear nobody knew what any of it was. Gemini and Aqua refused to move over to the food, concerned that one could poison the other. Kyle had begun slurping the drink and rummaging through the food. Marcus took a sip of a drink.

His face tightened, as his eye began flickering, exclaiming, "That's the same stuff we had downstairs. Have they never heard of sugar?"

He then shifted his attention to the food, picking up one item as he apprehensively took a bite. After a couple of chews, he opened his mouth and let the food fall out.

"Who would put mint in food! Mint is literally just used for cleaning your teeth!" shouted Marcus, throwing himself back on the sofa. "Why are we here? We've paid hundreds of thousands to fund a 'winery', that turns out to be the size of a small warehouse, where they don't even make wine! We've all been conned, they just wanted our money," continued Marcus, still furious.

Two knocks rattled the door. It hinged open and the head of security came around the corner.

"I hope you're settling in okay," said the security guard.

"Yes, everything's wonderful, thank you," replied Marcus, grinning as if he meant it.

"Good. I'm sorry to bother you, but I wondered if I could borrow you, Kyle?" asked the guard.

Kyle finished off his fifth drink and stood up, grabbing some of the food as he moved towards the door.

"Thank you, Kyle. As for the rest of you, if you head up two floors, you'll find your sleeping quarters for later tonight. We have two different types of bedrooms for you to fight over. If you head down the long corridor, first on your right is a bedroom with an en suite, as is the second on your left. The second and third on your right are bedrooms with balconies. And the first on your left is a bathroom. You can also find another lounge if you turn left when exiting the stairs. Have fun," concluded the guard, as he left with Kyle, closing the door behind them.

"Well, I'm taking one with a balcony," said Gemini.

"As am I," added Aqua quickly.

"I guess I'll take an en suite then," said Marcus, knowing he had no choice.

As the food and the drink weren't being touched, since Kyle's departure, they all made their way to the stairs. Gemini didn't mind walking in front of Aqua, confident she would set a trap as her only method.

They all headed two floors up and entered their respective rooms. Marcus took the first on the right, Aqua the second on the right, and Gemini took the third on the right. Gemini headed straight through his room and onto the balcony. He flipped his legs over the side and began lowering himself, trying to land on the thin ledge two floors down.

"Good luck!" shouted Aqua, as Gemini lowered himself out of her sight.

He carefully placed his feet in any grooves he found, trying to slow his descent. When he was about a metre above the ledge, Gemini jumped down, throwing his hands against the wall for balance. He wasted no time in getting back into the guest lounge; changing back into the guard's uniform before he left. Gemini hurried as he headed straight down the stairs. Time was against him now Aqua had become involved; she wasn't a problem that he couldn't deal with, but at the same time as The Vesper, he knew it wouldn't be easy. Gemini went past the wine room floor and continued one floor down, to the very bottom of the villa.

As he left the stairs, everything changed to white, the floors, the ceiling, the walls, everything was clean and white. Gemini turned to the right and went down the long, bright corridor, until finally reaching the door at the end. There were no signs on any of the doors, but as he slowly pushed the door open, it was clear as to the room's purpose. The room was used as a morgue. There were steel tables scattered throughout the room, all with huge lights looming over them. Over to Gemini's right was a freezer, big enough to hold over twenty bodies. He was about to look further into the room when a voice alerted Gemini.

"What are you doing down here? Guards are not allowed in this area," said the approaching surgeon, dressed in a white coat with a matching face mask and apron.

"I was looking for the bathroom," replied Gemini.

He knew his answer wouldn't get him out of trouble, but it would buy him enough time, whilst the surgeon came closer. The surgeon walked over to Gemini, unaware of his impending danger.

"I'm going to have to ask you to leave," persisted the surgeon, now only a few steps away from Gemini.

Gemini took a final look around the room, ensuring they were alone, and tightened his fist. With one hard knock on his nose, the surgeon fell to the floor, without enough time to even know what was coming. The surgeon was tall and skinny, so his uniform would be no good to Gemini. He dragged the surgeon back down the corridor until reaching the first room where no noise could be heard. He edged the door open and dragged the surgeon in once he was sure it was empty. It was a bathroom fitted with cubicles, so he placed the surgeon in one, locked the door and clambered over it, before leaving as cautiously as he entered.

The corridor was still empty, but Gemini had no plan to stick around. He went straight for the door ahead and went in. The room was used for changing and cleaning. Taking advantage of the empty room, Gemini began changing his clothes. Each item was hanging up separately, so he had no idea whether they were from the same set, but they did fit. He laid the guard's uniform down, with the rifle, behind a stack of gloves and masks, neither of which were reusable. Ensuring his mask was pulled to cover most of his face, with a hairnet covering the rest, Gemini used one of the two remaining doors. It took him into a room similarly sized to the wine room above. His eyes were immediately drawn to The Vesper, who was stood near a group of surgeons. The room had a few tables scattered around, but it was the centre of the room which was the most densely filled. There were more tables neatly placed to create a circle, each full of tools, and a much larger table in the middle. The room was well-lit, but the centre had lights that were as strong as floodlights, making the rest of the room appear dark. There were a group of surgeons huddled around the central table, making it hard to see it, with The Vesper paying close attention to their work. There were three guards, including the head of security, and a few surgeons stood slightly further away, so Gemini wasn't too concerned about looking out of place. It was clear that the staff from the entire floor were all working on this one project, all intensely focussed on what was in front of them. Gemini edged closer, desperate to look.

As he slid his feet closer and closer, their work began to become clear. Laid out on the table was Kyle. He was not strapped down, but was just lying there, his eyes wide open, flicking from side to side. He didn't talk, nor shout for help, and he didn't even scream, but just lay on the table, never moving. As Gemini got even closer, he could see more of what was happening. Kyle's body had been cut open; his intestines lay beside him, his heart in one of the surgeon's hands. Despite Kyle's silence, it was clear from his eyes that he could feel everything they were doing.

"Administering drug for trial one hundred and thirty-six," said one of the surgeons, as he moved towards Kyle's beating heart, holding a syringe.

The surgeon injected the heart and they all watched, as it began beating slower and slower. It quickly slowed to about ten beats per minute, when the surgeons began cutting the heart free of the body. They placed the heart in a dish on one of the tables and returned their attention to Kyle.

"The heart has maintained eight beats per minute. We will continue to monitor it, but initial results find trial one three six a success for heart removal. Now implementing synthetic replacement," said the same surgeon as before.

Another surgeon came over, delicately holding a different tray. Its contents were removed and placed inside the body. The silver object seemed to be solid and was perfectly spherical. The Vesper was clutching a tablet and, as soon as the object was in, he thumped the screen. Suddenly, the sphere started to lose its perfect shape and now appeared to be soft. Gemini found it hard to believe what he saw and struggled to make sense of their technology. The cluster of surgeons then tightened the circle around Kyle, making it hard to see what they were doing. But as Gemini edged closer, he could see all the arteries, veins and everything which was previously connected to the heart, being attached to its replacement. As they continued to reattach smaller tubes and nerves, Gemini gave it more thought. Whatever the sphere was, it was able to replace the heart, but he still couldn't think why it was being done.

As soon as the surgeons had finished, The Vesper thumped his tablet's screen again which seemed to make the sphere return to its original, perfect shape, as it became solid once again. Wasting no time, they then repeated the process on his brain, injecting the same liquid and replacing the organ with an identical sphere. They placed his brain inside a glass jar, filled with a green liquid and laid it next to his heart. At that moment, a change in the noise from the heart monitor could be heard throughout the room, the heart had stopped beating in an instant and had flatlined. All the surgeons stopped what they were doing and started clearing away, as if this had happened many times before. Now their attentions were no longer diverted, Gemini began trying to blend in by helping to clean up. The lead surgeon moved over to The Vesper; his head held low.

"Shall we talk in my office?" said the chief surgeon.

The Vesper showed no emotion, he just turned and headed for the room with a glass wall looking into the operating theatre. Gemini knew he couldn't miss the conversation and slipped back into the changing room, nobody even acknowledging his presence.

With his guard's uniform back on, he moved back into the corridor and over to the door which he was certain would lead to the office. He pressed his ear tightly against the cold metal door; he heard nothing. Gemini had no idea how important the conversation was, but given what he had just witnessed, he thought it was worth a risk. He carefully opened the door just enough to listen inside, hoping nobody would notice.

"It is at the same point we fail each time," said the chief surgeon.

Gemini was easily able to identify his distinctive voice, being somehow both squeaky and low-pitched.

"Do we need both organs for this to work?" asked The Vesper, his voice being just as easy to identify.

"Well, the brain is certainly needed. The original brain being here will be the only thing possible to communicate with a receiver implanted in the host. Without that, there is no way of controlling the host's actions," answered the chief surgeon.

"And what about the heart?" demanded The Vesper.

"We are not sure whether it is necessary or not, but from our research, it appears that we need to control the blood flow to the brain, and that can only be done by keeping the heart here as well. That way, we can control the entire host from here, and they would have no idea we were even controlling their minds. They would feel... normal, because we would allow them to," answered the chief surgeon, clearly hoping he would get no more questions.

"Next time try just the brain. If I can control their mind, then we can begin to control those who think they can order me about," said The Vesper.

"One more thing. We want to try a new way of storing the host's body prior to the operation. Instead of maintaining it as we have been doing, we think it will work better if you inject them with this new serum. It seems to age them by about 150 years, looks-wise anyway, making them somewhat unrecognisable, but that should help to maintain the brain's internal structure, as it almost absorbs the life from the outside, to maintain the life of everything inside. Surgery will allow us to restore their original looks, so no need to worry about that. Implementing a hair transplant would also be required, as their hair goes a similar way to their skin, in that it also ages. The expected result is that the hair will grow long and grey. We are unsure whether this new serum will cause the host any more pain, as they have felt nothing up till now, but I do suggest we try this before moving to a brain-only operation," said the chief surgeon.

"Well, the pain makes no difference to me. I don't care how much pain they are in. I expect this new serum to work, I must be able to control my superiors before it is too late," said The Vesper.

"I understand your predicament, but we..." started the chief surgeon.

"I don't want to hear any excuses, and you most certainly do not understand my predicament," interrupted The Vesper.

"I apologise. We will be able to control your superiors before they know what we plan. It will be karma," concluded the chief surgeon.

"There is no such thing," insisted The Vesper, before his tiny footsteps began to move towards the door.

Without wasting a second, Gemini turned and ran straight for the stairs. He jumped up several at a time and made it back to the ground floor before they noticed the door was open. He went back into the guest lounge, changed back into his suit and went up to his room, making it back without being seen.

As Gemini sat in his room, trying to work out what was going on, he heard a bell ring out.

"Lunch is served! Lunch is served!" shouted someone outside his room.

Gemini went back to his door and opened it, seeing a waiter head down the stairs. Aqua left her room next, turning to Gemini and smiling.

"Enjoy your meal. I hear we have a frangipane tart for dessert. I've never eaten anything which smells of bitter almonds," she said, still smiling, as she moved towards the stairs.

They all adjourned to the dining area one floor below and took their seats. The Vesper was the last to join and sat in the chair at the head of the table, which had been removed to ensure the seat wasn't taken. Course by course, the food was brought out in abundance. But neither Gemini, nor Aqua ever touched their food. Instead, they sat opposite each other, staring, refusing to shift their attention elsewhere. Whilst at the table, nobody said a word; Kyle wasn't mentioned once, just as Gemini's and Aqua's lack of eating went unnoticed. They were watching every move the other made, trying to get in each other's head, unsure whether the food could've been tampered with or whether they were playing games with each other. Gemini had many things to consider, Aqua had just one. Gemini knew she was taking too much of his attention, so decided to call her bluff and shift his focus back to The Vesper. He was hunched over his plate, munching on tiny bite-sized pieces of steak. Although he wasn't dribbling, the noise he made whilst eating gave that impression. Marcus, who was sat closest to The Vesper, had started to edge his chair away, trying to look in the opposite direction. After a while, even Marcus had stopped eating, unable to ignore his churning stomach caused by the foul noise beside him.

After over an hour of tense and nauseous dining, they had finally finished eating.

"Your tour will continue later today," said The Vesper, as he stood up and left the room.

"I don't get this place. We've invested in part of a drink. What else is there that can be included in a tour?" asked Marcus, now continuing his meal.

Gemini knew what else was in the tour, but decided to shrug his shoulders out of courtesy, trying not to worry Marcus about the room two floors underground.

"Why don't you meet me back at my room? We'll have a drink together. I'll even let you choose which glass to use," said Aqua, still showing her false smile, concerned she was no longer Gemini's prime focus.

Marcus lowered his head, pretending he didn't hear someone get chosen over him. Aqua had already left the room, knowing she'd done more than enough for Gemini's curiosity to make him join her. He stood up and walked halfway around the table until he was behind Marcus.

He tapped him on the shoulder, saying, "You're far safer down here," before leaving the room to follow Aqua.

Back upstairs, Gemini had reached Aqua's room and knocked on the door. The door slowly crept open, showing an empty room. Gemini knew she was playing with him; at least he was almost certain she was. He walked into the room, ensuring his footsteps were loud.

As he passed the door, she leapt out from one of the four wardrobes, shouting, "I could've got you!"

Gemini found it hard not to flinch, with his senses on high alert, but as soon as he had calmed, he put on a smile identical to Aqua's.

"But you wouldn't have, would you?" he said, maintaining Aqua's smile.

There was a table in the centre of the room, much like his, which had two drinks sat on top.

"Do you like games? I bet you do," said Aqua.

"Actually… I hate them," replied Gemini, offering her nothing with which to continue the conversation.

They both sat down around the circular table, pushed over to the left, which was pressed tightly against the wall they shared. The two drinks were dark in colour with a strong smell of almonds.

"I know it's a bit repetitive, almonds again, but this time there is a slight twist. One of these drinks contains enough of my home-made poison to kill anything. I'll let you choose your drink, and then we'll see who the winner is," said Aqua.

Gemini looked at the drinks; he knew he had little way of differentiating between them.

"If you turn your back, I'll choose," replied Gemini.

Aqua was clearly surprised by his choice.

Her smile started to fade, just for a second, before she turned away and said, "Okay. Usually, when I do this with my targets, they just take the poisoned glass and drink it. Although I tend not to tell them one is poisoned, it usually creates quite a tense atmosphere. You know I've been studying you, the way you eat and drink, which hand you pick your drink up in. Even your dominant eye makes a difference to your…"

Before she could continue, Gemini interrupted, saying, "Ready."

She turned around and looked at the glass in front of her.

"Excellent choice," she said, pretending to know which glass she'd been given.

They picked up their respective glasses and drained them, carefully placing them back on the table.

"How long will it take for the poison to work?" asked Gemini.

"Usually, a couple of minutes. It's my own poison, so I allow us sufficient time to talk," answered Aqua.

"What should we talk about?" asked Gemini, checking his watch for the time.

"Each other…" Aqua started.

Gemini held his hand out and gestured for Aqua to start, something she would likely do anyway.

"So… Gemini died three years ago," she continued.

He was hardly surprised by her direct approach to the questions, given the short time one of them had left, as she mimicked his direct approach from earlier.

"Straight to the point! Well, as you know, Gemini had made a lot of enemies, so, long story short, I placed the price on my own head. I waited for someone brave enough to find me, and I used it to disappear," he replied, taking another glance at his watch.

"Well, I'm here to collect the reward for you, or rather, on you, well, on you and from you, no matter who set it. I have killed thirty-seven targets this way and, obviously, I've never failed. I could've killed you countless times before; on the boat, at the dinner table, I could've even planted a trap for when you came back to your room in a hurry. But I'm patient, I decided to study you, to understand you," said Aqua, still confident he'd chosen the poison, unable to consider the possibility that she might have lost.

Gemini began shuffling in his chair, wriggling from side to side. He grabbed his collar, desperately trying to pull it away from his neck. He started dabbing his dry forehead, as his wandering gaze fixed on Aqua. She leant forward; her smile larger than ever.

"It was nothing personal," said Aqua.

Gemini's shaking hand reached for his glass, knocking it over in the process.

"Just kidding," said Gemini, as he sat bolt upright in his chair.

Aqua's face dropped, as she sat back in her chair, suddenly feeling faint.

"But how?" asked Aqua, who was now pale and scratching her own throat.

"Do you know why they called me Gemini? Because everyone thought there were two of me," replied Gemini, now leaning towards Aqua.

"But that was just a myth," she mumbled.

"It used to be. But I've changed. Now there really are two of us. You could never understand me," said Gemini, pointing out of the window towards Blindspot. "It was nothing personal," he concluded, as Aqua's hand slipped from her throat.

"A leopard never changes his spots," she mumbled, before her lifeless body slumped over in her chair.

"What I don't get, is how you knew which glass to choose, I never told you," said Blindspot, clearly confused.

"I started to think whether she could be bluffing, double bluffing, or doing even more bluffing. But then I remembered that she used to work as a bartender and she was good at it, that's where she picked up most of her targets. So, naturally, she would pour the same quantity into each glass, being the perfectionist she was. So, the one with more liquid must've had the poison in. Plus, if I'd got anything wrong, you would've stopped me, right?" said Gemini, now starting to doubt whether his method had more guessing than he'd initially thought.

"Well, I never saw her pour the drinks, so I didn't have a clue which glass was which," answered Blindspot.

Gemini sat in his chair for a moment, contemplating how easily he could've chosen poorly. After a moment of trying to ignore her final comment, he eventually stood up and grabbed his glass, tucking it into one of his many pockets. He walked to the door, turning to take one last look at Aqua, still slumped in her chair, and to ensure he left no trace of his presence.

"One down, one to go," said Gemini, as he released one long lungful of air and lowered his head, before leaving the room for the last time, realising his past was finally catching up with him.

"How are you finding your tour?" said The Vesper, stood outside Aqua's room.

Gemini froze on the spot, his heart thumping. He knew to be on his guard, unsure who The Vesper's next target would be. Slowly, Gemini turned to face The Vesper and the three guards just behind him.

"Very good, thank you," replied Gemini, watching every move they made.

The Vesper smiled and turned to walk away.

"Follow me," he said, parting the guards.

Gemini followed, hoping it would lead to his best opportunity to take out The Vesper. The three guards all stayed at the back, ensuring Gemini remained on course. He was led up the stairs to the top floor. As they stepped away from the final tread of the stairs, Gemini could see a door at the end of the long, narrow corridor labelled 'Guest Terrace'. It might've been a perfect place to escape, allowing Blindspot to cover him, if anything went wrong, but Gemini was led towards the other door, which was promptly unlocked by The Vesper, as he held his hand on a large panel next to the door. Gemini was taken into a dark room, with the two masked guards remaining outside and the head of security following Gemini in.

Chapter 11.3

Inside the room was a short corridor which opened into a room like the living and dining area two floors below. It was smaller and appeared to be set out for only one person, with one of most pieces of furniture. Directly ahead, there was a huge expanse of glass, spanning the width of the wall, which led to a terrace area almost as large as the inside. There was an open door to Gemini's right which was swiftly closed by The Vesper. Before it was closed, Gemini caught sight of giant bed, leading him to believe the final closed door to Gemini's left must be a bathroom.

"This is my room, completely private from everywhere else and entirely soundproof. So, it won't matter if you scream," said The Vesper.

The Vesper stood just in front of Gemini, but was immediately ignored, as Gemini focussed entirely on the guard behind. Gemini could hear the rustling of the guard's suit jacket as he raised his arms. The guard's fist tightened and one of his boots creaked on the floor, as he shifted his weight. Gemini flicked his head to the left with the rest of his body following. A long needle was thrust past Gemini's right ear and, before it could change direction, he grabbed the hand that controlled it. Using its momentum, Gemini steered the needle towards The Vesper, plunging it into his neck. The guard wrapped his free arm around Gemini's neck, allowing Gemini to slowly push the fluid from the needle. With about half the fluid gone, The Vesper swiped the needle from his neck, knocking it onto the floor. The

Vesper continued flinging his arms around, as if trying to swat flies from his face, whilst stumbling around the room. With The Vesper somewhat preoccupied, Gemini turned his attention back to the guard. Both the guard's arms were now wrapped around Gemini's neck, desperately trying to squeeze the life from him. Gemini took only a second to calm himself and concentrate, trying to not focus on gasping for air. With one kick, powerful enough to break open a door, Gemini cracked the guard's knee backwards. He released his grip instantly, as he grabbed his knee, shrieking in pain.

Gemini moved away from the grunting guard and picked up the needle. As he turned back around, he saw the guard hobbling towards the glass, still trying to ignore the pain. The guard pushed against one of the many panels and stumbled outside.

"Sub-target heading out onto the right balcony. Ensure he doesn't do anything he shouldn't," said Gemini with no panic in his voice.

The guard continued to hobble towards the edge of the terrace. As he crashed into the side, he leant over, about to shout out. But before he had a chance, he was suddenly sprawled out on the terrace floor, with one round hole in his head, covered in blood. His brain painted the terrace floor. Gemini took a towel from the adjacent bathroom and wrapped it around the whole of the guard's upper body, trying to prevent any blood from possibly dripping inside the apartment.

Gemini picked up the guard first, under his arms, and dragged him to the back of the living room, past the now motionless Vesper on the floor, where he found a set of screens. Before approaching them, he glanced back to The Vesper. He looked just like you would expect a 200-year-old to look if they were still alive, just like a mummy from a horror film. The Vesper had become even smaller, but, ironically, his hair didn't seem to look much different.

It was hard to think someone who was over 200 years old, in appearance, could still have the same insides as someone 150 years younger. He shifted the screens to the side, revealing another, more private, living space with an L-shaped sofa, a fireplace, and one painting of The Vesper on the left wall. Gemini continued to drag the guard's body into the secluded room and dumped him in front of the sofa, ensuring his body would be hidden from any quick glances into the room. As he started to move back into the main room to retrieve The Vesper and finish his job, he heard the door open and at least two guards enter.

They walked only a few steps into the room before stopping, right at The Vesper's feet.

"This must be the guy. I can't believe he's actually still alive. I'm not sure whether this technology is incredible or just odd," said one of the guards.

"I thought he was wearing a suit," questioned another.

Gemini slowly crept towards the screen and peered around, seeing only two guards, both looming over The Vesper's body.

"We don't get paid to think. Just pick up the body," insisted the first guard.

"I'm sure these were the clothes The Vesper was wearing," continued the second guard, clearly more observant than the first.

"Look, whatever the reason, The Vesper changed this guy into his own clothes. We don't know why, and we don't want to know why. Every time one of us thinks, somebody ends up getting killed, so pick the body up and do as you're told," demanded the first guard.

"Where is The Vesper anyway?" asked the second guard, as he swung The Vesper over his shoulder.

"He's probably hiding behind his own painting; the guy doesn't think we know about it," replied the first guard, laughing, as they both left the room, locking it behind them.

In the private space, behind the screen, was a painting of The Vesper. Gemini had a moment to wait, whilst the guards got further away, so he moved over to it. He tried removing the painting from the wall but found it wouldn't move an inch. Gemini then tried twisting the painting, followed by moving it up and down, and then left to right. He still had no luck, and nothing moved. It was then that Gemini saw the plaque at the bottom of the painting. It read, *'Hear no evil, speak no evil'*. Gemini thought for a moment, trying to figure out whether the missing, 'see no evil' could help. As he took a closer look, he noticed the eyes of The Vesper had a slightly glossy finish, compared to the rest of the painting with its grainy texture. He took a closer look, almost pressing his nose against the painting, as he realised the eyes acted as a scanner. Gemini lifted the chief security guard up, unwrapped his head, and pressed his face up to the scanner, witnessing no changes. He then tried the guard's fingers, as he pressed them tightly against the eyes. Making no noise at all, a door behind the painting began to swing open. Gemini moved inside, dragging the guard's body with him.

The hidden room was much smaller and had a very high-tech finish. There were computer screens, covering most of the walls, most of which showing cameras scattered over the five islands. Over to one side was a radar screen and an old radio. Whilst Gemini wanted to stay to see what intel he could gather, his mission was elsewhere. There was a ladder, on to which he climbed, leading to the floor below, and another, followed by yet another and even one after that, until he was on the ground floor. Although the ladders continued, it was the ground floor Gemini wanted to be on.

Pressing a big red button, Gemini had a little flutter of panic, uncertain what the button did. Shortly after, Gemini's hunch was correct, and the wall turned into a door which opened into a freezer. He was instantly faced with whole animals strung up on hooks, dangling above the cold floor. Through the meat, he could also see stacks of bags and boxes, but again, he had no time to inspect them. Gemini closed the door behind him and used the freezer door on his right to leave. The door itself comprised of two doors, where only one could be opened at a time, ensuring the room stayed cold. The door took him out into the corridor on the ground floor. Using the familiar walls, Gemini moved back into the guest lounge and quickly changed into the guard's outfit. It wouldn't get him all the way, but it would take him further than his suit.

With the outfit back on, Gemini headed back down the stairs and into the clean, white corridor, two floors below ground. Taking the time to change again, Gemini, now wearing the surgeon's outfit, headed into the office. He crept through the unlocked door and looked out through the glass windows to see all the surgeons huddled in the same circle, just as before. With everyone's attention diverted, Gemini sat down at the only desk and started up the computer. Although faced with a locked computer, Gemini wasn't bothered. He removed a small device from inside his sock, which he'd carried with him all along, and plugged it into the computer. The tiny device got into their system and copied everything to its own storage drive, before erasing all data, logs, and records of the experiments and research that had gone on in the facility. Once the tiny, green light began flashing on the device, Gemini ripped it from the computer and tucked it back inside his sock, before leaving the room. Taking the same path as before, Gemini went back into the large experimentation room, unnoticed.

He moved closer and closer until he could see The Vesper's body on the table. Despite only half the injection, The Vesper didn't look like he could be alive. But as Gemini took a closer look, The Vesper was very much alive, with panic clearly in his eyes. He knew exactly what was going to happen, as he had put so many people through the same ordeal.

"Removing the heart now," said the chief surgeon, digging his hands into The Vesper's chest.

Gemini could see The Vesper's eyes grow larger, as he looked exactly like Kyle, helpless. The Vesper's eyes continued to dart around the room, until meeting Gemini's. He slightly pulled his mask down, ensuring The Vesper knew who he was. His heart gave one final beat as his eyes calmed; the last thing he saw was Gemini, the man who took everything away from him.

"Another failure. This one was obviously too weak. Clean up and we'll go again. I'll let The Vesper know it hasn't worked," said the chief surgeon, as he headed back towards his office.

Without wasting any time, Gemini ensured he was among the few who wheeled The Vesper's unidentified corpse out of the room. They took him into the morgue and placed him to one side.

"Craig still isn't around; we'll have to do it ourselves," said one of the three surgeons.

One of them went to wheel The Vesper into the freezer but was instantly stopped.

"There are too many bodies in the morgue with no sign of bringing the dead back to life. This one's going in the furnace like some of the others. We want no traces left of our experiment," said the surgeon who stopped the trolley.

Gemini hung back, watching every move they made, as they wheeled him over to the large furnace. Together, they dumped him inside and switched it on, making the entire room turn red through the fiery light. With his job done, Gemini changed back into his guard's outfit and went back upstairs, this time taking the surgeon's clothes with him. He swiftly collected his suit, still stashed in the bathroom, and went back outside.

As Gemini left the house, he stopped by the pool, as he noticed all the guards were over to his left, pointing out to sea. He heard the gasps from the guards as they all expressed their shock.

"Do you see that?" said one guard.

"What is this, John?" demanded another.

Gemini looked out to sea and instantly saw what they were looking at. It looked like a meteorite shower raining down in the distance, just visible on the horizon.

"There're going to kill us all!" shouted another, as they ran back to the villa.

"There's no time to waste. VOICE says we need to get to our rendezvous point straight away," said Blindspot, still watching from his elevated position.

Gemini headed down the wooden, sloped jetty. With both his used disguise and suit he arrived in stashed inside a plain, black bag, Gemini strolled past the other guards without arousing any suspicion.

He climbed onto the only boat parked at the jetty and told the pilot, "The Vesper wants these delivered to port."

The pilot nodded his head, and they began moving back towards the port island.

***

"Jump off the boat three minutes into your journey. There'll be an oxygen tank weighed down next to the only large rock in sight. I'll meet you at our rendezvous point," said Blindspot, who was climbing down the ladder with all the gear he'd brought up.

Blindspot then climbed down the rocks and submerged himself back under the water and into the darkness, unseen.

Chapter 12 – The Satellite
February 13th
11:30 GMT

The wheels touched down on the cold runway, squeaking as they tried to slow the private jet. As it rumbled down the tarmac, it eventually slowed to a steady and manageable speed. The jet continued to the end of the runway and turned in, stopping in front of a group of cars. Apart from them, there was only a control tower a little way up the steep mountainside that encaged the runway. The door unclicked and swung down, allowing Alpha One to emerge, dressed in a black suit. The freezing wind filled the plane instantly, causing him to tense as his body tried to adjust to the harsh temperature. With his teeth clenched, Alpha One straightened his suit and began strolling down the steps. As he moved downwards, he took a sense of power and dominance with him, unthreatened by the huge presence of guards ahead.

"Mr Green, a pleasure to meet you. If you could just check in with my head of security…" started the woman stood in the middle of the group. Alpha One gave a slight nod in her direction, as she headed over to the head of security, adding, "Security is of the upmost importance, I'm sure you understand."

She was very well spoken, with her English accent which sounded almost put on, and was wearing a huge fur coat with the fur-lined hood covering much of her face. Alpha One crunched in the snow as he arrived in front of the head of security and removed the few documents from inside his jacket, handing them over. Elias Green was the assumed name that Alpha One had taken. He was a completely fictional character, but an entire life story had been written for him. Among many other tales, stories and lies, Elias was a businessman, who owned billions, and had a certain interest in space. It was the perfect alias to take on and one that had worked so far.

After the documents were checked, the head of security directed Elias over to one of the cars. They were all identical 4x4s, black, and with tinted windows. Just as he got to the car door, the guard grabbed his shoulder and heaved him back. The force almost knocked him of balance, but he ended up crashing into the guard, as he tried to play the part of an untrained businessman. He spread Elias' legs and began to frisk him, thoroughly.

"Awkward, isn't it?" said Elias, trying to show his humorous personality and the slight embarrassment which his alias would feel.

Once the guard had finished, and found nothing, he opened the back door and allowed Elias to climb in. The head of security was exactly how you'd expect a 6'4" security guard to look. He had a big head, matching his big build, and stubble covering the lower part of his face. He had in just one earpiece, attached by a curly, clear cord, running behind his ear. He also had a stark expression which was meant to make him look like someone to not mess with, but instead made him look miserable. The woman removed her coat and climbed into the car from the other side. Inside, the car was completely white. It struck Elias as a little odd, if the colours were inverted, they'd have a completely camouflaged car.

"My name is Emma. I'm in charge of the entire operation here in Switzerland. But before I continue, I'd just like to convey my thanks for the donation that you so kindly made. It really will go a long way," said the woman, who could now be seen clearly, as she interrupted his train of thought.

She had red hair tied up in a ponytail, wore a suit similar in style to the one worn by Elias, and wore so much make-up that it became impossible to see her true face. Her brown eyes were hard to see because of her dilated pupils. As Elias looked closer, he could also see the make-up around her eyes had smudged and was a little shiny, almost as if she'd been crying prior to his arrival. But due to her calm persona, Elias knew it was most likely because of the cold, harsh temperatures. Although, 'most likely' wasn't always true.

"Nice to meet you, Emma. It is hardly a problem investing in the future, and I am honoured that you've allowed me to come and visit the project, even if you took a bit of persuading," said Elias.

The cars drove off in convoy, with Elias and Emma two cars ahead of the central vehicle. Throughout the journey, there was silence. Elias was on his phone, acting the businessman who had too much money to spend, whilst Emma admired the giant mountains, hiding their peaks among the white sea of clouds. The convoy drove around, in between, and over only a few of the many mountains the Swiss Alps had to offer. The roads were covered in snow, enough to obscure them from above. The wind was strong, making it feel unsafe, as they drove close to the edge of the mountains, a long way up. After about twenty nail-biting minutes, they eventually reached a building. Its style was exactly what you would expect from a privately funded company based in Switzerland. The huge building was fitted with tinted windows, covering most of the unusually shaped walls, with huge doors leading from the car park. Although Elias couldn't see it from this angle, he also knew the roof was white, helping it to hide amongst the snowy backdrop. The car park was unused and covered in snow, but the presence of guards had increased as they got to the compound, as they patrolled the grounds in their white jackets.

The gates were opened, and all the cars drove to the front door, with Emma's car parking right in front. She got out, along with Elias and her head of security, and headed into the building, whilst the cars drove off and moved underground, without another person exiting their vehicle. Emma had once again put her coat on, just to walk the fifteen metres to get back inside. The doors slid open, revealing the sleek interior with clean, white walls, before automatically shutting behind them. Inside was warm, so Emma again removed her coat, this time handing it to a man who was waiting inside. He had short, black hair, was also dressed in a suit, although his top button was undone, and was holding a tablet in the hand with her coat. He looked like a secretary of some sort and began pounding away on the screen after she leant towards him and whispered something in his ear. The secretary looked to be in his early thirties at the oldest and had no visible stubble around his face. But the more Elias observed the secretary, the more something didn't seem right. He didn't seem very attentive to Emma and was more concerned with subtly taking quick glances at Elias. He also wore glasses, which in itself wasn't suspicious, but every time he looked up and down, the glasses didn't budge, as the temples seemed very tight. He could also look at things in the distance and very close to him without removing his glasses. Neither seemed overly unusual, as the temples could be tight due to being new, and glasses are more than capable of focussing on long and short distances with widely available modern technology. Despite the perfectly rational explanations, it was still enough for Elias to warrant keeping an eye on him. There was something about the secretary which Elias knew wasn't right; he just couldn't figure out what it was. Secretaries were always people Elias found suspicious, perhaps because they had the perfect opportunity to spy, or maybe because they had the word 'secret' in their titles. But before he could continue his observations of the secretary, Elias was swiftly pushed through a metal detector and then into a body scanner, before being ordered to empty his pockets completely. He wasn't allowed to take anything in with him; even his phone had to be left in a plastic box which was then placed inside a metal cage.

Once he was all clear, Emma finally began talking again.

"I apologise for all the security checks," she said, trying to make her voice sound compassionate.

"I quite understand. At least I know nobody is going to be able to steal the prototype," said Elias.

"If you would follow me, I'll give you the tour of our facility and then we'll conclude with the prototype itself, if that's okay with you, Mr Green?" continued Emma, holding her hand up to direct Elias forwards without giving him the opportunity to object.

"That's absolutely fine," Elias persisted.

They continued down the hall, its ceiling about three floors above them. It quickly became clear that the facility was built for show, rather than practicality, which started to make Elias wonder whether there was a prototype there at all.

As they walked down the corridor, Emma's arms began flailing around, pointing to things in all directions.

"As you can see, we have the best staff, from all areas, who work tirelessly," said Emma, as they passed countless staff that all looked greatly overworked.

They approached doorway after doorway, each containing a different department, all full of staff.

"This is our engineering department, with the science section next door. Or more specifically, the chemical section," continued Emma, still flinging her hands around as if they were out of control.

Elias hadn't taken anything in Emma had said whilst on their tour, but the mention of a chemical room did interest him.

He saw the potential to get hold of some supplies that could help him, so asked, "Any chance we can go in?"

Emma looked straight to the secretary but, by the time Elias had swung round to look in his direction, Emma answered, saying, "Why not? If you'd follow me."

Emma led the way into the science room with Elias, the guard, and the secretary all following closely. As they began to move through the doorway, the secretary was right behind Elias. Elias took a quick look behind him, trying to take anything else in. He saw the secretary continue to pound away at the screen, and although he couldn't see what was on the screen, he did notice the secretary's hands were surprisingly rough and coarse which was unusual for a secretary.

Elias entered the room, the rows of chemicals catching his eye. There were six scientists in the room, all with white lab coats. They seemed to be at their respective stations; some were looking through microscopes, others were on their computers.

Emma moved over to one of them and asked, "Can I borrow you for a second?"

The scientist looked annoyed that he had to stop his work but seemed equally pleased that he'd been chosen, despite him being the closest scientist.

"What can I do for you?" asked the scientist.

Elias was a little disappointed because he didn't have that 'mad scientist' look to him, not that he'd ever seen a scientist with that look. The man was in his forties, which looked to be about the same age as the others, and wore a white hairnet, completely covering his hair. His round, thin face looked drawn and tired with wrinkles and huge black bags surrounding his eyes. He looked clearly overworked and run down, despite his perked-up mood and attitude.

"This is Mr Green…" Emma started, whilst pointing at Elias. "He is our largest sponsor and is being given a tour of our facility. I was wondering if there was anything… exciting, that you could show him."

The scientist began smiling and said, "Yes! Yes! I can show you our new spacesuit."

Elias was a little confused by the fact that the chemical scientists were making the spacesuits, but once he'd been taken into an adjoining room, his confusion was cleared up. The next room was much smaller and had nothing but five suits hanging up on the right and a collection of canisters on the left.

"You see, these canisters here are all filled with our finest work. Obviously, I can't tell you what is in them, but when sprayed onto certain materials, the chemical, within the canisters, begins bubbling up. We actually discovered the reaction to these materials quite by chance, and after a little intentional modification, we have been able to create it so that it forms one bubble around the material which is what the suit is made of. There is no worry about a suit splitting, because the bubble formed is under so much pressure that nothing can get through. Also, the inside maintains an identical pressure to when the suit bubbles up and is painted with an oxidiser, for obvious reason, although it is a last resort, as the oxygen tank should be favoured…" said the scientist, before being abruptly interrupted,

"I think you might be boring Mr Green now. Shall we move on?" said Emma, directing Elias out of the door and away from the scientist.

"Can I take one of the suits?" asked Elias, expecting an 'I'm afraid not'.

Emma began saying, "I'm afraid…" before the secretary whispered in her ear. She had a remarkable change in attitude and started again, saying, "Why not? Could you fix him up with one?" she asked, as she looked at the scientist.

The sudden change had Elias even more concerned, and it became apparent that Emma was not as 'in charge' as she first let on. Whoever was running the place was speaking through the secretary and clearly had their eyes on Elias the entire time, which wasn't exactly surprising given the hundreds of surveillance cameras Elias had already identified.

The scientist packed up one of the five suits and added two cans of the chemical, saying, "The suit is 'one-size-fits-all', but I should warn you, the chemical is still experimental and it doesn't last as long as we would like."

"Thank you," said Elias, taking the suit and canisters.

The scientist got back to work as the other four all left the room and re-entered the corridor. They continued to walk, as Emma began explaining the history of the facility.

"Our organisation was originally founded in 1952. We didn't do much more than design planes, but then we were hired by the government. We assisted in the 'space race' and began designing rockets that could get to the moon and back. We were pretty good at it, but before long our objectives were shifted. We had to begin work on the 'Star Wars Project'. Unfortunately, it never entered production, because we lost all government funding and were once again a private corporation. So, we returned to what we were good at and began designing and producing the next generation of rockets," said Emma, as if she was remembering it from a script.

There was an uneasy feeling as they ambled along their tour. Elias wasn't sure whether it was just him being overcautious or whether there was something to be concerned about. Elias started to take in every piece of information Emma was throwing at him, whilst observing his surroundings. At that moment, he turned around to see the secretary had gone, though the head of security was still following, only a foot away. As they approached the final doorway, Emma carried on talking.

"And this is where we keep the prototype," she said, opening the door to allow Elias through.

The hangar would've looked huge if it wasn't being compared to the Molehill, with cars, fuel tankers, and a huge plane over to the right. It had a massive wingspan with giant engines at the rear. There was a little cockpit window at the front which was hard to see against the black paint the plane was covered in.

"We call it the 'Star Rocket'," said Emma.

At that moment, Elias heard a gun being cocked behind him. With a little glance over his right shoulder, he saw the head of security aim his sidearm at Emma's head. He was ready to pounce at the guard, when he noticed a small flash of light come from opposite him. Elias quickly realised there was a sniper aiming right at him.

Before he could even formulate a plan, a loud, crackly noise came from all the speakers, before a voice said, "Mr Green, we thank you for your contribution. Unfortunately, nobody is allowed to leave this compound alive. That does also include you, Emma."

Elias instantly recognised the voice as the soft, Irish accent on the other end of the call in the Dutchman's office. Emma was instantly filled with fear as she turned to see the gun pointing at her head.

"Who wishes to die first?" said the still unnamed voice through the speakers.

Elias gave no thought, as he shouted, "Me!"

"Very well," concluded the voice.

Bullets travel faster than even Elias could ever think of moving. They can travel faster than the speed of sound, so with a well-placed shot, you could be killed before even hearing the gun go off. To outrun a bullet would be impossible, but to avoid one has an element of luck. Elias knew this was his only chance to get them both out alive. He dropped to the floor, allowing the sniper's sights to go over Elias' head as gravity did all the work. When the bullet left the rifle, Elias was already halfway to the floor and the bullet flew past him and went through the guard behind. He jumped back up and grabbed Emma, dragging her around the corner, out of the sniper's sight. The head of security dropped to the floor, blood pouring from the hole in his chest.

Elias stretched over and picked up the guard's handgun that slid over towards him.

"I need you to take me to their security room," said Elias.

Emma nodded and started moving towards the closest door. Elias was right behind her, able to push her aside should they come up against any guards. The door led to a wide corridor which then opened to reveal a staircase. She led him up two levels and along another wide corridor. Two guards came running towards them, and Elias pushed Emma to the floor and aimed at them. He waited until they took aim at him, before firing two shots a split second apart. The guards dropped to the floor, dead. Emma was pulled back to her feet, and they continued along the corridor until they got to the third door.

Elias turned to face away from the door. He kicked his leg back and spun around as the door swung in and the handgun was aimed into the room, tightly clasped within his hands. There were four people sat in chairs around a computer system. They all jumped up but seemed unarmed.

"Get out!" barked Elias, as he bolted the door behind them.

He began getting up the surveillance cameras and trying to shut down the plane's security measures. Once all the cameras were up, he grabbed two earpieces, putting one in his ear and trying to give the other to Emma. She was curled up in the corner and had started to cry.

"I'm so sorry," she began, the words hard to make out through her tears. "I didn't know what I was doing. They told me to show you around the place, and they gave me exactly what to say. They have my family," she continued, still hard to hear.

"Emma. Emma, look at me. I know it wasn't your fault. But if you want to get out of here, I need your help," said Elias, trying to calm her down.

"I didn't know," she persisted.

Elias had to think of some way to calm Emma down, but little came to mind.

"Is Emma your real name?" he asked.

Emma nodded her head and said, "Emma Smith."

"Okay, Emma Smith. My real name is Scott. I work for a secret organisation. Now, we've saved the world before, so together… we can save each other," he said.

Emma had begun to calm down, enough for him to put the earpiece in her ear.

"Do you promise?" Emma asked.

Alpha One was confused and went to ask her to clarify, but Emma didn't need to be asked.

"Do you promise to get me out?" she asked.

Making promises wasn't something he liked doing, but in certain situations some sort of promise was needed. This was one of those times.

"I promise to do everything in my power to get us out, but I need you to do the same. Okay?" said Alpha One, choosing his words carefully.

Emma nodded her head again, unable to produce any words.

Alpha One only had part of a plan, but that was enough to start with. He got Emma over to the computers and sat her down.

"I'm going to need you to monitor these cameras for guards. Okay? You can watch my every move and follow me to the hangar. I'm going to release the plane. You can use the earpiece to talk to me. It's just like talking to me as if I was in the room. Okay?" said Alpha One, talking in a compassionate tone.

Emma continued to nod. She had stopped crying, but her eyes were red, and her cheeks still glossy with her smudged tears. Alpha One moved back over to the door with Emma closely following.

"Bolt the door behind me and open it for nobody except me," he said, as he moved through the doorway.

Alpha One checked it was bolted behind him and moved off, down the corridor.

With the handgun raised, Alpha One retraced his steps back to the hangar. He moved through each doorway, checking every corner.

"Stop," said Emma.

Alpha One froze, not knowing who was close. Three guards emerged from his right, and Alpha One hid in the tiny space between the wall and the open door. They crept past, unaware of his presence. Alpha One held his handgun up and aimed it at their heads; it was a last case resort, but there was little point in being unprepared.

The guards moved past without an issue, and Alpha One could again head towards the hangar.

As he returned to the hangar doors, he asked, "Is the hangar clear?"

"Yes. There's nobody in there," replied Emma.

Alpha One started to move forwards. "You're good at this."

"Wait! Somebody is in there," she said.

"Maybe I spoke too soon…" joked Alpha One, laughing to clearly show Emma it was a joke, before becoming more serious and asking, "Where are they?"

"He's hiding behind the barrels," replied Emma, pleased with her help.

Alpha One struggled to hide his impatience but proceeded to calmly ask, "Which barrels?" taking deep breaths to keep his voice relaxed.

"The red ones," said Emma with more confidence than he'd heard in her voice all day.

Alpha One decided that it was probably the most help he was going to get, so removed one of the giant mirrors that littered the walls and held it out in front of him. He slowly crept the mirror out, and twisted it on the floor, until eventually he saw a collection of red barrels. The glass mirror hadn't been shot, so the sniper was clearly trying to keep their location a secret. Alpha One studied the rest of the visible hangar and found no more red barrels. *They must be the right ones*, he thought. The only problem now was that they knew where each other was hiding, and it would be a sniper rifle against a handgun.

Alpha One abandoned the mirror and waited, coming up with a plan. Because of the time delay after the first shot, he assumed the rifle was bolt-action, so all he had to do was make the sniper miss their first shot, or at least make sure the bullet didn't penetrate his suit. Alpha One quickly slipped the spacesuit on and sprayed it with one of the canisters. The suit billowed up, covering everything except his face, which Alpha One thought was a little strange considering the difficulty they'd have breathing. He stepped out, ensuring the sniper had enough time to go for a centre of mass shot. There was a crack from the gun, as Alpha One was thrown back down the corridor. He quickly climbed back to his feet and looked down to see the bullet had been completely stopped by the bubble. He raised his handgun and emptied the entire magazine towards the red barrels, leaving nothing to chance.

"You got him!" shouted Emma.

At that moment, guards could be heard pouring in from outside. The presence of guards inside the facility was low, but outside housed enough to form a small army. Alpha One ran over to the nearby control panel, his legs moving almost too fast for his body. He grabbed hold of the panel, just clinging on as his legs tried to travel past. Thumping the controls, he eventually got the right ones, as the hangar door opened and the lock on the plane was released. Alpha One ripped off one of the side panels and tore out all the wires he could see. He was trying to stop anyone from undoing his work and ensure the plane could no longer be locked down. Unfortunately, it also triggered a fail-safe. The hangar doors began closing again. *It works in every film, but the one time I try it, it doesn't work*, thought Alpha One.

"Somebody's trying to get in!" shouted Emma, clearly panicked.

"Alright, I'm on my way back up. Don't open the door," said Alpha One, now picking up speed and heading back down the corridor.

"It's okay. It's one of the analysts," said Emma with a tone of relief.

"No! Don't…" started Alpha One, before he was swiftly interrupted by a piercing scream.

He travelled as fast as he could, leaping up five steps at a time. As he got to the peak of the stairs, Alpha One could see two guards stood outside the room. He began charging at them, and before they could even raise their rifles, Alpha One smashed into them like a rhino protecting its young. The guards were thrown to the floor, one knocked unconscious from hitting his head; the lucky one. Alpha One lifted the other guard by his collar and swung up with his tightly clenched fist, catching him under the chin. The guard made a slight groan, before lying motionless on the floor. Alpha One proceeded to thump the guard in the temple a further three times, ensuring he would be in no hurry to stand up.

He climbed to his feet and entered the room with such confidence in his bulletproof suit that the one guard left didn't even fire his gun. At the guard's feet, Emma was lying in puddle of red blood, the knife in the guard's hand still dripping. The guard threw his gun to the floor and held the bloody knife up.

"She was innocent!" bellowed Alpha One, full of adrenaline.

"My boss didn't think so," said the guard with a sly smile.

"And I don't think you're innocent," said Alpha One.

The guard let out a tiny laugh, as he lunged forward with his knife.

As the knife came close, Alpha One ducked down, allowing it to pass straight over his head. He thumped the guard in his torso, whilst he was off balance. The guard groaned, as he curled up into a ball. Whilst the guard was still in pain, Alpha One came from behind and grabbed his neck. He flung him into the wall, headfirst. The steel-handled knife dropped to floor, followed by the guard. Alpha One lifted him off the ground and swung his hand towards the guard. The punch was aimed at his nose, and it was on target. Alpha One punched and punched again, replicating his technique and hitting the same spot repeatedly. The guard was still conscious and could just about roll out of the way, as Alpha One stood back up.

"Finish it!" mumbled the guard, spitting blood onto the floor. "Finish it!" he persisted.

Alpha One stood over Emma's lifeless body, remembering the promise he had made.

"No, I will not be the one to kill you. But I won't stop you from dying," said Alpha One, refusing to take his eyes away from his failure.

Alpha One moved over to the generator and shifted his gaze to the guard.

"I will give you a choice. You can stay there and live, or you can try to strike me down and die," said Alpha One, in his now emotionless voice.

The guard climbed to his feet and ran at him with the knife outstretched. When the knife was less than a foot away, Alpha One stepped aside, allowing it to plunge into the generator. With a few sparks and thousands of volts surging through his body, the guard began shaking irreparably. Unable to release the knife, the guard was eventually thrown back to where he was standing. His smoking corpse sat there, ignored by Alpha One.

He bent down to Emma and carefully closed her eyelids. Alpha One then lifted her up, cradled in his arms, and carried her over to one of the cupboards. He carefully placed her body in and locked the doors, ensuring nobody else would find her before he sent another team in to retrieve her body. Alpha One took a deep breath and released a long sigh, trying to suppress his anger.

He got back to his feet and left the room, refusing to even glance at the guards littering the floor. He grabbed one of their rifles on his way out and moved back to the hangar. Once there, he realised where all the extra guards had gone. They had all been sent to secure the hangar. He looked down to his suit to see the bubble effect had all gone, so he couldn't just walk in. Without wasting the final canister, Alpha One jogged around the outside of the hangar to get to the other side, climbed the stairs, and eventually found himself stood over the sniper's body. He had three bullet holes and wasn't going anywhere. At the slight elevation, he was about level with the plane's wings. Alpha One grabbed the sniper rifle and shot one of the tankers over on the other side. It didn't explode, but the leaking fuel drew a lot of attention. With most of the guards now away from Alpha One, he climbed up the hangar's frame and reached the roof's supports. Edging along, he was eventually above the plane, only a very long way up.

He dropped the rifle onto the plane, testing the distance. It hit the plane a couple of seconds later. Alpha One knew it would hurt, but at least he could survive the drop. He lowered himself and hung from his arms, trying to decrease the drop distance and the pain. After a moment of pushing all his doubt out of his mind, Alpha One dropped down, hitting the plane just moments later. The landing wasn't elegant or quiet and, as soon as he'd climbed back to his feet, Alpha One grabbed the rifle and began firing at the guards around him. His right hip had started throbbing, after taking the brunt of the fall, but he knew it had to be pushed to the back of his mind. He used only one bullet for each guard, catching them all in their dominant shoulder. There was heavy fire coming from the other end of the hangar, but with the distance, the guards found it hard to hit anything. Alpha One took one step at a time, flicking the rifle from side to side, taking down everyone that was a threat, before eventually reaching the cockpit.

There was a small lever behind the cockpit, and after lifting it, the tinted glass sprung up, almost catching him under his chin as he dodged out of the way. As it swung up, it revealed the tightly packed cockpit below. Alpha One dropped in, closing the lid after him and encasing himself in the tiny tin box. There were very few controls, most of them on the wheel in front of him. A steering wheel wasn't exactly what Alpha One was expecting, but because of the tight space, the wheel had to be big enough to hold most of the controls. With the press of a big, green button, the engines fired up. Alpha One began pressing all the buttons, finding that the wheel itself could tilt up and down, and move forward and backwards. When he thrust the wheel forwards, the plane began moving towards the hangar doors. On the wheel were two covered buttons. Alpha One tried the right-hand button, firing a twin-mounted machine gun underneath. The plane was still getting closer to the door and had started picking up speed. Alpha One knew that if he eased off the power, he might run out of runway before taking off. He plunged his finger into the other button, firing a cluster of rockets directly ahead. They collided with the door, crippling it from the inside.

There was little space left, as Alpha One punched the wheel as far forward as it would go, causing his head to be thrown back against the chair. The acceleration of the plane was unthinkable, able to reach take-off speed within the hangar. He shot through the buckled hangar door, leaving in his wake a pile of guards thrown to the floor.

Chapter 12.2

As soon as he left the facility, everything looked white, despite it turning into a clear and sunny day. There was a mountain directly ahead, so Alpha One tilted the wheel down, lowering it to his knees, expecting the plane to angle up. This didn't happen, as the plane began hurtling towards the white, rocky mountain. He quickly tried tilting the wheel up, as far as it would go, as it was only stopped by the canopy. The plane eventually started pitching up, but the mountain had got a lot closer. He was holding the wheel as far up as it would go, trying to push it through the canopy. The plane lifted and headed up, close enough to the mountain that the snow was blown away.

"Why would anyone put the steering wheel on upside down!" bellowed Alpha One, as if he was shouting at the plane itself.

After regaining control, he began looking around the cockpit for the oxygen tank that should be fitted. To the right of his chair, there was a small, silver tank. He wriggled around in the tiny space, placing the tank under his deflated spacesuit and feeding the mask up through the collar. He didn't place the mask from the tank over his head, but instead fitted a mask that was connected to the plane. With the random press of a few more buttons, air began filling his mask. It started with a mix of oxygen and nitrogen, but with each breath, the air received contained more oxygen and less nitrogen. The masks were designed to purge nitrogen from the blood, and Alpha One would eventually begin breathing pure oxygen. This would prevent him from suffering any altitude or pressure sickness. It would also mean Alpha One wouldn't have to wait for hours whilst his pressure returned to normal to avoid getting the bends.

Once Alpha One had begun breathing 100% oxygen, he began his ascent. He angled the plane vertically, so it acted more like a rocket. It started shaking, as he headed up. The sky began to darken, but it was so slow that it became hard to notice the change. A couple of minutes of shaking and rattling had passed before the light blue sky had become black and sparkly, the stars brighter than Alpha One had ever seen. Whilst sitting in the tiny cockpit, admiring everything that was out of reach, he had to be patient. Alpha One switched off the engines and floated at the same altitude the satellite was orbiting in, waiting until he was in the correct position. When in position, he switched the thrusters on and headed in the opposite direction to the orbiting satellite.

A little while later, the satellite came into sight, well if that's what you could call it. Their images didn't lie, as this so-called 'satellite' seemed larger than a space station. Alpha One changed his mask to the portable tank, which also provided pure oxygen, and steadied the ship. As it got close, he activated the magnetic clamps which allowed the ship to fasten itself against the side of the satellite. Unfortunately, their intel was also correct regarding the Star Rocket, as it seemed to lack anything capable of connecting to the satellite's external hatch. Despite it being designed to fly back and forth to the moon, Alpha One couldn't quite make sense of the lack of a perfectly reasonable addition. He sprayed the final canister onto his suit, which bubbled up, sealing itself around the mask. Alpha One opened the small hatch above him and leapt towards the satellite. As he slammed into the side, his arms scrabbled to hold onto anything. He bounced down the length of the satellite, until he finally got hold of a metal pipe surrounding it. He wrapped his fingers around it as best he could, clinging on as if his life depended on it.

Alpha One mustered all his strength to propel himself towards the only hatch he saw, grabbing hold as he crashed into it. There wasn't much security on the outside of the hatch, with no locking mechanism. It was probably because they didn't get many people passing by, trying to get in, but this time they might've wished it had been secured. Alpha One spun the handle round and round until, finally, the door opened. He floated in, closing the door behind him. After taking a moment to relax, knowing he was somewhat safe, Alpha One moved over to a small panel on the door and began pressurising the small compartment. Because of its tiny size, it didn't take long to return the space to the same pressure as the satellite before he was able to proceed. It might have been officially documented as just a satellite but, inside, it was clear that it was more of a space station, backing up their images.

The station had some form of weak artificial gravity, but as Alpha One bounced down the narrow tube, his body still felt light. Although the space station was large, it seemed to be more of a rabbit warren with narrow corridors, ensuring the interior was as tightly packed as possible. As he moved along, he left his mask on, still breathing the pure oxygen. As he crept further into the station, there was an eerie feeling. There were no astronauts and no scientists, which was unusual for a space station, especially one of this size. Now Alpha One's mask was secured, his suit didn't allow him to hear any external noises, so he relied entirely on what he could see. The cupboards and drawers were all open, and all empty.

He rounded a corner, the close, domed walls giving a claustrophobic feel, despite its large area. Alpha One saw a body lying on the floor. He moved over to him and turned him over. He was dead, with two bullet holes; one to the chest and one to the head. As Alpha One continued along the only route, he began following a trail of death. There were eight bodies in all, each with two identical bullet holes. Alpha One's lack of weapons wasn't too much of a concern to him, given his suit. He approached a computer terminal, trying to access any logs, but found nothing. Everything had been wiped clean, and there was no trace of anyone ever being there. As he continued looking through empty file after empty file, he eventually found something of use. The entire space station had recently been filled with pure oxygen, making it likely that the culprit was someone who had recently arrived. Even a small compartment of pure oxygen would make the entire place extremely flammable.

Suddenly, an alarm began sounding. Then one of the giant dishes under the station changed its angle, twisting into a different position.

"Activating Operation Storm. Stand by for weapon firing," said a very calm and monotone voice through the speakers.

Alpha One didn't realise it straight away, but somehow the computer system was able to play the message and alarm through his borrowed earpiece. Alpha One began sprinting to the other end of the station, his body still light. He didn't know where he was going, but as the station was laid out as a set of long tubes, the other end likely held the answers he needed.

As he got to the end of the station, Red Viper was sat in the control room, facing Alpha One. Red Viper wasn't wearing a mask, as a smile crept upon his face, as he pressed the big, red button in front of him. The station began shaking.

"You're too late," said Red Viper in his Texan accent, somehow also through his earpiece.

Alpha One looked out of one of the many circular windows and observed, as the giant dish began spinning. He could see clouds begin to form down on Earth, covering what was below, like a huge, darkening blanket. Red Viper stood up and removed his knife, clenching it, opting against his gun due to the pure oxygen environment. His face could be seen more clearly, compared to at the nightclub, as his broad shoulders and red eyes came into view. It was clear his eye colour had been created using contact lenses, matching his assigned officer's colour. Red Viper looked to be about forty and 6'4", as he seemed an even bigger build than he had done at the nightclub. Alpha One still had his mask on, mainly because he didn't know how to remove it whilst the suit was still inflated, but it would offer him extra protection against the knife.

Red Viper pressed a few more buttons, this time turning off the gravity. Alpha One instantly became weightless; he didn't start floating, his feet were still on the ground, he just became weightless. Red Viper pushed his feet back, propelling himself towards Alpha One, his knife leading the way. As he got close, Alpha One pushed his feet down, sending him flying to the ceiling. As Red Viper flew past, unable to change his course of direction, Alpha One kicked back down, crashing into him. They both hurtled towards the floor, still interlocked. Red Viper began swinging his arm from side to side, trying to catch Alpha One with his razor-sharp knife. Despite the protection offered by Alpha One's suit, he still tried to duck and dive to avoid the knife, not wanting to let Red Viper find out about his advantage.

Alpha One grabbed Red Viper, pushing his face into one of the computer screens, sending them drifting apart in the process. Alpha One found himself in the centre of the tube, unable to grab any surface, as he slowly floated to one side. Red Viper again pushed off from the side and flew towards him. Alpha One tried to block the knife, but it hit his suit, making a heavy impact, despite inflicting no damage. They both hit the back wall. Red Viper looked down, trying to see the extent of Alpha One's wounds, but became confused, as he realised Alpha One seemed almost invincible.

Red Viper didn't stick around to ask any questions and immediately tried heading back to the control room, using Alpha One to propel himself forwards. Alpha One gave chase, but as Red Viper passed through the control room, he entered a small capsule docked at the back. On his way through the room, Red Viper plunged a lever down, compromising some of his speed, but setting all the alarms and lights off in the station.

"Self-destruct in T-minus, ten seconds," said the still calm voice through Alpha One's earpiece.

Red Viper climbed into the tiny capsule and began frantically pounding the screen in front of him. The door started sliding downwards, so Alpha One grabbed hold of one of the fixed chairs and used all his strength to push himself forward. He smacked into the door and slipped underneath it, just tucking his legs in as the door sealed shut.

Red Viper spent no time battling Alpha One, as he was solely focussed on trying to strap himself safely in his seat. A spark ignited in the station, setting the whole place alight and turning it into a ball of fire. The capsule was thrown away from the station, as Alpha One was pinned against the door. Debris collided with the capsule, as it created tiny, hairline splits in its surface. Inside the tiny tin can, they started spinning uncontrollably as they hurtled towards Earth. Through the small window in front of Alpha One, all he could see was the Earth and the burning debris, flicking by as if looking at a flipbook that had two colliding stories.

The damaged window began cracking under the immense pressure and heat, as they entered the atmosphere. Alpha One watched, helplessly, as the cracks began getting bigger and bigger. Red Viper stretched over to grab a parachute, knocking the others off their hooks in the process. As the three extra parachutes began rattling around the capsule, Alpha One was able to grab one, clutching it tightly in his arms. A few seconds later, the window gave way, the glass being torn out. The rest of the capsule began melting and buckling, as they travelled through the atmosphere, looking like meteorites crashing to Earth. They were both pulled into the open, as the capsule was turned to scrap metal. Some of the station's debris was also falling to Earth, whilst Alpha One was desperately trying to avoid it all.

Alpha One's suit protected him from the heat, but Red Viper didn't have such protection. As soon as he was torn from the protection of the capsule, his body was erased in a tiny orange flash as just an ownerless parachute was left. Alpha One continued spinning, trying to slip the parachute on whilst avoiding the falling station. Once the parachute was securely on, he attempted to stop spinning, knowing that if he pulled his chute he'd only get tangled up in it. He was making tiny hand, leg, and even head adjustments, all making a huge difference, as he eventually got back in control. His mask had started melting and had become scorched with the heat, making it even tougher to see through. The only thing that could be made out was the blue below him. It was almost as if he was facing the sky, but Alpha One knew he wasn't. Taking no chances, he ripped the cord out and released his parachute.

It yanked him back, feeling as if it had tried to rip him in half. Alpha One had dangled in the sky for less than a minute, as he felt his suit deflate. Taking no time to doubt himself, Alpha One ripped the mask off and could again see. He was a lot closer to the ground than he'd first thought, and it appeared the debris had either already landed on the surface or had completely burnt up in the atmosphere. Alpha One could see a submarine below and noticed people were stood on top. There was no chance of casually drifting off in the other direction, as they would've seen him. So, Alpha One glided down, pulling hard on its cords, before landing softly on top.

He quickly pulled the parachute in and wrapped it up so it didn't catch the wind and drag him into the sea. Alpha One turned around to see Alpha Four and Bravo One stood in front of him, their mouths wide open, clearly in shock. Their obvious confusion didn't faze Alpha One, who was trying to mask the same emotions they felt.

"I just thought I'd drop by; see how you're doing. Was your operation a success?" asked Alpha One, trying to be casual, as he knew the other two must've been in awe, despite it being a complete coincidence.

"Well... that's the enemy ship," said Alpha Four, pointing to a sinking submarine, a piece of the space station sticking out of the side.

Neither Alpha Four, nor Bravo One were able to take their eyes away from Alpha One. They still couldn't work out what had just happened.

"Should we get back to base? Oh, and I've got a couple of things for you and Suzy to work on and examine, one being a parachute that didn't burn up in the upper atmosphere, it could prove useful," said Alpha One, heading inside their submarine and passing the parachute to Alpha Four, a huge grin plastered across his face.

"One more thing, VOICE has said we've got an emergency mission sanctioned by Bosse. The details are scarce, but they've sent a helicopter to pick me... well... us, up. We should probably tell them you're here as well," said Alpha Four.

"I guess so. I'll do it, I've also got to get Bosse to sanction a mission back to the Swiss compound; recovery and capture," added Alpha One with Emma and the promise he'd made still firmly on his conscience.

Chapter 13 – The Reckoning
February 14th
02:02 GMT

Protected by the sweeping landscape, the Molehill was intertwined within the rolling hills. Inside, Mike and Anthony were the last to arrive. As they disembarked their aircraft, neither were greeted, nor informed where to go. To them, it was obvious there would be a meeting in Bosse's office. As they began to move towards a parked vehicle, to give them a lift, Samuel bellowed from another plane about fifty metres away. The noise he made couldn't be understood by either of them, as they certainly didn't hear any proper words being formed. They continued their path to the pickup truck and climbed on the back. Anthony stayed a couple of steps behind Mike, refusing to turn his back, even as they climbed onto the truck.

"Over to the guy that's waving," said Mike, leaning around the side towards the driver, before thumping his fist on the roof to indicate he'd finished.

"Oi!" shouted Samuel, unaware they'd heard him before.

The noise echoed throughout the Molehill, causing people to turn in all directions, as they tried to work out where the sound came from.

The truck drove past Samuel, slow enough to allow Mike and Anthony to leap off the side, their huge rucksacks weighing them down.

"I wasn't sure if you could hear me," said Samuel, oblivious to how far his voice carried.

"We heard you," said Mike, showing a false smile to hide the 'you stupid fool' which he wanted to add at the end of his sentence.

"Everyone's inside, we've got wheels up in ten minutes. Hopefully we'll actually be told what's going on now you're here," concluded Samuel, as he turned his back on Mike and walked into the plane.

Anthony again held back a few paces, ensuring he was behind Mike as they entered. The plane they entered was bigger than their modified C-17 and looked a lot more commercial in style. It was on four floors and had hundreds of fake windows down both sides. Whilst it had no firepower, it could travel to most places as just an ordinary commercial flight, but with the added benefit of it looking like a fortress inside and being able to fly around the world once without refuelling. They climbed up to the top floor and went through to the largest room. There was a table inside with the rest of Alpha team all stood around it. They each took a seat with VOICE stood in the corner. About five minutes later, the plane started moving. It was hard to notice, but as the floor began to lightly rumble, Scott felt its movement, placing his hand on the floor to check.

Moments later, Bosse strode in, closing the door. He walked around to the other side of the table without making eye contact with any of them.

He remained standing, leant forward and said, "I can't honestly say any of your ops were a success, can I? There have been reports of bodies turning up within a ten-mile radius of the airfield. Who knows who's going to get a hold of our technologically advanced bullets. The submarine was meant to be recovered but is now lying at the bottom of the ocean, surrounded by deep-sea divers, treasure hunters and conspiracists. And as for the satellite… well… congratulations, you've made headline news!"

Bosse rarely shouted, but throughout his admonishment,

he was as loud as his husky voice would allow. Mike then looked around the room and began to perk up.

"But my mission was a success. Does that mean I was the only one who did good?" asked Mike.

Bosse then picked up a piece a paper and began nodding, saying, "Your mission was a success; you killed The Vesper…" He then slapped the paper on the table in front of Mike, ensuring his hand made as much noise as possible. "…But you certainly didn't do 'good'," Bosse concluded, his right nostril twitching.

Mike leant forward and read what was on top. There was an image of Mike, dressed in his suit, playing the part of Gemini. His face was fully visible.

"This image is now everywhere. This image can now be seen by everyone. Last month, our presence was unknown because nobody knew to even look for us. How hidden do you think we are now?" asked Bosse, as his eyes moved across each member of Alpha team.

Scott had sat and listened to everything Bosse had said, whilst closely looking at every gesture he made. From what Scott could tell, Bosse showed strong signs of anger. Scott knew how much the organisation meant to Bosse, because he felt the same. But Scott had no intention of letting Bosse lay the blame at the wrong feet.

He stood up, his eyes fixed on Bosse's and said, "We are not the ones to blame. The submarine blew up because the satellite struck it, that's hardly Kenny's fault. The guards at the airfield were blown away because of a storm that none of us could've seen coming, so is hardly Sam's fault. And the satellite blew up because OUR enemy got to it first. So, before you come in here blaming us for everything, because it's convenient, I want you to look in the mirror and ask yourself, 'What did I do to help?', 'Could I have done more?', and 'What can I do better next time?', because having a next time is nothing to take for granted."

Scott finished his defence, but their eyes stayed locked together for the next few moments, before Bosse eventually broke his gaze and turned to VOICE.

"Fortunately, we have one remaining chance of finding whoever is responsible," said Bosse, as he handed over to VOICE.

"Thank you, sir. We are currently on our way to a private estate which, at present, is occupied by Heartfell and his family. He approached us, well, Bosse, with a suggestion. Heartfell will make his presence known to the organisation he used to be a part of. They are apparently still hunting him, so will send plenty of people to kill him. We will be there to protect him, and when they are unsuccessful, they will start up some natural disaster which I can obviously trace back to its origin now I know the signal I am looking for. Of course, I was unable to do that before, because they had been bouncing the signal off the satellite rendering their true location a secret, obviously," said VOICE, constantly turning to Bosse throughout.

"Obviously," mumbled Samuel.

Bosse then moved back to his central spot, shifting VOICE to the side.

"I know you don't trust Heartfell, but this will give you an opportunity to meet him. This is the only way that he can earn your trust, so please, just give him a chance," said Bosse, changing his voice from aggressive to being almost compassionate.

Bosse looked straight at Scott, asking for his approval. Despite Scott having little say, due to the plane already being en route, he gave a slight nod to show his approval, giving Heartfell a chance to prove his loyalty. Scott was certainly apprehensive about meeting Heartfell, especially as Diana hadn't found anything on him, and likely wouldn't for a while, but figured finding out whether Heartfell was trustworthy for himself was probably for the best, although Scott still had every intention of letting Diana conclude her investigation into Heartfell and his relation to Bosse. Bosse was pleased he had Scott on his side again, but the earlier disagreement had started to put him back in his place.

"Didn't taking down the satellite stop them from controlling the weather?" asked Kenny, as he tried to prevent another staring contest.

VOICE went to take the central spot but, as Bosse remained there, VOICE sat back down and answered, "No, the satellite acted as a receiver. It was almost something to boost the signal, which originated from elsewhere. It was kind of like a wizard using their wand to channel their power, rather than create it. The original signal likely comes from just one place and, without the satellite to mask its location, as I said earlier, as well as boost its signal, we should be able to pinpoint a location the next time it is used."

There was a lot of nodding throughout the room, where they hung onto the one word that actually answered Kenny's question.

"So... no, then. That's all you had to say, was... 'No'," added Samuel.

"We'll be arriving at about 1900 hours local time, so it'll be dark. We'll stay until they use their weapon. As soon as that happens, VOICE should get a lock on the location and we can move out, taking Heartfell and his family to an undisclosed location. This flight will be around nine hours, so if there are no questions, now would be a good time to get some rest. And before I forget, our research into the hooded figure you saw at the nightclub returned no results, as expected," concluded Bosse, hoping there wouldn't be any questions, as he gathered his paperwork and started heading for the door.

"I've got a question..." started Anthony. "Who was Gemini?"

Bosse stopped dead in his tracks, and Mike looked up from the piece of paper he had been studying the entire time.

"Just drop it," said Mike.

The rest of room were looking at the three who clearly knew more than the rest, and it was Bosse who decided to stay unnaturally quiet.

Anthony pressed on, saying, "No. That Aqua person knew who you were, and you knew her. I saw something in your eyes when you left The Vesper's villa, you..."

"Just drop it!" barked Mike.

At this point, Scott stepped in, knowing it certainly couldn't be dropped.

"Mike, tell us who Gemini was," he said, adopting a calm voice to try and counter Anthony's forceful approach.

Mike took in a huge breath of air and slowly released it. He gave a quick glance towards Bosse, who remained silent, before addressing the others.

"Well... My father, my birth father, was a hitman... or contract killer... or assassin, or whatever name you want to give. Or if you want to be precise, a hitman, as he was a member of TOOTH. And he brought me up to follow in his footsteps. From birth... I... I was taught to kill. Years later, I assumed the alias of 'Gemini' upon completing my first contract. When my father died, I became the target of all his enemies, and I devised a plan to escape which involved placing a contract on my own head and letting everyone think I was dead," said Mike, his head lowered allowing him to not make direct eye contact with anyone.

Nobody said a word, they were all listening intently, except for Bosse, who seemed to hear nothing new.

"How come I never heard this when we got everyone to join up, Bosse?" asked Scott, ensuring he couldn't casually slip out of the room.

Bosse had already been thinking of an answer, perhaps since they'd first started the organisation, as without hesitation he answered, "When we formed the organisation, I gave you a range of candidates to select from. I also gave you the details surrounding their lives. I knew Mike was concerned that you would think badly of him, so I decided to agree to keep it hidden. I am sorry if I've caused any… friction, but I did what I thought was best…" He then gave a slight pause, as he went to leave the room. Before the doors closed, Bosse turned to face back into the room and concluded, "We all make mistakes," before allowing the doors to close, leaving them alone in the room.

VOICE had also started casually heading for the door and disappeared quickly to get out of the frosty atmosphere.

"It's not fair on any of us to prolong this conversation. I know you're all tired, but I think we can agree this matter takes precedence, okay?" said Scott.

They all agreed without moving or speaking, as it was more a case of them only speaking when in disagreement.

"What Bosse didn't tell you was that he knew my father. Whilst I had no clue who he was until after my father's death, Bosse told me that he owed him a debt he could not repay. Computers were always my passion, certainly more than what I was forced into. So, when Bosse found me, I took advantage of the debt and asked him to keep it a secret from you," said Mike, his words clear and his voice meaningful.

"How did you know… Aqua?" asked Scott, still keen to find out everything.

"Well, I was the one who recruited her into TOOTH. She used to work in a bar, but my father saw something in her and sent me to… subtly, recruit her. As far as I know, she had no idea it was me who recruited her, but my reputation certainly did travel in front of me. And before you ask… My father was killed… with a knife… plunged deep into his heart," replied Mike, ashamed of what he was saying, yet with no signs of sadness.

Scott knew he had to ignore his feelings, it would be the team's choice and that was especially important with Daniel's absence.

Kenny was the first to speak, saying, "Over the past few years, I've had to trust you with my life… and I… I know it's... a quick judgement, but I'd still be willing to trust you. I've heard nothing to say otherwise."

Samuel began frowning in Kenny's direction. It looked like he was disappointed with Kenny's comment, but the truth was that he was disappointed he couldn't bring himself to say the same.

Anthony then looked at Mike and said, "I've also come to trust Mike over our time together, and I also don't see anything to change that. But... I don't know Gemini; I don't trust Gemini. So, which are you... Mike or Gemini?"

Mike then looked at Anthony, fixed eye contact, and said, "No matter what you heard at The Vesper's villa, and no matter what you saw at The Vesper's villa... Gemini is dead."

Mike didn't break eye contact, and there were no signs of him telling a lie, so with reservations pushed to the back of his mind, Anthony looked at Scott and nodded once, showing his approval.

The room then turned to Samuel.

He didn't waste any time in giving his verdict as he said, "I'm not as forgiving as these two. I don't take kindly to people lying to my face... But... I am willing to go with the majority. But just to make this clear, I don't trust you and I'm only going with the majority because I believe everyone should get a second chance. So, don't mess this one up, second chances only come around once."

Samuel had also taken to looking deeply into Mike's eyes, but instead of trying to find another lie, Samuel was making it a threat.

With the decision clear to Scott, he retook control of the conversation, saying, "I think our position is clear. You'll need to earn our trust again, but yes, that'll be done like the first time around, by earning our trust in the field. Now, all of you get some rest, we might have a long op ahead of us."

Scott then left the room, cementing his final say, as he took his own advice and got some rest.

Chapter 13.2

At precisely 1900 hours, their plane touched down at the nearest airport to their destination. The plane crept to the far end of the runway and began bounding across the rough and unused ground leading to an empty square of concrete. Once they had come to a complete stop, all five of the team left the plane and climbed into two identical 4x4s parked nearby. Alpha One got into the front, with Alpha Six in the back, whilst the others all entered the second car. Their drivers were local residents with ties to their own organisation, and after a little persuasion, they were only too happy to accept the 'donation' they received. Both drivers wore long-sleeved tops, despite the high temperatures, as well as plastic gloves so no DNA could be left in the cars, just in case something went sideways. They also wore baseball caps, which were pulled down, had scarves to pull up over their mouths and sunglasses to put on if necessary. It was clear they wanted to remain anonymous, no matter what happened. As they drove through the cities and towns, the streets were packed and the roads were dense with cars, bikes, and pedestrians all jostling for position. It took almost another hour to get through and finally arrive at their destination, which turned out to be an old embassy building that had been redesigned for residential use but with most of the security defences still in place.

The cars stopped outside the twelve-foot, imposing front gates, and they were allowed entry on foot after just a few security checks completed by a single guard. The guard seemed to be expecting them but didn't look ready for danger. He looked more like a bodyguard, rather than a security officer with his bald head, black beard, and big build. He was around 6'2" and had a straight expression that gave no sense of messing around. His black suit and contrasting bright, red tie seemed clean and well kept. The two cars drove off around the corner, where they could sit and wait out of sight and danger. The guard led them along a gravel path, separating two huge patches of grass, which finished at a dark wooden front door. The building itself was full of windows, which covered most of the walls. Alpha One immediately noted them and knew that it would make his job harder, despite the likelihood of them being ballistic glass. He knew that if the enemy could get a clear sightline, they would have a much more coordinated attack, because that's exactly what he would do. On the front patch of grass, there was also a small building unconnected to the embassy building. Alpha One couldn't work out its use, but he did notice it was well protected with reinforced walls. Inside, the embassy building had huge, great ceilings, with crystal chandeliers dangling above the glossy, oak flooring.

The guard led them through the front door and quickly directed them along one of the many hallways and into a room at the front. The room was full of books. Each of the four walls had shelves stacked to the top of the ceiling with books, all different sizes and all jumbled up. Alpha One couldn't see any pattern to the order but knew that even disorder had some sort of rhythm. He didn't concern himself, as his eyes fixed on the gentleman sat at the table pushed over to one side. His head was buried in a book, which he could only tear his eyes away from once the page had been finished. He picked up a narrow, but long, piece of paper, placed it in the book and carefully placed the book on the table. The man lifted his head and observed the team stood in front of him. He was dressed in a pale T-shirt and blue jeans which could just be seen under the table. His hair was short and brown, yet also extremely thick and had a bird's nest look to it. His face was round and his teeth were twisted, despite their bright white glare. He had green eyes and the early stages of facial hair with short, fluffy hair around his chin, helping Alpha One to put Heartfell in his early to mid twenties. His young appearance did surprise him, as he was expecting someone a little older, given the connections he seemed to have.

"I'm glad you could make it," said the man.

"I assume you're Heartfell," said Alpha One.

The man nodded and replied, "There is no need to assume, though, all you have to do is ask."

"Point taken... Er... well... nice to meet you," said Alpha One, quickly realising that conversations might be a little difficult to start.

"I don't like it when people hesitate," said Heartfell, looking straight at Alpha One.

"Oh dear... Should I go?" replied Alpha One, even less certain he would get the answers he desired.

The room hardly erupted with laughter, there was just some sniggering behind and a blank expression in front. Alpha One knew the signal to Heartfell's former organisation had already been sent, so didn't want to waste any more time.

"Where are the rest of your family?" asked Alpha One.

"I sent them somewhere safe, along with most of my security to protect them," answered Heartfell.

"Great..." mumbled Alpha One, expecting to have a squad of security to help him secure the embassy building. He looked around the room, thinking, before continuing, "Exactly how many guards are left?"

"There are six, which should be more than enough for a warrior of your repertoire. Two are securing the car park downstairs, one is in the operations building outside which you passed on your way in. There is access to it both above ground and through a secret tunnel underground. Two are patrolling the building, and the final guard is behind you," said Heartfell.

Alpha One released a long sigh, whilst he formed a plan. He didn't have much to go on but knew they would only have to hold the building for so long, he just didn't know how long.

Alpha One then turned to look at his team, saying, "Okay, Alpha Five, I want you in that operations room, it gives the easiest access to the embassy building and makes for the most likely place they'll attack. Alpha Three, I want you to join him…"

Before Alpha One could continue, Alpha Three gave a look that instantly said he wasn't comfortable with the arrangements.

Without making too much of a fuss, Alpha One continued, saying, "Actually, Alpha Three, I think I'd rather you went to secure our exfil, it makes more sense. Once there, set a few of your small charges, enough to prevent the enemy from following us should we need it…" He then turned back to face Heartfell and asked, "Are there any other secret passages, and is there a safe room?"

"Yes, and yes. The safe room can be accessed through a passage from this room, and this room only, and the only other passage is the one that leads to the operations building," answered Heartfell, as he moved around his desk and pulled one book out from the shelf.

He was about 5'10" and walked with a straight back and good posture.

Alpha One then looked back at his team and said, "Okay, Alpha Three, head to the car park, that's the second place they'll try and assault. Alpha Four, plant the traps, then get to Alpha Five's position. And Blindspot, I obviously want you on the top floor, you can give us an early warning of their arrival. I'll patrol the building as soon as Heartfell is in the safe room, and the security can stay doing what they're doing. Alright, that's everything, so let's get to it."

After Heartfell pulled one book out from the shelf, he slid the following seven books to the left, to fill the vacant places. Alpha One ensured he observed everything, even the potential of any sleight of hand. Heartfell then placed the book he had just removed in the one space that was left and pushed it to the back. With a couple of clicks and what sounded like a cog turning, sixteen planks of wood all lifted from the floor. Because they were all staggered, it was difficult to see there was a seam between the floor and the hidden door. Heartfell reverted the books to their original places and went down the steps the hatch revealed, closely followed by the one remaining security guard and Alpha One.

A little way down, they entered a tight tunnel, still with bare wooden structures holding back the visible mud and stone. At some points, the tunnel was so narrow they had to turn sideways to squeeze through. Eventually, they reached a steel door at the end, and after Heartfell pressed a few buttons, they were inside. It wasn't so much a safe room, but instead felt more like a safe house. It was similar in style to the one found at Mr Wilson's complex, just a lot bigger. They sat down at the table which was positioned in the centre of the room. Before Alpha One started to ask any questions, he couldn't help but notice the number of books in the safe room. Filling an entire twenty-metre wall was a bookcase full of books, again looking out of order. Although Alpha One had only seen a fraction of the rooms, it seemed clear that Heartfell valued books above most other things.

They both sat opposite each other, aware of the questions that would be coming next.

Heartfell didn't wait for the first question, as he immediately opened up, saying, "The organisation I worked for a year ago is called 'Fellscient'. Now, don't ask me where the name came from because it's been around for hundreds of years. In fact, the first recorded use of the word was back in 1665. And as for my involvement, well,

I was part of a team who created a machine that could control the weather. Its original use was to prevent weather disasters, not create them. But when Fellscient took over, its purpose was altered. The four tests couldn't have been avoided; in fact, it was after the first test that the machine's true purpose was revealed. You've got to believe me when I say all I ever wanted was to make the difference, and I never even considered the machine being used in this way. Now, before I left, I knew there was no way I could stop it; they would just get someone else to fix it if required and controlling it is pretty simple. But I did ensure it was built with just one error. If you plug this stick into the machine, it'll cripple it with a rather explosive outcome."

Heartfell then slid a small memory stick across the table which had just been taken from inside a draw underneath the table.

Alpha One held the device in his hand and stared at it, before turning back to Heartfell and asking, "What does it do?"

"In simple terms, it acts as a virus, except this is the kind of virus you can't recover from. It will attack the machine's nervous system and disable its security measures, allowing for the virus' final blow to destroy it from the inside, which is the machine's only weak spot. For them to continue using the machine, they would have to rebuild it from scratch, and I'm the only living person with the know-how to do that," answered Heartfell.

Alpha One knew to not interrupt Heartfell whilst he was talking, even if the information was of no use, because the flow of the conversation would yield more information than the irregularity of constantly asking questions. Heartfell could become reluctant to provide any more information than just the answers, and Alpha One couldn't be sure he had all the questions.

"Do you know who runs Fellscient?" asked Alpha One,

aware the time for their initial questions would be almost over, as the conversation started to dry up.

Heartfell lowered his head and said, "I'm sorry, but I was never told who was in charge. I do, however, know who runs this weather operation. Operation Storm, I think. He goes by the name, Crabble. He's overseen all the designing, building, and testing."

Alpha One gave a couple of small head nods, pleased he had a more concrete lead after the second time he'd heard this name, despite being unable to find anything on him.

"Why did you order The Vesper to be killed?" asked Alpha One directly.

Heartfell was taken a little by surprise, as he began to hesitate.

"Er… well… The Vesper was… er… well… when I left Fellscient… The Vesper was the one who was tasked with tracking me down… and… he found me. Although I got away, my only daughter didn't… and… well that's it really, I think that's good enough reason, isn't it?" answered Heartfell, ending the conversation abruptly.

At that moment, Alpha One's CAT started flashing. There was an orange light that was blinking on the screen. He immediately knew it was time to head back out of the safe room.

Alpha One stood up and began to move to the door, saying, "I'm afraid we'll have to cut our conversation short; I'm needed upstairs."

As Alpha One got to the door, he looked down to the floor and thought of one last thing he wanted to go out of the room with an answer for.

He looked back at Heartfell and asked, "What do you know of M.N.G.W.A.?"

Heartfell looked visibly confused, as his brows furrowed.

"Sorry, but again, nobody told me about another organisation. You've already been told I was someone who worked on the machine and nothing else," answered Heartfell, before going completely silent and picking up the closest book to him.

Alpha One left the room, closing the door. As he made his way back to the unhidden part of the embassy building, he thought about how he'd never mentioned M.N.G.W.A. was another organisation, yet Heartfell seemed to know it.

Once back upstairs, Alpha One immediately got in contact with his team.

"I'm back, what's happened?" he asked.

"There's an extremely high presence of firepower out front, currently sat in a few trucks. The civilians are nowhere to be seen, and the vehicles are all identical. There are four trucks, just like the ones we saw on the beach," answered Alpha Five.

"Okay, the most likely entrance point is still the front gates; they could easily ram them with those trucks. We've got to stop them before they get to the front door. If the embassy building is breached, we may lose our advantage. Is there anything else to report?" asked Alpha One.

"Car park's clear... well, the giant garage," said Alpha Three.

"All I can see from up here are the four trucks," said Alpha Six.

"From the operations room, we can also only see the four trucks," said Alpha Four.

"Good, let's stick with the plan. Let them make the first move," said Alpha One, as he started his patrol of the embassy building. "Oh, and one last thing, Kenny, you can tell Suzy that our CAT works where our comms don't, so if we can get our comms to work the same, that would be great," said Alpha One, as he began moving through the wide hallways.

There was only silence over the radio, which Alpha One observed for almost a minute.

He did start to wonder whether maybe he hadn't said anything, as he said, "Hello?"

With still no reply, he lifted his right arm and began tapping the screen. Within a few seconds, Alpha One had tested their communication devices and had found them to be disabled. Usually, their devices would be blocked by a nearby jammer which their earpieces could detect and would give a slight buzz to alert them. Somehow, their earpieces had been completely disabled, as if an EMP had disabled just those devices or they had run out of power. It was nothing Alpha One had experienced before but began to try and find a way to contact the rest of his team. Using his CAT again, he sent a short message, saying *'comms out'*, and had to hope it would get through, just as it could get through a reinforced wall. The message had to be brief and sent quickly; nothing else would be useful, as they all knew an attack would be imminent. At least, that's what he thought.

Chapter 13.3

Another three hours went by with still no assault. It was clear their tactic was not aligned with what Alpha One would plan, which concerned him for the rest of the strategy. Alpha One had more than enough time to visit each member of his team, confirming they did know their comms were down. Despite their enemy not following what Alpha One would do, he could still predict their most likely next steps. Due to the long wait, he assumed they were putting Alpha team on edge, trying to tire them and force them into a false sense of security. But four hours and twelve minutes in, the power went down. It took only a few seconds for the backup generator to kick in, but because of the vast energy usage of the safe room, the generator couldn't supply much power elsewhere. At the time, Alpha One was in the operations room. The cameras flickered, as Heartfell's security guard in the operations room started selecting where the backup generator's energy would go.

The guard said, "Our system allows us to select where to input the energy from the backup generator, allowing us to divert energy to and from different sources depending on where we need them most. It's rather like a game…" He looked back at Alpha One after a slight laugh, before swiftly clearing his throat and straightening his face, seeing that Alpha One was not seeing it as a game. "Where would you like the energy to go?" continued the guard, directing his question to Alpha One.

"Alpha Four, you're in charge of the operations room, it's up to you," said Alpha One.

He knew Alpha Four could be trusted, so he went to move back down the hatch, which led to the embassy building underground. As he lifted it, to start climbing down, there was a knock on their door.

As he moved back into the operations room, they all shared uneasy glances. The security cameras were still flickering on and off, but were becoming stable, one by one. However, they were blind to what was outside. Alpha One noticed the door wasn't reinforced after all, nor the rest of the building, it was just meant to look reinforced to deter attacks. Alpha One kept his rifle strapped to his back whilst drawing his sidearm, before moving towards the door. He ripped off a piece of card that was on the noticeboard next to him. As Alpha One moved to the door, he made his footsteps loud.

He held the piece of card to the small peephole in the door and stood to the hinged side of it, shouting, "Who is it?"

From the outside, it was clear when someone, or something, stood in front of the peephole because the light from it suddenly disappeared. A second later, a bullet punched its way through the card, flying straight into the wall behind. The door was immediately kicked in, swinging towards Alpha One. He softened the swing to a complete stop, before kicking it back closed. The door slammed back, pinning someone's arm in the process. They released their gun, poking through the doorway, before shrieking in pain, as they tried to free their arm from the door's grasp. Alpha One opened it again and fired one bullet straight at the masked assailant. They fell to the floor, their black mask covered in a slimy, green gel. Straight after, two more assailants came from either side of the door, one grabbing Alpha One's handgun. As his gun was pushed down to face the floor, Alpha One grabbed the first assailant. His hand felt around the assailant's tactical vest, as he wrapped his hand around a knife. Alpha One instantly tore it from its holder and dug it into the assailant's shoulder, causing him to free his grip on the gun. He raised his handgun and fired at the oncoming assailant, placing one bullet in the centre of their head, before returning to the other, who was drawing the knife from their shoulder, and shooting them in the same place. Alpha One looked up to see more armed and masked assailants moving towards the operations room, but as he switched back to his rifle, they each began dropping to the floor, one by one, before running back to dive into cover. Alpha One held his hand up, giving thanks to Blindspot who was clearly watching over him. As Alpha One moved back into the operations room, Alpha Five quickly barred the door, sliding all the locks, bolts, and steel bars across it.

Alpha One could see Alpha Four still working on diverting power to different areas of the embassy compound, so went back down the hatch, telling Alpha Five, "Ensure this building remains secure. We won't be able to talk, but you both know how we all work," before closing the hatch and charging back to the embassy building, underground and out of sight.

Alpha One moved as quickly as he could back to the front door, but as he got there, more assailants had already started to breach it. Through the many windows, he could see a group of almost twenty move away from the door and into cover, making it likely the door was about to be blown in. Without taking any risks, Alpha One took cover behind one of the many pillars in the hall, crouching down to stay out of sight of the windows. Two of Heartfell's guards moved towards the front door, but before Alpha One could warn them, there was a huge *bang*, as the giant doors were propelled inwards. One of the guards was hit by a door, as it rammed him into the wall behind. The other guard was thrown to the floor, but before Alpha One could even move in, the guard was swiftly gunned down, as he ended up lying in his own blood. Floods of assailants came flowing through the door who quickly caught sight of Alpha One. He fired his rifle at the hordes that were still entering, trying to spare no more than one bullet per target, knowing his precious thirty-round magazine had to be stretched out.

He counted the bullets down until he was completely out. Alpha One knew he wouldn't have enough time to reload before even more came in, and so did Alpha Four. As soon as Alpha One moved into cover, the chandelier illuminating the entrance exploded, sending tiny shards of glass in all directions. Alpha One wasted no time in reloading, as he began crawling towards the open doorway, ensuring he still couldn't be seen from outside. Continuing towards the door, the metal frame of the chandelier dropped from the ceiling. And as the cable, still tethering it, tightened, the metal frame swung towards the doorway. It clattered into the next wave of unsuspecting assailants, sending them crashing back down onto the grass behind. Alpha One looked towards the closest camera and held his outstretched, left palm up. He then thumped his right hand, which was also outstretched, on top, perpendicular to his left, almost as if he was giving his hand a karate chop, making the movement clearly visible to the camera. Within a couple of seconds, the shutters all began to fall, and Alpha One climbed to his feet, his rifle leading the way along the hall.

Within moments, the shutters were all down at the front of the building. Alpha One knew that putting them down might force the assailants to breach elsewhere so wanted them raised as quickly as possible, allowing him to control the influx. As Alpha One got to the entrance, he quickly checked the pulse of the security guard with numerous bullet wounds, confirming he was dead, before lifting the heavy door from the other guard. He was still conscious, as he was coughing and spluttering, gasping for air through the thick cloud of dust and smoke. Alpha One wasted no time in dragging the guard to his feet and helping him to the library room. He then dumped the guard in the closest chair and checked him for any critical injuries. With none visible, Alpha One again held his hands to the nearest camera and made the same movement as before, but this time in reverse, indicating for the shutters to be opened.

By the time he got out of the room, the shutters were already being opened. Alpha One crouched down below the window and took aim at the, now open, doorway. As more assailants came through, Alpha One dropped them as quickly as he could, but after another magazine had been emptied, he again had to ask for the shutters to be lowered. The huge, silver shutters slammed closed, separating the outside from the inside. This time, however, Alpha One circled his finger in the air, indicating he wanted them to regroup. Finishing the movement off with a quick flick towards the library room, he made the location they would meet clear. Still with cover from the shutters, Alpha One began charging down the other side of the hall, making his way down the steps he eventually reached. The steps went down a few metres, before opening into the car park. One of Heartfell's guards was slumped over the bonnet of a car, whilst the other was crunched up in the corner, using a different car for cover, as he held his head in his hands. Alpha Three had his rifle resting on the bonnet of the closest car, picking off anyone in the open.

Alpha One also began firing at the masked assailants, ensuring they were all suppressed, whilst he shouted, "We're falling back to position two!"

Alpha Three didn't take his eyes off the enemy, nor did he stop firing, but instead slowly rose to his feet and edged his way back to the stairs. Alpha One was beckoning to Heartfell's guard, trying to get him out of the room as quickly as possible, whilst he flung the dead guard over his left shoulder. As soon as Alpha Three got to the stairs, he began providing cover fire for Alpha One, who leant forward and grabbed the guard, dragging him around the corner and up the stairs. Alpha Three sealed the door behind them, knowing it would do nothing more than buy them a few crucial seconds. As they continued up, Alpha Three then detonated the charges he'd laid earlier. There was a small rumble, as the charges exploded, buying them a little more time to return to the library room.

Alpha One, with his hand still on the guard's shoulder, directed him to the library room. As they passed the guard, still lying in the entrance, Alpha One pointed to his corpse, standing out from the masked bodies he laid with. Alpha Three picked him up and carried him the final part, until they were all in the library room. Alpha Four and Heartfell's operation's room guard were already inside.

"Alpha Five's getting Blindspot," said Alpha Four, whilst looking at his CAT, which he had synced to the operations room.

One of Heartfell's guards started thumping the spines of different books, pushing each book about a finger's width behind the rest. Alpha One watched as he pounded every single one, remembering the order. After ten books had been pushed in, they all sprang back to their original place, before the whole section of the bookshelf began sliding out. Once it sat proud of the other bookshelves, it then started sliding to the left, revealing what was behind. There was a huge suit of armour pinned up on the wall, standing next to two thick sheets of metal and a Minigun.

"This should help," said the guard, as he backed away, making it clear he wasn't getting into the suit. Alpha Three looked at the suit, before turning to face Alpha One. He didn't say anything, as he didn't need to, Alpha Three's face did all the begging and pleading with his eyes larger than usual and his eyebrows pointing up in the middle.

Alpha One didn't reject his wish, as he said, "Fine," before he turned back to Alpha Four.

"They've breached the embassy building through the car park," said Alpha Four, who was still watching the cameras intently, waiting to activate more of his traps.

Alpha One didn't waste any time, as he checked he had a bullet in the chamber and left the room.

He crouched down beside the door, allowing him to quickly move into cover should he need to. As the assailants left the stairs and rounded the corner, Alpha One opened fire. He knew there would be too many to take out, so he worked on just suppressing them whilst waiting for Alpha Five and Blindspot to return to the library room. Firing a single bullet at a time, he continued to hit the furthest wall, ensuring he hit high and low points in a random pattern. Without being able to predict where the next bullet was going to end up, the assailants cowered behind the wall. Alpha One also ensured he didn't evenly space out the time between each shot, making sure they couldn't know when he was reloading. Within the next two minutes, only a couple of assailants ventured around the corner, but none of them returned. Alpha Five eventually came down the central, sweeping staircase with Blindspot just behind. Alpha One gave a slight break in his firing, allowing them both past. From his right, he could see sparks from the shutters at the front doorway.

Just as they were about to enter the library room, he said, "Alpha Five, you stay with me. Blindspot, tell Alpha Three to hurry up, they're cutting their way through the shutters."

Although Alpha One couldn't see, Blindspot nodded as he entered the room, whilst Alpha Five crouched down below the sealed windows.

They took it in turns, firing single bullets down the hall, trying to buy Alpha Three as much time as possible.

"Why did we fall back to the one place we don't want them to go?" asked Alpha Five, whilst waiting for his turn to fire his rifle.

"Well, my original plan was to draw them up to the top floor, because they'd never find a way inside the safe room…" started Alpha One, before taking his turn to fire his rifle. Once he'd emptied the next ten rounds, he was again able to concentrate on their conversation, continuing, "But they haven't exactly followed my plan so far, so I thought I'd switch things up a little. Plus, at least we can fall back inside the safe room… just in case." They continued to fire down the vast length of the hall, preventing anyone from making an advance, but as he watched them cut through more and more of the shutter on his right, Alpha One opened the library door and shouted, "Alpha Three, hurry up! They're almost through!"

Moments later, a cut-out section of the shutter fell to the floor. At first, nobody came through, so Alpha Five took the opportunity to get into the library room, whilst Alpha One covered him. Then, both the assailants from outside and the ones at the far end of the hall all flooded into the embassy building, simultaneously. Alpha One swung inside the room and allowed Alpha Five to bolt the door closed, before it was shrouded in bullets.

Alpha One looked up to see the final pieces of armour being placed onto an already hidden Alpha Three.

"Alpha Four, do what you can to slow them down," said Alpha One, knowing they hadn't bought enough time.

Alpha Four began touching the screen of his CAT, as he said, "A taste of their own medicine. I've placed small electro-pads on the wall, evenly spaced apart. They should provide an electrical charge between them and the metal shutters, electrifying everything… or rather, everyone, in between. It is a small charge, so it definitely won't kill them; it'll probably just slow them down… hopefully."

As he activated them, they gave off a noise which sounded more like Tesla coils along with the constant cries of pain as they tried to make their way through.

"Okay, I... am... ready," said a muffled Alpha Three.

He stomped over to the door, holding the Minigun, with two giant metal sheets strapped to his arms, which could be used as shields, just in case extra protection was needed. The armour was made up of two main layers, the armour itself and an exoskeleton under it. The exoskeleton was able to grant the wearer the extra strength needed to carry the vast weight of the armour and move in it. It also gave a little extra strength, enabling the wearer to move objects slightly heavier than they could before. He got to the door, as everyone else all moved to the wall that would be behind the door, ensuring they would be out of the line of fire.

"Any chance of some smoke?" asked Alpha Three, unable to turn to look at Alpha Four.

Alpha Four smiled, as he powered down the electro-pads which hadn't already been shot, and detonated several smoke bombs which he'd placed on the ceiling. Alpha Three opened the door, to see nothing except a thick wall of white smoke. He lumbered through and witnessed the few assailants that could see him stop in their tracks. Alpha One swiftly closed the door, bolting it shut again, until Alpha Three had pushed them outside.

Alpha Three stood in the hall, towering above everyone, with an imposing stance inside an already imposing suit of armour. The assailants began to slowly edge backwards, as if they didn't want an animal to catch sight of them. Then, Alpha Three lowered his Minigun and clipped it onto his suit. He raised both arms, to hold the shields in front, and began charging forward. Those who weren't close enough to see him could only hear the thundering footsteps become louder, before he emerged from the thick fog. The assailants quickly dispersed, as they rushed back out of the building. Some decided to stand their ground and attack the oncoming force. They fired countless bullets, most of them ricocheted off the shields and some dropped from the padded suit. As Alpha Three got close to someone, he swung his shield at them, sending them crashing into the wall behind. As the number of bullets hitting Alpha Three got less and less, he lowered one of the shields. There was an assailant stood to his right, frantically trying to reload. Alpha Three grabbed his throat, with one of his huge hands, and lifted him off the ground. The assailant began screaming, as he was lifted to face the monster that had caught him. The assailant continued to scream and shout, as he tried prising the monster's fingers apart, whilst Alpha Three started walking to the front door. The rest of the hall had now cleared out, so they could gain an advantage for when he stepped outside. Alpha Three stood in the doorway, watching as his enemy set up several machinegun nests. He threw the assailant several metres back on the hard ground, unthreatened by his enemy's presence. The screaming assailant instantly climbed to his feet and ran towards safety. Alpha Three's suit had a built-in microphone and speaker, so when he spoke, his voice was twenty times louder.

"Leave and you will live! Stay and your safety is not guaranteed..." started Alpha Three, before lifting his Minigun and concluding, "These rounds are real! You have been warned."

Then, without warning, the entire courtyard lit up, firing huge rounds of ammunition from six separate machine guns.

They were all protected by metal barriers that were quick to erect, but that also meant they wouldn't be as strong as more conventional methods. Alpha Three raised one of his shields, whilst he spooled his Minigun up. He then raised the Minigun and released a spray of bullets across the courtyard. The gun spat out hundreds of rounds within seconds, so he knew he wouldn't have much time to take out all the machineguns. Alpha Three lined up his target and shredded the cover they cowered behind, ripping each machinegun apart and leaving nothing whole. The rounds weren't accurate, but as hundreds flew across the courtyard, they chewed up everything in their path, leaving nothing but mangled shreds and lumps of metal. Quickly, Alpha Three dismantled all six machineguns and turned his attention to shredding the trucks they arrived in.

Whilst shooting the trucks, which were just visible through the fences, a rocket sparked from his left. It was an RPG which coiled its way towards Alpha Three. He raised one of his shielded arms just as it struck him. He was thrown back and smashed into the wall behind. The shield on his left arm had been completely disintegrated through the impact, and the armour on his left arm was black, smoking, and had almost entirely burnt away. So, as he was squashed within the wall, Alpha Three covered most of his body with the remaining shield and raised his Minigun to face forwards. He then waited, patiently, knowing he had to draw them in. Shortly after, the remaining group of assailants opened fire again. They began to close in, as Alpha Three's shield took the brunt of the firepower. They all took just one, slow step at a time, keeping their eyes and rifles fixed on Alpha Three, who was still merged with the wall. As they got to the door, he spooled his Minigun again; a whirring noise the assailants knew meant they had to move. An instant later, Alpha Three fired the remaining bullets and cleared the doorway.

He pulled himself free of the wall and stood up, having to balance on his knee first. He just managed to stand with the weight of the armour trying to pin him to the floor. He gave four strong, deep knocks on the library door, informing the others that it was clear to exit.

Alpha Five scanned the nearby area for heat signatures and, after a few seconds, said, "All clear."

Alpha Three then removed his helmet, exclaiming, "They need air conditioning in these things!"

They stepped outside and looked up to the sky, waiting for an incoming storm of some kind. As they waited, there was a loud crack. Initially, Alpha One thought it could be a crack of thunder but realised he knew the noise all too well. He turned around to see one of Heartfell's guards drop to the floor, bits of his head scattered across the pristine grass. They immediately dived back inside and ensured they couldn't be seen from outside. A storm then began to roll in, which they knew could turn lethal in seconds. Without wasting a second, they all headed into the library room, but as Alpha Three and another guard crossed the open doorway, Heartfell's guard dropped to the floor, lifelessly. Alpha One remembered the pattern to get back into the safe room, and he got them all inside safely before sealing the door.

***

The storm pounded the building for hours but couldn't break into the safe room. They all tried to fill their heads with entertainment, to pass the time, but found nothing except books in the safe room. Alpha Six spent his time addressing the wounds of Alpha Three, whose left arm was plagued with cuts and burns. Alpha Six cleaned them all with an antiseptic wipe, before patching them up with stitches, bandages or whatever they required. At no point was Alpha Six tender or gentle, receiving a few grunts and frowns from Alpha Three, as he had little concern about his pain. Due to the imposing nature which could be implied through the large presence of Alpha team, Alpha One had already decided against pressing forward with his questioning of Heartfell. Instead, Alpha One couldn't ignore the events surrounding their operation, nor could he find answers. As he delved deeper into his memory, more things began to not add up. Firstly, he couldn't understand how they could be so organised when assaulting the building. They were able to cut all radio feeds, except their own, they knew how to cut the power, and the best places to enter. They seemed far too prepared for an assault on an unsuspecting engineer. Alpha One also couldn't overlook how the two shots fired by the sniper were so accurate, yet both had hit Heartfell's security guards. It could've been little more than coincidence, but as Alpha One thought about how he would've planned things, it seemed the most likely target would've been Alpha Three, who had taken his helmet off.

Although Alpha One's mind was yet again working too hard, he knew that trying to think during an active operation wasn't going to yield clear, nor accurate, answers. From within the confines of the safe room, it was impossible to hear what was going on above. But, over four hours in, Alpha One's green light began flashing, although this time from VOICE. Alpha One immediately got up and started moving towards the door.

"It's time to move," he said, as he left the safe room.

The tunnel leading to the building was still intact, but as they entered what was once the library, they found very little left of the building itself. Although it was unlikely that the sniper had been able to maintain his position, Alpha One took no chances, especially given the localised effect the storms seemed to have. They all charged across the courtyard, using the rubble, which had dug itself into the ground, for cover. As they approached the road, they could see chunks of turf had been thrown onto it after the storm had ransacked the once idyllic grounds. As they got to the front gates, two cars pulled up.

They were the same two cars that had dropped them off, and Alpha One was pleased to see a welcoming face wind the window down and shout, "Get in!"

Bosse then closed his window and continued to sit bolt upright as if he was being chauffeur-driven around. A third car then pulled up, giving them just enough seats for everyone to squeeze into. Their tyres squealed and their heads were thrown back against the headrests, as they took off down the road, hastily heading back to their plane.

"VOICE was able to interrupt the signal to stop the storm. He doesn't know how long it'll last though, so we've got to be quick," said Bosse.

"He took his time, didn't he?" said Alpha Three, who was watching every window and door as they passed through the residential areas.

Without any further setbacks, they made it back to their plane and were able fly back to their hidden base.

Chapter 14 – The Island
February 27th
20:56 GMT

Bosse entered the, already assembled, meeting room. He brought his usual sense of power, as he sealed the doors. Everyone was already in their seats, including Daniel, leaving just three empty chairs over on the far side.

"I know it's been almost two weeks since we used our final lead, but it's finally yielded results," said Bosse, as he took his own seat and allowed VOICE to continue for him.

"Back at the embassy building, I was able to find the unique frequency that was used to create, and control, the storm. I then blocked the signal, upon finding a trace of the original source, which disrupted the storm. The trace I found had been bounced off countless other satellites, well, one hundred and thirty-two to be precise, as well as hundreds of signal receivers on the surface. For the past twelve days, I have been following the signal backwards, because it would be impossible for there to be an infinite number of, dare I say, dummy signals. The original satellite you blew up was technically able to produce an infinite number, so destroying it did still prove vital," said VOICE.

Everyone in the room was waiting for nothing more than a location, as they couldn't think why else they would've been brought back in after twelve days. VOICE then sat back down, giving the impression he had nothing more to say. Bosse then turned to him in confusion, as he started to make tiny gestures with his hands, lifting a few fingers up and rolling his hand. The room sat in silence, as they all shared glances with each other, some in confusion, others in anger.

Scott eventually broke the silence, asking, "So, are you going to continue? Do we have a location?"

VOICE then leapt back up and continued, "I did not want to just run through all the information, I know your brains are not quite as quick as mine, and I did not want to leave any of you behind. As for the location, yes... well, no... well, we kind of do."

"Well, I'm glad you could clear things up for our slow brains," said Samuel, causing a few suppressed laughs and sniggers which changed the tense atmosphere VOICE had created.

"Are you going to expand?" pried Scott.

"Yes. I have managed to narrow down the potential locations to three possibilities. One is located on top of a mountain, another in the Bermuda Triangle, and the third is underwater," said VOICE.

Three pieces of paper were then flung towards Scott, allowing him the first look before them being passed around after his analysis.

"Can't we just send drones over them or get Delta team to scout them out, then?" asked Bravo One, looking to Scott for the answers.

Scott scanned the documents and began shaking his head. "We can't send Delta team in, because they're all hard-to-reach areas. No drone would get a clear image under the sea. And we're dealing with someone who can control the weather, a drone wouldn't even get close," said Scott, unsure how to proceed.

"Satellite images?" asked Kenny.

Scott again shook his head, as he found yet another problem.

"Apparently, we tried, but both are covered by a thick layer of cloud," said Scott.

Kenny then started nodding his head, as he gave it more thought. "And obviously the other is deep under water, so we couldn't get an image of that, either," he said.

"It seems they knew the three best places to hide," continued Scott, as he began passing the documents around the table, clockwise.

"If our drone is shot down, then we'll know the location, right?" said Bravo One, still trying to use his plan.

"They'll know we have these three locations, and they'll know we won't assault any because it's too much of a risk. The only way to form an assault would be for us to all work together. And, if we choose the wrong location, they will have likely set a trap for us. Plus, we don't want them to know we know where they are. Losing a drone will take away any element of surprise we might have, which we need if we're going to strike before they start their weather weapon," continued Scott, as he came to the full realisation that Fellscient, and Crabble, were still an unknown number of steps ahead.

"We don't know if they're even at one of these locations," said Mike, creating an even bleaker atmosphere.

Daniel was the second to observe the documents and almost passed them straight on, before paying attention to one of the three. He stared at the location in the Bermuda Triangle, whilst passing the other two on to Samuel. He focussed on the coordinates of the possible base which said, '*Latitude 25.3049, Longitude -66.73*'.

"This is the place," announced Daniel, causing the entire room to face him. He then turned to Scott directly, and insisted, "This is the place."

Scott saw a similar sense of confidence in Daniel's eyes as he'd seen in Mike's when giving him the lead on the assassination.

"We're going to need a little more to go on than that. How do you know this is the place?" asked Scott, reluctant to make the same mistake again.

"We have worked together and have trusted each other for years. I don't see why this is any different. I won't be able to operate on this one, so this is the only way I can help. Now please believe me when I say, this is the one."

Scott was aware he might be led the same way as he was with Mike, but it would be unfair to lose any trust in Daniel because of Mike's… and Bosse's, lies. He looked around the room to see what the others thought. It was clear that they were all intrigued, and Bosse was probably the most intrigued, as he felt a lack of control facing the uncertainty.

"I'm willing to go with Daniel on this one. It's not the first time he's been right about this sort of thing," said Kenny, showing the same kind of trust he'd showed Mike.

The room was instantly filled with noises of agreement and nodding heads, as they concurred with Kenny, although not all the room joined in, as Bosse maintained his stare towards Daniel and Mike kept quiet.

"Okay, we've got a location," confirmed Scott.

"Very well done. Now I hope I don't have to inform you that this operation is time sensitive. The longer you take to execute the operation, the more likely they are to create another natural disaster. I have a contact who has some rather… useful assets in the area. I'll ensure you get sufficient air cover, so I'll arrange for our aircraft to rendezvous with the asset straight away. They haven't attacked any civilian sites since activating the extinct volcano, which could mean they're planning something big. So, don't waste any time when planning the mission, okay?" said Bosse, almost as if he was trying to assert his power and authority, as he left the room.

Scott took little notice of Bosse, ignoring the irritating nature of him stating everything he knew Scott would consider.

Scott addressed the teams and said, "The location puts it among the Bermuda Triangle which, as you know, is a long flight from here. The best thing is to plan on the way. I think it's a certainty that we'll be taking all our equipment with us, so ensure every piece of equipment that you think we might need is loaded onto one of the two C-8 Donkeys within the next two hours. We'll formulate our plan on the way, but we don't want to fly too close to the location, so we'll likely have to land on the mainland before moving in. And we'll all be given the specialist bullets. I know you haven't all used them before, but they do work. Just… don't forget that if you pick up an enemy gun… well, it will kill."

Everyone then started leaving the room without Scott needing to dismiss them. They were all aware of the ticking clock that would be working against them. Scott then turned to Daniel, who looked to be in pain as he stood up. As the table stopped hiding Daniel's injuries, it was clear he was held together with bandages and a back brace.

Scott then said, "I know you want to help, but the doctor said you shouldn't fly in your condition. You are healing fast, but the best thing you can do is rest…" Daniel went to say something, getting no further than opening his mouth, before Scott made it clear he was continuing, by raising his voice, saying, "When we get there, VOICE can rope you into our operation. You'll be able to follow everything we do, and I'm sure VOICE will need your help coordinating the whole thing."

Daniel felt he was being sidelined, no matter what the doctor had said, but he did know Scott was finding the best compromise, so lowered his head and headed for the door, knowing there was no chance of any negotiation.

Two hours later, they had all their equipment loaded into the two Donkeys, with Alpha and Delta team in the first plane and the other two in the second. From within their planes, they still couldn't feel the bumps and jolts as the two were lifted to the runway. Alpha One wasted no time, as he got straight to planning before the planes had even taken off. The four members of Bravo team and the two from Charlie team, who were present in the previous meetings, joined through a video link. Their faces could be seen, which was enough for Alpha One to gauge their silent opinions. VOICE was also present, as he coordinated their meeting from inside the safety of the Molehill.

"The coordinates VOICE has given us show a large area…" started Alpha One, before immediately being interrupted by VOICE.

"Well, I think I might be able to narrow down the coordinates further as soon as we get close." VOICE then went back to his laptop and buried his head in it.

Alpha One then continued, "Right, well, thank you. The signal appears to have come from the surface, so we're expecting it to be an island or a collection of islands. Whilst we don't know what defences they have, it's pretty much a certainty they'll have their weather weapon located there, as that is where we think they control it from…"

"Are we definitely going with 'weather weapon'? It kind of sounds a bit… I don't know… crude?" interrupted Alpha Four.

"Doesn't crude mean something that's vulgar, a bit like an innuendo?" asked Bravo Two.

"I don't really know. I was going for something like crude oil, you know, unrefined," replied Alpha Four, suddenly very confused.

"How about the 'weather wand'?" suggested Charlie One.

At his suggestion, Charlie Two turned to face him and rolled her eyes, tutting in the process.

"What about… 'storm-maker'?" asked Alpha Three, as he started nodding to his own suggestion.

Alpha Four then turned to him and gave a little chuckle, saying, "That's very good, I like that."

Alpha One had sat back down, holding his head in one hand. He knew interrupting them wouldn't help, as their minds might still be fixed on their juvenile conversation.

Their conversation went on for the next few minutes, before Alpha One decided to finally put a stop to it, saying, "How about we call it, 'Titan'?" A lot of agreeing noises followed along with nodding heads. With limited progress made, Alpha One tried to realign the focus of their conversation, saying, "Going on the assumption that it is an island, both Alpha and Delta teams will emerge from the water and will disable any air defences. Once that is done, we will get VOICE into their system to shut down any radar, sonar, and so on, as well as Titan itself. Then, Bravo team will enter from the water and provide a distraction, whilst Charlie team drop themselves, and their equipment, in by air. Obviously, if the island is too small, or has unsuitable terrain, Charlie team will be deploying without their equipment. From there... well, we take control of their base and prevent Titan from ever starting up with slightly more decisive methods than VOICE..."

He gave a quick glance at the device Heartfell had passed to him. He had previously got VOICE to run a few checks to ensure it would carry out its purpose and nothing else, and it had gained VOICE's approval.

Alpha One didn't want to draw any more attention away from planning, as he looked back at the teams and continued, "When we get close, VOICE will send out a short-range drone to try and take pictures. Its tiny size means it shouldn't be picked up on any radar, but due to its limited range, we will only get the images close to us moving out. If he's successful with that, then I'll call another meeting to make the plan more detailed, but if not... then we adapt accordingly in the moment. We all know how each other thinks, so we'll all have to use our own initiative."

"Fingers crossed for the drone footage then," mumbled Blindspot, too quiet for anyone that wasn't stood next to him to hear.

There were a couple of seconds of silence, whilst everyone made sure Alpha One had finished.

"Sounds good," said Charlie One.

"Fine by me, too. I'll pass the plan on," agreed Bravo One.

"It's good by us, too," added Delta One, as Bravo and Charlie team disappeared from the meeting.

Everyone dispersed from around the table and started checking over their equipment, ensuring everything was prepared for the terrain they could be facing.

"Can I have a word?" asked Alpha Five in a quiet tone.

Alpha One nodded and led him to a quiet room away from everyone else.

They went into the small room tucked away in the corner of the plane.

Once inside, Alpha Five shut the door and started, "I'm more than capable of hacking into their system. I am the 'computer guy' after all! But since VOICE has pushed his way in, I'm feeling more and more redundant. Adrian was never brilliant with computers; he was just the best coordinator…"

Before he could continue, Alpha One stepped in, aware of what was coming next, and replied, "VOICE isn't taking over from you. We are already one man down, and I can't afford for you to be preoccupied with your computers when someone else can do it. I need you to help make up the numbers in Alpha Two's absence, and that means operating, not hacking. Now is your head in the game?" Before Alpha Five could answer, Alpha One continued, adding, "Because if it isn't, you've got a few hours to make sure it is. Okay?"

"Sure thing… boss," said Alpha Five in his still quiet and distant tone.

Although his head was down, he maintained eye contact with Alpha One as he left the room. Before they parted ways, Alpha One passed Heartfell's device to Alpha Five, allowing him to shut down Titan. It was nothing which would change much; it would just allow Alpha Five to have a more involved role.

The flight might have been long, but it felt short. There was little time for Alpha One to sleep, after prepping his equipment. Whilst he spent the little spare time in his hammock, he watched Blindspot sat staring at an empty shell casing. He took it everywhere with him. It was a shell casing from Westbrook, which he'd received in the post days after a clean-up crew had recovered all assets from the building wreck. In fact, it was one of the only things they did recover, with no body recovered. Alpha One was always aware of Westbrook's death, but up until a few days ago, Blindspot had never given him the name of the man who'd ordered his death; Crabble. He knew this operation was close to home because of Echo team and Adrian, but for Blindspot, it was made even worse. Blindspot also told him how the entire mission was a hoax, with no sign of any nuclear weapons nearby, adding yet another mystery to the increasing list. As they neared the mainland, the drone came back, taking multiple pictures which Alpha One included in his plan, along with Bosse's assets which were already in position. There was little to change, it was more adapting their already sound plan. As soon as the Donkey's wheels touched down, their plan was put into motion. Both Alpha and Delta teams travelled straight to the island, separately, balancing speed with silence.

Chapter 14.2

After hours of clinging on to their military-grade aqua jets, they could finally see the base of the island. Alpha team would enter from the beach on the south-west side of the island and disable the closest surface-to-air missile turret, whilst Delta team would enter from the beach on the south-east side and disable the other SAM turret.

Alpha team were still submerged in the dark waters. Their aqua jets had a pump behind the propeller blades which removed any vacuum of air that might occur. The blades also started to spin very slowly as they got close to the island, which did mean their journey took longer but it also meant they could stay unnoticed through the lack of bubble cavitation. As they crept closer to the island, the water didn't become shallow as expected. They got to the island and pressed themselves against the rocky wall to stay hidden, as their feet still dangled above the seabed just visible through the murky water. Still submerged, they removed their fins, along with their aqua jets, and tucked them into a bag Alpha Four had brought with him. They then swam to the sea floor and searched for something to fasten the bag down with, but with no hooks or poles on the seabed, they quickly gathered stones and pushed them into the bag to hold it in position. The final things they removed were their rebreathers. After one huge lungful of air, they tucked them into the bag and sealed it up, before swimming to the surface, still undetected, and now a few metres away from the rocky bank.

They used just their legs to keep themselves under the surface of the water, with their arms clutching their rifles. Alpha One slowly emerged from the water, with no more than his eyes peeking out. When he was sure their coast was clear, he gave two little flicks of his right foot. Seconds later, another four pairs of eyes slipped through the surface of the ocean. They all drifted towards the edge of the island, slowly raising their heads as they got closer. As they got to the edge, their rifles emerged from the water, watching, as Alpha One climbed up onto the grass ledge, about a metre above sea level. Whilst Alpha One scanned the surrounding area, the other four all climbed up, two at a time, ensuring they could quickly react should they be ambushed. Thanks to the images taken by their drone, Alpha One led the way straight to the SAM turret they would be disabling, despite there being yellow shrubs rather than the expected sand at their infiltration zone. Alpha One was also very aware that obtaining the pictures could've given away their element of surprise, so moved with caution.

The island wasn't the size of a country, but it was large enough to have different terrains. Over towards the most northern side, there was a mountain which overlooked the entire island. The rest was divided, with open, grass-filled landscapes, forests, and a settlement, right in the very centre, which seemed to house the island's residents.

They still had their jet-black wetsuits on, so their best camouflage would be during the night. With little time to waste until the sun illuminated the island, Alpha team crouched as low as they could and crept through the short grass. Crawling would've always been the first choice to maintaining their secrecy but travelling across the stretch of grass, whilst prone, would've taken too long. The grass hardly covered their ankles, but Alpha One knew their wetsuits would be enough to obscure them, as they wouldn't be noticed unless someone was looking for them specifically. It took them a while to creep through the grasslands but, eventually, they made it to the first SAM turret, surrounded by guards, concrete buildings, and small fabric tents. With little over half an hour until sunrise, Alpha team moved into position to strike.

The SAM turret and its surrounding guards were all in an area recessed into the ground, giving it more protection. It also gave Blindspot the perfect opportunity to provide cover for them. He covered from above, as the others slid down the sloped bank leading into the den. They landed softly on the mud and moved behind the closest building for cover, whilst they regrouped.

"Hold," said Blindspot in his very calm but flat voice.

They waited patiently in the shadows, not questioning his call. Moments later, two guards wandered past, paying no attention to anything but their own conversation.

"Just the two," he added.

Alpha One held his right hand up, so it was visible to the others, and held four fingers up followed by five. Alpha Four and Five crept out from the shadows and placed their rifles on their backs. Alpha One slightly emerged to watch their backs, whilst Alpha Three covered ahead. They both stayed low but moved quickly, allowing the guards to make just a few steps before their throats were constricted and were then swiftly dragged back into the shadows.

"Clear," said Blindspot.

They moved on and between the small concrete buildings and the fabric tents, drawing no attention to themselves.

"Hold. Four from next right," said Blindspot.

There was talking coming from all directions, but as Alpha One turned his head to the right, he could hear them getting closer. But as he moved to take cover, he found few places to hide.

"Drop them," ordered Alpha One, as he positioned himself behind a low brick wall.

A few seconds later, four guards wandered around the corner, one of them peeling off to the nearest building. The lonely guard fell to the floor, unheard. As the other three started to approach the slightly obscured Alpha team, the guard nearest the back fell to the floor. The other two spun around, unaware of what was happening, and the next then fell. As the realisation started to hit the final guard, he went to shout out in desperation, but he never had the chance, as he too fell, silenced.

As soon as the final guard dropped, Alpha team all took one guard each to stash them away. Alpha One went to grab the guard furthest away, but as he got close, the corner of his right eye caught two further guards approaching.

Without hesitation, he slumped the guard through the closest window and followed him in, saying, "Hold."

The two guards knew something was wrong, and they approached with caution, after seeing something climb through the window. Alpha One waited patiently, with his sidearm drawn, as the guards edged closer to the window. One of them leant through and poked his head inside the dark room. Alpha One grabbed the guard's bulletproof vest and placed his handgun under his chin, causing the guard to freeze.

"Execute," said Alpha One, as he pulled the trigger and yanked the guard inside. Whilst looking back into the open, he saw Alpha Four was already dragging the other body towards him. They threw the final guard inside and headed further into the centre of the makeshift village.

"I'm blind around the next corner, but there's lots of smoke," said Blindspot, as his view was becoming blocked by the tallest building.

"Copy, move to a better location. We'll move in now," said Alpha One, in a quiet voice, as they moved towards the next corner.

They pressed themselves tightly against the wall, as Alpha One slid one eye around the corner. He took in every piece of his surroundings and committed them to memory.

"There's no quiet way through. I counted thirty-two guards, likely more out of sight. They are all sat around a large fire, with the SAM turret at the other end of the courtyard about thirty or forty metres away," said Alpha One.

"I'm in a better location. I can guide you around the fire. Limited numbers away from the courtyard," said Blindspot, giving them their best opportunity.

"Moving out," concluded Alpha One, as he bent down and aimed his rifle towards the campfire.

The other three ran across the open space, with Alpha Three stopping to cover Alpha One as he crossed. Once across, they followed Blindspot's instructions through the winding path, until they finally reached their destination, still undetected.

As they approached the other end of the courtyard, they could see the SAM turret clearly. Over to their right, there was also another building which stood out from the rest. Its walls looked to be metal and was unlike the other buildings, as there were also no window holes. As Alpha One observed the SAM turret, he traced a group of cables all leading to the metal building.

"Alpha Five, plant the device to allow VOICE to hack into their network," said Alpha One, whilst pointing towards the metal building.

Alpha Five headed straight over to it, keeping his head low, as he crossed any open paths and keeping close to the walls whilst alongside the buildings. He entered the room and swept it clear, with no sign of any guards. He then went to plug the device in, but as his hand got to the computer, he stopped. Alpha Five then dragged over the nearest seat and began getting into their system himself.

"What's the problem?" asked Alpha One, getting no reply. He then pressed the question, asking, "What is the problem?"

Alpha Five knew that another unanswered radio message would lead to them coming in, so he replied, "I'm doing the hack myself. I won't be long."

"Plug the device in and get out," insisted Alpha One.

Alpha Three caught sight of a few guards moving towards the building, drawing Alpha One's attention to them with a light nudge.

"Targets approaching. Get out now!" shouted Alpha One, in the loudest whisper he could make.

There was still no reply, so they took aim at the approaching guards, aware they might be about to make their presence known.

"No! No, no, no, no! Er... we've got a problem. I've tripped a fail-safe. The room's sealed!" shouted Alpha Five, as he thumped his hand on the table in anger.

Once the room was completely sealed, a hissing noise could be heard. Alpha Five moved over to the source and noticed a thick, green gas flooding from the floor vents. He quickly placed his small gas mask over his nose and mouth and sat back down in the chair to continue his work.

"I'm fine, just disable the SAM turret," said Alpha Five with his now muffled voice, as he persisted on the computer.

Just moments later, alarms rang out around the sunken camp.

Swiftly moving to a rarely made plan B, Alpha One said, "We're blowing the thing up; I'll ready the charges. Bravo team, move in and make as much noise as you can, it looks like we're doing the same."

Guards began moving towards the building, ready to surround it.

"I've got your backs covered," informed Blindspot, as the other three found cover, ready to fire.

Once in position, they opened fire, dropping everyone to the floor. There was no need to watch their backs; they had to trust Blindspot could manage any number of guards approaching. They all began firing at staggered intervals, ensuring that only one of them would need to reload at a time. But as more came into view, it became harder to take them out as they also began to take cover.

"Alpha Three, head up to the roof… You should get a clear shot at the explosives," said Alpha One, paying more attention to the guards ahead.

Alpha Three began to move to the side and climb the closest building, as he paused and asked, "What explosives?"

"These explosives," answered Alpha One, as he drew his attention to the bag lying at his feet.

"But those explosives aren't going to be enough to take down the SAM turret," said Alpha Three in confusion.

"No, but they will be enough to destroy the munitions next to the turret, and they should be enough to destroy the turret itself," replied Alpha One, confirming his plan.

Alpha Three didn't question his orders any further, despite his reservations, and climbed up to the roof. Once there, he lay prone and dragged himself to the edge.

"Ready," said Alpha Three, still not sure whether the plan would work.

He edged his head over the side and fixed his eyes on the bag of explosives. Alpha One picked them up and ran towards the metal building. As he ran towards it, he swung his arm round and yelled out as the bag flew across the courtyard, landing only a few metres away from the stockpile of missiles accompanying the turret. Alpha Three didn't need an invitation, as he fired just one bullet into the stationary bag, causing it to burst into flames and ignite the nearby ammunition. They all took cover, as the courtyard turned into a huge fireball stretching high into the sky. Even Blindspot dived back as the heat hit him, allowing the shockwave to fly overhead.

***

28 MINUTES EARLIER
Delta team arrived at the beach and started climbing out of the water. Delta One led the way across the sand, as the other five followed in single file to hide their numbers and limit the chance of discovery. They wore completely sealed clothing with tactical masks covering their faces. It wasn't something everyone used, due to the restriction in sight, but with the visors able to pick out heat signatures, Delta team preferred to be with them. Although they were miles apart, Delta team crossed the field in the same way as Alpha team, staying low but moving quickly. They also made it across the field without seeing anyone and, with the radio still silent, their plan seemed to be working. They approached their SAM turret site, which was laid out in an almost identical style to the other. They lay prone to observe the sunken encampment. Whilst watching, they could see only a limited number of guards patrolling the surrounding area and saw no guards on top of the roofs.

"We can go across the roofs," said Delta One.

"It'll be hard to spot any guards, plus they might notice if we all start leaping from rooftop to rooftop," added Delta Two, giving her less confident opinion.

"Delta Two and Four, you will be with me, disabling the turret. Delta Three, I want you staying here. Delta Five, you can go to the east side, and Delta Six on the far side. We should have all directions covered and three of us moving across the rooftops will be better than six," said Delta One, as she clarified her plan and signalled for them to move out by rolling her right hand in one complete circle.

Delta One led them down the sloped bank and ran straight towards the building in front, scaling its wall and lying prone until they were all on top.

"You're clear," said Delta Three.

They stayed prone until both Delta Five and Six were in

their designated positions and able to help. They started leaping from building to building, following Delta One.

"Hold," said Delta Five, causing them all to instantly drop to the floor of the roof.

They waited patiently, unsure who was close.

"One guard heading towards the ladder, I think he heard something," said Delta Five.

"He's heading up now. Six o'clock from Delta One's position," added Delta Three.

With the position of the guard firmly in mind, they rolled over to the raised edges of the roof and tucked themselves as close to it as possible. The guard's head popped up one building back. He climbed onto the roof and began searching. From where he stood, Delta team was completely obscured, so with nothing identified, the guard moved back down the ladder.

"Clear," said Delta Three, causing a sigh of relief from those on the roof.

They continued along the rooftops, as they moved towards the turret. Delta Five was the only one who could see it and helped to direct them. They leapt to the final rooftop and, again, observed everything in the immediate area. Delta One took note of guards, exits, windows, and buildings with access straight to the courtyard, along with everything else which might come in useful. The raging fire in the centre of the courtyard was the first thing to catch Delta One's eye, as she thought of a way to use it as a distraction. Meanwhile, Delta Four fired a cable which imbedded itself in the building opposite, allowing him to hang above the SAM turret.

"You know what to do, wait for my signal," said Delta One, as she moved three buildings back and crouched down close to the fire.

To her right, there was a rifle resting against a wall. She removed the magazine and ripped out each individual bullet, placing them all next to her. Using her knife, she split the bullets by removing the tops and tipped the gunpowder into the empty magazine. Once she had emptied all the shell casings, Delta One flung the contents into the fire and quickly ducked down out of sight. The gunpowder gave a crackling sound, quiet enough to not put the guards on high alert, but loud enough to draw the guards towards the fire.

Delta Four saw the signal and began sliding across the cable. Once above the turret, he lowered himself and began fiddling with the wires and computer within the turret itself. Whilst he was disabling the turret, Delta Two steadied the cable. She could hear a faint ringing in the distance, as she turned her head to focus on the sound.

"Bravo team, move in and make as much noise as you can, it looks like we're doing the same."

The voice was clearly Alpha One's, as the message got relayed to all the teams. The guards at Delta team's location suddenly became more on edge, as they moved away from the fire and spread out across the encampment. Delta Four lifted himself back up and was pulled along the cable by Delta Two, before they both moved away from the edge and met back up with Delta One. There was then an orange flash over to the west side of the island, shortly followed by the noise of an explosion.

"This is Delta One. Our SAM turret is disabled. There was an explosion towards Alpha team's location, unsure if the airspace is clear," said Delta One, as nothing but silence followed.

Everyone on their channel was waiting for a response from Alpha team. Eventually, a coughing and spluttering voice came through a crackly radio.

"Airspace is clear... Charlie One... you're cleared to move in hot," said Alpha One.

Chapter 15 – The Promise
February 28th
10:51 GMT

Towards the north side of the island, Bravo team had positioned themselves at the foot of the mountain. They were spread out across a hundred-metre line, ensuring one lucky grenade couldn't take them all out. There were four machine guns mounted on the steel sheets they used for cover. Bravo team had no intention of advancing; they just held their position to draw in as many of the Night Vipers as possible. The four machine guns tore into any of the Vipers attempting a frontal assault, whilst the other eight prevented any sort of flanking manoeuvre, as they were aided by the steep mountain on one side. The Night Vipers edged closer, as they stormed the front defences, trying to overpower the machine guns. Bravo team staggered the times they opened fire, so they would always have at least one gun operational at a time. But as Bravo Eight began to reload, the Night Vipers turned their guns on her. Without being able to return fire, the gun began smoking. Unable to use the machine gun again, Bravo Eight grabbed her rifle and crawled to the left, taking herself away from the sparks and shredded gun. With one gun down, the Night Vipers continued with their new-found tactic and targeted the next machine gun. As the Vipers continued to close in, Bravo team were quickly being overrun.

"This is Charlie One. We are making our landing run now," said Charlie One, giving a much-needed sense of hope, as Bravo team hung by a thread.

***

A few kilometres away from the island, Charlie One was on the plane, flying only a few hundred metres above sea level.

He tried to make his voice heard over the screaming winds entering the cargo bay door, as he shouted, "We are all going to drop on the north of the island. We'll meet up with Bravo team stationed at the foot of the mountain. Because of the height we must fly at, our descent will be quick, and we'll likely land in the middle of the Night Vipers, or a long way out of the action. That's why most of you will either be in a vehicle or will land behind Bravo's line. Good luck and remember the part we're playing."

Within seconds of concluding his words of encouragement, he leapt from the back of the plane, followed by other members of Charlie team, all quickly opening their parachutes. As soon as they were clear, tanks and APCs were pulled out of the plane by their, already open, parachutes. The sky filled with people and vehicles all floating down, like spiders lowering themselves with their webs.

Charlie One softly hit the floor, as he ran to keep his balance. He wrapped up his parachute and moved to meet Bravo team as quickly as possible. He knew that his team had been scattered over the top half of the island, but he had no fear in their ability to survive as some headed to help Bravo team and others began their assault on the main compound. A minute later, Charlie One finally met up with Bravo team, who had already started to push their way forward, thanks to the assistance they had recently acquired. It took them time, but they eventually managed to push the Vipers back up the mile-long path, rejoining with every member of Charlie team who had dropped individually. They started moving from cover to cover, but as the momentum picked up in their favour, Bravo team stood in a long line, with Charlie team scattered between, as they marched up the path. The Night Vipers ran back to the main compound, trying to get in before the doors were inevitably sealed, but they couldn't even get that far, as they were felled, one by one.

***

Near the top of the path, Charlie Two was sealed within one of the four armoured tanks that blocked the way. They had cleared the limited number of Vipers who'd stayed back, which allowed the two APCs to offload their cargo of Charlie team. A further twenty members climbed out and scattered themselves off the path, taking cover from the fleeing Vipers.

"Vipers heading to… point 'Ambush 4'. They're armed with nothing more than rifles," said Charlie One, clearly getting out of breath, as he tried to keep up with Bravo One charging up the path.

"Copy… It sounds quite tiring. I'm glad I'm sat in here," replied Charlie Two.

There was no comment, but she wasn't expecting one, as she gave out a huge sigh as if she was exhausted. Everyone else could hear Charlie One's message, as their heavy vehicles came to a stop, so the front of the tanks, the most armoured side, faced the unknown part of the path, whilst the turrets were swivelled round to face down to where the Vipers were running from.

After just a few minutes of waiting, with their fingers pulsing over their triggers, a group of Night Vipers flocked around the corner. They stopped dead in their tracks, as the thirty or so remaining guards were faced by four imposing turrets.

"Firing non-lethal rounds," said Charlie Two, as she thumped a large metal canister into an even bigger tube. "Fire!" she shouted, as a single metal canister flew out of the turrets of all four tanks.

They landed in amongst the Vipers, spread out, as they exploded. The green gel, which was the same as in their bullets, spewed out and covered everything within a twenty-metre radius. Any that didn't get caught by the gel were quickly dispatched by Charlie team, hiding beside the path. Moments later, Bravo One flew around the corner, closely followed by his team and a very out of breath Charlie One.

"Six o'clock!" barked Bravo One.

A giant tank glided round the corner, facing the line of Charlie team's tanks, which now looked insignificant. The Vipers' tank dug into the mud, as it came to an instant stop. It looked double the width of an ordinary tank, as its tracks were pressed tightly against each bank of the dirt path. The whole vehicle was black, with no visible doors or hatches, and no signs of any weaknesses. The thick turret on the top twisted to face one of the smaller tanks. A plume of smoke left its five-metre-long turret, as Charlie Two's tank was hit with an immense force. An explosion shrouded them in fire, as the projectile itself ripped most of the front shielding clean away but left the rest of the tank looking like it hadn't been touched. The startled crew all stumbled to climb out of the top hatch, despite the gaping hole in front, with Charlie Two making sure she was the last to leave.

"We are far superior to your primitive technology. That was a shot from our weakest projectile. You choose your fate; surrender your arms, or know the true power of the Vipers' Venom," came from a hidden set of speakers outside the tank.

Charlie One looked towards Bravo One and said, "The Vipers' Venom; isn't it a bit pretentious?"

"I'm surprised you know what that means," added Charlie Two, as her ears stopped ringing.

Charlie One ignored the comment and once again became serious, as he ordered, "Maximum firepower, lethal force is authorised."

Bravo One had moved a few paces back to talk to VOICE. "Is our escort in position yet?" he asked.

There was a slight delay, before VOICE eventually replied, saying, "Yes, I can get a message to them if you need me to, whilst we wait for Delta team to get there."

"Good, I need a favour. Mark the coordinates of my position," said Bravo One, as he tapped Charlie Two on the shoulder and asked, "Can you get everyone to move back as far as possible?"

"Okay, your coordinates are marked. Why did you want me to do that?" asked VOICE.

"Don't worry, I know your plan. I'll get VOICE up to speed," said Alpha Two, joining the conversation from his position back at base.

He knew Bravo One would only start getting angry, especially with his short fuse, so felt he had to step in.

"And remember, the target is about fifty metres south-south-east of our location," added Bravo One, as he joined everyone else falling back.

"Final chance!" bellowed the Viper from within the enemy tank.

Seconds later, it started to change its target, as its turret locked on to the next tank, and fired another shot. The tank was completely vaporised, as molten lumps of metal were thrown over the path.

"Coyote is down. Fall back!" shouted Charlie One.

As they all started to move back, whilst nearby members of Charlie team were pulled to their feet and dragged into cover, Charlie team's two remaining tanks and two APCs had also started to move back, prompting the Venom to edge forwards, thinking they were in control. The Venom continued to fire, hitting the ground beside the retreating Charlie team. But as Bravo One paused to look up, he saw what he was waiting for, as a surface-to-surface ballistic missile flew into the enemy tank, exploding as it made contact.

Now in the distance, Bravo One watched as the smoke began to clear, revealing the still operational enemy tank.

"Perfect shot, but we need more, a lot more!" shouted Bravo One, as he continued to run back.

The Venom had clearly felt the last shot, as its shell looked out of shape and it struggled to move, jolting forwards until it finally started to gain traction again. Before it could start to close the ever-widening distance from Bravo and Charlie team, several more missiles shrouded the tank, concealing it in fire and smoke. Despite the distance they had put between themselves and the Venom, both teams were thrown to the floor, as they covered their ears. As the explosions stopped and the smoke cleared, Bravo One could see the damage. There was little left of their previously damaged tanks, but as he shifted his gaze further up, he could also see what was left of the Venom's carcass. It was just a pile of smoking metal, its shape unrecognisable before it eventually gave in.

"Nobody is invincible, and nothing is indestructible," said Bravo One, as he started checking the motionless members of Charlie team, lying on the dirt track.

Eventually, they continued their path up the track, now close to the main compound.

"We're almost making entry. What's your ETA until entrance?" asked Bravo One.

He waited a few seconds, with still no word, when Alpha Two came back over the radio, saying, "Alpha team and Delta team have been in and out of contact. We're not sure what's causing it. I know Delta team have moved back to secure any cover fire that's necessary, so they'll hopefully be on board soon. I'll get back to you when we re-establish contact with Alpha team."

They continued up the path, maintaining a spread-out approach, ensuring nobody could slip past undetected.

"Bravo One, that's a good copy. ETA is unknown. We will try to secure transport. Hold at the perimeter until we are in position," said Alpha One.

***

He was trying to lift the huge pieces of concrete, all reinforced with thick rebar, which had been blown into the metal building Alpha Five was in. Alpha Four was aiding in the removal, as they both tried to get some movement in the broken concrete wall. Eventually, they did manage to flip it over, revealing a small gap where it had torn a hole in the metal building.

"Alpha Five! Alpha Five can you hear me? Mike!" bellowed Alpha One, getting louder with each word, but still receiving no reply.

"I think Delta team could hear you," mumbled Alpha Four, not being as quiet as he would've liked.

Alpha One flicked his head round and threw him a look that could kill, causing Alpha Four to lower his head and stand in silence. They continued to roll the smaller blocks away, giving themselves just enough room to squeeze inside.

Alpha One dropped into the room, turning back to say, "Wait there," to Alpha Four.

The room looked as if it had been spun in a washing machine with desks, tables, shelves, chairs, and computers all in pieces jumbled up across the floor. He slowly moved around the room, looking at the floor. Finally, his eyes caught sight of Alpha Five under a filing cabinet. He charged over the debris and lifted the cabinet up, pushing it aside. Alpha Five was conscious, as he was checked for any injuries. Alpha One lifted him up and helped him back towards the hole, which Alpha Four had made even wider. As they stumbled back over the destroyed furniture and back out of the building, they both remained silent.

At the top, Alpha Three had also joined them, refusing to look at Alpha Five. Alpha Five caught his breath and made sure he was the first to speak, not that anyone else was going to.

"I'm sorry, okay. There's not much more I can say. I was just trying to make amends and earn your trust back, and I messed it up. I know that, and I'm sorry," he said.

"We've no time to discuss this now, as we've got something more pressing on our minds. Mike, can I trust you not to do something stupid again?" said Alpha One.

Alpha Five didn't say anything, he just nodded a couple of times, slowly, with his shoulders sinking. Whilst the lack of a verbal answer wasn't what Alpha One was looking for, his body language gave a clear enough answer to show how sorry he was. Without the exchange of any more words or opinions, they swiftly left the burning site and joined back up with Blindspot, who had continued to watch over their every move.

On the horizon, a fast-moving truck came into view. Blindspot was the first to identify it, using the scope on his rifle.

"That's going to be our quickest way to the compound. Let's wait for it to come closer and strike before they alert the compound of our presence," said Alpha One.

"I'm pretty sure they know we're here; we weren't exactly quiet," replied Alpha Three.

After a long sigh and a quick glance back at the smouldering embers of the SAM turret, Alpha One added, "Yes, but they don't know we're still alive, nor do they know how many of us are here. Now, let's get out of sight."

Whilst it would've been easy enough to allow the truck to pass by, unaware of their presence, Alpha Five had already put them behind schedule and prevented them from staying under the radar, so the quicker they got to the compound, the better their chance of surprise would be. The truck continued to get closer, kicking up a trail of dust in its wake. Before long, it was almost on top of them. Blindspot went to take the driver out, but with Alpha One's hand holding his rifle down, it was clear another plan was in motion.

The truck pulled up only metres away from them, as eight Vipers climbed out to peer down to the sunken SAM turret site. Alpha team were in a line, lying prone, as they watched the guards through their sights. Without a word to each other, five of the Vipers were dropped. The other three swiftly followed, unable to draw their guns to their invisible enemy. Alpha team had shot the first five in the order of their assigned positions, with Alpha One taking out the furthest to the left, and Blindspot taking the sixth Viper from the left. With nothing left to slow them down, they followed Alpha One towards the guards, where they each hastily retrieved some outer clothes and slipped them on. Now they could pass for the guards from a distance, and the truck could get them close enough. It struck Alpha One as odd that the SAM turret was guarded by ordinary guards, along with the patrol that arrived. With the possibility that the Vipers might be running low on numbers, he didn't let it concern him, confident they would come face to face with enough Vipers as they entered the compound. They all climbed into the truck, with Alpha Four driving, and headed towards the compound, as the fiery orange sun illuminated the island.

By the time they'd reached the main compound, the sun was high in the sky, as it started to break up the thick layer of cloud which hung above the island. Surrounding the compound was an unscalable wall, standing over ten stories high. Alpha One and Four lowered their guard's caps over their faces, as they knew, despite it being one of their own, that all eyes would be upon an approaching vehicle during an assault. They drove up to the only open part of the wall, where a group of Vipers controlled the checkpoint. One of them stepped forward and held his outstretched hand in the air to signal Alpha Four to slow the truck to a stop. The brakes squealed as the truck jolted to a stop, as the Vipers approached without any suspicion.

"Get ready to floor it," whispered Alpha One, as one of the Vipers approached from his side.

Alpha One already had his handgun clutched within his dry hands, obscured and out of view. He lowered the window to speak to the Viper but, as soon as the Viper stepped up to the cabin, he saw Alpha One's face in full and realised they weren't the same people that had left. Before the Viper could react, Alpha One lifted his suppressed handgun and fired one muffled shot under his chin. The gel splattered onto his neck and knocked the Viper out instantly. Without drawing too much attention, Alpha One caught the Viper and leant him into the truck, making sure his feet stayed on the truck's step. From the outside, it looked as if he was leaning in to find something, which did start to raise some unwanted attention, but not nearly as much as the guard flat on his back. Fortunately, they were wearing the same clothes, so he leant him back out of the truck, and held his own hand up to the other Vipers, with his thumb held high, making out it was actually the unconscious guard's hand. It didn't look particularly convincing from the truck, but the Vipers seemed to buy the act.

"The poor guy isn't a puppet," whispered Alpha Four.

The gates were promptly opened, and they were beckoned through.

"Yes, he is... they all are. Now floor it!" replied Alpha One.

Alpha Four slammed his foot on the throttle, causing them to leap forwards, with all four wheels grabbing the dirt. Alpha One let the unconscious Viper drop to the floor, as they accelerated towards the open gates. The other Vipers soon noticed what was wrong and signalled for the gates to be shut. But as everyone in the truck ducked down to avoid the spray of incoming bullets, the truck squeezed through the closing gates and was on the tarmac road within the compound. Alarms rang out an instant after squealing around the first corner, as one wheel tried lifting off the road.

They wasted no time in leaving the truck, as Alpha Four ploughed into the corner of a building. They climbed out and went inside, clearing the room and sealing the door shut, likely only buying them a few crucial seconds. Making the vehicle crash gave the impression they were panicking and might just give them their only chance to strike without the full force of the Vipers on their tail.

"Bravo One, begin your assault," said Alpha One, as they flowed through the building checking every corner with their rifles primed.

Alpha team swept through building after building as quickly as possible, trying to break their scent trail from the hunting Vipers.

Then, a welcomed voice began to speak, as Alpha Two said, "Okay, our geo-scan is complete. According to this, the compound itself is more like a miniaturised city, but there is also activity under the surface. It looks like the island's lifeline is underground, so that'll be a good place to start looking for Crabble. There should be several access points near your current location. Head into the next building and up the stairs, there's a chute in the first room on the right which leads underground. I'm not sure if it leads into the series of tunnels, but it's worth a look."

Whilst he provided extra information about the island, Alpha team continued to clear the buildings and moved into the next one. Instead of heading straight out of the other side, Alpha One led the way up one flight of stairs. The first room on the right housed two Vipers who were swiftly dropped, whilst Alpha One opened the hatch on the far side. Alpha Four removed two glow sticks from his pocket, cracked them, and dropped them down the chute. The glow sticks rattled down and hit a solid base two and a half seconds later, before illuminating the bottom in an eerie, green light. The chute was plenty wide enough for someone to move up and down, so Alpha One wasn't concerned with it being a one-way trip.

But to ensure they didn't all end up in a pile at the bottom, he looked at Alpha Four and said, "Head down and see if there's a way out."

Alpha Four didn't give any argument or objection, as he placed his rifle on his back and started to edge down the chute.

Alpha One looked around the room and grabbed a rope. He attached one end to the metal pole that ran perpendicular to the chute and dropped the other to the bottom. The rope knocked Alpha Four, just as he reached the bottom, startling him.

He looked up and shouted, "You could've warned me!"

"True, I could have," answered Alpha One, as he looked down to check on Alpha Four's progress.

"We've got movement downstairs," said Blindspot, who had just entered the room after watching the stairs for any presence of Vipers.

"It's now or never. Is there a way through?" asked Alpha One, as the other three started taking cover behind tables and other furniture capable of providing protection.

They didn't close the door, knowing that it would be easy enough for one of the Vipers to slip a grenade through. This way, they had just as much opportunity to get it back out of the room. Alpha Four started to kick the sides of the metal chute, until finally releasing what seemed to be another hatch.

"Yes, I'm through," said Alpha Four, as he retrieved his rifle and began to check his surroundings.

They could then hear footsteps approaching their doorway, so Alpha One took cover and said, "Copy, we may be a little delayed. Bravo One, have you made entry yet?"

***

"This is Bravo One, we are making entry now," he said, as he took cover behind one of the two remaining tanks.

They both fired two single shells at the steel gate which blocked their path. The impacts blew it clear of its hinges, allowing the two tanks to ram the gate crippling the final threads that kept it standing. Their advance was slow, as they crept into the open. Both APCs held their position at the gate, with a small group of Charlie team, ensuring no Vipers could escape out of the back. Bravo One knew they didn't have the firepower for a full assault, but their main objective was to create the biggest distraction. As they moved forward, they removed any Vipers who came into their sights, using the two tanks for cover. There was a constant spray of bullets pounding the tanks' armour which sounded like sitting under a glass roof in a rainstorm. They held their position only a few metres inside the towering walls, drawing all the Vipers away from the assault which mattered most. Charlie One caught sight of a grenade flying towards them.

"Down!" he barked, as they hit the floor and the grenade landed on the other side of the wall which Bravo One was behind. The grenade detonated, letting out a loud '*pop*' and a bright flash. It was nothing which would kill Bravo One, but it was enough to disrupt his hearing for a few seconds. Even the tanks' turrets were muffled, as he stayed in cover.

"I don't know what the fuss is about. My hearing wasn't affected," said Charlie One, as he knelt beside Bravo One.

Within just a few seconds, Bravo One was back up, pushing forward with their tanks.

"We are in position on our escort. The two frigates, the destroyer and the aircraft carrier are all ready to make their assault. The carrier is full of our aircraft and helicopters. Just give the word," said Delta One, now on the central ship in the formation.

They could provide covering fire on the island, as well as provide protection for the aircraft carrier behind. The carrier's top deck was full of various aircraft, all able to bombard the island or provide a more targeted attack to protect the ground operatives. As all the aircraft were from the Molehill, they carried various enhancements to help. The most noticeable upgrade was the propulsion-fuse drive which Suzy had fitted to all the aircraft. The design was still experimental but, in the short burst it could sustain, the drive provided an extreme increase in acceleration, meaning aircraft requiring a six-hundred-metre runway only needed a runway half that length to reach take-off speeds.

***

"We're about to head underground. It's unlikely we'll have any sort of radio contact, so Bravo One has full control of the naval escort. We'll be a long way underground, so no need to worry about our precise location as no explosion should be felt," said Alpha One, as they held the Vipers at the open doorway.

"They're still coming through!" shouted Alpha Five, as he ducked behind a metal filing cabinet to protect himself from the barrage of incoming bullets.

"We're going to have to head underground, there's no way we can hold them back forever. Alpha Three, set a charge on the chute, we don't want them to follow us," shouted Alpha One, trying to hear his own voice over the gunfire.

Alpha Three ripped the pin from a grenade and flung it out of the room. It let out a bright white flash and a piercing noise, dazing everyone outside. It provided enough cover for Alpha Three to run over to the hatch and slap a pack of explosives inside the chute. He then pulled himself inside and started his descent, sliding down the rope.

"Blindspot next, then Alpha Five," said Alpha One, using the break in gunfire to speak at a normal volume.

Blindspot followed his instructions, as he moved towards the hatch and climbed down before the Vipers could continue firing.

"Moving!" shouted Alpha Five, as he quickly headed for the hatch.

But before he could make it, a cluster of bullets flew across the room. He dived behind the closest table and covered his head, as they pounded it. Alpha One pulled the pin from an identical grenade and threw it to the other side of the table he was using for cover. He covered his ears tightly and counted to five. Once done, Alpha One leapt up, flicked a tiny switch on the side of his rifle to fully automatic, and pulled the trigger back hard.

He sprayed every remaining bullet towards the stumbling enemies, as he shouted, "Move!" to get Alpha Five out of the room.

Alpha Five jumped to his feet and ran to the hatch, slamming into it as he arrived. He scurried down and out of sight, leaving only Alpha One in the room. As soon as the magazine was empty, he swung his rifle behind him and removed his handgun. Without waiting for any more Vipers to enter the room, Alpha One started to head towards the hatch. He didn't need to turn around to hear the footsteps creep around the corner and rifles being raised into the room. Alpha One propelled himself forwards, as he leapt over a table, making it impossible for the Vipers' rifles to keep up with him. As he flew over the table, his body twisted to face the Vipers. He raised his handgun and managed to fire six shots before he disappeared behind the table. On landing, his shoulder took the brunt of the impact and, as he rolled over, he used his momentum to rise straight back up. Now close to the hatch, Alpha One jumped back up and threw his feet through the square gap, shortly followed by the rest of his body. Just before his head was submerged into the darkness of the chute, he turned to see six Vipers keeling over, each with one shot to the head.

He fired two remaining bullets before vanishing, each one hitting another unsuspecting Viper. Alpha One tried to use his feet to slow his descent, as the rope eluded his grasp, but soon after leaping down, he crashed to the bottom, falling out of the side, and smacked onto the concrete floor underground.

"Blow it," he said, as he was aided back to his feet by Alpha Four.

They moved a few paces away before Alpha Three detonated the charge, igniting the room and sealing the chute with part of the building above. Bricks fell down the chute with a huge cloud of smoke. They headed along the wide, open corridor confident they couldn't be followed.

Chapter 15.2

Inside the system of tunnels, there was a cold, damp feel as they moved through the concrete pathways. They only walked through a few intersections before quickly realising that, without VOICE, it would take them a long time to cover the ground. The following intersection had three ways to go, aside from where they had come from, so they split up to cover more ground with Alpha One going alone. Alpha Three still wished to stay away from Alpha Five, so he headed to the left with Alpha Four, leaving the other two to take the tunnel on the right. They had the capability of pinging each other, despite being amongst a maze of concrete tunnels, so they would always be able to regroup should something be found. After a while of moving through the tunnels, with even their sound-absorbing boots making a slight clomp as they echoed through the warren, Alpha Five and Blindspot eventually came to a room of interest.

They both crept in and cleared it, taking note of the huge machine in the centre. There was only a small space that was accessible, with the machine sealed behind glass and clearly unreachable by anyone. Alpha Five started to look through various files on the only computer in the room. Blindspot looked over his shoulder at the computer flicking information up and down, as multiple screens of data were raised at once. It was nothing he could make sense of, and as it started to make him feel a little sick, he left the technical side of the mission to Alpha Five. Whilst he waited, Blindspot admired the monstrous machine behind the glass.

"So that's how they do it!" exclaimed Alpha Five.

Blindspot was curious but had no intention of taking the bait, knowing an explanation wouldn't make any sense.

"They disturb the magnetic field. They start a chain reaction of excited particles, which eventually reaches the magnetic field, allowing them to control even the slightest fluctuations. They control one of the smallest parts of science which ends up controlling one of the biggest. Well, that's how they control the storms, anyway, which means they aren't strictly real but are instead more like synthetic ones. Although, it still doesn't explain how they started an earthquake and caused an extinct volcano to erupt," continued Alpha Five.

"Was any of that supposed to make sense?" asked Blindspot, getting nothing in return. "Thought not. So in future, keep it to yourself," he concluded, still amazed by the engineering he was looking up at.

Whilst Alpha Five continued to make himself look useful, Blindspot did the same by ensuring the tunnels remained clear. By the time he'd looked up and down the empty tunnel to see nothing but chipped walls and hear an echoing, dripping noise from somewhere within the underground network, Alpha Five had climbed on top of the desk and had started removing ceiling panels. He dropped the thin panels on the floor and started to remove some wires. With some more overly complicated fiddling of the wires, he cut some and rejoined them in different places. Blindspot still wasn't interested, as he went to check the tunnels again, finding nothing new. Alpha Five jumped off the table and attached the final wire to his CAT, allowing him to communicate with those above ground through the relays used to control Titan.

"VOICE, I'm sending you everything on how Titan works. Once you have it, set the reactors to 'overdrive' and activate the device Heartfell gave us which is plugged in to port twenty-four. I've already shut off the pulse generator, so it should destroy everything here, just hopefully not us," said Alpha Five, as he tore the wire from his CAT and ushered Blindspot out of the room.

He sent a signal to the other three, resulting in an orange flash, to indicate Titan had been shut down. On their way out, Blindspot gave one final look at the machine, as he noticed Heartfell's device sticking out of one of the many USB ports. And as they continued through the tunnels, only Crabble was left to find.

***

"This place looks derelict," said Alpha One without thinking about the fact that nobody could hear him.

The signal sent by Alpha Five bounced throughout the underground and finally reached Alpha One, as the small light started flashing orange. The only path he chose was forwards, so he wouldn't have a dilemma each time the tunnel split. As he walked on, he couldn't help but think he was within a labyrinth and could at any moment come across a Minotaur. But eventually, Alpha One came across his first door, directly ahead. He edged closer to it, trying to make as little noise as he could, until finally reaching for the handle. Slowly, he twisted it and pushed the door in. As it swung open to reveal the room, Alpha One was faced with a room full of Night Vipers. There were about fifty in front of him with potentially a lot more surrounding the circular floor in the centre of the room. Knowing he couldn't take them all, Alpha One slowly closed the door again to give himself time to contact the rest of his team. As he clicked the door closed, whilst screwing his face up to try and make it quieter, everything started shaking. The walls, the floor, the door, everything shook with an immense force, causing Alpha One to stumble back, just after calling the rest of Alpha team to his location. Moments later, the ceiling of the tunnel began to crack, before eventually giving way. A huge cloud of dust engulfed Alpha One and the tunnel, as debris fell through the weakened structure.

***

3 MINUTES EARLIER

Charlie One took cover behind his advancing tank, as he was shrouded in heavy gunfire.

"Take cover!" he shouted, as enemy machine guns lit up the road they were trying to advance on.

"There are multiple machine gun nests within the tall building, eleven o'clock from our position," shouted Charlie Four in his high-pitched and squeaky voice, as he took cover beside his leader.

The building beside them exploded, as an RPG hit the wall. Charlie Four covered his round head and chubby face with his short fingers, trying to protect himself from the blast. His helmet ended up crooked on his head, as it hung to the side. Despite his high number in Charlie team, he was only twenty-four and left Charlie One to make the plan.

"Charlie Two, we've hit a slight setback, we'll be a little late to our rendezvous. How goes your progress?" shouted Charlie One.

"Quite well, we've hit no problems and have met light resistance. I hardly expected you to be on time. Having too much fun?" replied Charlie Two.

"There is nothing fun about this, we have met heavy resistance. Cougar, hit the building at eleven o'clock, we've got to bring it down!" shouted Charlie One, against the relentless machine gun fire.

The tank they were behind twisted round and aimed up, until its turret pointed directly at the building. With one deafening blow, the tank jolted back as it sent an explosive projectile at the building. It struck its target, grazing only the outside.

Charlie One could hardly see the damage, as he took a brief look from behind the tank.

"Delta One, I need a heavy strike at the following coordinates. It needs to be targeted and powerful, you're hitting the tallest building in the location," shouted Charlie One.

Only a few seconds passed, with the machine guns tearing up the road, before he got an answer.

"Copy that. Hawk and Eagle are heading to the marked location for a contained strike. They've been advised of close, friendly contact, so mark your location with orange smoke," said Delta One, calm and relaxed on her heavily guarded destroyer.

Charlie One and everyone around him started throwing small canisters of orange smoke into the open, before taking hard cover behind any building they could find.

Two jets flew overhead, too quick for Charlie One to even see through the orange smoke. Their noise, however, was unmistakable, as the two A-10s boomed past. Moments later, there were multiple loud explosions as the two jets emptied what sounded like their entire payload at the building.

"This is Hawk, the building is still standing. We are going to make another pass. This time, we'll hit the floor in the hope of toppling the building," said one of the pilots, as they circled around and made another pass from the opposite side.

"Danger close!" shouted Charlie One, as everyone hit the floor and covered their heads for the impending strike.

The two jets flew past again, creating an even louder set of explosions in their wake. As silence descended at the location, they could soon hear cracking as the building started to fold in on itself.

"That's a good hit. The building is going down," said Hawk, as the two jets headed off into the distance to refuel and restock their ammunition.

The building slowly disappeared, as it got swallowed up by the ground, dragging any surrounding structures into the hole it left. There was cheering, as Charlie team celebrated the small victory before proceeding with their assault.

***

Below ground, Alpha One was desperately trying to get his breath back, as he regained his orientation. The thick cloud of dust had started to clear, but it was still difficult to even see a foot in front. As his senses came back to him, he could hear Vipers approaching from the doorway. It was still hard to see them, but he wasted no time in taking cover behind one of the many fallen lumps of concrete. It didn't take much longer for the dust to settle, allowing Alpha One to see part of a building had ruptured the casing of the tunnel. It blocked the other entrance and had clearly weakened the surrounding walls and ceiling of the tunnel, despite only a small amount of the building poking through. The Vipers continued to get closer, moving around the fallen rocks and lumps of concrete scattered across the floor. Alpha One looked around for his rifle but couldn't see it anywhere. He slowly drew his handgun and formed a plan, as he risked a tiny look around the debris he hid behind. His look was quick, and he got little information. However, he did see his rifle in the hands of one of the Vipers. He also saw too many guards to be dispatched with one sidearm. Replacing his handgun back at his side, Alpha One took out his knife and final grenade. Knowing a grenade could bring the whole place down, he had few other options, as he waited for them to edge closer.

Finally, they were close enough, but as Alpha One shifted his position, one of the Vipers caught sight of him. Within a second, they had all opened fire on him, as he lay prone behind the block and covered his face from the spitting concrete, as the Vipers' bullets chewed through it. He didn't have long, as they edged closer, firing everything at the shrinking block. Alpha One ripped out the pin and tossed the grenade over, as he screwed his eyes up and cupped his hands over his ears.

As soon as the grenade went off, Alpha One leapt up with his knife clasped firmly in his right hand. He hurdled the thin concrete block and lunged towards the closest Viper, who was dazed by the grenade. The knife was plunged into the Viper's side, before quickly being drawn back out. He dropped to the floor and held his wound, as blood rushed from the red gash, allowing Alpha One to move on to the next. He raised the knife and buried it in the following Viper's shoulder. The Viper reached up to grab what caused the pain, as his hand began to wrap itself around the handle. Before he could get any grip on it, Alpha One tore it out, slicing the Viper's hand as it exited. The knife was then briefly thrust into the third Viper's torso to distract him, before his head was thrown against the wall. The Viper slid down it, his hand resting on his damp, red clothes. By this point, the Vipers had started to regain their senses, as Alpha One lowered his body and grabbed the back of the fourth Viper's knees, using all his strength to lift them off the ground, sending the Viper crashing to the floor. Alpha One finished the move off by digging the knife into the Viper's chest, ensuring he couldn't get back up, but didn't hit any major organs. Whilst still low to the ground, he swung the knife round and sliced the two closest knees, toppling the Viper and allowing Alpha One to catch his arm with the knife as he went down. The Vipers were fully focussed, as they started to take aim at Alpha One. Without taking the time to think, he leapt forward and grabbed the closest Viper, pushing the knife against his throat, trying to prevent him from moving. The Vipers had no concern with shooting one of their own, as they opened fire on the

Viper Alpha One was hiding behind. He dug his knife into the lifeless corpse he was hiding behind and grabbed the Viper's rifle. He knew he had little other choice, as he lifted the rifle up and emptied the entire magazine towards the Vipers ahead.

They fell back, as Alpha One pushed the corpse forward to meet the rest of what felt like an endless line of Vipers. Once the rifle was empty, he dropped it along with the corpse and rushed in amongst the hostiles, taking his knife with him. The knife darted from person to person and limb to limb, acting more like a pinball. He stayed low and created a sense of disorientation, as he manoeuvred between them all, preventing anyone from getting a clean shot. As he inflicted more and more wounds, taking down Viper after Viper, they started to get desperate, as they fired within the group, sometimes hitting the walls, sometimes taking out their own team. Alpha One eventually reached the doorway with little energy left, but as he went to step into the giant circular room, he saw what looked like hundreds of Vipers all waiting for him. He grabbed the closest one, pulled the pin out of their grenade hanging on their vest, and pushed them back through the doorway, closing it behind them. Alpha One hung onto the door, ensuring nobody could throw it back, as just seconds later the door was blown into the tunnel, its fall softened by Alpha One. As he lay under the door, his vision blurred, he centred his focus and grabbed the closest gun, despite it only being a handgun. Two Vipers down the tunnel were climbing back to their feet but were quickly disposed of, as the main group of Vipers opened fire on everything within the tunnel. Alpha One stayed under the door, as anything that moved was swiftly torn to shreds.

He waited until a slight break in their firing, where they would most likely be reloading, and swung his arm around the door firing the handgun. Although he could only see as he peered round the side, every shot was perfect and well placed, and he was able to take down twelve Vipers with the twelve bullets in the gun. As he stood up to take advantage of his momentum, he dropped the handgun and retrieved another, full of ammunition. He continued along his path without cover, grabbing a second handgun to start firing two at a time, aware this could be his last stand. Upon reaching the open doorway, he took cover behind the concrete surrounds and picked up two remaining handguns. Another rumble could be felt throughout the system of tunnels. He swung his body around the corner, unsure whether the entire place was about to collapse. But as he faced the circular room, he was suddenly pushed forward by an unstoppable force which threw him inside.

***

Alpha One couldn't be sure how much later it was, but as he opened his eyes to see the muzzles of multiple blurry rifles pointing at him, all he could hear was ringing and buzzing. It didn't take long for his mind to take control, as he was in complete survival mode, considering nothing but his own safety. He grabbed the barrel of one of the rifles and pushed himself to the right, flinging his leg round to catch any close Vipers off balance. He pulled himself up, taking the Viper's knife as he raised himself. He struck the Viper repeatedly, as he lunged towards another, pushing his rifle to the side. The Viper opened fire, causing bullets to be strewn throughout the room, hitting anyone in their way. Alpha One continued to take down everyone within reach, but they soon became too far away to catch with the razor-sharp blade. He threw the knife towards an enemy, catching him in the right of his neck, in what he thought would be his last act. As he closed his eyes to the circle of Vipers that surrounded him, his body froze. Gunfire filled the room.

***

Moments had passed, as Alpha One remained standing. His brain couldn't quite contemplate the situation, as he slowly opened his eyes to see every Viper lying on the floor. Still in shock, Alpha One looked up to see his team on the mezzanine, one floor up. It was a sight he'd never been so pleased to see. Everything seemed slow and quiet, as he looked around the room, compared to the adrenaline rush that was wearing off. Thanks to the trackers Suzy had recently installed in all of their grips, he quickly gathered his rifle, sidearm, and found his knife, covered in blood and dust. Alpha One then moved over to the final person that he'd hit. From above, Alpha Three could still see the knife sticking out of their neck, as Alpha One bent down to take a closer look. He couldn't think why his leader had taken such an interest, as he saw him remove the Viper's helmet and mask while he continued to stare at his face.

Before long, he shouted down, saying, "We think Crabble is above ground somewhere. It's only a matter of time before we find him."

It was enough to break Alpha One out of his trance, as it caused him to move away and start climbing the ladder that went to the very top. Every rung he climbed, he caught sight of his blood-soaked hands constantly flashing in his face.

Chapter 15.3

It didn't take long for them all to reach the surface, even with Alpha Three looking directly ahead as he carefully took each step. Alpha One climbed out and aided the rest, as they got to the top. And as each one got out, they covered a different direction, looking up and down the road they had surfaced on. Alpha Three was the final to be pulled out, as he had to roll to the side, not wanting to take any steps near the open hole. The compound had drastically changed in appearance since they were last on the surface, with buildings on fire and smoke billowing from everywhere. As they waited to move, four friendly Apache helicopters flew overhead, heading towards the main source of the fire and smoke. Now back in radio contact, Alpha One was about to announce their return but was interrupted before he could even start.

"This is Charlie Two. I have eyes on Gold Viper and a possible ID on Crabble," she said.

"Charlie Two, do not engage. Tail them loosely if possible, but do not engage," replied Alpha One, making it clear they'd returned to the surface.

***

"Copy that, Alpha One. Engaging in a tail will be difficult, but we will do our best," concluded Charlie Two. She then went off comms and said, "Continue your assault, Charlie Five. You're in charge. I want you seven to follow me, we're going to tail Crabble," as she directed her comment to the seven closest members of Charlie team.

She knew trying to keep up with them as an entire unit would be difficult, but eight of them would find it a lot easier to follow in the shadows whilst the rest provided a distraction. Charlie Five seemed extremely laid-back, as he gave just one, slow, nod whilst giving an equally slow blink. He was more than capable of leading the splinter division, which allowed Charlie Two to move off with confidence.

She moved into the closest building and started to follow Crabble, staying out of sight. They all followed in double file, as it was the best compromise between stealth and safety. Building after building, they travelled alongside the road to where they last saw Crabble and his security escort. By the time they reached the end of the line of buildings, Crabble had moved on. Charlie Two leant out of the door and looked up and down the road to try and find him. With no sign of them, Charlie Two then looked directly ahead, where she saw a door swinging open and closed, banging against the wall in the wind. She felt something wasn't right, as if it was almost too good to be true, so she updated Alpha One on their position.

"Alpha One, we've lost Crabble but have a potential lead. We think they've entered the barbershop on street… one three two. Should we follow them inside?" asked Charlie Two.

"Negative, hold position. VOICE, are there any other exits to the building?" replied Alpha One, as he tried to further the likelihood of Crabble being inside.

"No, according to our scans, there is just that one entrance. But there does seem to be a tunnel inside. It appears unconnected to the main network of underground tunnels, but a small, unmapped route into them is possible," said VOICE.

"Charlie Two, we're about ten minutes away. Watch the exit and we'll enter together," concluded Alpha One.

"Copy, holding position," said Charlie Two, as she began

making hand signals, causing the other seven to spread out.

She watched the building for the next two minutes, seeing no change. But at that moment, Charlie Two caught site of movement to her right. She couldn't see much, but someone had crossed the road and entered the building they were holding position within. There was no need to inform her team of the potential threat, as they all turned towards the entrance. The door swung open, and Gold Viper slowly emerged, holding his hands in the air, showing nothing in them.

He slowly stepped forward, approaching the eight operatives who were all aiming their rifles at him. It was the first time any of Charlie team had got a clear look at one of the coloured Vipers. He had a black helmet, with two gold stripes running down it, and half a black mask, showing nothing except his mouth. The rest of his outfit was black and gold, which looked too thin to have any real protection, as he looked slim, yet still muscular, himself.

"Stop!" shouted Charlie Two.

Gold Viper continued to walk forwards, as a sly smile began to emerge across the only visible part of his face. He then, very slowly, removed his mask and helmet, dropping them to the floor. His face was also thin, and he had no facial hair. The hair on his head was blond, but only just visible due to its very short length. He was about 5'11" and in his mid-thirties, but the most eye-catching feature was the long scar which ran down the full stretch of the left-hand side of his face. As Charlie Two looked closer at the scar, she also noticed his eyes looked gold in colour. They weren't like Alpha Three's amber eyes, but were gold, which meant he was clearly wearing contact lenses, taking his role too seriously.

"I won't ask you again. Stop!" shouted Charlie Two once more.

But he didn't stop.

Charlie Two had hoped to keep him conscious to obtain

knowledge of Crabble's whereabouts, but she knew she had just one choice left. With the sedative rounds loaded, her finger pulled the trigger. The bullet was lined up with his head but was stopped only a few centimetres away. It looked to be floating in the air, as it held its position. The other seven operatives then all opened fire, sending an abundance of bullets towards Gold Viper. But no matter how many they fired, none of them reached him. As the bullets started to stack up, it became clear that they were being stopped by a perfectly colourless sheet of ballistic glass or plastic which was attached to his suit. As soon as they started to reload, Gold Viper unclipped the sheet and pulled out a knife from behind his back. He lunged forward and dug the knife into Charlie Eight's chest, somehow cutting through his tactical vest as if it wasn't there at all, before grabbing Charlie Twenty-Seven, pressing the knife against his throat, and holding him to face the other six. The cold, metal blade cut into his throat, as they all watched Gold Viper intensely. Nobody dared to move, as blood started to trickle from where the knife was held so close. After just a couple of seconds, Gold Viper drew the knife back, spraying a jet of blood towards the others. They flinched, as the blood covered them, giving Gold Viper just enough time to move forwards. He cut through them all, inflicting multiple wounds. It seemed impossible, even for a group as skilled as Charlie team, to get a clear shot, as Gold Viper leapt from walls, slid on the floor, and performed acrobatics which shouldn't be possible. It felt like he was everywhere at the same time. He darted between them, killing the operatives one by one, as they desperately tried to block the bombardment of strikes. In his blur of movement, it almost seemed like he was able to jump over the bullets to avoid them. Within just a few seconds, only two were left alive. He retrieved his knife, buried under Charlie Nine's chin, as he watched the remaining two. Gold

Viper hadn't escaped without any wounds, and certainly looked a little worse for wear, with one gunshot wound to his left shoulder and a stab wound to his right thigh.

Both Charlie Two and Sixteen had lost their rifles in the fight but had their sidearms trained on Gold Viper. They shared uneasy glances, as the green gel on his left shoulder hadn't put him to sleep. He did, however, seem to be affected by the shot, as it looked like he was struggling to stay focussed.

"An adrenaline injection makes you invulnerable to your bullets. I entered this room prepared, did you?" said Gold Viper, as he looked towards Charlie team's vulnerabilities. Their bodies were covered in tiny lacerations which Gold Viper had inflicted during the brawl. Gold Viper's left hand was behind his back and, before Charlie Two could order him to raise it, their sidearms suddenly felt odd. Gold Viper placed his hand in front of him, showing a small, round, black object. Charlie Sixteen pulled his trigger, but nothing happened. Charlie Two did the same and had the same outcome. Whatever the device was, it had disabled their sidearms.

"No guns," said Gold Viper, as he slowly drew a handgun from behind him and laid it on the floor with the round device.

Charlie Two and Sixteen did the same, slowly placing their useless sidearms on the floor.

"No cheating, there is only honour," added Gold Viper with a laugh, as they all held their own knives in front of them.

They all stood motionless for the next few seconds, watching every twitch and flinch the others made. Charlie Sixteen's hand started to sweat, as he clutched his knife tighter. With the flicker of Gold Viper's eyelid, Charlie Sixteen charged forward, holding his knife at arm's length ahead of him. Charlie Two followed shortly behind, knowing they would have to attack simultaneously, but it was too late. As Charlie Sixteen lunged forward, Gold Viper kept his cool and flicked his body to the right. He let his knife slip from his hands, as he raised his flat, right hand under Charlie Sixteen's knife, flicking it out of his sweaty grip and into the wall behind. Charlie Sixteen's momentum took him out of the way, allowing Gold Viper to focus on his next target. His knife had landed on his foot, but he wasted no time in flicking it back up, instantly returning it to the safety of his right hand. They both took several swings at each other, missing every lunge, as they both dodged and attacked. Charlie Sixteen retrieved his knife from the wall and started to move towards the duelling pair, but both saw him approaching and, without hesitation, Gold Viper rolled his knife in his hand and threw it at Charlie Sixteen. The knife was heading straight for his heart, but before either of them could even comprehend what was happening, another knife cut across its path, adjusting its trajectory. The knife buried itself deep in Charlie Sixteen's left shoulder, sending him stumbling back. Gold Viper was confused for only a second, until he turned to see Charlie Two had sacrificed her own knife to counter his.

This time, Gold Viper made the first move, as he charged towards her. After a few failed punches, they found themselves locked together. With the test of strength leaving them at a stalemate, Charlie Two raised her left knee up to her chest and found enough room to kick Gold Viper in the torso, sending them stumbling apart. She wasted no time before charging at Gold Viper, taking him down to the ground. They continued fighting, neither getting a clean hit as the other blocked perfectly. Eventually, Charlie Two gained the momentum she needed, as Gold Viper got impatient and went to strike too soon, allowing her to get a hit under his chin. The punch dazed his senses for just a split second, allowing Charlie Two to wrap her hands around his throat and squeeze. But instead of resisting,

Gold Viper kept calm and pulled the pin from a grenade hanging on her vest. It released a loud bang and a bright white flash, as they were both disorientated. Charlie Two lost her grip on Gold Viper, as they started stumbling around the room. After a moment or two, they could start to see again and locked onto each other. They were stood metres apart, with several corpses lying between them. Charlie Two bent down and started running towards him, confident she could win again. Gold Viper knew it as well and, before she got halfway, he drew another handgun from behind his back and fired just one bullet.

Charlie Two wasn't fazed by the gunshot, as she tackled Gold Viper, forcing him back into the wall. He grunted in pain, as the gun slipped from his grasp. They hit the back wall, causing a wooden noticeboard to fall off under the force of the impact. She continued to throw his head against the wall, time after time, until he was finally able to retaliate. With a lucky hit, Gold Viper caught her in the midriff, causing her to stumble back, as she let the pain fuel her wrath. Their fight only continued for the next thirty seconds, but as they both sustained multiple blows, it felt like an eternity waiting for the other to tire. Eventually, Charlie Two moved for another tackle; this time she grabbed him from his thighs, and lifted him up, before throwing him to the floor. Gold Viper landed on the wooden noticeboard, as his back cracked over it. He let out another groan, whilst desperately trying to ignore the pain. But after looking back to Charlie Two, there was a remarkable change in his demeanour, as he saw the extent of her injuries. He laughed, as she also noticed the gunshot wound just above her bulletproof vest gushing with blood. Charlie Two felt the pain increase and looked around to see the extent of her blood loss covering the floor. With little time left, she grabbed two knives from beside her and, with all her remaining strength, she buried each one deep into

Gold Viper's hands, and through the wooden noticeboard, until no part of the blades were visible. That was the first time anyone had heard him scream.

Moments later, Alpha One ran through the open doorway, but the time for helping had passed, as the battle had been both won and lost. Charlie Two was on her knees when he entered but keeled over shortly after. She lay on the hard floor, as blood continued to pour from the wound. Alpha One rushed over and immediately started applying pressure to the hole in her upper chest. With a quick glance behind, he saw Charlie Sixteen on the floor with a knife in his shoulder. He wasn't going to die, but he seemed in no condition to help. The rest of Alpha team had gone ahead to breach the barbershop, so he needed to obtain assistance from elsewhere.

"Charlie Two has been hit. She needs immediate medical attention. VOICE, send them my location," said Alpha One, applying even more pressure to the wound. "You'll be alright," he said, trying to make her more comfortable, as he removed a rifle from behind her head.

"We both know that's a lie," she replied in a weak and frail voice.

It didn't take long before Charlie One stumbled around the corner and saw her. He bent down and allowed his huge fingers to softly stroke her warm cheek. She reached up and held his other hand, as a tear slowly trickled down her cheek, stopping at Charlie One's index finger.

"It looks like you're going to have to find someone else to nag you all the time," mumbled Charlie Two, as with every blink her eyelids became heavier.

"Don't talk like that. Charlie Seven will be here in a few seconds, and he'll patch you up. You'll be back to nagging me in no time," said Charlie One, confident in his answer.

Charlie Seven entered the room shortly after and got straight to work.

"Alpha One, we've hit light resistance but are closing in on Crabble's position," said Alpha Three.

"Go get him," said Charlie Two, softly.

There was little more either of them could do whilst Charlie Seven tried to save her. Alpha One nodded, smiled, and slowly stood up to leave the room and rejoin his team, knowing it wouldn't be the last time he spoke to Charlie Two.

As he stepped outside, his attention was briefly directed above him. He looked up to see an eagle circle the local area, before swooping down and perching on the edge of the barbershop's building. It stared down at him, its eyes fixed and its head at a slight tilt. The eagle was motionless, as it continued to watch Alpha One, with its wings clasped tightly behind its back, in an imposing and judging stance. It didn't take its eyes off Alpha One until he finally moved out of its sight and into the building.

***

In the building opposite, the rest of Alpha team had entered a much smaller tunnel, hidden at the back of the barbershop. Although it was small and narrow, its length wasn't, as it seemed to continue forever. They'd moved through slowly, but hadn't met any heavy resistance, despite only finding one tunnel. The tunnel was lit with flickering lamps, strung up on the ceiling, which were completely out of place with the modern feel of the compound. They continued on, until they could finally see a light marking the end of the tunnel. As they edged closer, two additional paths came into view opposite each other. Although they had every intention of moving straight ahead, they approached with caution. As they closed in on the crossroads, they stopped, waiting for everyone to advance at the same time. Alpha Three gave one nod, just before they all moved forward simultaneously. Alpha Four flicked left and Blindspot flicked right, as they both cleared their respective directions, finding them both to be nothing more than alcoves. Alpha Three and Five continued to watch forwards, whilst they waited. Both stared down the long tunnel towards the light, with little of the room visible from their range.

Suddenly, Alpha Five shouted, "Sniper!"

Everything tensed, as he tightened his grip on his rifle and ploughed into Alpha Three, pushing him into the alcove on the left. They clattered against the rough rock wall, as Alpha Five looked over to his right shoulder to see blood pouring from a wound.

Alpha Three instantly leapt up and started moving his companion's shoulder about, finding out the bullet had exited Alpha Five, as he said, "You'll be fine. It is merely a flesh wound."

"It doesn't feel like a flesh wound. I know it isn't going to kill me, but it feels much worse than a flesh wound," replied Alpha Five, raising his voice, as he sat in pain unable to move his shoulder freely.

"No, you don't get it, it's... Oh, don't bother... But... thanks for... Well, thanks," said Alpha Three, as he turned his attention to the sniper.

Blindspot had already thrown down two smoke grenades which had billowed up and blocked any sightlines through the tunnel. He then raised his sidearm and shot the cable that ran between each light, as they ran in series. The bullet hit the cable but didn't penetrate it, as it left a wide, green smudge on the ceiling.

With a loud sigh, Blindspot then cut the cable with his knife and attached an additional sight on his rifle, as he mumbled, "Stupid technology."

He then lowered himself, looked through the thermal sight, and slowly edged out. It didn't take long before he fired a single shot.

"Sniper down," he said, as they stood up and made their way down the tunnel, with Alpha Five staying in the alcove and watching their backs, clutching his sidearm in his left hand.

They continued down the tunnel and reached the room at the end. The sniper was slumped over the table he'd used for cover. There was only one other person in the room, as Alpha Four and Blindspot checked everywhere. It also seemed to be a dead end, with nowhere left to run. Over in the corner, Blindspot found a small stack of guns, including rifles and shotguns, which were probably intended for use as a last stand, but with nobody left to fire them, they seemed useless.

The man was sat over on the other side of the room, in a chair all by itself. Alpha One joined them only moments later, and he immediately approached the man. He was a little younger than Bosse, in his fifties, with short, black hair, which was clearly going grey in places, and a tiny nose that was completely out of proportion to his chunky face. The man was slightly squinting, suggesting he struggled to see properly, though there was no sign of any glasses. He had hazel eyes, very thin eyebrows, and bright red, rosy cheeks. But what intrigued Alpha One the most was his missing ring finger on his right hand. It looked amputated, rather than being missing from birth, but it wasn't what Alpha One considered an urgent inquiry and could be asked about it back at the Molehill. The man's blue suit was pressed without a single crease, as he sat upright in a refined posture in the middle of the mucky, bare-boned room.

"I understand you have been looking for me. Well, allow me to introduce myself. My name is Crabble, I don't believe we have had the pleasure of formally being acquainted," said the man in the chair, unthreatened by their presence.

He had a weak voice with a soft, Irish accent and one side of his mouth drooped down slightly, giving Alpha One the impression Crabble had suffered from a stroke.

"Tell us everything you know about Fellscient,"

demanded Alpha One.

He knew there would be time to interrogate Crabble back at the Molehill for the less pressing questions, but there were a few things he wanted answers to, without Bosse's presence.

"Wow! No hanging around. I like it. I would ask for your name, but I already know it. In fact, I know all your names..." started Crabble.

Although he didn't start to answer the question directly, there was every chance he'd get to the point.

"I've been interested in all of you for some time now. Fellscient wished to recruit you, but clearly Bosse got to you first. You see, we'd obviously singled out the same people, because everyone you failed to recruit was picked up by us..." he continued.

"So, your organisation is full of rejects," said Alpha Four, interrupting the flow of the conversation.

Alpha One wasn't best pleased with the interruption, despite him trying to hide his annoyance.

"I don't think you should have said that, Kenny. Or should I say, Trevor?" whispered Crabble, as he leant forwards towards Alpha Four.

"Back to the point," ordered Alpha One.

"I apologise. Where was I? Ah, yes. Fellscient wanted to recruit you all. It is something they still want, actually. You see, my role in this organisation was to recruit you. The entire weather... situation was just to get your attention, which is obviously why I haven't attacked any civilian sites, or ordered the destruction of any relief aid, since you were hot on my tail. Of course, the killing wasn't something I atoned for, in fact, I rather enjoyed it. But anyway, you wanted to know about my involvement, didn't you? Well, we, or rather, I, have been following you for a very long time. Long before you joined your organisation... What was that called again?"

Only silence followed, as they both maintained eye

contact.

"No? Well, we weren't sure of its name either. We had no code name to assign to this operation, but everyone knew the silence resembled you, a team who can't even define their own purpose. But you never noticed me, even after the first couple of attacks, so I had to grab your attention rather forcefully, which is why I had Echo team killed. A needless sacrifice, if only you had noticed me. There were certain strings I knew to pull to get you involved, from shall we say... previous knowledge. In fact, I also tried to force some of you towards Fellscient, creating that sense of distrust within Mike's father's little group of hitmen, killing poor old Daniel's family and, of course, having Westbrook killed as well," continued Crabble, able to speak without interruption, despite the tense atmosphere he'd created.

"I must say, it is nice to finally put a face to that voice of yours. In Gert's office, at the Swiss compound, it was all you, wasn't it?" asked Alpha One, trying to prevent Crabble from controlling the conversation.

Whilst letting him speak was providing useful information, it was also an easy way to avoid the questions Crabble didn't want to answer.

Although Alpha One couldn't see, he could feel Alpha Three's confusion, as he turned around and said, "Gert was the Dutch guy."

Alpha Three gave a few small nods, as if he knew all along.

Crabble ignored the tangent, as he answered, saying, "Yes, it was all me, very perceptive of you. Now, as for Fellscient, which you keep drawing me away from, I am sure you have heard much speculation and many rumours. Yet, the thing with those is they are rarely true, or else they would be called fact, wouldn't they? So, allow me to clarify. I am both puppet and puppet master, but I am afraid I do not know who my puppet master is. In fact, that is why I hired M.N.G.W.A. in the first place, to find out who is at the top of my chain. Naturally, I had to include them legitimately. Mr Wilson became the accountant for Fellscient, whilst I handed the Night Vipers over to Gert, although Hailey still ran them; I wouldn't have trusted Gert with any responsibility. I also got M.N.G.W.A. to carry out the attacks, but that was just to keep them occupied. I'm sure Mr Wilson will tell you they didn't enjoy doing it, maybe he even said they felt threatened by us. Hmm, he is a very accomplished liar, which is both a gift and a curse, I believe. Unfortunately, Gert was not. He was a fool, and I had to have him killed. I'm sure M.N.G.W.A. will have me killed for it, I understand he was a valued asset to their close-knit team of just five, but I am willing to live with the possibility... or rather, die with it, I suppose. Plus, it was a good way to test our new helicopter. Its first outing and it killed a member of M.N.G.W.A., not bad I suppose..."

Crabble then took a slight break in his long outpouring, pretending he'd finished and trying to make Alpha One ask about The Vesper again. But Alpha One still refused to give Crabble what he wanted, as he was more occupied with Crabble thinking the HAHA had killed Gert, not the mystery figure with the huge hood.

Without any prompting, Crabble continued, "And The Vesper, who isn't, or rather wasn't, a part of M.N.G.W.A., well, I hired him to dispose of any unwanted assets... officially, anyway. But the main reason was because of his research. Not the research about bringing people back to life; that was just a dream with no reality... Well, as far as I know, anyway. You see, I wanted his research so I could use the 'brain control' technology. I knew all about it, even though I had to pretend not to, because he thought he was going to use it on me..." Crabble started to chuckle to himself at the thought, before continuing, still without Alpha One's persuasion. "Unfortunately, he was killed, by your assassin, which is a shame, but all good things must come to an end. Where is Mike, anyway? I do hope he hasn't perished as well," said Crabble.

Alpha One brought the discussion back to his previous line of questioning, to prevent Crabble from controlling the conversation, despite him already suspecting the answer.

"What I don't get…" he started.

"What don't you get?" interrupted Crabble.

Alpha One ignored the interruption and started again, saying, "What I don't get is why you allowed me to have the spacesuit back at the Swiss compound. If you planned to kill me, what was the point?"

Crabble smiled and shook his head at Alpha One, as he answered, "I can't believe you haven't worked it out. I knew you would survive, and I wanted you to get to the satellite. The plan did go a little sideways, as Red Viper was meant to bring you in, but after all this time, you still don't get it, do you? My boss wants you to join him. It's more than my job's… in fact, it's more than my life's worth to kill you."

Alpha One kept a straight expression and moved on with his line of questioning, refusing to take the bait which Crabble continued to lay out.

"And what of Hailey and Kale?" asked Alpha One, still not finished with his questions.

"Well, Hailey is the true head of the Night Vipers, who I sent elsewhere, if that's what you're asking. And Kale, well, he was a decoy I'm afraid. He was just there to lure you out of hiding. His name isn't even Kale. We just ensured he would answer to that name through fear of us. Sorry about that, but it was fun watching you cut through the Night Vipers as you did. It quickly became clear why my mysterious boss wanted you for himself. If you're interested, though, we got the name Kale because there's another member of Fellscient with that name, who I knew you would've wanted to catch after obtaining the hard drive, a lower level than myself, obviously, but he'll probably step up in my temporary absence. He is the obvious choice after all," answered Crabble.

Alpha One hadn't heard much he wasn't expecting, so decided the interrogation could be concluded back at the Molehill.

"Is there anything you want to add?" asked Alpha One, with mixed feelings about whether he wanted him to continue.

"I am so glad you asked. As a matter of fact, there was something. As much as I hate to plant seeds of doubt in your minds, I feel it is my duty to tell you this. Bosse is not someone you can trust. All this time, you thought you were the gun, right? You knew you were being pointed in a certain direction, but at the end of the day, you decided whether or not you would release a bullet. Well, that's wrong I'm afraid. I'm here to tell you that you are actually the bullet itself, with no control. Bosse has been the one to play your side of the game, as well as his own. I guess that means he will always win, but I would see it as he will always lose. That doesn't seem all that trustworthy, does it?" added Crabble.

Whilst Alpha One had no intention of trusting Crabble over Bosse, he couldn't deny it was impossible to ignore the seed that had been planted.

"And that's coming from the villain," said Alpha One, trying to prove his loyalties to Bosse.

Crabble looked deep in thought, before replying, "Am I the villain? Or am I just stood on the wrong side of history? After all, it seems my boss has orchestrated all of this. My boss wanted you here, and here is where you are. It seems they've played both sides and have manipulated us into being here at this very moment. But I do wonder how long they've been controlling both sides. Don't you?" said Crabble, again trying to get Alpha One to answer his question, no matter how irrelevant it seemed.

With Alpha One sure he was going to get no answers

with any gravity, he concluded the interrogation.

Alpha One went to walk out of the room, but before he made it, Crabble cleared his throat, indicating he had not finished.

"Something the matter?" asked Alpha One.

Crabble then smiled and said, "No, nothing's the matter. It's just, I have… more. It is not any more information, as such, it is more of a profound statement I think applies to you and your… morality. Just think, if this was a book and you turned to the final page first, you would just assume that I am the villain, because I lost and because history is famously written by the victor. But am I really the villain here? Or is that something you have just been told? Perhaps, it is because without context, the ending is meaningless. After all, it's the journey that matters, not the destination."

"You really got your job lot of fortune cookies, didn't you?" said Alpha Three, receiving no visible reaction.

Crabble started to laugh at Alpha Three's comment, as he went on to say, "I will very much enjoy our future together. I have so much more to tell you. I doubt this will ever come to the surface though, will it? I'm sure it will be our little secret. After all, ensuring nobody hears this story and nobody finds out the truth, makes this little… story, fiction, doesn't it? Well, I can't wait to tell you more… but, till the nex…" Suddenly, Crabble's head exploded, with chunks of flesh and blood splattering the walls, as a deafening bang echoed throughout the room.

Alpha One, along with the two next to him, turned around, looking at each other on the way. As they looked behind them, they saw Blindspot, holding a shotgun which still had smoke pouring from its barrel.

"What have you done!" shouted Alpha One, with blood splattered on his face.

Blindspot didn't break his gaze at Crabble's decapitated body, as he slowly opened his mouth and quietly said, "I… I made a promise."

Epilogue – The Allies
February 28th
22:01 GMT

The rain was battering the windows of a building five stories high. Inside felt cold, with no fires lit and no heating on. There was little in the office, aside from a desk and chair. But sat in the chair was a hooded figure. He just sat, motionless, surrounded by almost nothing. The room was lit by a bulb on the ceiling, with no shade around it, so the room seemed bright, despite the black outdoors sucking out as much light as it could. On the desk in front of him was a teacup, on a saucer, and a pot of sugar with a teaspoon sticking out of it. The door creaked open, and a woman slowly emerged. It was LoLa.

She smiled and said, "I bring good news. Crabble has been killed."

"Good, but that doesn't excuse your lateness," replied the man, as he stayed motionless.

His voice was very soft and quiet with a faint, but slightly croaky, North London accent.

They both observed each other in silence for a few seconds, before LoLa checked her watch and replied, "It took me the extra minute to get up the stairs."

"Well, make sure it doesn't in the future, deadlines are set for a reason," he replied.

Another bout of silence followed, until she asked, "Where is everyone?"

"We're changing location. It seems they're, once again,

on our tail. The building is clear, I was merely waiting for you to arrive," said the mystery man.

"So, this business with Fellscient hasn't put them off our tail, then?" questioned LoLa, as she looked out of the window still being bombarded by the rain.

The mystery man shook his head, as he answered, "Unfortunately not. It seems our enemy's focus is far more aligned on hunting us than it is on aiding Fellscient. We have assisted Scott and his team five times now; it might be time for them to return the favour. Do you think they took your little hint or was it too subtle?"

"Well, it was obscure, but I would be surprised if Daniel didn't pick up on it. He was certainly suspicious of me, but I think he might be struggling to allow his two lives to coexist. All his training tells him to switch off his operator life when away from the Molehill, and yet it's his operator life which protects him the most. Daniel is recovering well, though, so should I contact him?" asked LoLa.

The mystery man took a moment to think, before he said, "Maybe... but I think there are better ways of contacting them. After all, Scott knows of me from killing Gert and knows that I am not a threat. Perhaps, a little... manipulation is needed first."

The door swung open again, and another man emerged, smartly dressed in a blue suit and brown shoes. It was difficult to see anything other than his short, black hair and greying stubble, as he darted around the room.

He looked slightly flustered and in a panic, as he said, "They're here. We've got to move."

The mystery man didn't share his concern, as he stayed in his chair and calmly said, "Thomas, you need to relax. Miss Cadlow is more than capable of dispatching a couple of scout operatives..."

Thomas then interjected, still panicked, as he said, "No, they've sent two of their tanks to weaken our defences, before the rest come in."

The mystery man released a sigh, before momentarily pausing.

"Very well, go and get the car ready. We will hold them back," he replied, still in his chair.

Thomas followed his order and left the room, whilst Miss Cadlow stood beside the closed door. The mystery man then picked up the teaspoon with his right hand and sprinkled a level teaspoon of sugar into his teacup. He placed the spoon into the liquid and moved it back and forth, silently. After just a few seconds, and without the spoon ever touching the cup, he removed it and allowed the few drips of tea to return to his drink. Once done, he placed the teaspoon behind his teacup, on the saucer, completely parallel with the side of the desk closest to him.

They both waited in silence, as they listened for any movement. Only a few moments later, two sets of heavy footsteps could be heard thumping down the corridor. They moved slowly, clearly wanting to be heard, as stealth couldn't inflict fear. But neither were threatened by their presence, as they allowed them to come closer and closer. The footsteps continued to get louder, before finally coming to a sudden stop. They had to observe more silence, as their enemy tried to build fear in the room. But it still didn't work, as they both kept their cool and waited. Shortly after, the door was thrown off its hinges and burst into the room.

"It was unlocked. You could've simply opened the door," said the mystery man, as he watched the two giants stomp into the room.

They were both almost 7' tall and had to duck down to enter the room. Neither wore anything except trousers and a sleeveless vest, with no sign of any protection apart from the combination of fat and muscles that surrounded their bodies. Even their tiny heads were wrapped up in their natural armour which prevented them from even looking side to side.

"You know why we've come. Your debts are long overdue and only your head will suffice as payment now," said one of the two men, in a deep growl.

The mystery man smiled. Although his face was still obscured, he slightly looked up to show the smile creep along his face but left the rest of his face in the shadow of his hood.

"How very charming. But I'm afraid it won't be me losing my head today, so I suggest you watch out," the mystery man said, as he shifted his gaze towards Miss Cadlow, out of their visible range.

The two men were unable to see anything which wasn't directly ahead of them. So, as Miss Cadlow began to move, she was completely unseen. She put her right hand flat and outstretched, before swinging it into the closest tank's throat, disturbing his windpipe and causing him to start wheezing and gasping for air. Whilst one of the tanks was preoccupied, she turned her attention to the other. Whilst strength was on his side, speed was on hers, so she leapt up and swung herself towards his head. Miss Cadlow then wrapped her legs around his neck and started to shift her weight forwards in an attempt to topple him. But the tank didn't even stumble, as he grabbed her and threw her against the wall. She crashed against the furthest wall, bashing some of the plasterboard in and leaving a gaping hole as she fell to the floor. As she brushed off the dust, she could see the first tank had started to breathe properly and was heading towards the mystery man, still sat calmly in his chair.

"One of them is heading my way," he said, gently, as he pointed to the approaching tank.

"Well, why don't you help and take him out!" replied Miss Cadlow, as she became angrier with his lack of involvement.

"Very well," the mystery man replied.

The tank approached slowly, making thundering footsteps and cracking his knuckles as he went. But the mystery man remained relaxed, as he sat in his chair. Suddenly, the mystery man thrust his right arm towards the tank. His hand completely detached itself, as it flew towards the tank, with the fingers wrapping themselves around his neck. Although they couldn't reach around the back, the fingers dug themselves into his neck to secure the hand. It squeezed tighter and tighter, as the tank dropped to his knees, desperately trying to pull the hand away from his constricted throat. The mystery man continued to maintain his cool, as he reached forward with his left hand, which wasn't prosthetic, and twisted the teacup 180 degrees, clockwise, so the handle faced to his left. Still watching the tank on his knees, he delicately picked up the teacup, pinching his thumb and forefinger under the top of the handle. With his middle finger under the bottom of the handle for balance, and the other two tucked out of sight, he raised the teacup to his lips. Before it reached his lips, he let out a noise of approval, as he watched his right hand keep the tank alive, but motionless, as it toyed with his life. The mystery man took his attention away from the tank only to look inside the teacup, as he took a sip of the translucent, brown liquid.

He placed the teacup back on its saucer and readdressed the tank, as he said, "Please, forgive me for using my left hand to raise the teacup. I know it is not particularly good etiquette, but my right hand is somewhat, preoccupied." He then turned his attention back to Miss Cadlow.

She was pinned to the floor by the other tank, as his chubby hand covered her entire neck.

"Have you… got… yours yet?" she asked, struggling to form the words.

"Yes, I'm all done. You can drop the act now," he replied, whilst taking another sip of tea.

"Finally," she muttered.

Although it looked like the tank had all but finished her off, she suddenly took control of the fight. She wrapped her legs around the tank's outstretched arm and squeezed them together. With just a single movement, she twisted his arm and applied a huge force against the outside of his elbow, bending it inwards. As the tank's colossal weight was used against him, his elbow cracked inwards, causing the bone to rupture the many layers of fat and muscle surrounding it. He stumbled back and groaned, with his teeth tightly clenched together, as he tried to push through the pain. With the bone sticking out of the inside of his elbow, he tucked his left arm out of the way before starting to charge towards Miss Cadlow. She moved two steps forward and turned her back to the tank. He got closer and closer to her, but before he could make a move, she started to run forwards. She ran towards the wall, took two leaps up, and pushed herself backwards. Miss Cadlow flew over the tank and gracefully landed on the ground, bending her knees only slightly to give herself a soft landing. The tank wasn't so graceful, as he ran headlong into the wall with an immense force. She then calmly walked over to the desk and felt around the rim. By the time the tank had finally picked himself up, using the wall to climb back to his feet, Miss Cadlow had removed a katana. Holding it high above her head, she drew the blade and held it towards the tank. He didn't seem fazed, as he again went to tackle Miss Cadlow, but just like last time, his efforts were in vain. As he approached, she dodged to the side, slicing through one of his legs. The tank fell to the floor, smacking his face against the smooth wooden boards. Miss Cadlow slowly approached the wounded tank and raised her katana back in the air, facing down. Without hesitation, she plunged the blade deep into the tank's chest. He had just enough time to grab the blade before his final breath left his pierced lungs.

The mystery man took his final sip of tea, leaving a minute amount in the cup, and stood up, saying, "If they want my head, they're going to have to wait. In the meantime, why don't we leave them a little present of the same... calibre?"

He then tucked his teacup and other accompanying items into a small box, which he'd removed from his desk, and pointed towards the other tank that was only allowed to take tiny breaths. The mystery man held his arm towards the tank and his hand shot straight back, leaving the tank gasping for air on the floor. By moving his fingers around, he checked the connection and calibration of his hand, until satisfied.

He then moved to the doorway, saying, "Make sure you're not long in removing his head. I'll be waiting in the car."

Then, without waiting for a response, he left the room, leaving the door open for Miss Cadlow to follow shortly behind.

"Sure thing, Mr P," said Miss Cadlow, as she turned her attention to the remaining tank.

As he walked away from the room, with the box tucked under his arm, all he heard was one strike of the blade followed by a lifeless thud.

If you're reading this, then I'm going to assume that you've reached the end of the book. Hopefully, you're a little sad about finishing it, but eager to read the next edition. If you did enjoy it, then please feel free to leave a rating, a review, and maybe even add your favourite chapter to it, because these will all help me immensely.

Once again, thank you for giving your time to read this book and I hope you really did enjoy it.

COMING 2024

OPERATION
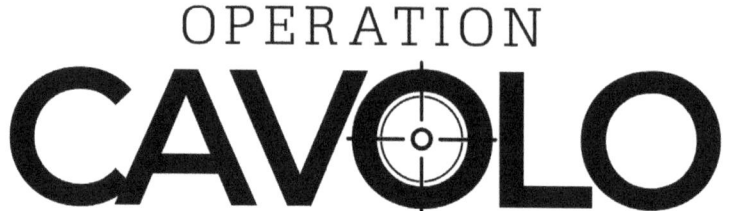

The Silent Codename Series Book Two

Milton Keynes UK
Ingram Content Group UK Ltd.
UKHW042058240924
448733UK00006B/396